KING OF HAWTHORNE PREP

USA Today Bestselling Author
JENNIFER SUCEVIC

King of Hawthorne Prep

Copyright© 2020 by Jennifer Sucevic

All rights reserved. No part of this book may be reproduced in any form or by any electronic or mechanical means, including information storage and retrieval systems, without written permission from the author, except for the use of brief quotations in a book review.

This is a work of fiction. Names, characters, businesses, palaces, events, locales, and incidents are either the products of the author's imagination or used in a fictitious manner. Any resemblance to actual persons, living or dead, or actual events is purely coincidental.

Original Cover Design by Mary Ruth Baloy at MR Creations

Special Edition Cover by Claudia Lymari of Tease Designs

Interior Formatting by Silla Webb

Editing by Jenny Sims Editing 4 Indies

Subscribe to my newsletter for a free book!

SUMMER

1

My gaze wanders over the water as white-capped waves roll rhythmically toward the sandy shore. When the wind picks up, a warm breeze rustles through my hair, and I tip my face toward the sun before stretching.

Could life get any better than this?

Doubtful.

A family friend was kind enough to let us borrow their beach house in Door County for the week. Mom and Dad surprised us with the impromptu vacation a few days before we were supposed to leave.

The house we're staying at isn't like one of the newly renovated million-dollar monstrosities that flank us with their gargantuan square footage, swanky pools, and perfectly groomed lawns. But it's steps from the beach and has breathtaking views of Lake Michigan. At just fifteen hundred square feet, this house has three cramped bedrooms, an outdated kitchen, and a ton of seashell décor. Even so, there's something charming about it.

Sweat beads my forehead as I haul myself from the chair I'm sprawled on and saunter to the water's edge. It might look as inviting as the Caribbean cast in varying shades of cerulean and turquoise, but it doesn't feel like it. Especially when my skin has been crispifying for hours beneath the sweltering sun.

A breath hisses from my lips as the frigid liquid rushes past my ankles. The first couple of steps are the worst. As soon as numbness sets in, it gets better. Braving the water, I continue forward as the waves swirl around my calves. I do a little dance, bouncing up and down on my toes, trying to get used to the cold as it sinks into my bones.

I force myself to move deeper until the water reaches my hips.

It's now or never.

With that brief pep talk, I suck in a breath and dive beneath a wave as it peaks and curls. Water rushes around me, instantly chilling my overheated flesh. After a moment, I break through to the surface and expel the lungful of air from my body.

It's easier to submerge myself the second time as I dive to the bottom before trailing my fingers through the fine-grained sand in search of clamshells. When my lungs burn, I pop up again before floating on the surface so the sun can warm my skin. With my eyes closed, I stretch my hands and legs, allowing the waves to rock my body. My mind drifts as the rhythmic motion lulls me to a contented place. Every once in a while, I lift my head and search for our little blue one-story cottage to make sure I haven't drifted to far down the shore.

My plan is to make the most of our little beach vaca before returning to Chicago next weekend. There's so much that needs to be accomplished before senior year begins in the fall.

A couple of months ago, I registered for an introductory astronomy class at a local university about thirty minutes from the house. Next on the agenda are campus visits. I've scheduled tours for the University of Chicago, Northwestern, and the University of Michigan in Ann Arbor. My three dream schools have impressive astronomy programs. To round out the summer, I've snagged a volunteer position at the Adler Planetarium. I'm scheduled to start next Monday at nine o'clock sharp.

Long after my fingers turn pruney, I drag myself from the water. As I trudge toward shore, a bleached clamshell glints in the sunlight from the bottom and catches my attention. Stilling my movements, I bend over to inspect it. A wave crashes over me, stirring up the sand and covering the shell. Once the debris settles, I turn, brushing my fingers across the bottom until they land on it again.

"Nice view."

I yelp and swing around, straightening to my full height only to come face-to-face with the most gorgeous boy I've ever seen. My breath gets lodged at the back of my throat as his mahogany-colored eyes pierce mine with unwavering intensity. Rooted in place, it's all I can do to take in the thick slashes of his eyebrows before my gaze slides to the slant of high cheekbones, and then on to a perfect cupid's bow of a mouth.

Damn.

He's seriously hot.

Like...*way out of my league* hot.

My heart riots painfully against my chest as I continue to stare. His brows rise as humor sparks to life in his eyes.

Is he waiting for a response?

Did he ask a question, and I wasn't paying attention? I hit the mental rewind button and quickly sift through our limited conversation.

Nice view.

Nice view?

Wasn't I bent over at the time with my ass in the air?

Heat slams into my cheeks with the force of a tsunami. That's *exactly* the pose I'd been striking. When he said *nice view*, he'd been commenting on my behind. The very same behind barely covered by a thin strip of fabric because the beach has been fairly empty since we arrived on Saturday. This guy is one of the few people I've seen.

"Ummm, thanks," I force myself to respond.

His lips slide into a smirk as if I've amused him.

I need to pull it together before I humiliate myself any further. Although, let's be honest, that ship has already set sail. Right now, I'm operating strictly in damage control mode.

Is it possible that he hasn't noticed my awkwardness?

Any chance of clinging to that unlikely prospect is blown out of the water when he tilts his head. "Did you just thank me for admiring your ass?"

All right, so he noticed.

The heat radiating from my face intensifies a few hundred degrees until self-combustion seems likely. Not to mention, welcome.

"Yeah," I mumble, attempting to rip my gaze from his, but that proves to be impossible. It's as if I've become ensnared by the dark depths assessing me in such a forthright manner. "Apparently I did."

The sound of his deep chuckle reverberates throughout my entire body before darting straight to my—

"I'm Kingsley." He steps forward, closing some of the distance between us. His proximity makes my heart pound faster. "And you are?"

Humiliated?

Embarrassed?

Mortified?

It's a dealer's choice.

"Summer," I mutter instead. When you daydream about talking with a really hot guy, this isn't exactly how you picture it playing out.

Relief rushes from my lungs when his gaze flicks from me to the house I'm standing in front of. There's something powerful about his stare, leaving me to feel as if he's able to pick through all my private thoughts, and it's a disconcerting sensation. I want to run and hide, but my feet refuse to move. I'm frozen in place.

He points at the house on the dunes. "Is that yours?"

"Yes." I clear my throat along with those disconcerting thoughts. "We're renting for the week."

He nods as his attention returns to me where it stays put. That same feeling of nervousness fills me. "Who knows, maybe I'll see you around, Summer."

A wave of heat wafts over me at the sound of my name sliding from his lips. I tamp down the response and shrug, trying to play it cool even though it's much too late for that.

"Yeah, maybe."

He flashes a wide grin as if not fooled by my nonchalance before taking off at a brisk pace down the beach.

Now that his attention is no longer focused on me, I'm free to look my fill as all those well-honed muscles shift and bunch as he jogs away. We're talking broad shoulders with a broad, muscular back that tapers into a trim waist. Loose black athletic shorts cover his trunk and thighs. My gaze drops, wanting to commit every detail to memory. Damn, even his calves are well-defined.

There's no way a guy built like that is in high school. He's definitely in college. I'd like to know what university he attends so I can submit an application. As his figure grows smaller in the distance, I realize I don't even care if they offer astronomy as a major.

I chuckle and shake my head at the thought of planning my future around a boy I spoke with for all of two minutes.

Never.

Going.

To.

Happen.

I have plans. Lots of them. And I would never derail a single one for a guy.

No matter how good-looking he is.

Once the boy fades from sight, I blink out of my thoughts and head back to the house. In all likelihood, I'll never see him again.

SUMMER

2

As the brightly shining sun climbs in the cloudless sky, I drag my folding chair across the sand to the water's edge. Once settled, I grab a hardcover book from my bag and open it to the page where I left off. Up until this point, I've been devouring every word. But yesterday, I couldn't focus on a single sentence. How could I when a mental image of the dark-haired hottie kept materializing in my head?

Clearing my throat along with those thoughts, I start at chapter twenty and turn the page. But the words refuse to register, and I can't remember any of the details that should be fresh in my mind.

Damnation. I'm thinking about him again.

Kingsley.

Interesting name. It sounds so *royal*.

I glance left and then right, but the beach remains empty. A vast stretch of sand as far as the eye can see. Disappointment settles in the pit of my gut as I fidget restlessly on the chair.

This is ridiculous. I'm here to read and enjoy the sun. Maybe go for a swim. What I'm *not* doing is waiting around for a boy. Now I have to push Kingsley whatever-the-hell-his-name-is out of my head and focus on spending a little quality time with myself. Which I was perfectly content to do the past couple of days.

"Hey, there."

I squeak in surprise as my head twists toward the sound of his deep voice. No matter how much I don't want to admit it, I'm doing a happy dance inside and screaming at the top of my lungs.

"Oh, hey." *Good.* That's the perfect amount of disinterest. *Play it cool, Summer. No need for him to think you've been sitting here, waiting for him to show up and make your day.*

A smile simmers around the edges of his lips.

Have I mentioned how seriously kissable they look?

Or that I'm dying to feel them sliding over mine?

His tongue peeks out to lick at his bottom lip before biting down on the plumpness.

Holy hell. Liquid heat pools in my core, and a small sigh slips from my mouth.

Oh God, please tell me that didn't just happen.

Cautiously, my gaze darts to his to determine the situation. The smile curving his lips turns decidedly cocky. That, coupled with the knowing glint in his eyes, makes me realize he's well aware of the effect he has on me. If I were smart, I would pull the plug on this disastrous interaction by gathering up my stuff and vanishing inside the house.

The only thing getting me through this unfortunate moment is the knowledge that I'll never see him again. It's not like we live in the same city. Or go to school together. He's a random guy on the beach.

See? I feel better already.

He tilts his head as his dark eyes dance. "Any chance you've been waiting for me?"

"*What?*" I force out a disbelieving chuckle. "A little full of yourself, aren't we?" I grab the book from my lap and hold it up as proof. "I was reading."

"Hmm." My guess is that he doesn't believe me.

Apparently, we can add intelligent to his growing list of attributes. It goes right up there with gorgeous and muscular.

"That's too bad because I was hoping to see you again."

Be still my heart.

I blink. Did he really just say that?

This dreamy hunk of a guy was actually *looking* for me?

Me? No way.

I'm pretty sure my brows just slammed into my hairline with

disbelief. Wait a minute. I'm supposed to be playing it cool. I need to pretend hot muscly jocks talk to me all the time.

"Oh?"

"Yeah." He steps closer. "I was planning on taking my boat out today and was wondering if you wanted to join me."

Is he kidding?

Hell yeah, I do!

Instead of jumping out of my chair and straight into his arms, I keep my ass firmly planted in place while tapping a finger against my lips. "Hmm, I don't know. As you can see, I've got a packed day planned out."

His lips tremble. "You do look busy."

"Give me a moment to consult my calendar." Before he can say anything further, I continue. "All right, I've checked it. If I shift around a few things, I can squeeze you in."

"Wow." His broad shoulders shake with silent laughter as humor fills his eyes. "I really lucked out, didn't I?"

"Right?" I give him an overly bright smile, finally feeling like I'm on even ground with a guy who could easily be mistaken for a Greek god.

Just like in the movies, he stretches out his hand, and I almost squeal in delight—but keep all the joy trapped deep inside where it can't stroke his ego—before placing my fingers in his. Once his hand closes around mine, he pulls me effortlessly to my feet.

So.

Many.

Muscles.

I grab my canvas bag, which contains my cell phone, towel, coverup, sunscreen, sandals, and a bottle of water. All the necessities for a day on the water. I toss the book inside before hoisting the straps over my shoulder.

Voilà. I'm ready to go.

He glances toward the tiny blue house. "Do you need to tell your parents you're taking off?"

What does he think I am?

A baby?

"Of course not," I scoff before fishing around in the bag for my cell. "But I'll shoot them a text, so they don't worry." My fingers fly over the keyboard as I fire off a quick message before tossing it back inside the oversized tote. "Okay, all set."

"Cool." A smile curves his lips as he shifts his weight in the sand. "Should we get moving?"

"Definitely."

We walk for about fifteen minutes and pepper each other with light questions. As we head north, the houses continue to get more gigantic until they look like the beach version of a McMansion. We stop in front of a massive gray two-story with bright white trim painted around the windows.

With his hair blowing in the wind, he jerks his head toward the house. "This is me."

"Wow." I'm sure my face registers the shock coursing through me. This place is easily three thousand square feet and sits on prime lakefront property. I can't begin to imagine what a house like this costs.

We walk up the sand path that cuts through the wild grass that grows on the dunes until we hit a manicured lawn with a diamond pattern mowed into it.

Fancy.

There's a rectangular-shaped pool of crystal-clear water and a hot tub near the back of the house. The patio has a massive stone fireplace and an inviting gray wicker couch with plush blue cushions. An oversized umbrella shades the seating arrangement from the sun. I can almost imagine curling up there with a good book.

This definitely doesn't have a rental vibe to it. My guess is that Kingsley's family owns it.

My toes sink into the lawn as we move toward the sprawling house. The grass is plush beneath my feet as if it's been watered and fertilized to an inch of its life. I stop and fish my sandals out of my bag before throwing on my coverup. Instead of heading inside the house, we detour around the property until arriving at a faded red brick driveway.

He pulls out a set of keys from the pocket of his boardshorts and clicks the locks on a sleek silver Range Rover. "Why don't you hop in the car, and I'll run inside and grab my shoes."

I nod as he trots up the wide porch steps and slips inside the glass front door. By the time I'm settled on the leather seat, he's jogging toward the SUV. I glance at the house and realize it's even more impressive than it looked from the rear.

Maybe Kingsley is an *actual* king.

The thought brings a smile to my face.

A moment later, he slides in next to me, and the engine purrs to life. We pull out of the circular drive and head north. My gaze flits from the lush green landscape beyond the passenger side window that whizzes by to the handsome boy sitting to my left. It's difficult to fathom that an hour ago, I was pretending not to look for him, and now, we have plans to spend the day together on his boat.

"Exactly where are we headed?" That's probably a question I should have asked before locking myself inside the vehicle with him.

He shoots me a quick glance before focusing on the ribbon of black pavement stretched out before him. "The boat is docked at the marina. It's about a ten-minute drive from here."

My guess is that he's talking about the swanky country club where boat slips are available to its members for an astronomical fee. Less than ten minutes later, we pull into the parking lot. Pristine yachts and speed boats are anchored at the slips. Seagulls float overhead, squawking in the cloudless sky as they search for food. It's the perfect day to be out on the water.

We exit the Range Rover, and Kingsley heads to the trunk before popping it open and grabbing an olive-green cooler from the back. Once he slams it shut, we walk through the gravel parking lot to the pier.

Kingsley points at a massive speed boat. "That's mine."

Holy crap...can you say ginormous?

"Oh, good. I was afraid it might be tiny." I give him a bit of side-eye before adding, "That would be really embarrassing for you."

He snorts as his hand settles on the small of my back. The heat of his palm burns a hole through my coverup and singes my flesh. "I assure you, *nothing* about me is tiny."

I burst out laughing. "Did you *seriously* just say that?"

His shoulders shake as he chuckles. "Guilty."

"Well," I say primly, squashing the humor from my voice, "I won't be finding that out for myself. And if that's a problem, you should take me home right now."

"Hey," he says with an easy shrug, "you're the one who brought up size."

"Of your boat," I add as the gentle breeze off the water blows the loose hair away from my face.

"Noted." Even though his eyes are shaded by a pair of aviators, I imagine they're dancing with mischief. "Should we proceed?"

My feet slow as I arch a brow. "Can I trust you not to bring up the size of your vessel again? That was super uncomfortable."

His lips twitch as he removes his hand from my back and lays it on his chest over his heart. "You have my promise. There will be no more talk about vessel size."

"Then I'll continue with our voyage," I say in a magnanimous tone.

"Excellent." He dips his head in acknowledgment. "You've made the crew very happy."

We both grin before traversing the pier to where the glossy boat waits. The closer we get, the more impressed I become. I don't know anything about boats, but even I can tell this one costs a shit ton of money. Probably as much as our house in Chicago, which is a crazy thought.

With athletic grace, he jumps onto the wooden platform at the back before reaching out his hand for me to take hold of. My heart skips a beat as I make the leap with his assistance.

I guess we can safely add gentleman to the growing list of attributes.

Kingsley shimmies past a seating arrangement to the steering console before setting down the Yeti cooler. I follow him, taking the boat in as I do. The interior is clean and sparkling as if it's brand spanking new. There's a hard-top canopy over the steering console with a window to take in the view and a small white pad in the front that has a railing wrapped around it. As Kingsley moves through the preparations of getting the craft in operating order, I settle on the curved seating arrangement at the back of the boat and observe him. I'm not going to lie; it's seriously sexy watching him check fluids and flip switches. The process is obviously a familiar one because his movements are precise and economical. He knows what he's doing.

Before we're able to take off from the dock, he jumps off the boat and unties the heavy ropes that anchor the vessel in place before settling on the leather chair at the controls. The motor hums to life as he checks his surroundings and carefully navigates the boat out of the harbor.

The farther we get from shore, the more the wind picks up, blowing through my hair as we fly over the waves. I reach into my bag and grab a rubber band, pulling my long hair into a topknot so it's not in my face. As Kingsley accelerates, I watch the shoreline grow distant before my gaze shifts to the boy manning the helm. Mirrored sunglasses shade his eyes as the wind whips through his short dark hair. Today, he's wearing a navy-colored T-shirt that clings to his chest and biceps along with plaid boardshorts that reach the top of his knees. My girly parts twitch in male appreciation.

He's kind of perfect.

Actually, there's no *kind of* about it. And from our limited conversation, it's safe to say that he gets my quirky sense of humor. Other than my twin brother, Austin, not everyone does. So he definitely gets points for that.

After about fifteen minutes, Kingsley cuts the engine and drops the anchor. I glance around. It's like we're in the middle of nowhere. He pulls off his aviators, dropping them in a cup holder on the side of the steering column before yanking the soft cotton T-shirt over his head and tossing it onto the leather chair.

"Want to go for a swim?"

"Sure." I straighten to my full height, which is at least eight inches shorter than him. I'm five foot seven, so he has to be well over six feet. I slip my sunglasses into the canvas bag before stripping off the mesh coverup and removing my sandals. The rhythmic rocking beneath my feet takes some getting used to. I grip the edge of the chair so I don't take a tumble.

This morning, I'd decided on a light blue bikini. The bottoms are tiny but settle high on my hips, and the top is more like a strip with thin arm straps that hold everything safely in place.

"Ready?" he asks.

"Yup." I follow him to the wooden platform at the back before we step to the edge.

As waves lap at the boat, a bolt of fear arrows through me. Kingsley slips my hand into his larger one before giving it a gentle squeeze. A zing of electricity shoots through my fingertips. I glance at him to see if he's noticed the strange burst of energy. His gaze searches mine for a moment before his lips quirk. With our hands enclosed, he squats, preparing to jump.

A spurt of nerves flutter at the bottom of my belly. *"Wait!"*

He pauses, slowly straightening to his full height. "What's wrong?"

"Umm." I glance at the water. It's so much darker out here than at the shore. Exactly how deep is Lake Michigan? I rack my brain for the information but can't come up with an answer. "Are you sure it's safe?"

"Safe?" His brows slide together. "Of course. We're in open water."

Yeah, that's part of the problem. I always feel better when my feet can touch the bottom. That's not possible here.

"Do you think there are a lot of fish this deep?"

He tilts his head, and says carefully, "I'm sure there are a few."

My face scrunches. "You think they're big?"

"I'm not sure. I read somewhere that freshwater salmon can grow anywhere from fifteen to thirty pounds."

Holy shit! That's *not* the answer I was looking for.

"That's huge." Not to mention scary. When I swim at the beach, I never worry about that. Half the time, I don't wade out past my waist. And if I see a few fish, they're small. No bigger than my palm.

When he tugs my fingers, my gaze snaps to his. "I won't let anything happen to you."

His words leave my heart spasming. "Promise?"

"I promise." His eyes search mine for a long moment, and something indescribable passes between us. "You're safe with me."

I gnaw my bottom lip with indecision. I only met this guy yesterday, and already it feels like we're doing one of those horrendous trust-building exercises. Yet, for some inexplicable reason, I trust him to protect me. How crazy is that?

"All right," I finally mumble, reluctantly giving in.

"If you're uncomfortable, we don't have to stay in the water. Okay?" He waits a beat. "Whatever you want to do is fine with me."

I blow out a steady breath, his reassuring words making me feel marginally better.

"You ready to do this?"

I jerk my head into a tight nod.

"One, two, *three!*" he yells.

With our hands tightly clasped, we jump off the edge of the swim platform before sliding beneath the surface and sinking into the cold depths of Lake Michigan. My warmed skin goes into shock as the frigid water surrounds my body. I hold my breath and squeeze my eyes tightly shut before untangling my fingers from his and propelling myself to the surface with a flutter of arms and legs. When the bright sunlight hits my face, I suck in a deep breath as my eyes pop open. I glance around frantically only to find Kingsley bobbing beside me with a grin.

"That wasn't so bad, was it?"

I shake my head. No, it was actually kind of fun.

The waves lap at my chin as I tread water. We're about five feet from the boat, and a ladder hangs off the end in case a hasty exit becomes necessary. Now that my body has gotten used to the coldness that surrounds me, it feels refreshing. I take a few exploratory strokes with my arms. Kingsley keeps pace with me as we circle around the boat.

As I start to relax and enjoy myself, something smooth slides along my leg. I yelp, dog-paddling toward him before throwing my arms around his neck and locking my legs at his waist.

"What's wrong?" he asks, laughter simmering in his deep voice.

My head swivels, peering into the water as if I'm able to see down to the bottom. "Something brushed up against me."

One of his hands goes to my backside as he presses me closer.

"Are you sure?" he whispers against the shell of my ear.

My arms tighten around his neck as I frown. "I don't know." Whatever it was scared the hell out of me.

After a few silent moments tick by and the Lake Michigan equivalent of Jaws doesn't leap from the waves and drag us to a watery grave, I realize how intimately I'm pressed against the steely strength of his body. My muscles tense as a surge of arousal slams into me before settling in my core. This level of attraction isn't something I'm familiar with. My gaze widens before fastening on to his heated one.

"Sorry," I murmur, unsure what to do next. I should probably untangle myself from him, right? It's like he can read my thoughts as they flicker across my face, and his grip tightens on me in response.

"There's no need to apologize."

As we bob on the waves, the tension gradually leaks from my body. His fingers splay wide on my bottom as he draws me closer.

Mmm. That feels so good.

I keep the groan locked deep inside as I rest my chin on his shoulder while he kneads my behind.

Holy moly. Has anything ever felt this good?

We stay locked together, the heat of our bodies warming us in the chilled water. He's barely touched me, and arousal is already wreaking havoc on my system. All of my senses feel heightened with awareness.

Kingsley shifts his lower body away from mine before clearing his throat. "You ready to get out? I packed us a lunch."

Hmm. Lunch *does* sound good but staying here in the water with him sounds even better.

Although, I can't really say that, now can I? "Sure."

Funny how I was so reluctant to get in the water.

And now?

I'm even more reluctant to leave.

SUMMER

3

With no other choice but to untangle myself from Kingsley, I swim toward the metal ladder hanging off the edge of the boat. My fingers cling to the rungs as I hoist myself from the water while he waits. Goose bumps break out across my skin as a thick tension permeates the air.

Needing to break the energy that hums dangerously between us, I pause midway up the ladder. "You really need to stop checking out my booty."

Even though he chuckles, the sound is deep and low as if he's battling the same arousal as I am. "How do you know that's what I'm doing?"

I peer over my shoulder, giving him a wink. "Because you're a dude."

"You got me there," he says, voice simmering with humor. "I wanted to get a good look at what I'd been squeezing in my hands."

The admittance sends an avalanche of tremors sliding through my body.

"In all fairness," he continues as if we're discussing something as mundane as the weather, "it's a nice booty."

Warmth that has nothing to do with the sun fills me. "Thanks, I do a lot of squats and follow Kim Kardashian religiously. She's my booty guru."

He chokes on a laugh. "I'm not sure how I feel about that."

Once on the deck, I pad over to my bag and grab my coral and black floral-colored towel before wrapping it tightly around my body, shielding my skin from the sun and his view. Walking back from all this flirting seems like a smart idea. The attraction between us feels dangerously close to spiraling out of control, and I'm not ready for that to happen.

"Good," I say, lightening my tone, "that was a test, and you passed with flying colors."

Kingsley snorts before moving past me. His chilled flesh brushes against mine as he drops to his haunches to grab a navy-colored towel from the cabinet beneath the bench seat. He pops up before pressing the plush material to his face and rubbing his hair.

With unhurried movements, he strokes it over his perfect pectorals and six-pack. His dark gaze stays pinned to mine as I watch with undisguised interest. A flash of heat streaks to my lower belly before exploding like a firework. Any desire I had stomped out moments earlier flares back to life with a vengeance.

Good Lord, he's sexy.

I'm slightly disappointed when he finishes up, then tosses the towel over a chair to dry in the sun. Another quick dip off the back of the boat seems to be in order. Although, it's doubtful it would do anything to cool me off. The feel of his hands squeezing my ass has been singed into my mind for all eternity. Once I return to Chicago, I already know that I'll take this memory out and relive it a million times.

Kingsley grabs the cooler and brings it to the front of the boat where there's a flat, padded area that's perfect for a picnic. I unwind the towel wrapped around me and place it on the deck before sitting down next to him. The boat sways gently beneath us as he unloads the Yeti.

"They call this the bunny pad," he says conversationally.

Seems like an odd name. "Do you entertain a lot of bunnies here?"

We both know what I'm asking without voicing the question. My guess is that he does.

His gaze pins mine in place. "Not as many as you might suspect."

"Good to know." I glance away, breaking eye contact to stare at the white-capped waves. There's something infinitely calming about being on the water.

He clears his throat and changes the subject. "I packed sandwiches, chips, a couple of oranges, and a few bottles of water."

This guy knows how to do a picnic lunch up right.

Now that I'm staring at all this food spread out between us, my belly growls, and I realize how famished I am. For breakfast this morning, I had wolfed down a protein bar. I think we all know that I was more interested in getting my ass to the beach and waiting for Kingsley to make an appearance.

"Wow, thanks! This looks amazing," I say with appreciation.

We dig in, eating our turkey and cheddar sandwiches first. He plows through two of them. The guy has a big appetite. But I'm used to that because my brother is the same way. Mom can't keep food in the house because he's like a human garbage disposal. It doesn't take long for us to demolish our meal.

With a full belly and the scorching sun blazing down on us, I grow drowsy. Kingsley packs up the Yeti and takes the cooler back to the covered part of the boat before returning with his towel. He spreads it out next to mine before dropping beside me.

When his fingers tangle loosely with mine, I glance at him, unable to stop the flutter in my belly and the smile of contentment as it curves my lips.

So far, this has been the best day.

He squeezes my fingers, and I turn my face toward the sun, allowing my eyelids to close. The rhythmic rocking of the boat makes it easy to doze off. When I wake, my skin feels hot. I stretch and realize that my fingers are still entwined with Kingsley's larger ones. I prop myself up on my elbows as the haze clouding my mind clears.

Sunscreen. I should probably slather more on. My skin is fair, so the last thing I want is to get burned. As reluctant as I am to break contact, I gently attempt to pry my fingers from his. When I do, Kingsley's grip tightens. Unable to help myself, my gaze roams greedily over his prone body. He's all tightly honed strength stretched out on the towel. His muscles stand out in sharp relief against his sun-kissed skin. Another swift punch of arousal hits me.

"I need sunscreen," I whisper, mouth going dry. With his mirrored aviators covering his eyes, I'm not sure if he's awake or not.

With a soft grunt, he releases my fingers, and the connection between us is broken. I rise unsteadily to my feet, walking to the enclosed part of the boat and rummaging through my bag for the spray bottle. As I pull it from the bottom, I can already tell it's empty. I dig around some more, shifting things, hoping I brought another. Usually, I dump a few in for just this kind of occasion. As I'm about to give up, my fingers wrap around a small squeeze bottle.

Bingo!

Unsure if Kingsley needs to reapply, I set the bag on the table and make my way to the front of the boat. Lowering myself to the plush towel, I shake the bottle and squirt a dollop onto my palm to rub it into my arms and legs. Kingsley's head twists toward me, and even though I can't see his eyes, I feel their heat as I massage the lotion into my chest and belly.

When I reach around to get the tops of my shoulders, his voice rumbles from beside me, breaking the silence. "Need help?"

Thick tendrils of sexual tension spark to life and simmer in the surrounding air.

That's probably not a good idea.

"Sure." The word is out of my mouth before I can stop it. I pass him the tube as he pulls himself up to a seated position before stretching his legs out in front of him so there is a slight bend in his knees.

"Come sit here." He pats the space between his thighs.

I gulp before pinning my lower lip with my teeth and resettling in front of him. Even with the sun blazing down on my exposed skin, a chill scuttles along my spine as he works the lotion into my flesh. The way he massages my muscles has my eyelids feathering shut. He starts at my neck before gradually working his way lower until reaching my bikini briefs.

By the time he finishes, my body is humming with need. Silence descends as the tension ratchets up between us. A fresh wave of nerves skitter across my over sensitized flesh. It's the best feeling in the world.

"I think you're good," he says gruffly.

What I think is that I'm on fire.

I twist around as he passes me the bottle. My gaze crawls over the powerful lines of his chest. There's not a spare ounce of fat on the guy. He's all chiseled strength. I'm dying to lay my hands on him. "Want me to do you?"

Even from behind his shades, his brows skyrocket across his forehead. The comical expression is enough to break the sexual tension building between us.

"That didn't come out the way I intended," I laugh before clarifying the question. "Would you like me to apply some sunscreen?"

When he jerks his broad shoulders, my mouth turns cottony. "Sure, why not?"

He turns so I'm treated to the wide expanse of his back. His muscles ripple with every movement.

Traps.

Deltoids.

Scapulae.

Oh, my...

It takes a moment to realize that my hands are trembling as I squirt a quarter-sized dot on the palm of my hand before rubbing them together to warm the lotion. I draw in a shaky breath before laying my hands against his shoulders. The flesh beneath my fingers is hot as I work my way down his back, making sure to get the sides. His muscles are hard yet pliable as I massage them. I could do this all afternoon.

When I reach the band of his boardshorts, I clear my throat along with the dirty thoughts that have invaded my brain like a swarm of bees. "Okay, all done."

Unfortunately.

Instead of stretching out, he flips over onto his stomach, resting the side of his face against stacked hands. I lower myself to the towel, allowing my muscles to loosen before melting into the cottony material.

A pang of sadness fills me at the thought of never seeing Kingsley again after this vacation comes to an end. Even though we've only spent a brief period of time together, already I realize that he's someone I'd like to get to know better.

"You never mentioned where you're from," he says, deep voice interrupting my thoughts.

"You never asked," I shoot back, turning my face toward him. Our time together is limited. All I want to do is drink him in so I can create a series of mental snapshots I'll be able to pull out when I want to remember what an amazing day this was.

"Touché."

When he says nothing further, I clear my throat. "Chicago."

He nods, his expression turning thoughtful.

"What about you?" I ask, wanting to know every little insignificant detail about him until a clear picture is painted in my mind.

"I'm from a small town a few hours west of here in the middle of the state."

I don't ask for specifics since I'm not overly familiar with Wisconsin. We drive through Milwaukee and Green Bay to get to Door County. That's about all I know.

"Are you here for the rest of the week?" His fingers reach over to ensnare mine.

"Yup, until Saturday morning." Today is Tuesday, which means we have three days to spend together. If that's what he wants. Maybe I'm jumping the gun and won't see him again after he drops me off. A tightness gathers in my chest at the notion. Anxiously I ask, "What about you?"

"We're heading home on Sunday. Football camp begins next week, so I need to get back for that."

I *knew* he was an athlete. "What college do you attend?"

"I'm not in college." A grin flashes across his face. In the sunlight, his teeth are almost blinding in their intensity. "I'll be a senior in high school."

"Really?" Holy moly. I find that difficult to believe. What happened? Did he flunk a few grades?

"Yup." He seems pleased by the compliment. "You thought I was older?"

"Well, yeah."

"How come?"

"Because..." Exactly what am I supposed to say? *You're so freaking built and muscular, you couldn't possibly be in high school?*

"Because?" he prompts, twisting toward me and propping himself up on his elbow. All those well-honed muscles ripple with the movement.

A smirk curls his lips as he notices my reaction. "Come on," he cajoles, "I'm waiting."

My guess is that Kingsley is used to girls falling all over him. Not only is he hot but he's also a nice guy on top of it. Even with my limited experience, I know that's not easy to come by.

Instead of answering, I grumble, "I plead the fifth."

He chuckles before lifting his hand and stroking his fingers against my jawline. "You're adorable when you're embarrassed."

Then he must find me adorable quite often.

Is it weird that all I want to do is press myself against him?

"Summer?"

I blink out of those thoughts. "Yeah?"

"I'm going to kiss you," he murmurs, voice filling with heat.

"Okay."

Thank God.

He scoots closer, removing my glasses before doing the same with his own. His body hovers over mine as his lips descend. When the velvety softness of his tongue brushes over the seam of my mouth, I tilt my chin upward.

There's a sweet tentativeness to his exploration. As if he doesn't want to push me too far, too fast. I don't realize my arms have tangled around his neck until I'm dragging him closer. His lips slide into a smile, and our teeth scrape against each other.

"You taste so sweet," he murmurs before delving in for more. He's all controlled finesse, only giving me a little when all I want is everything now. The need pooling at my core is a new and heady sensation. Guys have kissed me before, but not like this. Not like they actually knew what they were doing.

When he finally draws away, my lips feel swollen and sensitive. As he picks up his head, I gradually blink back to the present and glance around, realizing with a start that the sun has dipped beneath the horizon, and the air has a distinct chill.

Exactly how much time has passed? It feels like only a matter of minutes.

"We should probably head back to the marina," he murmurs.

Disappointment surges through me. How can the day be over already? It went by much too fast. All I want to do is hang out on the boat and feel his mouth roving over mine as the blistering sun beats down on us. I want to swim in the water and wrap my body around his. What I don't want is to leave him.

"Okay," I agree, knowing it's the responsible thing to do.

Kingsley searches my eyes before pressing another kiss against my lips. His tongue slips inside my mouth one last time before he groans and rolls onto his back. He throws a muscular arm over his eyes, his breath erupting in short, choppy bursts.

My gaze roves over him, sliding from his partially covered face to his broad chest, tight abdominals, and—

I flick my wide gaze to his face, but his arm continues to shield his eyes. My attention is drawn back to the thick erection tenting his boardshorts.

Holy crow!

My teeth sink into my lower lip as I stare. I'm so tempted to reach out and stroke my fingers over the hard length. Instead, I squeeze my hand into a tight fist. A gasp leaves my lips when he jerks up, jumping to his feet.

"Sorry," he mumbles, rushing toward the back of the boat.

"I—"

Have absolutely no idea what to say.

Silently, I rise to my feet before following. I find him standing in front of the steering console, staring at the dials and buttons. A guarded expression has settled over his features. The easygoing boy I spent the day with has vanished.

I want him back.

What's the protocol for a situation like this? Am I supposed to pretend I didn't notice his boner, or do I crack a joke to ease the strained atmosphere? I don't have a clue. The thing is, we've had such an amazing day. I don't want it to end on an uncomfortable note.

Carefully my hand flutters to his bare shoulder. "It's not a big deal."

He glances at me, his lips quirking before he jerks his shoulders to downplay the situation. "You turn me on."

Happiness bursts inside me like a bubble. "You do the same to me." Knowing that we'll probably never see each other again after this week prompts me to be more honest than I'd normally be comfortable with. There's no reason to lie or hide my feelings from him.

His smile stretches into a genuine one as we exchange a long, heated look.

"We should go," he says, clearing his throat.

I nod and take a seat on the bench, curling my legs beneath me before slipping the glasses over my eyes as Kingsley starts the engine, and we head back to the marina.

This has been the best day of my life. And if I'm lucky, I'll get to spend the next three with him.

SUMMER

4

I wake the following morning with a grin plastered across my face. I haven't been able to stop smiling since Kingsley dropped me off yesterday evening. We kissed for a solid thirty minutes in the front seat of his SUV. It was difficult to drag myself away from him.

We made plans to spend the entire day together, and I can't wait.

With a squeal of excitement, I toss back the covers and hop out of bed. Even though Kingsley won't be here until ten, there's no way I'll fall back to sleep. If this were a Disney movie, birds would chirp on my windowsill and I'd be holding giddy convos with mice about what I'm going to wear on my date. Since that's not the case, I dig through my suitcase to find a pink-striped bikini before changing. Then I throw on a coverup and float down to the kitchen to grab breakfast.

As if I could eat a bite...

I stumble to a halt at the sight that greets me. Mom is racing around, stuffing everything we brought with us for the week into bags. Dad is on the phone in the adjoining family room, pacing back and forth in front of the windows.

"Mom?" My gaze darts between them as a sinking sensation fills my belly. "What's going on?"

This is not normal parental behavior. Yesterday, I came down to them sitting on the weathered deck, staring at the waves as they rolled toward shore, sipping their coffee, and looking less stressed than they had in a long time. It was nice to see. This kind of manic behavior resembles the crazy mornings in Chicago with Mom attempting to hustle us out the door so we aren't late for school and she can make her eight o'clock meeting on time.

Another bad sign—her face is pale and drawn. The lines on her forehead are more pronounced than yesterday.

Mom doesn't spare me a glance as she gathers up clothes, shoes, and books. "Your grandmother died this morning."

"*Grandma Rose?*" My face scrunches as the question falls from my lips. Considering that my mother's parents died years ago, it's the only viable option.

"Yes."

My gaze slides to my father before bouncing back to her.

This will sound terrible, but we don't have a relationship with Grandma Rose. She and my father had a falling out years ago before my brother and I were born, so she's never been a part of our lives. I've seen her a handful of times, and honestly, from what I remember, she was kind of scary.

I wait for a bolt of grief to strike me, but it never materializes. Death, no matter who it happens to, is sad. But even so, that doesn't explain what she's doing. "Why are you packing everything up?"

Mom straightens before swinging around to face me. "Because we have to leave." She glances at the clock on the microwave before huffing out a breath. "We need to be on the road in thirty minutes." I can almost see the wheels spinning in her head as she mentally ticks off the tasks that need to be accomplished before we go. "Can you do me a favor and make sure your brother is awake? You both need to get packed up and then bring your bags down so your father can load them into the car."

"Leave? But why? We didn't even know Grandma Rose."

Shitty as it may sound, the words pop from my mouth before I can swallow them back down. Doesn't Mom understand that I met the most amazing guy yesterday and am nowhere near ready to say goodbye?

Her brows jerk together as she blinks in surprise. "Because your grandmother died, Summer, and now your father needs to plan a funeral." Her fingers flutter to her temples as she carefully massages the sides of her head before sucking in a breath, holding it for a heartbeat, and then releasing it. "I realize you were looking forward to spending time at the beach, and I'm sorry our vacation will be cut short, but there's nothing we can do about it. We have to go back."

I bite my lip, hating myself for sounding like such a selfish brat. That's not who I am. Well, not normally. Before she can say anything more, I blurt, "It's all right, Mom. I'll make sure Austin gets out of bed and packed up."

"Thanks, sweetie." She throws a grateful smile over her shoulder as she moves into the family room.

All the giddiness pounding through me moments ago seems like a distant memory as I trudge up the staircase and knock on my brother's bedroom door. "Aus?"

Nothing.

Ever since arriving on Saturday, Austin hasn't been crawling out of bed until ten o'clock at the earliest. Back home, he's up with the sun before leaving for practice. My brother lives for football. It's his drug of choice. He's been playing on the high school varsity team since he was a freshman. It's probably the only reason he's excited about school starting in September.

Unlike me, academics have never come easy to Austin. He was diagnosed with dyslexia at the end of third grade. By the time it was caught, it was too late, and he'd already come to hate school. If he didn't have football to keep him in line, the guy would probably have major truancy issues. As his twin, I've always been there to help him, doing my best to smooth over issues with teachers and make his academic life more tolerable.

When thirty seconds slide by without so much as a rustle of sheets from inside the room, I knock again and raise my voice. When he fails to respond for a second time, I suck in a breath, squeeze my eyes tight, and fling open the door. I send up a quick prayer that he hasn't slept in the buff. We might be twins, but I'm not looking to inflict any mental scars on myself.

Once in the darkened room, I take my chances and crack open an eye.

Phew. Totally covered.

"Austin," I whisper-yell, "wake up!"

He grumbles and rolls over so that his back is to me. With an aggravated sigh, I step farther into the room and give his shoulder a good shake.

"Stop it," he mumbles. "Can't you see I'm sleeping?"

"Yeah, I know, but you need to get up."

"Why?" The word comes out sounding more like an unintelligible grunt.

Knowing that Austin feels the same way I do about our grandmother, I don't bother sugarcoating the situation. "Grandma Rose kicked the bucket."

"*Who?*" Some of his grogginess falls away. He sounds genuinely perplexed, which only reconfirms that Dad's mother wasn't the kindly old granny she should have been to us.

"You know, the woman who birthed our father?" I pause before adding, "I guess she died this morning, and now we need to head back to Chicago." At least, I assume that's where we're going. We packed for the beach, not a funeral. I have nothing appropriate to wear. None of us do. A mental image of us showing up at the gravesite in full-on swimwear is enough to make me snort.

"The really mean one?" he asks, as the picture in my head dissolves.

Exactly. "Yup, that's her."

"Ugh." He flops onto his back and throws an arm over his eyes to shield them from the nonexistent sun that should be pouring in through the windows. This place is like a cave with room-darkening curtains. "That sucks."

I don't bother to clarify if he's talking about Grandma Rose's death or the fact he needs to haul ass out of bed at this ungodly hour. If I were a betting woman, I'd go with the hour of the day.

Now that my work is done here, I head for the door. "Mom wants you up and packed so we can leave in thirty."

"You've got to be shitting me," he gripes.

"I wish I were," I murmur sympathetically.

"Fuck me."

My sentiments exactly.

"Language," I joke in my best Mom voice.

When he grumbles, I walk out of his bedroom and into my own. Thankfully, I never unpacked my clothing. I've been living out of my suitcase, so everything is still neatly folded inside.

I glance at the black clock on the wicker nightstand next to the queen-sized bed. Maybe if I pack quickly enough, there will be time to stop at Kingsley's place and say goodbye. We never exchanged numbers. The thought of leaving without a way to contact him makes my heart clench.

I don't know if he wants to stay in touch or if this was nothing more than a way to pass the time. Contemplating the issue, I grab the dirty clothes from the floor and stuff them inside the bag. Then I head to the bathroom and clear all the makeup and hair products from the counter.

"We're leaving in fifteen," Mom calls from the bottom of the staircase.

I haul my suitcase out to the hallway and pause outside Austin's bedroom. Since he's crashing around inside, swearing like a sailor, I assume he's out of bed and packing up his stuff. Decision made, I drag my bag down the steps and park it by the front door at the pile of luggage. Dad huffs and puffs as he jogs up the front porch stairs to grab more stuff.

"I'm sorry to hear about Grandma," I say before stepping closer and wrapping my arms around him.

"Thanks, Summer." Somberness fills his voice. "I appreciate it."

That's all it takes for Grandma Rose's death to hit me and become real. It's not that I've lost a grandmother or someone I was close to, but more that my father has suffered the loss of his mother. They had their issues, but now both of his parents are gone. If he'd been holding out any hope that they might one day put the past behind them and reconcile, the possibility has been snuffed out with her passing. And for that, I'm sorry. Whatever state their relationship was left in is how it will now remain.

Before I can offer additional condolences, he changes the subject. "Is your brother up?"

"Yup, he's packing."

"Good. We need to get moving." Even though the day has only begun, he blows out a breath as if already exhausted. "We've got a long trip ahead of us."

"Do I have time to run over to my friend's house and say goodbye?"

"Umm." He glances at the sports watch adorning his left wrist. "Sure. Just be quick about it, all right?"

A smile of relief curves my lips as I press a kiss to his cheek. "Thanks, Dad. I will!"

With that, I race out the door and down the porch stairs before hitting the gravel driveway. Then I head north, jogging along the side of the road. Only now am I wishing that I'd paid more attention to where his house was located. If memory serves me correctly, it was a gray two-story with white trim. Hopefully, I'll recognize the place when I see it.

If not, I'm screwed.

Even though it's early, and the temperature is in the low eighties, a fine sweat breaks out across my forehead and gathers at the back of my cotton shirt. It feels like I've been running for half a mile. Did I somehow miss it?

Time is running out. My parents have enough on their plates without me delaying our departure. My feet slow to a stop, and I'm about to turn around when the gray behemoth comes into view. Nerves explode in the pit of my belly as I haul ass up the brick drive. Parked near the front door is Kingsley's silver Range Rover.

This is definitely the right place.

I pound up the front porch stairs and peek through the beveled glass door. Nothing stirs from inside. Sucking in a breath, I rap my knuckles tentatively against the glass and wait. As the seconds tick by, my nerves stretch taut, and I hop from one foot to the other. When there isn't a response, I knock a little louder.

My efforts are met with more silence.

I chew my lower lip before huffing out a breath. One more time and then I have to take off. There's nothing more I can do. Maybe this fledgling relationship with Kingsley wasn't meant to be anything more than a couple of amazing hours spent together in the sun.

When I knock again, the sound reverberates loudly, and I wince. The last thing I want to do is wake up his parents.

Movement from inside catches my eye. As the person grows closer, I realize it isn't Kingsley. I'll apologize profusely, and hopefully, they'll understand the situation. The door swings open, and an older, dour-looking woman glares at me from the other side of the threshold.

"Hello," I say anxiously, "I'm so—"

"Can I help you?" she asks, cutting me off with a clipped tone.

Maybe it's better to get right to the point. "Yes, ma'am, I'm looking for Kingsley."

"He's still asleep." Her sharp gaze rakes over me. Only now do I realize that I'm a sweaty hot mess. "You'll have to return later." She tacks on with a grumble, "Or preferably not at all."

"Oh, I—"

"Look, young lady," she snaps, "it's early, and the household is still asleep. You need to vacate the premises before I'm forced to call the police."

"*Call the police?*" I echo in disbelief, eyes popping wide. "What for? I haven't done anything wrong."

"You're trespassing and refuse to leave." The woman folds her arms across her chest as she stands in her robe.

"But I'm not trespassing," I say with frustration. "I'm friends with Kingsley."

A skeptical look flickers across her face.

"I am," I gulp. Obviously, this was a terrible idea. I shouldn't have come.

With her lips pressed into a tight line, she glares until I shift awkwardly beneath the scrutiny. Unsure what else to do, I point at the road beyond the driveway. "I'm going to leave."

"Excellent idea," she grunts before slamming the door in my face.

Birds chirp from the trees that surround the property as I stare at the glass door in shock.

What am I supposed to do now?

My cell phone rings, breaking into the whirl of my chaotic thoughts. With shaking fingers, I pull the slim rectangle from the pocket of my shorts before sliding the green button across the screen.

"Summer?" There's a pause. "Where are you?"

Dad.

I squeeze my eyes tightly shut. I'm out of time. There's nothing else I can do but leave.

"I'm on my way home right now. Sorry it took so long."

"All right." He sighs. "We're all packed up and ready to go. Just waiting on you."

"Be there in five." With that, I disconnect and slip the phone back into my pocket.

Well, this sucks. Then again, maybe it's better this way. No hurt feelings.

What would have really happened between us?

I guess the world will never know.

SUMMER

5

As Dad's Volvo crawls through town, my brother and I press our faces against the glass so we can check out the place we now call home.

"I can't believe you moved us here," Austin grumbles from the seat next to me.

In the rearview mirror, I watch Dad's lips smash into a tight line. Even though I don't echo the sentiment, I secretly agree with my twin. What the hell was Dad thinking? How are we supposed to go from living in an overcrowded metropolis to *this*? A town with—count them—three stoplights.

My gaze fastens on the window and the storefronts beyond as we roll down Main Street. People stop and gawk, turning our way with a mixture of curiosity and hostility shining from their eyes. It's like they know who we are. Or maybe they've never seen out-of-state plates before. Who knows? Whatever the reason, it's creeping me out.

There's a tiny theater with a single box office window in the center of town. The old-time marquee is surrounded by bulb lights and advertises a movie we saw two months ago.

"Are you seriously shitting me?" Austin exclaims as he catches a glimpse of the sign. "Not only are you moving us to bumfuck nowhere but you somehow went back in time."

I snort and press my lips together to stifle my laughter.

"Language," Mom snaps, irritated with our unfiltered reaction to our new digs.

"It's a theater that plays last-chance movies for cheap," my father mutters.

"I think it's charming," Mom soothes, attempting to put Dad at ease.

Austin is right. This is horrific. Would you like to know who we have to blame for this?

Grandma Rose. Her death is the gift that keeps on giving. We found out after the funeral that she left the family company to Dad in her Last Will and Testament.

Sounds like amazing news, right?

Wrong.

In order for Dad to claim his inheritance, which was appraised at a hundred million dollars, he has to move here to run the company. Condition number one, he can't sell the business for ten years. Condition number two, he can't sell the family estate. If Dad attempts to get rid of either property, all proceeds revert to a trust which then gets dispersed to the charities of Grandma Rose's choosing.

Pretty fucked up, huh?

Instead of giving Grandma Rose the middle finger like she so richly deserves for trying to control us from the grave, we've been forced to uproot our lives. No way was Dad going to turn his back on all that money. Not when the two of them have spent most of their adult lives scraping by. I can't totally blame my parents for making that decision. It would be tough to pass up, but still...

I'm about to start my senior year of high school and had everything planned out. Summer volunteering. College visits. A course at the local university. And it was all blown to shit with one ill-timed phone call.

Not to mention leaving all my friends behind.

With one glance at Austin, I know my brother is beyond pissed. He had the starting QB position locked down tight and had reached a certain level of popularity because of his football prowess. Now he'll have to claw his way to the top all over again as a senior. And then there are the academic challenges he faces.

Sure, I'm mad. But he's the one I feel most sorry for in all this. Even though I've tried to put on a good face, telling him it won't be so bad, it hasn't worked. I have a feeling it's only a matter of time before my brother blows like Mount Vesuvius.

A suffocating silence descends over the car. Mom breaks it when she swings around and forces a cheerful smile to her face. "How cool is it that they named the town after us?"

The town, in case you're wondering, is named Hawthorne.

Austin doesn't make eye contact as he slumps on the seat and broods. "Super cool, Mom."

I glance at my brother, knowing I'll have to ratchet up the excitement for the two of us. "It's pretty neat. Why is the town named after our family again?"

She glances at Dad before rubbing his shoulder. "Because your great-great-grandfather was a real entrepreneur and founded Hawthorne Industries almost a century ago. I believe they manufactured engine components or something like that for the car companies in Michigan. After about a decade, the town sprung up around it and has been thriving ever since."

"You might want to rethink the word *thriving*," Austin mumbles under his breath.

Ignoring him, Mom looks at Dad. "Isn't that the way the story goes?"

"More or less," he mutters through stiff lips. If she's expecting him to shade in a few more details regarding our family history and the town, she's in for a disappointment.

"Hmm," I say in lieu of an actual response. Again, I have to agree with Austin on this point. There doesn't seem to be much in the way of thriving with a handful of stores, shops, and a few restaurants dotting the main drag. Compared to where we came from, it's sadly lacking.

A few minutes later, we reach the outskirts of town.

"I hope no one blinked," Austin says, "you would have missed the thriving metropolitan known as Hawthorne."

"Enough!" Dad snaps.

My brother scowls, slouching further against his seat. I lay my fingers on Austin's hand before giving it a gentle squeeze. When his sullen gaze cuts to mine, my lips lift into a tentative smile, and his eyes soften. His head jerks to the window as we turn into a sprawling subdivision that seems strangely out of place in a countryside speckled with red barns and open fields.

In surprise, I blink at the enormous estates we roll past.

Who would have expected a shit town to have such humongous houses? Actually, these don't resemble anything as common as mere houses. These are mansions. And not the McMansion variety slapped together in a matter of months with cheap finishes. They're grand old estates that scream generations of wealth.

With wide eyes, I shoot my brother a stunned look. He sits up a little straighter as shock registers across his face.

"*This* is where we're going to live?" I ask in wonder.

"Yup," Mom says. "We'll stay at Grandma's house for the time being until we can get everything sorted out, and then we'll decide what the plan is."

Mom throws another bright smile over her shoulder as if to say- *See? This isn't so bad.*

The jury is still out on that one, but I keep that thought to myself.

Even though no vehicles are behind us, Dad flicks on his blinker as we pull into a long, weathered brick driveway.

My mouth falls open as I glimpse the two-story stone mansion set away from the street on a perfectly manicured lawn. My gaze slides over the architecture, noticing that the roofline has several elevations and most of the windows are arched. I press closer to the glass, unable to believe how extravagant the place is. I mean, look at the entryway...it's flanked by columns. *Columns!* Impeccably trimmed shrubbery hugs the perimeter.

"*This is our house?*" I squeak again.

"Yes," Dad says, "it is."

"Holy shit," Austin exclaims, shaking off his sulky attitude.

"Language," Mom scolds, but it's more of an afterthought and not an actual rebuke. Her wide-eyed gaze is glued to the mansion in front of us.

Dad parks the SUV near the wrought-iron gate in front the

garage. I shake my head, completely blown away by the recent turn of events. When he turns off the engine, we all sit quietly and stare at the house.

"So," I say, needing him to reconfirm this information, "you grew up here?" This will sound stupid, but I never put it together that Dad came from money. We're talking generational wealth that gets passed down through trust funds. Unless you turn your back on your family obligations, needing to forge your own way in the world, because apparently, that gets you disowned.

"Yeah," he answers succinctly. It became obvious early on in our trip when I tried peppering him with questions that he didn't want to talk about anything having to do with Hawthorne or his childhood. "The moving company should have arrived yesterday and unloaded the furniture. We'll need to unpack the boxes."

We continue to sit in the car, staring up at the house as if it isn't ours until Dad clears his throat. Then it's like we're all waking from the same dream before exiting the vehicle. The four of us walk through the portico flanked by huge concrete urns that contain small evergreen trees. As we stand at the massive front door, I stroke my fingers over the smooth wood.

Dad pulls out a key from his pocket and shoves it in the lock before turning and pushing the door open. Even though I have no desire to take up residence in Hawthorne, I'm dying to explore every nook and cranny of the house. We step into a two-story foyer with a white marble tile floor and find a sweeping staircase with a fancy scrolled wrought-iron banister that curves to the second floor. A baby grand piano sits near the arched window in the entryway where a steady stream of afternoon sunlight filters in.

Holy shit, we're now the proud owners of a baby grand piano!

I spin in a circle, trying to take everything in at once. The entryway is as big as the first floor of our house back home. A sparkly crystal chandelier hangs from the second-story ceiling. Similar to the architectural detail outside, arches are present in every room and hallway.

For the first time since finding out about the move, a flicker of excitement fills me. Maybe Mom is right and finishing out my senior year in Hawthorne won't be so bad.

I shoot her a cautious glance only to find her grinning at me. A smug look dances in her eyes. An answering smile curves my lips as I shake my head. I'm nowhere near ready to capitulate. For the time being, I'm reserving the right to withhold judgment. At least until after the first day of school.

And then, we'll see.

SUMMER

6

A few hours later, I rap my knuckles on Austin's closed bedroom door. Both of our rooms are on one side of the house, while our parents' master suite is located on the other. We could probably get murdered in the middle of the night, and they wouldn't hear a thing. It's a disconcerting thought. I grew up in the cramped quarters of a tiny house in the city where we were always on top of each other, so to have all this space feels luxurious.

More amazing than that, we both have private bathrooms. Like the rest of the house, they're well-appointed with jetted tubs and walk-in showers!

Do you have any idea what it's like to share a bathroom with your brother?

In a word—disgusting.

Now that he shaves, there's always a dusting of hair on the countertop and around the toilet, making it resemble a Chia Pet. And his aim hasn't always been the best. I won't even mention how many times I've fallen into the toilet during the night because he forgets to put down the seat.

So to have a bathroom all to myself?

Yes, please!

I might not be ready to admit it out loud, but the list of positives keeps growing one impressive feature at a time. Which brings me to the heated pool in the backyard. Not only is there a rock formation waterfall but the pool has a stone hot tub attached!

It's totally crazy!

I didn't notice it earlier, but all the houses on our side of the subdivision butt up against an eighteen-hole golf course, so we don't have neighbors in the rear. In Chicago, houses are built side-by-side on tiny postage stamp-sized yards, making it feel like they're sitting on top of each other. I could stand with my hand on the side of our brick house and practically touch our neighbor. So all this space is fantastic.

And the air smells so fresh and clean. It's a mix of pine trees and wildflowers. I kind of like that as well. I don't miss choking on car fumes or the aroma of takeout food that permeates the air from the Indian restaurant on the corner of our block.

When Austin doesn't answer, I knock louder before pushing open the door and poking my head inside. Like mine, his room has already been set up with a queen-sized bed and dresser. There are a few antique pieces that remain. It's a mix of old and new furniture.

Austin lies stretched out on his bed with his arms folded behind him. His head rests on stacked hands as he stares at the tray ceiling. He's so zoned out that he doesn't notice when I walk in.

I wave a hand in front of his face to get his attention. When his gaze slides to mine, I ask, "You want to run out and pick up a few school supplies?"

If we were still in Chicago, we wouldn't be going back until after Labor Day. But here, school starts tomorrow, three weeks earlier. Our parents had assumed that Hawthorne Prep (yup, it's also named after our family) was on the same schedule as our old school. Turns out that's not the case.

Austin's green eyes flicker to mine before he shakes his head. "Nah."

Ugh. I hate when he gets all moody. "Come on, Aus," I cajole, "don't you want to explore a little?"

"Explore what?" he asks with a sneer. "That sad-ass excuse for a town? Hard pass."

I settle on the bed next to him. "I know this sucks—"

"It's more than that," he snaps. "This ruins *everything*."

"You're right, it does." My shoulders slump under the heavy weight of his words. It's hard not to acknowledge the truth.

His face contorts with a mixture of rage and bitterness. "The old bat should have hung on for a year instead of fucking up my life."

Ouch. I wince at the uncharitable sentiment.

"Maybe it won't be so bad here. I mean, think about it. How much competition could there be for the quarterback position? You've been playing football since you were four years old. You've done a bazillion of camps and clinics. Not to mention all the agility training. It's like you said earlier, we're in the middle of bumfuck nowhere. How could these kids possibly be as skilled as you are? Have you ever considered the possibility that they might be thrilled to have such a talented player join their team?"

It's now official. I've become my mother.

I can almost see the words circling through his head as he considers their merit.

"I don't know," he begrudgingly admits. "Do you really think that will happen?"

"Definitely." I hoist my smile, relieved that I could lift his spirits even a fraction. It's better than the sad bastard impersonation he's been doing for the past two months. I was less than thrilled to be thrown abruptly into school tomorrow, but maybe it's for the best. Maybe then Austin will see that he won't have any problems fitting in with the team. I can deal with this move being difficult for me, but I need it to go smoothly for my brother.

Changing the subject, I ask, "Have you FaceTimed Alice?"

That's the girl he's been seeing. Even though the relationship had been fresh, it's another thing snatched away from him.

"Nah. I broke it off a couple of days ago." He shrugs. "With us moving, there didn't seem to be much point. I'm not really into the whole long-distance thing."

"Oh, I thought you liked her."

His expression turns sly. "What I liked is how much she put out."

I roll my eyes in disgust. "You're kind of a pig, you know that, right?"

"The ladies don't seem to mind one bit." His lips curve. It's the first genuine smile I've seen out of him since Grandma Rose died and blew our lives to shit.

"Ugh." I rise from the bed and walk toward the door. "On that note, I'm out of here."

Austin's attitude toward the female sex doesn't surprise me. The girls at our old school used to pant after him like they were in heat. I'm sure it'll be the same for him here. They seem to find him charming and handsome.

The handsome part I get. He's a good-looking dude with inky-colored hair and mossy green-colored eyes.

Charming, on the other hand?

Definitely not. He can be moody as fuck.

I pause over the threshold. "Sure you don't want to come with me? Maybe getting out of the house would do you some good."

"Nah." He scooches up to a sitting position before draping his arms across his bent knees. "Hey, Summer?"

"Yeah?"

A crooked smile pulls at the corners of his lips. "Thanks."

"For what?" I blink in surprise as the tough façade he usually puts on dissolves, leaving a rare vulnerability in its place.

His gaze darts away as if he's embarrassed. "For being your usual upbeat self."

I flash him a grin. "Don't worry, bro, I got you."

With a shake of his head, he laughs before stretching out on the bed again. "Whatever you say."

As I close the door, he yells, "Pick me up a few notebooks and pencils."

"Will do," I respond before walking through the airy hallway. My footsteps echo off the cavernous walls as I jog down the sweeping staircase to the first floor. As the entryway comes into view, I'm once again bowled over by the opulence surrounding me.

One thing is for sure—we have definitely moved up in the world.

Once in the foyer, I turn to the left where the dark wood panel study is located. Hundreds of leather-bound books line the shelves.

Situated across from them is an oversized fireplace with an elaborately carved mantel. A thick Persian rug in muted red and gold tones covers a portion of the wood plank floor. An antique mahogany desk with curved legs sits in the middle of the room as the last rays of sunlight pour in through the arched window that overlooks the rolling front lawn. My parents are seated on two high-back chairs in front of the window. Their heads are bowed together as they talk quietly. As soon as I step into the room, their attention snaps to me.

I skid to a halt, almost feeling like I've interrupted a private conversation.

"Hey, honey," Dad says, clearing his throat. "Settling in all right?"

"Yup." I shuffle farther into the room. "Do you mind if I borrow the car? I want to run into town and pick up a few supplies for tomorrow."

A smile bows Mom's lips as her face lights up. "What a fantastic idea!"

Well, I wouldn't go that far.

"I just want to be prepared," I say with an easy shrug.

They're acting weird. But then again, the past two months have been surreal, so I can't blame them for being a little off-kilter. We all are. Hopefully, once we've had a chance to make ourselves at home, everything will get back to normal.

"We can always count on you to take everything in stride," Dad says, gratitude bleeding through his words.

Even though it's meant to be a compliment, I stiffen as a prick of irritation blooms inside me. It feels like a pointed comment made toward my brother. The retort tumbles from my mouth before I can stop it. "I don't think you realize how difficult this move has been for Austin."

We might be twins, but I'm five minutes older and have always been more like the big sister. Not that he necessarily needs me to fight his battles but jumping to his defense isn't an impulse that can be easily shaken off. I've been doing it since we were kids.

"We understand that, honey." Mom sighs, familiar with my

protectiveness where Austin is concerned. "Your dad is simply trying to express his appreciation that you're always willing to go with the flow. It wasn't meant to be a criticism toward your brother."

I jerk my head into a tight nod as Dad fishes around in his pants pocket before tossing me the keys. I snatch the jangling metal midair with one hand.

"Good catch," he says with a wink.

That's all it takes for my earlier snappishness to dissipate as my lips lift.

"Drive safe," Mom adds, "and don't get lost."

I give her an—*are you crazy* look. "That would be kind of hard to do."

"The town isn't *that* small," Dad grumbles with a roll of his eyes.

"Whatever you say." With a wave, I grab my purse from the credenza in the front hall before walking out the door and heading to the Volvo. I start it up and pull out my phone to search for the closest Target. It takes a moment for a response to pop up.

Hmm. Apparently, the nearest one is over a hundred miles away.

All right, let's look for Wal-Mart.

That also turns out to be a no-go. I rack my brain, trying to recall if I saw any big-box stores when we drove through town. But let's face it, I was a little shellshocked at the time and had stopped processing my surroundings. As I search for the closest store, the only thing that comes up is a place called Rothchild's.

Never heard of it.

With little in the way of choices, it's a simple decision. I tap the screen until the map sets with turn-by-turn directions before easing the SUV out of the drive and onto the street toward town. I switch on the radio and flick the channel until Billie Eilish explodes from the speakers and some of the tension filling me drains away.

I press the button on the door handle, and the window disappears as the lush green scenery passes by. The sun casts its last rays of light before dipping beneath the horizon. I guess all those twangy country songs are right. There is definitely something to be said for country roads and wide-open spaces. Fields of tall grass and trees that spear up into the sky, and the smell of fresh air as it hits your nostrils. I'm more used to bustling city streets crammed with cars, people, and skyscrapers.

Twenty minutes later, I pull into the parking lot of Rothchild's, located on the opposite end of town, and cut the engine. It's a single-level, squat white brick building. The kind of store that probably would have been popular before Target and Wal-Mart took over the market. I swipe my purse from the front seat and exit the vehicle. The parking lot is about a fourth of the way full.

Apparently, this is the place to be on a Sunday evening. I push through the front door into the vestibule and grab a cart. It's like my head is on a swivel as I wheel past aisles of greeting cards, cleaning products, health care goods, and a small selection of furniture and clothing before hitting the jackpot.

Happiness fills my heart at the wide assortment of school supplies.

I'm one of those dorks that secretly enjoys shopping in July for materials. If my life hadn't been turned upside down, that's exactly what I would have done. Usually, I have a list of everything I need for the first semester, but today, I'll have to wing it. I run my fingers over the covers of plastic-bound notebooks before tossing a few in the cart. I grab a couple of packs of mechanical pencils and gel pens, which are, hands down, my favorite. My fingers are already itching to open them and doodle in a notebook. A few binders and folders get added. Who am I to resist a box of colored pencils and Post-it Notes in various pastel colors?

Hmm, should I get a calculator?

If my schedule mimics my old one, calculus will be one of my classes. And my calculator has gone MIA in the move.

With only a couple of options to choose from, I pull one from the rack, turn it over, and study the list of capabilities. It's more than a hundred dollars. I don't want to spend that kind of money if it's unnecessary.

I'm in the middle of making a side-by-side comparison when two girls turn into the aisle. They're chatting and laughing. One holds a small basket that dangles from her arm. I scout them out, all the while pretending to be engrossed in the calculator packages.

The first thing I notice is that both are wearing short shorts that barely cover their ass cheeks and shirts that hug their curves. It's the same kind of outfit girls at home would wear. I suppose that's a positive. It can't be totally ass-backward here if the fashion is similar, right?

My gaze gravitates to the girl with long blond hair. She's the one who has been doing most of the talking and gives off that whole *I'm in charge* vibe. The other has brunette hair pulled back into a ponytail. Both are pretty. I try not to make it too obvious that I'm eavesdropping on their conversation. Although, the blonde is loud in an obnoxious way, so it would be difficult *not* to hear what she has to say.

From the intel I've gathered, there's talk of a get-together tonight. A couple of hotties from the football team will be there. And blondie has a thing for one of them. She also yammered on about a dried-up old English teacher named Ms. Pettijohn. I'm almost tempted to follow them through the store to hear more. They seem like an endless fount for Hawthorne gossip.

I wonder if these girls attend Hawthorne Prep or the small public school in the next town over. It's on the tip of my tongue to ask because they look to be around my age. How nice would it be to meet a few people tonight instead of walking into school cold tomorrow morning? Who knows, they might ask me to tag along to the party they've been dishing on.

As I work up enough courage to introduce myself, the blonde flicks her blue gaze to mine before pinning me in place. "Stare much?"

I blink, thrown off balance by the blunt question.

Holy shit. Is she talking to me?

When I remain silent, a nasty glint enters her eyes as she waves her hand with exaggerated movements in front of my face. "Hello? Is anyone in there? Or are you deaf and mute?"

The girl at her side giggles as a rush of heat floods my face. All I want to do is melt into the floor.

"She's probably slow," the dark-haired girl says, sounding bored as if she isn't talking about me right in front of my face. "How tragic."

"I'm not mute or deaf," I mutter, forcing out the rest, "just shocked at your rudeness."

The blonde's sculpted brows rise across her forehead. "Well, I'm not the one who was gawking like a weirdo." She smirks before flipping her hair. "Let me guess, you're into chicks." Her gaze flickers over me before she wrinkles her pert nose. "No thanks. Not interested."

My mouth falls open. Who talks to a perfect stranger like this?

The other girl snorts. "There's no question about it, you're strictly dickly."

The blonde laughs. "I know."

"I wasn't staring," I mumble, cutting into their conversation. "I was wondering if you go to Hawthorne Prep."

I wince. *How could I let the question slip free?* Now, I'm hoping the answer will be no. I don't want to be anywhere near these two mean girls.

"Of course, we do." The blonde's upper lip curls into a sneer as one of her hands settles on her hip. "What do we look like, townies?"

Great.

This time, I keep my lip buttoned. There is no way in hell I'm going to tell her I'll be starting at the exclusive prep school tomorrow. I have no idea how many students attend Hawthorne, but I'm hoping that I don't run into this nasty girl and her sidekick any time soon.

When her gaze flits over me for a second time, I become aware that I'm still wearing black capri yoga pants and an obscure band T-shirt that has seen better days. This is what comfortable travel wear looks like.

"From the regrettable state of her outfit, it's obvious she's a townie." Blondie makes a frowny face. "So sad."

Humiliation burns through me as I throw the calculator into the shopping cart and rush away. The two girls barely wait for me to turn the corner before bursting into peals of laughter.

Holy crap, where the hell have my parents moved us to?

In a small way, I was kind of excited to start school tomorrow, meet some new people, and settle in. Now?

Not so much.

If these two girls are in any way a reflection of the student population at Hawthorne, senior year will be a living hell. And there's not a damn thing I can do about it.

SUMMER

7

With my gaze trained on the ceiling, I lie awake in my bed. I've spent the past hour tossing and turning, trying to get comfortable. Those two beastly girls from Rothchild's keep popping into my head. I don't think I've ever encountered such rude people, and I grew up in Chicago. I've *experienced* rude but that was like a whole new level.

Now I'm nervous about tomorrow.

There is no way I'll be able to fall asleep. And if I do, my nightmares will be filled with bitchy and bitchier.

Another spasm of agitation slides through me, leaving a thick coat of restlessness in its wake. Lying here for another moment is out of the question. With a huff, I toss off the covers and pad to the window before pulling back the curtain and staring through the screen. My gaze drops to the illuminated patio below. It's still unfathomable that we own such a kick-ass pool. Dad plans on calling a company tomorrow to service it so we can get it up and running. There's a heater and we'll be able to swim until October. It could snow by then, and we could be outside swimming.

My gaze travels over the thick lawn. Dad mentioned earlier that the house sits on an acre of land. Trees and bushes border the sides of the property, offering a bit of privacy from the neighbors. A few pines spear up into the sky at the rear of the yard to delineate our estate from the lush landscape of the golf course.

As soon as I catch sight of the night sky, I press my face against the screen until there's a definite possibility of the mesh lines becoming permanently tattooed on it. There are so many pinpricks of light. Have I ever seen so many stars crowding the sky?

Only at the planetarium. And that was just a projection.

Swinging away from the window, I look around before grabbing an afghan from the end of my bed and moving to the screen door that leads to a tiny deck off my room. I hurry down the stairs and hit the concrete before skirting the pool area and stepping onto the plush lawn with bare feet. Immediately my toes sink into the velvety softness.

Now that I'm outside, the distant strains of music hit my ears. I turn toward the sound of voices as they carry on the wind. It's not a massive party, but there are probably a dozen people hanging out next door. There's a mix of higher-pitched female voices and deep male baritones. My steps falter as I glance over at the neighboring property, but the trees and shrubbery obscure my view. After what happened at the store earlier this evening, there's no way in hell I'm going to creep over there and spy.

Or, God forbid, introduce myself.

For all I know, it's the same party those girls were yapping about.

As curious as I am about our new neighbors, I'm more concerned with self-preservation.

Ignoring the noise, I cut across the lawn and head to the far side of the property away from the neighbor's house. It takes a moment to scout out the area and find the perfect spot before arranging the blanket on the lawn. As I settle on my back and take in the view, my breath gets clogged in my throat. My gaze skims across the vast expanse of the solar system that stretches across the sky.

It takes effort to empty my mind and focus on my inhalations as I remind myself to breathe deeply from my diaphragm. I repeat the process a dozen times until every muscle loosens and my body sinks farther into the green carpet that cushions me. Only then does a sense of peace steal over me. When I'm out of sorts, this is one trick I use to help center myself.

Hands down, this has to be one of the most breathtaking skies I've ever gazed at. It almost feels like I could reach up and trail my fingers through the pinpricks of light illuminating the inky blackness.

What's most mind-boggling is that scientists have only discovered four percent of the universe and that it stretches far beyond what anyone can possibly conceptualize. Or how about that it's billions of years old? In reality, the earth is an insignificant speck in the universe. And the people who fill it are even less consequential.

I blow out a steady breath, emptying my lungs completely. Those thoughts are usually enough to put my problems into perspective and settle everything rioting inside me.

But that's not the case tonight. The dread pooled at the bottom of my belly stubbornly remains.

SUMMER

8

At precisely six o'clock the next morning, my alarm goes off. With a groan, I roll over and grab my phone before hitting snooze. Even though I've been awake since five, I stayed in bed, hoping to fall back asleep.

No such luck.

Those two snots from the store are all I can think about.

My greatest fear is that they're the norm and not the exception. How will I survive an entire year of that? The thought is enough to make my stomach tighten with nerves. They roil in the pit of my belly, making me feel like I might throw up.

After I returned home from the store last night, I dropped off Austin's supplies. With a laugh, he had asked if anything eventful happened in town. For a split second, I considered telling him about the girls, but immediately nixed the idea. He's already pissed off about being here. There's no reason to add fuel to that particular fire. If I know my brother, he'll stride into Hawthorne Prep with an even bigger chip on his shoulder than there already is. And that's the last thing we need.

When the alarm goes off for a second time, I realize I can no longer delay the inevitable. I drag my ass to the bathroom and jump in the shower. As warm water sprays over my body, I'm hoping it'll wash away my lingering dread. Once I dry off and slip into my panties and bra, I grab the outfit that was waiting at the house when we arrived yesterday.

Mixed feelings churn inside me about being forced to wear a uniform. I've always attended public school and could wear whatever I wanted within reason.

I pull on the navy, green, and gold plaid skirt until it settles around my waist and then shove my arms through the sleeves of the white button-down before tucking the excess material into the waistband. I run my hands over both the shirt and skirt to smooth out any visible wrinkles. I shrug into the navy blazer with the gold crest stitched on the upper left corner and pull on the matching knee-high socks before staring in the bathroom mirror.

The girl who meets my gaze in the reflection brings a smirk to my face. If my friends could see me now, they would be on the floor rolling around with laughter. And I can't say that I would blame them for it. I look like I stepped off the set of *Gossip Girl*.

I rotate one way before turning to the other side to check myself out from every angle. When I catch a glimpse of my ass, a frown pulls at the corners of my lips as I tug at the material in the back.

Why the hell is this so short?

Isn't showing off this much skin at a private school considered sacrilegious? All I have to do is put my hair in pigtails with matching plaid bows and I could star in a creepy schoolgirl porno. That's definitely not the look I'm going for. My plan is to fly under the radar, so the last thing I want to do is invite unwanted attention. At least all the other girls will be wearing the same thing.

Not in the mood to mess around with my hair, I pull the inky-colored strands into a topknot and fasten it with a rubber band along with a few strategically placed bobby pins. I swipe on a bit of golden eye shadow and some pink lip gloss before calling it a day.

On my way down to the kitchen, I rap my knuckles against Austin's closed door. When it's met with silence, I call out, "You up?"

All I get is a grunt in response. It's not like I'm excited and in some big rush to get to school, but I don't want to be late for the first day either. My goal is to blend in with the masses until I can get the lay of the land.

I head down to the kitchen, where Mom and Dad are enjoying their coffee at the table. Sunlight filters in through the bank of windows overlooking the backyard. Mom is wrapped in her fluffy white robe, and her ebony-colored hair is a tangled mess around her shoulders. Dad is already dressed in a gray suit and looks ready to take on the day.

They both perk up as I enter the room.

Mom quietly surveys the outfit. It doesn't take long for her shoulders to shake with silent mirth. A smile quirks Dad's lips.

"Don't say a word," I mutter.

"Ahh, the old Hawthorne uniform. I see nothing has changed in that regard." He eyes the hemline with a frown. "Seems like the skirts have gotten a tad shorter."

"Yeah, I noticed that," I grumble before tugging self-consciously at the fabric, but it doesn't budge an inch. My legs are on display for everyone to see. I ran cross-country and track my freshman and sophomore years, so I'm used to shorts that leave little to the imagination. The difference is that I wasn't walking around in school with them.

"My advice is that you try not to bend over, sweetie. I'll call the office and see if we can get you a skirt in a larger size."

"That's not the problem." I slip my fingers beneath the waistband and tug it away from my abdomen. "It's the length. I need a tall or extra long."

Her brows scrunch as she considers the situation. "Maybe we can let out the hem an inch or two." She drums her fingertips against the table. "We'll play around with it when you get home from school. Unfortunately, you're stuck with it for today." A smile lifts the corners of her lips. "It's one of the curses of having long legs, I guess." She pauses. "I was about to start the griddle and make pancakes for your brother." With her coffee in hand, Mom rises from the chair. "Do you want a couple?" Before I can answer, she tacks on, "I have a fresh pint of blueberries. We can add them to your pancakes."

Under normal circumstances, I would be all over that offer, but not this morning. Food of any kind sounds like a disastrous idea.

I wrinkle my nose and shake my head. "No, thanks. I'll stick with coffee."

Mom clucks her tongue in disapproval. "Are you sure? I want you to be well-fueled. Breakfast is the most important meal of the day."

"Yup, I'm positive." I go to the glossy cherry cabinets before pulling open the first door and peering inside only to find plates and bowls. I slide over to the next cabinet and try door number two, only to find a stack of glasses.

Irritation bubbles up inside me. "Mom, where are the mugs?" How is this place supposed to feel like home when I don't know where anything is? It's like I'm a guest in someone else's house, forced to live someone else's life.

You know what?

I want my old one back. I want to go home and stop this farce. But that's not possible. So I do the only thing I can and stuff all the sadness and frustration deep down inside where I can't dwell on it.

"Next one over." She points, oblivious to the misery swirling inside me.

I huff out a breath and pull open the cabinet only to find a row of neatly stacked mugs. I grab an oversized one, already able to tell that it's going to be a shitty day. With my mug in hand, I pour a gigantic cup of coffee and dump two heaping spoonfuls of sugar into it before stirring. Today, I'm going to need all the help I can get. My eyelids flutter shut as I take my first sip and allow the java to course freely through my veins.

Better. Much better. If I'm lucky, it'll be enough to help me survive Hawthorne Prep.

As I lift the mug to my lips for another sip, Austin strolls into the room wearing his navy blazer, crisp white button-down, and tan pants. His dark hair has been combed into an effortlessly messy style.

"Well, don't you look all *School Ties*." I can't resist mocking.

"Huh?" He blinks as his forehead wrinkles in confusion, not getting the movie reference.

Our parents snicker before Mom says, "Let's hope real life doesn't echo cinematic expression."

True that.

I search my brain for an updated reference he'll understand. "You're channeling Chuck Bass from *Gossip Girl*."

Not thrilled with the comparison, he scowls his displeasure. I'm saved from a barbed rebuttal when Austin's attention gets snagged by Mom flipping a fluffy pancake onto a plate next to the stove.

My brother stabs a finger at the three-stack tower already glistening with butter. "Please tell me those are for me. I'm starving."

"All yours," she says with a smile.

"Awesome." He grabs the plate and a fork from the drawer before settling at the table. We all stare silently as he plows through the hotcakes at record speed. It's almost impressive the way he can demolish a plate of food in a matter of minutes. I've never witnessed anything like it. Somewhere out there is a food challenge circuit missing their crowned champion.

Once he pops the last bite into his mouth, he glances up. "Are there any more? That didn't even make a dent."

With a strange mixture of amazement and disgust filling her face, Mom shakes her head. "How is it that you don't weigh three hundred pounds?"

Austin flashes a grin before patting his flat belly. "Fast metabolism." It's a rare bit of happiness from him that we're dazzled with.

For a moment, it's like everything is normal again.

"Well, you certainly didn't inherit that gene from me," she grumbles.

After my brother demolishes another plate of pancakes, we grab our backpacks and head to the front door.

"Wait a minute, I almost forgot," Dad says, tossing a set of keys at us.

Austin snags them from the air before I have a chance. He smirks before opening his palm. I expect to see the keys to the Volvo with their familiar four-leaf-clover key chain that my dad has had forever, but it's not there.

My brother frowns before we both glance at our parents in confusion. "What are these?"

Huge smiles break out across their faces.

Dad shrugs, enjoying every moment of this surprise. "Beats me, maybe you should look out front."

Austin and I stare at each other for all of two seconds before scrambling through the kitchen to the foyer. The slap of shoes striking the marble echoes throughout the house. When we reach the front door, Austin elbows me out of the way and flies through the entrance before skidding to a halt under the portico. I slam into the wide expanse of his back before peeking around him, trying to catch a glimpse of the surprise.

"Holy shit!" Austin exclaims, hands going to the sides of his head as if to keep it from exploding. *"No way!"*

There, in the middle of the brick drive, sits a shiny black Mercedes G-Class SUV.

I grin and wait for Mom to reprimand Austin for his language, but she ignores it.

"This is just a little thank you. We know that neither of you wanted to uproot your lives and move here. Hopefully, a brand-new set of wheels to share will make everything a little easier to contend with."

All I can say is that it doesn't hurt.

"I can't believe you bought us a G-wagon!" Austin crows, echoing my thoughts exactly, before whipping out his phone and snapping a few pics to add to his Insta story.

"Thanks," I say, rushing toward my parents before throwing my arms around them.

They squeeze me tight before Mom whispers, "All right, you two better get moving. We don't want you to be late on your first day."

Since Austin is already sliding behind the wheel with the keys in hand, I head for the passenger side door before settling onto the buttery soft leather seat.

Mom bites her lip before waving a hand at us. "Should I come with and make sure there aren't any problems with your registration?"

Good Lord, no. Sometimes Mom forgets that we're not in kindergarten anymore.

"Nah," Austin says, dumping his backpack into the back seat, "we're good."

My brother and I grin at each other as he slips the key into the ignition. The engine purrs to life, smooth as silk. That new car smell inundates me, making me almost dizzy. It's all sumptuous leather, smooth natural grain wood trim, and expensive additions. I can't even imagine what this vehicle costs. Or that my dad bought it. He's been driving our Volvo for at least ten years. Austin turns on the radio and cranks up the music as we roll to the end of the driveway. Mom and Dad wave before heading inside the house.

As we're about to leave, a red convertible flies past us, going way over the subdivision speed limit. My brother slams on the brakes and grumbles under his breath as I whip forward against the seat belt. If Austin had pulled out a couple of seconds sooner, we would have been T-boned.

I stare at the red taillights and wonder if that was the neighbor I heard having a party last night. My assumption is that anyone who lives in a fancy subdivision probably attends Hawthorne Prep rather than the public school. As long as it's not those nasty girls from the store, I don't give a damn who it is.

"Sweet Mustang," Austin mutters, grudgingly admiring the car as I try to get a look at the driver.

As soon as the sports car is a couple of hundred feet away, Austin's lips pull up into an impish grin as he presses his foot against the gas pedal, and the Mercedes shoots onto the road. When the Strokes come on, he cranks up the volume until its eardrum splitting as we belt out the lyrics. It's doubtful Julian Casablancas has anything to worry about as far as us taking over the band.

Twenty minutes later, we turn onto the paved drive that leads to the school parking lot. There's a line of traffic waiting to get in. With wide eyes, I stare at the elaborately gated property. On either side of the driveway are ornate stone pillars. I'm not sure what I was expecting, but nothing this fancy in the middle of nowhere.

"Toto, I have a feeling we're not in Kansas anymore," my brother murmurs, breaking into my thoughts.

I almost snort.

No, we most certainly are not.

I notice the red Mustang that had whizzed past earlier is a few cars ahead of us. The top is down, but all I can make out is a boy with short dark hair. As intrigued as I am by our neighbor, I'm more concerned about how the next couple of hours will play out.

Austin drives through a sea of high-priced sports cars and SUVs. He crows in disbelief, rattling off the price tag of each vehicle we pass. It takes a few minutes for us to find an empty spot and park. These people are in a league all of their own, and I don't understand how we're going to fit in with them. As if in a dream, I turn and fumble around in the back seat for my bag before hauling it onto my lap. Not making a move to exit the Mercedes, I glance at my twin, who stares silently out the windshield.

"Austin?"

My gaze slides from him to the sprawling gray stone building looming in front of us that looks like it could belong on a vast estate in England. There's something charming and idyllic about the ivy that clings to the walls.

"Why are they staring?" Austin mutters from beside me.

"Huh?" I rip my gaze away from the three-story building and realize there are pockets of students watching us. If it were simply curiosity on their faces, it would be one thing. Their expressions remind me of the girls from the store last night. A shiver of unease slithers down my spine.

"I don't know. Maybe they don't get a lot of new people here." Let's hope that's all it is. I glance at my phone and realize we need to get moving. "We're supposed to be in the office already. It took us longer than expected to get here, and the first bell rings in fifteen minutes."

Austin hands over the keys since I'll be driving home by myself while he stays after for football practice. I drop them in my bag and take a deep breath before forcing myself to get out of the vehicle.

Now that we're standing in the parking lot, more people stop and stare. They bend their heads close together as their lips move. Hushed tones fill the air but don't quite reach our ears. The strange fascination they have with us continues to grow as we move toward the entrance of the imposing stone building.

From beneath my lashes, my gaze scans the crowd, but there's not a friendly face to be found. This feels like a nightmare, and a punch of nausea hits me full force. Thank God, I didn't eat breakfast. Blueberry pancakes making an encore appearance on the front lawn is not the first impression I want to make.

I throw a worried glance at my brother. The smile he had been wearing ten minutes ago has been replaced with a scowl and a hard-edged stare. Thick tension radiates off him in suffocating waves. My brother is no stranger to fistfights. And he doesn't have a problem throwing the first punch. Or the second and third.

When we were younger, Austin took a lot of shit for being slow. What our classmates didn't understand was that he wasn't stupid, he just learned in a way that made him different. It took him a little longer to figure things out. After a while, it got to a point where if anyone commented about him not catching on quickly enough or pointed out a bad grade, they would get pounded an inch within their lives.

I don't want to see Austin slip back into that mindset again.

My fingers flutter to his arm. When his head twists toward mine, I hoist my lips, wanting to give the illusion of being unconcerned. After a moment, he gives me a terse nod as if he understands my silently conveyed message. We'll call it a twin thing and leave it at that.

As we walk past more clumps of people, chatter and whispers hit my ears until the tips burn in mortification. This town must be seriously lame if our arrival has sparked this much interest.

"Bunch of fucking hicks," Austin grumbles as we walk up the wide stone stairs before yanking open the glass door to the building.

I give him a tight smile, hoping things get better and we're not treated like pariahs for the rest of the day.

My steps stutter as my gaze sweeps over the entryway. I'm just as bowled over as when we arrived at the house yesterday. I want to stop and take everything in all at once. The floors are a sea of glossy black-and-white checkered marble tile that stretches down the corridors. Near the staircase in the entry is a bust of a man displayed on an ornately carved pedestal. My guess is that it's a likeness of Herbert

Hawthorne, who founded the school. Gold framed pictures dot the upper portion of the cream-colored walls, while the lower part is paneled in black cherry wainscot. I glance up at the timber-covered ceiling and the massive gold chandelier that hangs from above.

Students force their way past us, their gazes crawling over our bodies, but none offer help, and I'll be damned if I ask for it. There has to be a sign somewhere. My gaze travels around the corridor until it lands on black lettering etched onto a frosted glass door.

Relief floods through me as I point. "There's the office."

Austin remains quiet as we move through the crowded hallway. The farther into the school we walk, the more out of place I feel. It's a disconcerting sensation. One that makes the hair at the back of my neck prickle with unease. My brother and I are dressed exactly like everyone else, yet we've been marked as outsiders.

With fingers that tremble, I grab the knob and push the door open, wanting to escape from the hallway and get away from all the prying eyes watching us. Once we step inside the office, I'm tempted to lean against the door in relief. I never want to go back out there again.

"Why hello there, you two," a kindly voice greets from behind a massive desk strewn with papers.

It's the first friendly face we've encountered since rolling into town yesterday.

I blink, wanting to make sure the older woman is speaking to us. When my gaze locks on hers, a smile adorns her wrinkled features. Her gray hair is pinned up in a bun, and a navy-colored cardigan is draped across her shoulders. Whenever I've pictured what a sweet old lady would look like, this was it. In other words, the complete opposite of my grandmother.

Her friendly gaze shifts back and forth between us. "I assume you're Summer and Austin Hawthorne?"

"Yes!" I snap to attention before shaking my head in embarrassment. "Sorry."

"My name is Mrs. Baxter, and I'm the office secretary. I pretty much do everything around here, so if you need anything, all you have to do is ask." Her lips lift as she claps her hands together with excitement. "It's so thrilling to have another generation of Hawthornes roaming these halls again. It's been..." her brow furrows as she does a bit of mental math before giving up with a sheepish shrug. "Well, since your father was here. We're all delighted by your arrival."

The quick glance Austin and I exchange speaks volumes.

Thrilled is not the word I would use to describe how we've been welcomed. It's more like we're lepers freshly released from the colony. I'm tempted to tell her so but hold my tongue at the last minute. In no way do I want this woman to think we're ungrateful for her kindness or that we expect to be greeted like royalty.

"Anyway," Mrs. Baxter continues, interrupting my thoughts, "I'm sure you would like to see your schedules for the semester."

"Yes," I agree while Austin remains his stoic self, "that would be great."

Humming under her breath, the older woman shuffles around a few papers before discovering what she's searching for. "Here you go, young lady." She gives me the slip before turning to my brother. Her movements stall as she blinks at him.

"My goodness, you certainly are a handsome young lad." The secretary waggles a finger at him as I attempt to rein in my laughter. "You're the spitting image of your father at the same age." She shakes away the memories. "Remarkable."

A dull red color stains Austin's cheeks as he squirms beneath her open perusal. He's grown accustomed to the staring but not the forthright inspection. Most take one look at his sulkiness and give him a wide berth while admiring him from afar.

"Um, thank you?"

Now that we have our schedules, we study them in silence. I have—English lit 12, calculus, physics, AP French, AP environmental science, AP psychology, a blow-off class. It's identical to what I would have had in Chicago, which is reassuring. I peek at Austin's class list and notice his is the same. Pre-calculus, chemistry, English lit 12, physical education, regular psychology, French III, and study hall. I can help him with all of those classes if he needs it.

"I've asked two students from council to stop by and show you around." She flashes another pleasant smile as if trying to put us at ease. "Hopefully, that will help your first day run smoothly."

"Thank you," I say, voice brimming with gratitude.

"It's not a problem. Everyone here wants you to feel at home." She waves away my appreciation before glancing toward the closed office door inside the spacious room. "The headmaster was looking forward to greeting both of you. Unfortunately, he was called into a meeting. It'll have to wait until another time."

Let's hope not. It's been a long-standing joke in our family that my parents should bite the bullet and rent office space for Austin next to our former principal since he was a frequent visitor. As those memories roll through my head, the door leading to the hallway opens, and a petite blonde with soft blue eyes walks in.

"Good morning, Mrs. B," she greets.

"Morning, Delilah." The older woman glances at the clock on the wall. "You're right on time."

Mrs. Baxter waves toward my brother, and the girl turns to us with a ready smile on her face. Austin straightens to his full height. I give him a bit of a side-eye and notice how he's staring at the new arrival.

"This is Austin. If you wouldn't mind giving him a brief tour before first hour and showing him where his classes are located, that would be helpful."

Delilah's eyes widen as color rises in her cheeks before she glances away. My brother takes a step toward her before grinding to a halt. A strange tension crackles in the air between them that changes the energy in the office.

Uncomfortable with Austin's unwavering interest, Delilah clutches her books to her chest before clearing her throat. "Can I see your schedule?"

Even in the silence of the room, her voice is barely audible. She's not the first girl to get tongue-tied in Austin's presence, and she won't be the last. I almost want to pat her on the shoulder and advise her to steer clear. I love my brother more than anything, but the guy can be kind of a man whore. And this girl looks way too sweet to survive him. He'll chew her up and spit her out before she even realizes what's happening.

Instead of handing over the schedule, Austin closes the distance between them, crowding into the girl's personal space so she is forced to look at the paper as he holds it in his hand.

I almost roll my eyes at his antics.

"It looks like we have a few classes together," Delilah croaks, turning redder by the second.

Poor girl. I can't tell if she's thrilled by the prospect or dreading it.

"Great," my brother murmurs. "You can walk me to class."

Her gaze darts to him before skittering away. Another hot stain creeps into her cheeks. She clears her throat and glances anxiously at Mrs. Baxter before her gaze touches upon me. "Should I show her around, too?" A hopeful note threads its way through her voice.

The secretary shakes her head. "Sloane should be along momentarily to pick Summer up for her tour."

Delilah's slender shoulders fall as she gnaws her lower lip. "I guess we should go."

"Yup." My brother grabs the office door and jerks it open before a charming smile curves his lips. "After you."

Uh-oh. I recognize the predatory gleam in Austin's eyes. I don't envy this girl one bit. My guess is that she has no idea how to handle a guy like my brother. Sadly, I think she's going to find out.

"Thanks," she murmurs, shooting us a look full of dismay as she steps over the threshold into the bustling hallway. Austin stays close before tossing a glance my way. "I'll see you at lunch."

I nod in bemusement.

That girl is toast.

After the door closes behind them, the secretary says, "Your brother is going to be trouble, isn't he?"

I snort as a smile tugs at the corners of my lips. My guess is that Mrs. Baxter will rue the day Austin drove through the gates of

Hawthorne Prep. Girls will be in the counseling office bawling about their broken hearts and fighting with each other over him.

Now that my twin and his student guide have taken off, the older woman frowns before consulting the clock on the wall. I follow the direction of her gaze and realize the bell will ring for first period in five minutes.

"I hope Sloane didn't forget to stop at the office," she mutters before huffing out an exasperated breath. "I should have asked someone a little more—"

The office door is thrown open as a tornado of energy rushes in. "Sorry I'm late, Mrs. B! The parking situation was crazy. The front row of the lot should really be reserved for seniors. That would make life *so* much easier."

I wince before my belly does a painful flip.

Oh, God. Please...not that voice.

All last night, it circled around in my thoughts like a hungry shark. My nerves, which had settled, seize up with dismay.

"The parking is the same as it's always been, Sloane," the secretary says wearily.

"Well, that might be true, but it's the platform I'm going to run on for senior class president."

Not bothering with a response, Mrs. Baxter clears her throat and points in my direction. "This is Summer Hawthorne." Her kind gaze settles on mine. "Sloane will give you a quick tour before first hour begins."

"Welcome to Hawthorne Prep!" The rude blonde from the store last night whirls toward me. "It's so nice to meet you!"

I blink, knocked off-balance by her warm greeting and the toothy smile plastered across her pretty face.

This *is* the same girl from the store, right?

"Summer?" Mrs. Baxter prompts when I remain silent.

"Sorry." I force my lips into a slight smile. "It's nice to meet you, too."

Sloane's beaming face transforms into one of sympathy. "I'm sure this is all super overwhelming for you. New town, new school, no friends—"

"Summer already has a copy of her schedule," the older woman interrupts.

"Great!" The blonde plucks the slip from my fingers before her gaze slides over it.

"You should probably get moving," Mrs. Baxter encourages. "There isn't much time before first hour begins. Perhaps you could help Summer locate her locker in the senior hallway and then head to class?"

"Sure thing, Mrs. B!" she chirps. "Maybe we can do more of a tour at lunch."

"That's a wonderful idea!" the secretary says, nodding her approval.

The other girl's lips stay quirked as she turns to me. "Ready to go?"

"Yup." I blow out a steady breath, unsure what to make of the situation. I'm almost positive it's the same girl from last night, but it's like she's had a personality transplant. I don't understand what her deal is. Maybe she doesn't recognize me?

Sloane grabs the door and holds it open before calling out a jovial goodbye to the office secretary as the bell rings. Anyone loitering in the hallway scurries to class until it's empty. Once the door closes behind her, the lock clicking audibly into place, Sloane's smile melts from her face. A spiteful expression morphs in its place before she crumples my schedule in her hand and drops it to the tile at her patent leather heels.

"Good luck, bitch. You'll need it."

That being said, she elbows me in the arm and leaves me standing alone in the vacant corridor.

SUMMER

9

With my mouth hanging open, I watch Sloane stride away, her long blond hair swinging like a thick curtain behind her as her heels click against the marble. Once she vanishes around a corner, I blink out of my stupor. The corridor which had been filled earlier is now eerily silent.

I should have known.

Same girl. Same bitchy behavior.

Welcome to Hawthorne Prep!

Releasing a breath, I squat down and snatch the balled-up schedule from the floor before rising to my feet and flattening the half slip of paper in my palm.

Now what am I supposed to do?

I take a moment to contemplate my next move. Maybe I should find my locker and drop off my backpack. After that, I'll head to first hour. If I'm lucky, I won't run into Sloane again.

Ever.

Although that seems unlikely.

What the hell is her problem?

For the time being, I push that question to the back of my mind. It takes over five minutes to find my locker and then another handful to figure out how to open the stupid metal contraption. I grab a notebook and pen from the bag before stuffing it inside the barren locker and slamming the door closed.

Now off to first hour.

I spend the next five minutes walking in circles through intersecting corridors before finally getting my bearings and winding up at the door to my English lit classroom. This has to be the most confusing building I have ever been in. Whoever numbered the rooms is an idiot. Some aren't even in order. What's the point of using a numeric system if you aren't going to use it properly?

Naturally, the classroom door is closed.

My shoulders slump with the realization that there will be no quiet sneaking in for me.

Unsure what to do, I fidget for a couple of seconds, nervously smoothing down a few wisps of hair that have escaped from my bun before forcing myself to wrap my hand around the brass doorknob and turn it. Other than a slight rattling noise, the wood doesn't budge.

Seriously?

I'm having the worst luck ever.

The only way I'm getting inside is to disrupt the teacher who is already lecturing at the podium in front of the class.

It takes a full sixty seconds to work up the courage and rap my knuckles against the door. Through the thin rectangle of glass, I see a few heads swivel in my direction with curiosity. When a smug blue gaze locks on mine, I gasp.

Sloane's glossy pink lips lift into a cunning smile before she leans forward in her desk and whispers something to the brunette parked in front of her. That girl quickly flicks her bored gaze toward me before flashing a grin at Sloane.

Heat scalds my cheeks as I recognize the other girl as the sidekick from last night. Thirty excruciating seconds crawl by, and no one bothers to answer the door.

I'm going to have to knock again.

Sloane continues to watch me with barely suppressed giddiness as I lift my arm and tighten my fingers into a fist. If these bitches think I'll slink away like a coward, they have another thing coming.

This time, I make sure the knock is loud enough for the whole damn class to hear. The teacher's monotone voice falls off abruptly as her gaze slices to mine through the glass before she purses her thin lips and walks from the front of the room toward me.

After she unlocks and opens the door, she stands at the threshold, barring my entrance. "Ms. Hawthorne, I presume?"

I clear my throat, realizing the entire class is eavesdropping on the exchange. "Yes."

"You're late." Her lips thin even more than they already are.

I bob my head. "Yes, I—"

"No excuses. From now on, you will arrive at my class in a timely manner. I do not tolerate disruptions." She huffs out a breath as if my lateness has been an ongoing issue that she's had to contend with. "Today, I will excuse your tardiness, but I will not do so in the future. Have I made myself clear?"

"Yes," I whisper meekly, embarrassment blistering my cheeks.

"Excellent." Only then does she step aside before extending her arm magnanimously toward the room. "Please take a seat so we may continue."

Silently, I scurry to the first open desk I find before sinking onto the wooden seat. Already my mind is conjuring up a list of reasons I can give my parents as to why it would be better to transfer to the local public school. There is no way it can be worse than this. Although considering this school is named after our family and it's Dad's alma mater, I highly doubt my parents will go for that.

I flick my gaze toward the overly thin woman at the front of the room as she drones on about her expectations. English has always been one of my favorite subjects. I love to read a wide variety of books and to write. Somehow, I don't think that will be the case this semester.

I open my notebook and jot down a few notes as Ms. Pettijohn continues to lecture. As I do, I shift on my seat with the disconcerting sensation of being watched. Ever since I stepped foot on campus, people have been staring. Without bothering to glance around, my guess is that half the class is inspecting me as if I'm a strange species they've never encountered before. As much as I try to ignore the unease prickling at the back of my neck, it only grows stronger.

Unable to stand another moment of the scrutiny, I lean against my chair as my gaze sweeps over the neat rows of students that surround my desk. A few who had been openly appraising me jerk their attention away when they realize I've caught them. Interesting. Maybe they aren't so bold after all. As I continue to peer around the room, my gaze collides with a familiar one.

One I never expected to see again.

Certainly not here.

I blink as my heartbeat speeds up, jackhammering almost painfully against my breast.

There's no way...

There's just no way.

Except it is.

It's him.

Kingsley observes me through narrowed eyes that hold a strange intensity. It's like he recognizes me but doesn't. An odd mixture of emotion swirls through his eyes.

Recognition. Confusion. Hatred.

Wait a minute...hatred?

That can't be.

The time we spent together was amazing. He has no reason to hate me. The last time we saw each other, his lips had been stroking over mine. We'd made plans to spend the next day together on his boat.

Swimming.

Sunbathing.

Making out.

The muscles in my belly contract as my lips lift into a tentative smile and I raise my hand in a wave. Instead of receiving a similar expression, his mouth twists into a scowl. Animosity burns brightly in his eyes before he pivots away, dismissing me with one icy look.

My hand, which had been suspended midair, falls to the desk with a heavy thud. I gulp down my disappointment and stare sightlessly at the notebook on my desk as confusion whips through me.

Why would Kingsley act like that?

Is he angry that I had to leave without saying goodbye? I tried to tell him what was going on. For goodness' sake, his mom or whoever that was threatened to call the police on me! What else could I have done?

For the rest of the class period, my attention strays to him, but he stares straight ahead. It's like I'm not even there. When the bell rings, marking the end of class, Kingsley rises from his desk and walks out with another boy. Not once does he glance in my direction.

His blatant rejection sends an avalanche of hurt and confusion cascading through me. There hasn't been a single day when I haven't, at least once, thought about him and wondered what he was doing. I've fantasized about different scenarios where we would run into each other. And now that it's happened, he glares at me like I'm nothing more than sticky, sun-warmed gum on the bottom of his shoe.

His behavior makes little sense.

I have two choices. One, I let Kingsley leave and forget I ever met him. Or two, I suck it up and confront him. What makes the situation more complicated is that he's the only person I know at Hawthorne. Hell, in this entire godforsaken town. And having at least one friend by my side would make all the difference in the world.

When you look at it like that, there's only one option. Mind made up, I rise to my feet and take a step toward the door, hoping to catch Kingsley before second hour. The sooner I get this situation cleared up, the better I'll feel.

"Ms. Hawthorne?" A sharp voice cuts through the low hum of student chatter. "A word, if you please."

Damn.

The air escapes from my lungs in a rush as I swing toward the front of the room where Ms. Pettijohn waits.

"Ma'am?"

A few classmates linger, watching the exchange with piqued interest.

The older woman keeps her thin lips pressed together until the last of the stragglers take their leave. "I hope you don't think special exceptions will be made for you because your family founded the school."

My eyes widen as I shake my head. "Of course not."

"Good." She nods as if satisfied with the answer. "That's not the way Hawthorne Prep works. It would behoove you to be humble about your heritage."

My heritage?

What is that supposed to mean?

When I stare blankly, she flicks her wrist toward the exit. "I would encourage you to make a better impression on your remaining teachers than you did on me this morning."

Ouch.

I point at the door. "I should go."

She tips her head. "Excellent idea."

With that dismissal, I scurry from the room and search the hallway for the dark-haired boy I haven't been able to stop thinking about since meeting him this summer. Whatever changed his opinion of me, I want to clear it up.

Trying to find Kingsley in an ocean of navy blazers is like playing a game of Where's Waldo. A zip of electricity shoots through me when I catch sight of him slamming his locker door shut before heading to second hour. Uncaring if I'm late for my next class, I take off after him with a determined stride. With my gaze pinned to his tall figure, I push my way through the crowd, attempting to catch up to him. When I'm within striking distance, I reach out and lock my fingers around his bicep.

"Kingsley, wait up!"

Without glancing at me, he jerks out of my grasp and keeps walking.

What the hell?

Is he really this angry?

What did I do?

"Stop!" Unwilling to give up, I reach out again and tighten my fingers around his arm. "Give me a chance to explain!"

My heart lurches when he unexpectedly whirls toward me. Fury fills his eyes, and my hand falls away as I stumble back in surprise.

His lips twist into a scowl as he advances, forcing me to scurry away from him.

The thick crowd of students pressing in on me scatters, forming a circle around the two of us as my back hits a metal locker. It's like they can sense that something volatile is about to happen, and no one wants to miss it. The space between us gets eaten up until he's so close I have to tip my chin to hold his flashing gaze.

"Why didn't you tell me you were a Hawthorne?" he growls by way of greeting.

He's so close that his warm breath feathers across my lips. A couple of months ago, I was drunk with the feel of it, but now it frightens me more than I care to admit.

"*What?*" I scrunch my face, wondering if I misheard the question.

Even though there's barely a whisper between us, he presses closer. "Why didn't you tell me who you were?"

The hallway goes silent. It's like they're all holding their collective breath.

"I didn't realize it would matter," I murmur, not understanding the direction this conversation has swerved in.

"Of course, it matters!" he scoffs before stabbing a finger at my chest. "You let me think you were an ordinary girl, and that's not the truth, is it?"

Confusion swirls through my brain. What else would I be if not an ordinary girl? I shake my head, attempting to deny his words, but that only incenses him further.

With a snarl, he wraps his hand around my throat and shoves me against the locker. The back of my head reverberates off the metal, the sound of it echoing throughout the corridor.

"*Kingsley.*" My eyes widen.

It's only then that I realize the two boys may be identical in looks, but this is not the same one I spent time with at the beach. That guy had been kind, sweet, and funny. There is nothing charming or nice about this one. The anger wafting off him in heavy waves is almost suffocating in its intensity.

He lowers his face until the tip of his nose practically touches mine. "Keep my name out of your mouth, do you understand? You and I don't know each other." His rage-filled gaze examines mine. "Don't talk to me. Don't look at me. Don't even *think* about me."

With unhurried movements, his grip tightens around the delicate skin of my neck until it becomes difficult to breathe. My hands rise to claw at his arm, but I'm powerless against his strength. His jaw ticks as he continues to squeeze.

"*Help!*" My widened gaze flutters to the students crowded around us. Not a single one does anything to stop Kingsley from choking me.

What's wrong with these people? Why are they all standing there silently watching this unfold?

"*Help,*" I whisper again, my voice growing faint. It's becoming more difficult to suck in air yet, no one moves a muscle.

"Don't look at them for help. They won't lift a finger to assist you." He applies enough pressure for wetness to sting my eyes. "Do you know why?" He waits a beat. "Because no one wants you here, Hawthorne."

A lone tear leaks from the corner of my eye before trekking down my cheek. When I begin to feel light-headed from lack of oxygen, Kingsley is shoved away. As soon as the pressure on my throat vanishes, I gulp a deep lungful of air before doubling over. With my elbows propped on my knees, I brace myself to keep from falling to the floor. Tremors wrack my body as tears fill my eyes.

He could have killed me.

"You touch her again, and I'll fucking wipe you off the face of the earth! Do you hear me, asshole?" a deep voice roars.

Thank God for Austin.

I lift my head in time to see my brother pin Kingsley against a locker. The two boys scowl at each other before Kingsley smirks and shoves Austin away. Both are tall, muscular and evenly matched.

Kingsley whips his hair back before straightening the lapels of his blazer. "Stay the fuck out of my way, Hawthorne." His gaze jerks to mine, and I shrink away from the hatred pouring off him. "Both of you."

As soon as he saunters away, the crowd disperses. Hushed whispers echo throughout the corridor. More heat scalds my cheeks as our name is continuously murmured. It's like the incessant chirping of birds.

Hawthorne.
Hawthorne.
Hawthorne.

SUMMER

10

My gaze stays focused straight ahead as I twist the dial of my combination. From all around me, whispers bombard my ears in a persistent chatter that refuses to be silenced. I had to listen to the steady hum of it in every class. No one will talk to me or even acknowledge my presence, but they sure as hell find pleasure in gossiping about me.

Thank goodness I've been able to avoid Kingsley. Every new classroom I forced myself to enter, my footstep would falter over the threshold as I held my breath, carefully searching the room for his dark hair and eyes.

Even though I don't have an appetite, I pull my brown paper bag from my backpack.

"Hey."

My gaze flicks to Austin, who now lounges against the locker next to mine as I slam the metal door closed.

"Hi." Besides Mrs. Baxter and Delilah, he's the only friendly person I've encountered. Even the teachers are stone-faced and chilly toward me. It's like I've done something wrong or have a reputation that precedes me. Teachers usually love me. I'm not a student who causes problems in class. I'm quiet, smart, and turn my work in on time. What's not to like?

So this, I don't get. It's like I've been dropped into the Twilight Zone, where nothing makes sense.

Kingsley's words continue to circle through my head.

You let me think you were an ordinary girl.

What the hell does that mean?

I'm as ordinary as they get.

"Ready to head to the cafeteria?" Austin asks with his paper bag in hand.

My eyes widen at the question.

I have zero plans to go anywhere near the lunchroom. It would be akin to walking into a lion's den. And I have a fairly high sense of self-preservation. The last thing we want to do is invite more trouble.

I shake my head and clutch my bag with fingers that bite into the paper. "Let's eat at the library or maybe head outside, if it's allowed."

"Forget that," he snaps. A potent concoction of stubbornness and anger flashes across his face. "We're eating in the lunchroom with everyone else."

No!

"Aus, please." My voice drops as I plead with him to reconsider his tactics. "I don't want to be anywhere near these people. Just for thirty minutes. *I* need a break." Otherwise, I'll be the one who breaks. And I don't want to give them the satisfaction of watching that happen.

"Suck it up, buttercup." He folds his arms across his broad chest. "I won't allow a bunch of hicks to dictate what I do." He waggles his finger between us. "We need to stick together. If these assholes think they can intimidate us, this bullshit will only get worse." There's a pause. "You know it's true."

My shoulders droop under the weight of his words because we both know he's right. These people are like sharks scenting blood in the water. If we don't make a show of strength, they'll grow bolder. It'll be a free-for-all to see who can rip us apart first.

Why does this have to be so difficult?

"Fine," I agree reluctantly.

A cocky grin tugs at the corners of his lips before he throws an arm around my shoulders and hauls me close. "We have each other, and that's all we need. We're Hawthornes."

A shiver of unease runs through me.

Yes, we're Hawthornes, but why does that now seem to carry such a negative connotation?

Halfheartedly, I allow Austin to steer me toward the cafeteria. He seems to know where it is. Apparently, his tour of the building this morning was more informative than my nonexistent one.

The closer we get to the lunchroom, the louder the babble of voices grow and the more my feet drag. The beat of my heart picks up speed, thudding painfully in my chest. I don't want to go in there. The smell of mass-produced food assaults my nostrils, and my belly flips upside down, threatening to revolt even though I haven't eaten today.

From beside me, Austin's body tenses. I glance at him and notice the stiff set of his jaw and the muscle that twitches there. He's bracing for a fight. My brother doesn't want to do this any more than I do. That knowledge only strengthens my resolve, and I lift my head higher, unwilling to let these jerks tear us down.

Austin gives me a wink before we step into the spacious room. A hushed silence falls over the student body as all eyes turn to us. If I wasn't expecting it, the sheer weight of their collective stare would be enough to have me stumbling to a halt before turning tail and running.

"Keep it moving," Austin growls from the side of his mouth. "Don't let these assholes sense your fear."

Easier said than done. I gulp down my rising panic, knowing he's right. They'll fall on me like a pack of jackals if they realize how frightened I am. I blank my expression and stare at the far wall of the cafeteria. As we move through the rows of students, I wait for an attack.

"There's an empty table to the left," he mutters.

I suck in a breath as my gaze skitters across the room before landing on a vacant table against the edge of the rectangular-shaped space. Together we stride toward it before sliding across from each other at the far end. The thought of enduring this hell for an entire year is enough to bring a hot prick of tears to my eyes.

I'll never make it.

Austin settles with his back to the crowd as I sit across from him. If I lift my gaze, I can scan the entire cafeteria. Instead, I block them out and refuse to make eye contact. There's no reason to provoke the inmates.

As soon as we're seated, Austin doesn't waste time in emptying the contents of his lunch onto the table. Two PB and J sandwiches, apple slices, a bag of chips, a protein bar, and a bottle of water. When I make no move toward mine, he raises a brow, prompting me to follow suit. Mechanically, I pull out the sandwich, apple slices, bag of Sun Chips, and a bottle of water before staring at them. There's no way I'll be able to force down a bite. The thought is enough to stir the nausea roiling in my belly.

"You need to eat," he prods with a frown.

I shake my head, wishing it were that easy. "I can't."

My shoulders slowly lower from around my ears as the din of conversation picks up again and people go back to conversing about whatever the hell they were previously discussing. As it does, my gaze travels cautiously around the room.

Like in the corridors, wooden beams cross the vaulted ceiling. Arched stained glass windows allow shards of sunlight to flood in, giving the space a warm feel. More gold-leaf framed pictures dot the walls, and heavy wooden chandeliers with white candles hang from the two-story ceiling. There are three lines of tables strategically placed in rows throughout the space. Without the food service off to the side, it almost resembles a church.

Except there is no peace or sanctuary to be found here. I'm more afraid of being ripped to shreds by the parishioners.

I continue to study the architectural details until my gaze collides with a dark one a few tables away. A current of electricity shoots through me, flooding my body with awareness. The wise thing to do would be to avert my eyes, but Kingsley has the power to trap me within his stare. The boisterous noise and people who surround us fall away until we're alone.

Similar to this morning when his fingers were wrapped around my throat, it becomes difficult to breathe. My hand flutters to my neck, but nothing is constricting my airways. How is it possible to feel the pressure of his fingers from across the room? A shiver of unease runs through me as his lips lift into a smirk. It's like he knows exactly what kind of response he's capable of eliciting.

With a flick of his gaze, he dismisses me. His expression transforms into one of playfulness as a girl stops beside him before reaching out and trailing her fingers over his arm. In one quick movement, he snags her hand and tugs her onto his lap. Pain blooms in my chest when I realize it's Sloane. Her arms loop possessively around his neck before she pulls him close. Her lips go to his ear as she whispers a secret.

Look away!

Stop staring!

It's a relief when Sloane tips her head back and laughs, loose blond hair bouncing around her shoulders, obscuring my vision. A moment later, she tilts her body, and he comes back into view again with his gaze pinned to mine. His eyes are frozen chips as a slow grin spreads across his handsome face.

The pain he's inflicting is deliberate.

Why is he doing this?

I almost shake my head in frustration before catching myself at the last minute. There's no way this is the same boy I met earlier this summer.

"Hey." Austin reaches out and grabs my lifeless hand from where it lies on the table between us.

Reluctantly, my attention jerks to him. "What?"

He points at my lunch with his other hand. "You need to eat."

I glance at the untouched food and grimace. "I'll eat later."

"Everything will be fine," he mutters, attempting to comfort me. "Give it some time to settle."

I snort out a disbelieving laugh. I'm the one who is usually the eternal optimist, not my brother. I'm the one who is always there, championing him, lifting him up, propelling him forward. It's disconcerting to find our roles reversed.

"Are you still going to football practice?" I ask.

Having polished off his lunch, he picks up his bottle of water and guzzles the rest of the liquid. "Yeah. Why wouldn't I?"

Even though I had been encouraging Austin to go out for the team only last night, now I'm rethinking my position. These people are frightening. I don't want him anywhere near them. Especially alone.

"Like you said, they're a bunch of assholes, and I don't think you'll be any more welcome on the team than we've been in this school."

He shrugs before an evil grin settles on his face. "Want to guess who's the bigger asshole?"

A mirthless chuckle escapes from my lips. Leave it to Austin to compete for that particular title.

When I don't respond, he tilts his head. "Isn't it your job to disagree and tell me how amazing I am?"

"I think you have me confused with our mother." Tension leaks from my shoulders. "And for the record, you already seem to know how amazing you are."

Humor flickers in his eyes. "Of course, I do. But it's always nice to hear."

"You're amazing, Aus," I rasp, hot emotion stinging the back of my eyelids. There's no way I could get through this moment without him.

He nods, looking pleased with himself. "Right back at you, sis." He pauses for a beat before adding, "These people won't break us."

Movement from the corner of my eye captures my attention, and my gaze slides from Austin's green eyes to Kingsley. I'm jolted into awareness when I find him watching me from beneath a thick fringe of dark lashes.

As his unfriendly gaze holds mine, I get the feeling that Kingsley would like nothing more than to break us.

Me, specifically.

SUMMER

11

I stare at the clock on the wall, willing the seconds to tick down. Two more minutes and this hell that has been Hawthorne Prep will be over.

For today.

Only one hundred and eighty-nine more days to go until I graduate and never have to step foot in these hallowed halls again. Sad that it's my first day and I already can't wait for it to be my last.

Mr. Timmons, the AP psychology teacher, drones on, but I've tuned him out as I fidget restlessly on my seat, a mental countdown running through my head.

Ten.
Nine.
Eight.
Seven.
Six.
Five.
Four.
Three.
Two.

My muscles stiffen with anticipation.

The bell rings, and I grab my notebook and pen before hauling ass to the door. A handful of grumbles follow in my wake as I shove people out of my way. They can fuck off for all I care.

With my head down, I maneuver through the crowded hall to my locker before shoving my books into my backpack and going in search of my brother. His locker is a couple of classrooms down from mine.

I stride toward him as he shoves his books on the shelf. "Are you still planning to stay after?"

Kingsley mentioned playing football when we spent the day together on his boat. After what happened this morning, I don't want my brother anywhere near him. Austin isn't afraid to throw down. And it would seem like Kingsley isn't either. That makes for a particularly dangerous mix.

A renewed look of determination settles over Austin's features. Deep down, I know what his answer will be. He only confirms it when he says, "I already told you at lunch that I was going."

My teeth sink into my bottom lip before worrying it.

He has no idea that I met Kingsley at the beach this summer. I should probably give him a heads-up so he isn't thrown off if something gets mentioned. But the words stay locked deep inside where I can't set them free. After today, all I want to do is forget I ever knew the guy.

"I wanted to make sure you hadn't changed your mind before I took off."

My brother shifts his weight as a hard glint enters his eyes. "If they don't want me here, they'll have to force me to quit."

Austin's life revolves around football. He performs in school solely so he can step onto the field and play. You take that away, and his whole entire world would crumble. It's a scary prospect.

"Okay." I sigh as my shoulders wilt. "I'll see you at home later."

"Bye." He hoists his backpack onto his shoulder and takes off.

Silently, I watch as he strolls down the hall before vanishing around the corner. It takes me a moment to realize I'm alone.

A more unsettling word flashes through my head.

Vulnerable.

I need to get out of here before anyone takes advantage of that situation.

With my shoulders hunched and my gaze trained on the marble floor, I move swiftly through the building, trying to draw the least amount of attention to myself. Whispers dog me through the corridors. My anxiety ratchets up, reaching a fever pitch as I burst through the heavy glass doors into the late summer sunshine. Fresh air hits my cheeks, and my feet stall as I draw in a shaky breath before expelling it from my lungs.

Keep it moving.
One foot in front of the other.
I'm almost out of here.

With my hands clutching the strap of my backpack, I weave through the parking lot. Students congregate in pockets. They stare, but no one says a word as I rush past. I keep my gaze averted until I'm a row away from where Austin parked the G-wagon this morning. With a sigh of relief, I lift my gaze and grind to a halt as my mouth falls open.

Dozens of broken eggs dot the black paint. Cracked white shells mixed with bright yellow yoke cover the hood. It looks like a bunch of angry birds dive-bombed the Mercedes. A white gloppy mess resembling shaving cream covers the windshield.

Are you freaking kidding me?

Giggles explode from around me. I swing toward the sound, glaring at the students, some doubled over with laughter.

Anger erupts from inside me like a geyser. *"You're all a bunch of assholes!"*

"Take the hint and go home, Hawthorne!" comes a shout from the crowd.

"No one wants you here!" another person adds.

As more people pipe up with comments, I grapple with my backpack and pull out the keys. My fingers tremble as I click the locks and slide behind the wheel. I toss my bag onto the seat next to me and shove the key into the ignition before starting up the engine. I white knuckle the black leather steering wheel and stare blindly at the windshield but can't see a damn thing because a thick coat of shaving cream covers the glass. Tears sting the back of my eyelids as I fumble with the buttons until the wipers slide across the glass, pushing away enough of the mess to make out the parking lot. Heat slams into my cheeks when I realize that everyone is still standing around gawking as if I'm the paid entertainment.

Inhale and exhale.

Don't lose it.

I shift the car into reverse and pull out of the parking spot. Once I'm able to put the SUV into drive, it takes everything I have inside not to stomp on the gas pedal and squeal out of the parking lot. Instead, my fingers strangle the steering wheel as I fall in line with the other high-end cars before driving through the gate and turning onto the main road.

Now that I'm away from school, fury swirls through me. I'm halfway to the house before realizing that I can't show up with the Mercedes in this condition. Not unless I want to explain how shitty my first day at Hawthorne Prep was and how god-awful these people are. I wouldn't put it past Mom and Dad to call the headmaster—or worse, pay him a visit—and then I'll be known as a snitch on top of everything else.

I ease the vehicle over to the side of the road and search my phone for the nearest place to clean the SUV. Once I have an address, I set it for turn-by-turn directions. Since the town is small, it doesn't take long to find the one and only carwash. The attendant gives me a funny look when I roll up and hand him my credit card before asking for the premium wash and wax.

I stay in the G-wagon, squeezing my eyes closed as it moves through the different wash cycles. It's sad that this is the most enjoyable part of my day.

When the two guys are done wiping off the SUV, I dig around in my wallet for a couple of bucks and roll down the window before handing over the bills. "Thanks. It looks great." Better than it did this morning.

One of the attendants scratches the side of his head. "You're lucky the egg wasn't on there for long. It would have taken the finish right off."

Fuckers.

"Yeah." I force my lips into an anemic smile. "Lucky."

I stew the rest of the way home. As I pull into the drive, I notice that my parents are both home. I was hoping they would be at

Hawthorne Industries, and I'd have a little time to collect myself before having to put on a show.

Had an amazing day!

So glad you moved us here!

Everyone was so warm and fuzzy!

I park behind the Volvo and grab my backpack before exiting the vehicle. It takes everything I have inside to paste a smile on my face as I let myself in through the front door.

"Hello," I yell, dropping the backpack onto the floor. "I'm home."

"In the study, sweetie!" Mom answers in a cheerful voice. "How was your day?"

Complete and utter shit.

I want to move back to Chicago.

Is homeschooling a viable option?

"It was fine," I say instead.

"Just fine?" she asks with a tilt of her head.

I step over the threshold into the study before screeching to a halt. Yesterday, I'd thought all the dark paneling lent a lavish, cozy feel to the room. Now it only reminds me of Hawthorne Prep. I back up a step, not wanting to move any farther into the space.

Dad is seated behind the desk that once belonged to Great-Great-Grandpa Herbert. For half a century, it sat in his office at Hawthorne Industries. His laptop is open, papers and manila folders are scattered across every square inch of the polished top. Apparently, he's delving in headfirst. Mom is curled up near the window, enjoying a cup of tea.

"Yeah." Little does she know what a stretch *just fine* is.

"Well, it can only get better from here, right?"

That's doubtful. My biggest fear is that it'll get worse. That thought is enough to send a quiver of dread through me.

"Did you make any new friends?" she inquires before taking a sip of her drink.

"This isn't kindergarten," I mumble, rolling my eyes.

"Well, I hope everyone was nice to you and your brother."

Ha! We were lucky they didn't eat us alive for lunch.

I give her a noncommittal grunt in answer.

"How about your teachers?" Mom is bound and determined to pull something good out of me. "Did you like them?"

Not particularly. They were as crappy as the kids.

"I guess," I say, trying to throw her a bone so she'll lay off with the interrogation tactics.

"Were your classes the same as back home?"

Home.

That one word is enough to send a fresh wave of wistfulness crashing over me. I blink away the hot sting of tears that burn the back of my eyes. I would give anything to go back home.

Anything.

The small cramped house. Sharing a bathroom with Austin. A school that isn't prestigious. Broke and living paycheck to paycheck. I'd take all of that over this.

"Oh, honey," Mom murmurs, noticing the emotion that has gathered in my eyes, "there's no question that first days can be rough. It'll get better, I promise. Dad and I appreciate how great you've been through all this. Give it a couple of months. After that, we'll be settled in, and Hawthorne will feel more like home. You'll make new friends and won't feel so much like an outsider."

Again, doubtful. Mom doesn't understand how much these people hate us.

"I hope you're right." Another step backward brings me into the hallway. "I'm going up to my room to start homework."

"That's my girl, already hitting the ground running," Dad pipes in, attention focused on the computer screen. "Think how good a prep school will look on your college applications."

"Yup." For the first time in my life, I don't give a damn about my college apps. I care about making it through the week without having a nervous breakdown.

Before Mom can bombard me with more questions or platitudes, I flee from the study, grabbing my backpack from the foyer on the way and pounding up the staircase two at a time. Once inside the safety of my room, I close the door and sag against it.

One day down. Only a hundred and eighty-nine more to go.

That thought is enough to make me cry.

I lock away all the heavy emotions simmering near the surface before dumping my books onto the bed. I wasn't exaggerating when I mentioned having homework. What I learned today is that Hawthorne Prep has rigorous academics. Maybe even more so than my old school. The next two hours are spent working out calculus problems and reading a chapter from my psychology textbook.

I'm finishing up my last calc problem when I hear Austin's door slam shut. All the anxiety from earlier comes crashing back as I hop off the bed and make my way to his room. I pause at the door and listen, but there's only silence. Softly, I rap my knuckles against the wood. When there's no answer, I turn the handle and poke my head inside. I find Austin sitting on the side of the bed, staring down at his hands. He doesn't look at me as I inch my way into his room.

"How did practice go?" Even as I ask, my intuition tells me it wasn't good.

When he remains quiet, nerves gather at the bottom of my belly, and my voice rises. "Aus?"

He glances up, and a puff of air leaves my lips when I see the shiner under his left eye. I rush toward him, grabbing his face to get a better look. "Oh my God!"

"It's not a big deal," he grumbles. That being said, he remains still, allowing me to inspect the damage. "It happened at practice."

I narrow my eyes. "Bullshit."

He shrugs but keeps his lips tightly pressed together.

"Who did this?"

My brother huffs out a breath and drags my hands away before rising to his feet. "No one."

"Austin!" I snap. "Who hit you?"

"Just drop it, okay? It doesn't matter." He points at the bathroom. "I need to take a shower and then hit the books."

My shoulders slump. It's useless to keep pressing him for an answer. I know my brother, and he won't snitch on whoever did this. Even to me. "Do you need help?"

He pauses. It's hard for Austin to ask for assistance, which is why I always offer it.

"Yeah," he mumbles, moving toward his dresser to get a fresh change of clothes.

"I already finished, so I have plenty of time tonight."

Some of his anger drains as the tension leaks from his shoulders. "Thanks, Summer."

"Let me know when you're ready to work."

He jerks his head into a tight nod before stepping toward his private bathroom and hesitating over the threshold. "Everything go all right after school?"

I swallow down the truth as my gaze darts toward the window and the rolling green lawn of the golf course in the distance. I should tell Austin about the G-wagon, but he's already dealt with enough shit today. The last thing I want to do is add more to it. Hopefully, the vandalism was a onetime thing.

"It was fine."

"Good." Relief floods through his voice before he disappears into the bathroom and closes the door.

For the first time in our lives, Austin and I are keeping secrets from each other. Out of all the changes this move has created, that shouldn't be one of them. Something tells me that our situation here is going to get far worse before it gets any better.

SUMMER

Mom's comment about the first day being the hardest couldn't have been more wrong.

Every hour I spend at Hawthorne Prep is agonizing. For the first time in my life, I dread going to school and count down the hours until I'm able to flee from the property at precisely half past two.

By the time Friday rolls around, I could almost weep with joy. Two blissful days spent away from Hawthorne seems like a much-needed reprieve. I never thought I'd say this, but I'm beginning to hate the sound of my own last name.

I sleep late Saturday morning and spend the rest of the day exploring the house. Mom convinces me to go grocery shopping with her in town, where everyone steers clear of us and is unfriendly as fuck. Mom pretends not to notice. Instead, she's smiling and waving at everyone we meet before chatting up the clerk at the checkout. After we load groceries into the back of the Volvo, she tells me that small-town folks aren't always open to newcomers, and we have to kill them with kindness.

Honestly, I would just prefer to kill them.

That muttered comment earns me a frown along with a gentle rebuke.

Whatever.

Her tune would change mighty fast if she spent a week at Hawthorne Prep.

I help cook dinner Saturday night—fish tacos, a family favorite. Once night falls, I grab a blanket and head outside to get lost in the stars. It's one of the few reprieves I have.

On my way across the yard, I hear voices coming from the next-door neighbor's property. Raucous laughter mixed with shouting. With a flash, I remember the red convertible Mustang that zipped past us the first day of school. With everything else going on, I had forgotten about him.

Hmm. My eyes narrow. Is he one of the assholes who egged my SUV?

I really hope not.

Sunday morning, I finish my homework and help Austin with a few assignments. He still won't tell me about the black eye or if there have been any other problems at practice. It's beyond frustrating.

While unpacking the last few boxes of my belongings, I come across my running shoes and decide that now is as good of a time as any to get back into it. I search through my drawers and find a black crop tank that hugs my chest, camo mesh running shorts, and a pink cap to shade the sun from my eyes. Then I grab my AirPods and head to the front door.

"Going for a run?" Mom asks, carrying a vaseful of fresh flowers to the black Steinway by the staircase.

"Yup."

"Good." She nods before setting down the Waterford crystal container and rearranging a few stems. "I think that's exactly what's needed to make you feel better."

"We'll see," I say evasively.

My mother is an eternal optimist. I was too before moving to this hellhole.

"Use your GPS if you get lost."

"I will, but I don't plan to run that far," I say before closing the front door behind me.

As I leave the house, I shove the buds in my ears, choose a playlist, and move through some quick stretches. Then I hit the driveway before turning onto the tree-lined subdivision road. I don't have a particular route in mind as I set out. After about a block, I pick up the pace and explore the entire subdivision. It's one monstrous mansion after another, which is strange, given that the town of Hawthorne is in the middle of nowhere.

Do all these people work for Hawthorne Industries, or are there other businesses in the area? When I find a second way into the sub, I head out onto the main country road. After about a mile, I hit the front entrance that Austin and I take to school.

By the time I wrap around, I'm winded and have to push myself to finish strong. It's been months since I laced up my running shoes. My chest is tight, and the muscles in my legs burn with fatigue. The endorphin high has hit me hard, and I'm zoned out as the music blasts in my ears. From the corner of my eye, I notice a car pull alongside me. I glance at the driver and nearly stumble when my gaze locks on Kingsley. He's wearing the aviators I recognize from the beach along with a scowl.

As much as I want to turn away and ignore him, I'm powerless to do so. Even though I can't see his eyes, their intensity burns a hole in me.

After a handful of seconds, I realize three other guys are crowded into the convertible with him. The blond sitting behind the driver's seat makes lewd gestures with his hands as he leers. It makes me wish I'd worn looser-fitting clothing. I gnash my teeth together and curl my upper lip at him. Not put off by my reaction, he grins.

The tires spin as Kingsley floors the gas and takes off. Gravel spits up from the road, spraying my legs.

"Fucker," I mutter, keeping my gaze pinned to the red Mustang as it zips through the neighborhood.

Oh no.

Red Mustang.

No.

No.

No.

A burst of adrenaline shoots through me as I pick up speed, pushing my legs so I can keep an eye on the sports car as it screeches around a curve before whipping past my driveway.

Keep going.

Just keep going.

I hold my breath, hoping it'll zoom past the neighboring property, but deep down, I know that won't happen. My feet slow as I watch him zip into the driveway next to ours. I'm slammed with the realization that it was Kingsley and his friends I've heard partying it up.

Goddammit!

Kingsley is my neighbor.

Ironic how I spent most of the summer wishing I could see him again. Just one more time. And now...

Now I wish I'd never met the guy.

SUMMER

13

Monday rolls around much too quickly. I wake with a pit the size of Texas sitting in my gut and nothing I do banishes it. My new plan of action—or inaction—is to keep my head down, my mouth shut, and hope that people forget about my existence. When I make it through the first two hours relatively unscathed, the thick knot of tension gradually loosens.

The bell rings, signaling the end of second hour and the beginning of a five-minute passing period. Mr. Demsky dismisses the class with a reminder that there will be a calculus quiz on Wednesday. A wave of groans ripples through the room as I gather up my books before hustling through the crowded hallway to third hour.

An unexpected shove from behind sends me careening forward. My arms pinwheel to break my fall as I slam into the marble tile with a grunt of pain. Students stare but keep walking. No one offers to help me or pick up my books, which are scattered throughout the hall. I've seen enough movies to realize this is usually when the attacker gets in a few vicious kicks to the ribs.

Even though sharp shafts of pain shoot through the palms of my hands and knees, I quickly flip over onto my backside, hoping I didn't flash everyone my panties.

The humiliation around here is never-ending.

A pair of navy-colored lace-up heels come into view. My gaze moves up the matching knee-high socks, over a blue, green, and gold plaid skirt, white button-down shirt, only to find Sloane scowling at me.

Her upper lip is curled in a snarl like I'm the one who shoved her. "Stay the fuck out of my way, or you'll end up on your ass every time."

"I wasn't in your way," I mutter.

When she shifts from one hip to the other, I tense and wait for her to kick me with her pointy-toed shoe. For reasons I don't understand, this girl has been nothing but hateful since the first time she laid eyes on me at Rothchild's.

When a pair of beat-up brown loafers step beside her, I stifle a groan. A one-on-one fight I can handle. Unfortunately, my odds of coming out of this intact dwindle significantly if more people join in the fray. My gaze shifts, locking on Kingsley.

Of course he's here to partake in any kind of embarrassment or hazing that involves the Hawthornes. Humiliation burns my cheeks as he glares down at me.

Why can't they leave me alone?

Sloane's pink-slicked lips lift into a smug smile as she loops her arm through Kingsley's before pressing her breasts against him.

Not only do I hate this girl for being a major bitch, but it's become painfully obvious that she and Kingsley are an item. I've seen them walking together in the halls and talking in the cafeteria at least half a dozen times. Even though his recent behavior should have killed everything kindled on the boat, it hasn't.

That knowledge only makes me more of a pathetic loser than Sloane thinks I am.

"Can I give you a piece of advice?" she sneers.

"I'd prefer if you didn't."

Ignoring me, she continues. "Go back to wherever you came from. No one wants you here."

She's not wrong, that does seem to be the general consensus.

"You know," I retort, "I was kind of wondering about the lukewarm reception I've received. Thanks for explaining it to me."

That response wipes the smile off her face. "Hawthornes aren't welcome here," she growls.

My voice grows stronger. "I guess that's what you'd call an ironic situation, considering that the town, company, and school are named after us."

A few tinkers of laughter erupt in the swelling crowd. Sloane glares, and the sound dies a quick death. When she steps toward me, I scooch back as Kingsley grabs her around the arms and drags her away.

"Let's go." His cool gaze falls on my person, freezing me on the spot. "She's not worth your time."

His indifference sends a bolt of pain shooting through me.

As if realizing that Kingsley has his arms wrapped around her, Sloane melts against his body, giving him her full attention. "You're so right." She flicks her narrowed gaze at me before smiling at him. "Hopefully, the trash will take itself out."

Ouch.

In this scenario, it's obvious that I'm the trash she's referring to.

After they vanish through the sea of gawkers, everyone disperses. I draw in a breath and rise to my feet before picking up my books. My shoulders collapse when the bell rings, signaling the start of third hour.

No matter what I do, I can't seem to win. Relief rushes through me when I spot a bathroom down the hall. I need a few moments to collect myself in private. I'm not sure how much more of this I can take.

Once safely inside the small room, I fight back the tears stinging my eyelids before splashing cold water on my face and patting it dry with a paper towel. After my emotions have been locked down tight, I glance at the mirror above the sink.

I'm disturbed by the reflection that greets me.

There's a hollowed-out look in my dark eyes, and my face is thinner than it was a couple of weeks ago. Most days, my stomach is tied up in knots, making it impossible to eat breakfast or lunch. At dinner, I pick at my food, pushing it around my plate to cover up how little I'm fueling my body. And I'm running more. Other than stargazing, it's the only thing that allows me to forget about how shitty my life has become. It's a bit of a shock to realize that I'm slowly becoming a shell of my former self.

I grip the sink basin with my fingers as my head rolls forward.

Keep it together.

Thoughts of skipping out for the rest of the day flood through my mind. More like the rest of the year. But I refuse to allow these assholes to jack with my future. So, as much as I don't want to go to third hour, there's no other choice in the matter. With a huff of breath, I push out of the bathroom door before skidding to a halt.

SUMMER

Icy cold tendrils of fear squeeze my heart when I find Kingsley leaning against the lockers with his arms crossed against his chest. The anger simmering in his eyes intensifies as his gaze pins me in place.

How is this cruel boy the same one I fell for at the beginning of summer?

He doesn't say a word as he pushes away from the bank of lockers before sauntering toward me.

Run!

Instead of listening to the voice inside my head, I remain paralyzed. When he's close enough to reach out and touch me, I blink to awareness and take a hasty step away. The need to put as much distance between us pumps through me, and I retreat until my back hits the bathroom door with a painful thud. Panic slides through me, when I realize there's nowhere to go. I'm trapped in a small alcove by the bathroom. Even if a teacher stepped out of their classroom and looked down the hallway, they wouldn't see us.

A merciless smile lifts his lips as he invades my personal space until I'm flattened against the door.

He leans one arm against the wood, partially caging me in. "Afraid, Hawthorne?"

"No."

Deathly.

I have no idea what he's capable of. And that's a scary realization.

He chuckles before picking up the thick length of my ponytail and playing with the blunt end of it. "You should be."

My mouth dries, making it impossible to swallow. When my

tongue darts out to moisten my parched lips, his gaze drops to the movement. Desire flashes in his eyes, and I find that more unsettling than his hostility.

"Why do you hate me so much?" The question tumbles from my lips before I can stop it.

His jaw clenches, and a muscle twitches in his cheek. The arousal that had flared to life in his eyes is snuffed out as quickly as it was ignited.

"Feigned ignorance won't absolve you," he sneers, his grip tightening on my hair.

What the hell does that mean? It sounds like a riddle. It's obvious that everyone hates the Hawthornes, but no one will give me an explanation as to why.

"What are you talking about?"

His gaze carefully examines mine. It almost feels like he's able to pick through all of my thoughts and feelings. "You don't know anything about your family, do you?"

It's only when I shake my head that I remember the hold he has on me. I wince and hastily still my movements. "No."

He presses closer, tugging my ponytail so that my chin lifts.

"You're hurting me," I whisper.

"Good." A slow grin spreads across his face. "That was the intention."

I whimper when he yanks it again, my chin jerking up with the movement. Only then do I notice how close his lips are to mine.

"Even now, you still want me." His voice is full of scorn as his breath drifts across me.

Images of us kissing on the boat and in the car flicker through my head like a slow-motion picture show. Again, pain radiates through my scalp when I try to shake my head.

"Are you a liar on top of everything else?"

On top of what?

If I could get a few straight answers, then maybe I could figure out what he's talking about. What everyone at this stupid school seems to allude to, but no one will come out and say.

When his lips ghost over mine, everything rioting inside my head empties. I'm mortified by the bolt of lust that shoots through me before exploding in my core.

After the way he's treated me, how can I possibly be attracted to him?

What the hell is wrong with me?

His lips crook as if he knows how deeply the realization bothers me.

"Should I kiss you, Summer? Like I did on the boat?" There's a pause as his voice dips, turning husky. Seductive. It strums something deep inside me. Something I don't want to acknowledge but find impossible to ignore. "Do you ever think about how good it felt?"

Not only do I think about it, but I've also touched myself to memories of him dozens of times.

I squeak in surprise when he nips at my lower lip. Pain floods through the plump flesh before he sucks the fullness into his mouth as if to soothe the dull ache he caused before releasing it with a soft pop. His gaze stays locked on mine. My brain turns fuzzy with the hormones that have ignited a firestorm throughout my body.

With one hand wrapped around my ponytail to secure me in place, the other grazes my bare thigh below the hemline of my skirt. I inhale a sharp breath as his fingertips trace lazy patterns against my leg. Each arc brings his hand dangerously close to the apex of my thighs.

"You could scream for help."

A whimper leaves my lips as his grip tightens on my hair.

"Go ahead," he encourages, "*yell.*"

"Why are you doing this?"

"Because I can."

My eyes widen when his fingers brush over the thin cotton of my panties. Another round of explosions burst in my core. Confusion tumbles through me. As much as I want him to stop, I want him to continue even more.

The tip of his tongue darts out to trace my lips as his fingers stroke my heat. He focuses the pressure on my slit, and I have to stop myself from spreading my legs so he can touch all of me. Instead, I do the opposite and press my thighs together.

With a jerk of his hand, he yanks my ponytail. "Open for me."

A hiss leaves my lips as pain radiates throughout my scalp.

I tell myself that I have no other choice but to obey his commands, but deep inside, I know it's a lie. I could scream and fight him off, but I remain silent, craving his touch as my body burns with fire.

The moment I suck in a shuddering breath, he thrusts inside my mouth. Our tongues tangle as he caresses my pussy. It doesn't take long for my hips to gyrate against his hand, matching the rhythm. As wrong as this is, I'm powerless to stop it from happening. When he lifts his lips from mine, his eyes are hard and unforgiving.

Even as he strokes me closer to orgasm, he says, "Did you know that your great-great-grandfather didn't start the company alone?"

There is so much pleasure pumping through my system that it's almost impossible to focus on the sound of his voice, let alone the words tripping off his tongue.

"*What?*" It takes effort to fight my way out of the thick fog that has descended, clouding my better judgment.

"Or that Herbert Hawthorne tricked his partner into signing the company over to him?"

Wait a minute...Hawthorne Industries was co-owned? I don't remember hearing that part of the story.

As my body tenses and I'm about to splinter apart, the pressure of his fingers disappears, and a harsh whimper of protest falls from my lips before I can rein it in. My heart thumps under my breast as I fight to catch my breath.

"Here's what you don't understand," he murmurs against my mouth, "the entire town was ecstatic when the last Hawthorne finally kicked the bucket. We don't want any more in *our* town."

The lips of my pussy throb with painful awareness as the orgasm that had been moments away from crashing over me dissipates, leaving behind a deep achiness to take its place.

The hold on my hair disappears as he steps back so we're no longer touching.

"Disappointed?" A nasty sneer curves his lips as he says with faux pity. "And you were so close to coming."

An avalanche of humiliation buries me alive. Thankfully, he doesn't wait around for a denial. My knees nearly buckle as I sag against the door in relief.

Or maybe it's regret rushing through my veins. I don't know.

If I hadn't already realized it, I do now. Kingsley is dangerous. Even more so than Sloane. Or anyone else at Hawthorne Prep looking to hurt me. I need to stay as far away from him as I can get. What I don't know is if that's possible.

But something tells me I'm going to find out.

SUMMER

15

"You're becoming a real regular around here," the carwash attendant says with a grin.

Unfortunately, this is true.

When I give him a tight smile in response, he asks, "You want the premium wash again?"

"Yes, please." I hand over the credit card.

Before he runs it through the machine, he asks, "Have you considered purchasing a monthly package?" There's a pause. "It might save you a couple of bucks."

This is my fourth time through the carwash in little more than a week. The little fuckers don't egg my SUV every day, but it's pretty damn close. I'm trying to figure out a way to sneak out of sixth hour a couple of minutes early, but so far, Mr. Timmons has been a stickler about dismissing us after the final bell.

By that time, it's too late, and I have to do the walk of shame through a crowd of my peers eagerly waiting for me to have a meltdown. I refuse to give them the satisfaction of seeing me lose my shit. I'll cry and scream in private, thank you very much. At school, I'm an iceberg. Nothing they do can touch me.

"Yeah," I grumble, "I'll buy the monthly package."

He nods as if agreeing with the decision and rings me up.

After the carwash, I drive straight home. Kingsley's words circle madly through my head. We're not going to talk about how he was touching me when he gave me a brief history lesson on my family. We're also not going to talk about why I'm a little fuzzy on the details. I park behind the Volvo in the driveway and make a beeline for the house. I have questions, and I'm hoping my parents will give me answers.

"I'm home," I announce the moment I step into the cavernous foyer.

"Hey, hon!" Mom calls back.

Now that all of our belongings have been unpacked, she's in full-on cleaning and redecorating mode. Some of Grandma's furniture has been wrapped up and moved to one of the unused garage stalls until they figure out what to do with it. Mom is happier than I've seen her in a long time. Both my parents used to work long hours to make ends meet. With the high cost of living in Chicago, they were always playing catch-up.

In Hawthorne, life is different. The pace is slower. Mom has found her rhythm and is enjoying small-town life to the fullest. Dad goes to the office every day but works a lot from home. He's still trying to wrap his brain around the business side of the company. There seems to be a steep learning curve involved. Honestly, I haven't asked a lot of questions. I've been too focused on keeping my head above water and surviving. But now, it seems a part of my survival hinges upon me figuring out the Hawthorne family history.

I peek in the study since that's where I usually find them when I return from school. Both smile as I hover over the threshold, leaning against the doorjamb. I'm still not a fan of this room and go out of my way to avoid it.

"How was school?" Mom asks like she does every day.

I shrug instead of giving an actual answer.

"It'll get better," Mom promises with a confidence that almost makes me believe her. It's reassuring that at least one of us has remained the same. Austin is so filled with rage that I'm afraid of what will happen when he finally blows. And Dad has become more withdrawn. He's constantly poring over paperwork and muttering to himself.

And me?

We all know the hell I'm going through. Barely hanging on by my fingernails. At any moment, I'll lose the battle and plummet to a grisly death. A part of me wonders if it would be better that way. Exactly how much harassment is one person expected to withstand?

"We'll see," I mutter cautiously, gaze falling to my father. "Hey, Dad?" I wait for him to glance up from the papers he's shuffling around. "Would you mind telling me a little more about the company?"

He blinks before taking off the wire-framed glasses perched on the bridge of his nose. "Why do you want to know about that?"

His guarded expression takes me by surprise. I was expecting him to be delighted with my interest.

"I don't know." I shrug. "I remember you saying that the town is named after us because the company was founded here."

Dad leans back in his chair as he carefully contemplates the comment. "Yeah, that's right."

"The school, too."

"Yeah," he says in a clipped tone. "That as well."

"It's almost like they loved the Hawthorne family so much, they named everything after us." Nothing could be further from the truth, but it seems like a good place to start this fishing expedition.

His lips thin, and I get the distinct impression he disagrees with the statement. "Herbert Hawthorne did that." There's a pause. "A lot of people claimed he was a narcissist, which is why he named everything after himself."

"Huh." My gaze flickers around the space, touching on the window, fireplace, and bookshelves. The smell of aged leather-bound volumes permeates the air. That, coupled with the scent of lemony wood polish, must be what reminds me of Hawthorne Prep. "So, if everything in town is named after us, that must mean he started the company by himself."

"No," he admits reluctantly, "in the beginning, Great-Grandpa Herbert had a partner."

A prickle of unease fills my belly when I realize that at least one piece of information Kingsley gave me was accurate.

"Oh," I say carefully, "that's interesting. Who was his partner?"

A frown settles on Dad's features as he sits forward, resting his elbows on the desk and staring at me with narrowed eyes. "Is there a reason you're asking?"

Surprised by the suspicion that fills his expression, I jerk my shoulders. "Just curious. It's our family history and the reason we had to uproot our lives and move here." I wave a hand toward them. "Aren't you two always encouraging me to ask questions?"

"She's right, Griffin," Mom chimes in, looking as perplexed by her husband's odd behavior as I am.

Dad's lips flatten before he begrudgingly continues. "Herbert's partner was a man named Gerald Rothchild."

Rothchild? Why does that name sound so familiar?

The store in town where I picked up my school supplies had the same name. There's no way that's a coincidence. It must be the same family, right?

"Like the store in town?" I ask, the wheels in my brain spinning, integrating all this newly gleaned information.

"Yes."

I wait for him to pepper in a few more details, but he remains stoically silent. Normally, if I ask Dad a question, he expounds on the topic ad nauseam, giving me way more information than I wanted.

With no other choice, I tilt my head and try to get him talking again. "Do the Rothchild's still own part of the company?"

"No."

Herbert Hawthorne tricked his partner into signing the company over to him.

Is that what really happened?

My frustration grows as Dad remains tight-lipped. Why do I have to drag every little detail from him? "When did that happen? Did they part amicably?"

Dad forces out a chuckle, but the amusement doesn't reach his eyes. "What's with all the questions, huh? Are you really this interested in our family history?"

In this particular case?

Absolutely.

Every day, it becomes painfully clear that the people of Hawthorne hate us because of something that happened in the past. Until I'm able to get to the bottom of what that is, I can't understand or fix the problem.

Shifting my weight, I hastily manufacture an excuse. "I was thinking about writing a paper on the topic for English class."

The lines of tension bracketing his eyes and mouth grow more pronounced. "That's probably not a good idea."

"Oh?" I perk up, ready to pounce. "How come?" He needs to give me something here other than the runaround.

"It's just not," he says tightly, flicking his gaze to his wife before forcing a smile. "There are more interesting topics to focus on, like astronomy."

"Yeah, I guess."

That's not going to happen. Now I'm more determined than ever to figure out our past. Even though I'm tempted to keep asking questions, intuition tells me it would be prudent to drop the topic for the time being and come at it again at a later point.

I take a step into the hall. "All right then, I should probably—"

"Wait!" Mom says, cutting me off. When I raise my brows in question, she continues. "Did I mention we're going to host a party at the house over Labor Day weekend?"

"A party?" I frown, my brain switching gears at that bit of news.

Who the heck does she plan on inviting? No one in this town will even talk to us.

She nods, a smile springing to her lips as her eyes crinkle. "Yup, I thought it would give everyone a chance to get to know us a little better. It might make things easier at school."

You know what that sounds like?

A disastrous idea. But I don't have the heart to tell Mom that and rain on her parade when she's obviously excited about it. I glance at my father to gauge his thoughts, but his expression remains shuttered.

The only thing this conversation has proven is that Dad knows more than he's willing to admit. Kingsley mentioned two things this morning. One, Great-Great-Grandpa Herbert started Hawthorne Industries with a partner. And two, the partner was cheated out of his stake in the company. As much as I want to believe Kingsley is a liar, I can't. He's right about at least one thing, and my gut tells me he's probably right about the other.

I need to figure out what happened and why.

SUMMER

16

I lay on the horn for the second time.

Where the hell is Austin? Why is he taking so long?

If he keeps this up, we'll be late. A shiver works its way through my body. I wouldn't necessarily call it fear, but it's pretty damn close. I've been doing my best to fly under Ms. Pettijohn's radar. Waltzing in late for the second time in a matter of weeks won't help that objective.

With my palm resting against the horn, I'm about to lay on it for a third time when the front door opens, and Austin rushes out with his head down and shoulders hunched. He's been especially surly lately. My gut tells me that his foul mood has everything to do with football, but he's remained frustratingly tight-lipped about it.

Once he slides into the passenger seat, I grumble, "What took you so long?"

"Woke up late." His words are barely audible.

"Ever consider setting your alarm?"

I wait for him to fire off a snarky comeback, but instead, he says, "Yeah, I'll do that from now on."

I glance at him from the corner of my eye as he silently stares out the passenger side window at the house. Something feels off about his behavior, but I can't put my finger on what it is.

"Aus?" I lay a tentative hand on his shoulder. "Are you all right?"

"I'm fine." He shrugs off my touch. "Just drive, okay?"

Surprised by the curt dismissal, my mouth tumbles open.

What the hell is wrong with him?

When I walked out of the house this morning, Austin had yet to appear for breakfast. Mom said something about him oversleeping.

Come to think of it, I never saw him last night after practice. He had slammed into the house and shut himself away in his room. I'd knocked on his door, asking if he needed help with homework, but he'd claimed not to have any. I didn't push the issue because I had a quiz to study for.

Suspicion grows inside me. "Austin," I blurt, angling my body toward him, "look at me."

"No."

My heartbeat hitches as my mouth turns cottony. "Why not?"

"Summer, can you just drive?" There's a pause as his voice drops. *"Please?"*

"Not until I see your face."

For a long moment, he remains still, and I wonder if we'll sit in the driveway all morning. Finally, he huffs out an exasperated breath and swivels toward me. My eyes widen as I clap a hand over my mouth. His nose is bruised and swollen. The damage around his eye from last week had only begun to fade.

"What happened?" Before he can say anything, I growl, "And don't tell me it happened at football!"

His lips lift into a humorless smile. "Well, it *did* happen at football, just not practice."

My mind whirls at the implication. "In the locker room, then?"

"They want me to quit, and I'm not going to." His voice turns belligerent. One of Austin's best qualities is that he's relentless. In this instance, it's a detriment to his health.

"Who? Who wants you to quit?" I really hope Kingsley doesn't have anything to do with this. Why that matters, I don't know, but it does.

He presses his lips together, refusing to answer.

"Austin?" I search his battered face as he glares out the windshield.

"You wanted to see what happened, now you've seen it. So drive. I don't need to be late on top of everything else."

This is getting out of hand.

"Maybe we should tell Mom and Dad," I murmur, pulling the car out of the driveway and heading to the main road.

He barks out a laugh. "What the hell are they going to do about it?"

I chew my lower lip and contemplate the question. It's the same rationale I used for not mentioning the vandalism to the G-wagon. Mom is under the delusion that throwing a party will fix all our problems.

It won't.

My belly pinches with nerves as I turn onto school property and pass through the gate. It's been less than two weeks, and I hate Hawthorne Prep along with the kids who attend it. I glance at the clock on the dashboard. We have ten minutes to get to class. At least we won't be late. For one more day, I'll escape the wrath of Ms. Pettijohn.

We exit the vehicle and walk toward the entrance of the stone building. Conversations ground to a halt as we pass by. For fuck's sake. This is the second week of school. Why are we still garnering this much attention? It sets my teeth on edge and sends a prickle of unease scuttling down my spine.

Austin yanks open the glass door as we head to our lockers. It's definitely not my imagination. More people are staring than usual. Smirks and whispers get shared behind cupped hands. There's an air of anticipation that permeates the atmosphere.

A feeling of foreboding gathers inside me. Instead of stopping at my locker, I follow closely behind Austin to his. Half of the football team is hanging around, talking in small clumps. Most go silent when they catch sight of us. The tension becomes even more stifling, and I tug on Austin's arm to stop him.

He shoots me an impatient glance. "What?"

My gaze flits around nervously, trying to pinpoint what the problem is. "I don't know," I mutter, "but something's going on."

His lips flatten into a tight line. "They can't do anything to us here."

If only that were true. Doesn't Austin realize that these people don't follow any rules other than their own?

One of the football players straightens when he sees us. A malicious glint enters his eyes. "Looks like Hawthorne tripped again and landed on his face," he says in an overly obnoxious voice before laughing. "Maybe you're not coordinated enough to play football, bud. Ever think about taking up checkers? Might be the way to go."

My brother grits his teeth as every muscle becomes whipcord tight. His hands gather into fists. I recognize his body language for what it is. The not-so-calm before the storm. Dread pools inside me. I have no idea how to avoid the inevitable.

The blond guy with stormy gray eyes appears to be the ringleader. Next to him is the girl who showed Austin around the first day of school. Delilah. Looking distinctly uncomfortable, she gnaws her bottom lip before whispering something in the douchebag's ear. When he ignores her, she reaches out and tentatively lays a hand on his bicep. He jerks his gaze away from my brother long enough to scowl before shaking off her touch.

"Who is that?" I mutter from the side of my mouth, glaring at the guy. I know an enemy when I see one.

"Jasper Morgan."

Even his name sounds douchey.

"Let me guess, he's the first-string quarterback."

"You guessed it."

For a moment, I squeeze my eyes shut. This is the guy who's been messing with Austin.

Fuck.

"That would about sum it up," Austin mutters.

"Why are they all standing around your locker?" The hallway is jam-packed with people. More than usual.

"My guess is that we're about to find out." Austin's tone and expression don't betray him. He's become a master at hiding his genuine feelings. If the past has taught him anything, it's to keep your vulnerabilities buried deep inside where people can't use them against you.

As we move through the corridor, a whiff of something rancid catches my attention. I inhale again and try to figure out what it is and where it's emanating from. Although, I'm pretty sure I have a sneaking suspicion.

"Aus," I claw at his arm, attempting to stop him, "forget about your locker. Let's head to class."

He shakes me off, unwilling to back down from whatever confrontation is about to unfold. His new teammates have brought the battle to him, and Austin has never backed down from an altercation in his life. When you're used to fighting for every scrap of respect, it becomes second nature. Sometimes I think he enjoys it.

"Maybe you should listen to your hot sister and get your pussy ass to class," Jasper yells.

Austin snarls in response. I feel the pent-up adrenaline rushing through his blood.

I glare at the guy dead set on provoking my brother into a reaction while his monkeys stand behind him. Delilah looks miserable. For a moment, a twinge of pity fills me before it's quickly quashed. No one is forcing her to date an asshat.

That's her choice.

As we arrive at my brother's locker, the stench becomes almost unbearable. The guys are all laughing, trying to contain their giddiness. A punchline is coming, and I'm afraid of what it will be. More than that, I'm afraid Austin will lose his shit and go berserk.

Even though my brother's face is an inscrutable mask, he understands how this will go down. He flicks his wrist left, then to the right, before twisting left again and arriving at the number twelve. When he yanks on the handle, the door pops open.

My hand flies to my mouth as an avalanche of manure tumbles out of the locker onto Austin before landing on the floor. The locker has been jam-packed with it. The blazer he'd left hanging in there last night is ruined along with his books.

A battle roar erupts from deep in Austin's chest before he spins around and lunges for Jasper. As soon as he does, the blond boy throws his books to the floor and meets my brother halfway before they collide. The surrounding crowd erupts into chants of—*fight, fight, fight.*

In the blink of an eye, all hell breaks loose. Austin's fists fly with an amazing amount of velocity. Grunts soon follow. I'm not sure if the sounds originate from Austin or the other guy. When it becomes apparent that Jasper isn't thrashing my brother with ease, a few more football players join the fray.

Fuck!

There's no way I'm going to stand here and allow them to beat the crap out of my brother. With so many players throwing punches, he'll get pummeled, and these assholes will stand around and watch. I drop my backpack to the floor and advance toward the group of grappling boys when strong fingers grip my arms and yank me backward until I land against a muscular chest.

"*Let me go,*" I yell, struggling against the tight hold.

"You're not going anywhere," a voice growls against my ear.

Kingsley.

His arms band around me, making escape impossible.

"*Please, I need to help him.*" Even though it's futile, I twist and turn in his arms.

"No."

It seems like forever before a couple of teachers poke their heads out of their classrooms and jog down the hallway when they see the ruckus taking place.

"Hey!" Mr. Timmons yells, "Break it up right now before everyone gets suspended!"

"Get to class!" another man bellows.

Now that teachers have appeared on the scene, the crowd splinters apart. I search the sea of faces for Austin. He's on the ground, wrestling with Jasper. The two male teachers wade through the football players before prying the two boys apart.

"Both of you get to the headmaster's office!"

I jerk out of Kingsley's hold and rush toward my brother. His face is more swollen than when we arrived fifteen minutes ago. With a growl, I swing around and shove my hands against Jasper's chest.

Not expecting the attack, he stumbles back a step as hatred materializes across his face. "Someone needs to teach you a lesson, you little bitch!"

Even though there are adults in the vicinity, he takes a menacing step toward me. I stand my ground, straightening to my full height. If he thinks he can hit me and get away with it, let him try. It'll be that much easier to get his ass expelled from Hawthorne.

"Morgan!" Kingsley barks, and Jasper stops, turning toward him with a snarl. The dark-haired boy shakes his head. "Don't even think about touching her."

My eyes flare at the power Kingsley wields.

"Mr. Morgan and Mr. Hawthorne," my AP psychology teacher snaps, "get to the office. *Now*."

Then he turns to Kingsley and me, who I realize are the only other students loitering in the corridor. "Both of you get to class before I write you up."

I shake my head and step closer to Austin. "I'm going to the office with my brother."

Mr. Timmons purses his lips but doesn't argue before turning to Kingsley. "Mr. Rothchild, get to first hour."

Rothchild?

With wide eyes, I swing toward Kingsley.

He's a Rothchild?

He was talking about his great-great-grandfather?

Even though a small piece of the puzzle has fallen into place, it's not enough to have a clear picture of what happened and why everyone in this town hates us. Unfortunately, I can't think about that right now. Something tells me we've got bigger problems.

SUMMER

17

A ustin and I sit silently across from the headmaster in his office.

Jasper was the first one called in, and after five minutes, he was sent back to class. I have no idea what was said to him or if he was even reprimanded for the shit-filled locker or the fight. From the smirk he flashed at us on the way out, it's doubtful.

Mr. Pembroke, the headmaster, steeples his chubby fingers together as he glares at us. "I'm not sure what kind of school you attended in Chicago, but fisticuffs are not tolerated at Hawthorne Prep. Students are encouraged to reach peaceful resolutions by elevating themselves intellectually with discussions and debates. They do not settle disputes like Neanderthals by using their fists."

Is this guy for real? My guess is that he doesn't have a clue about what takes place in these hallowed halls.

When it becomes obvious that my brother isn't going to defend himself as he slouches on the chair, giving Mr. Pembroke a blank stare, I realize that I'll have to take matters into my own hands.

As soon as I open my mouth to tell our side of the story, the headmaster turns his attention to me with a scowl. "I was told that you, young lady, attempted to attack Mr. Morgan after the fight had been broken up by Mr. Timmons and Mr. Smyth."

Please...I hardly *attacked* that jerk.

His beady gaze returns to my brother. "I could suspend you right now for two weeks, and the board wouldn't have any objection to it."

I inhale a deep breath before blowing it out, attempting to rein in my frustration. If I don't get my anger under control, I'll blow like a geyser. Austin isn't the only Hawthorne with a temper. It may take more to ignite my fuse, but it can be done.

"Mr. Pembroke, I did not attack Jasper." When one of his brows jerks in disbelief, I admit begrudgingly, "I pushed him, that's it."

"That is not the story I heard, my dear."

Grrrrr.

"All the witnesses I spoke with," he continues, "verified that it was your brother who threw the first punch."

"Well, yes—" I say, needing to clarify why that occurred.

A triumphant smile curves his fleshy lips. "Then we're in agreement. Your brother started the fight and will be suspended for two weeks."

"*What? No!*" I yell, jumping out of my chair. "Austin may have thrown the first punch, but he was provoked into doing it. Jasper filled his locker with cow shi—"

The headmaster clears his throat and gives me a look chock-full of warning.

"Manure," I finish awkwardly, falling back onto my seat.

"And you have proof that it was Mr. Morgan who did this?" the headmaster questions.

Other than him loitering in the area and gloating? "Um, no, but—"

Mr. Pembroke lifts his hands in the air as if there's nothing more he can do about the situation before shrugging. "Without proof or witnesses, we can hardly say without a shadow of a doubt that Mr. Morgan did anything to your brother."

I press my lips together until they feel bloodless before admitting, "Austin's eye was blackened at football practice last week, and then yesterday, he was hit in the nose."

The balding man shakes his head. "Football, I'm afraid, is a brutal sport. Participants know this going in."

My mouth falls open. "It happened in the locker room, not on the field."

Mr. Pembroke's gaze shifts to my brother. "Is that true, Mr. Hawthorne? Have you been hazed or bullied by your peers?" *Transla-*

tion—*are you a snitch who is getting his ass handed to him by the popular kids?*

When Austin remains silent, I elbow him in the ribs. "*Tell him, Aus,*" I plead, needing Pembroke to see that my brother isn't the troublemaker he has pegged him to be. The blame for this shouldn't be heaped solely on him.

"No," he grunts.

The headmaster's gaze returns to me. I can practically see the satisfaction simmering in his watery blue eyes.

Grrrrr!

"Our vehicle has been egged in the parking lot at least four times," I blurt in desperation. Pembroke is operating under the delusion that Hawthorne Prep is a utopia of higher education and perfectly behaved students.

It's far from it.

More like a horror show.

"I'm sorry to hear that." His voice fills with faux concern. "I assume you filled out an incident report with Mrs. Baxter. What's strange is that I haven't seen a single episode of vandalism come across my desk."

When I remain silent, he raises his brows in question. I'm really beginning to hate when he does that.

"You filed a report in the office, correct?"

"No," I ground between clenched teeth.

"No *what*, Ms. Hawthorne?"

"No, I did not fill out an incident report," I force myself to say calmly. It takes everything I have inside to keep my temper under wraps.

His eyes widen. "Why ever not?"

I wince as Austin's probing gaze settles on me.

"Did you take any pictures? Perhaps with your phone? You kids seem to enjoy snapping photos of everything and plastering it all over social media. I'm sure you must have at least done that."

Heat suffuses my cheeks. Already I can see where this is heading. "No, I didn't take any pictures."

"Without a doubt, you reported the incident to your parents. They must have corroborating knowledge of this."

Ugh!

"No! I didn't tell anyone about it!" My voice escalates as I strain forward. Any moment, I'll leap over the desk and strangle this fleshy excuse of a human being. "I was embarrassed! I wanted to forget it ever happened!"

"Ms. Hawthorne, calm yourself!" Mr. Pembroke jerks on his seat as he straightens his shoulders. "Must I remind you to speak in a controlled manner when addressing a faculty member?"

I slump on my chair with defeat. None of this is going the way I expected. Or maybe it's going *exactly* how I feared it would.

A timely interruption comes in the form of a knock on the door.

"Come in," Mr. Pembroke says.

Mrs. Baxter sticks her gray-haired head in the room. "The children's parents have arrived."

"Perfect timing," he says with a pleasant smile. "By all means, send them in."

As my parents rush through the door, I slouch further onto my seat.

The headmaster rises from his chair as he ushers them into the small office. "Perhaps the children should wait outside while we discuss matters."

I open my mouth to argue when Dad swings toward me with a harsh glare. *"Do as Mr. Pembroke says and wait outside!"*

I rise to my feet as Austin does the same, and we slink out of the headmaster's office with our tails tucked between our legs. The door closes firmly behind us as my brother flops onto a chair. My guess is that Pembroke will spin the situation so it appears as if we're the problem.

Austin flicks his gaze to me. "Why didn't you tell me about the eggs?"

I shrug and stare straight ahead, not wanting to meet his questioning gaze. "I don't know. Enough was going on without worrying you over a stupid prank."

His voice drops, filling with barely suppressed anger. "You shouldn't have kept it from me, Summer."

Wanting to defuse the thick tension brewing between us, I press my lips together and admit, "You're right, I'm sorry."

Instead of dropping the conversation, he growls, "You need to stop hiding crap from me. And while you're at it, stop trying to fight all my battles. I'm more than capable of fighting them myself."

"That's not what I was doing," I mumble, shifting uncomfortably on the scratchy fabric of the chair, though, when it comes down to it, that's *exactly* what I was doing. What I didn't realize is that *he* would understand it. I've spent most of my life in protective mode where my brother is concerned. It's a hard habit to break.

Austin's lips lift into a ghost of a smile. "You might be five minutes older than me, but we're still the same age. Believe it or not, I'm capable of taking care of myself. You don't need to treat me like a baby."

I shake my head. "I don't—"

"Yeah," he says, cutting me off, "you do. All the time. I might be dyslexic, but that doesn't mean I'm an idiot who can't deal with his own shit." He winces before raising his voice. "Sorry about the language, Mrs. Baxter."

"Don't worry about it." She waves her hand from behind the desk she's sitting at. "I've heard much worse."

Lowering my voice, I whisper, "I don't think you're an idiot." It pains me that he would even suspect that. Being diagnosed with dyslexia has been difficult for Austin, and his self-esteem has taken major hits throughout the years because of it. All I've ever tried to do is be a good sister and smooth the way for him. Is that so wrong? Wouldn't he do the same if the situation was reversed?

He raises a brow. "You sure about that?"

"Of course! You're the furthest thing from an idiot. I..."

"You *what*?" he asks, voice sharpening.

"I just love you, Aus. And I want to help you any way I can." I shake my head and stare down at my entwined fingers as emotion gathers in my throat. "Being protective doesn't mean that I think you can't take care of yourself."

"Well, that's the way it feels."

"I'm sorry." It was never my intention to hurt Austin. He's the one person I want to see succeed in life more than anyone. If I've overstepped my boundaries, it was done out of love.

"How about from now on, you let me deal with my own problems? You might not realize this, but you won't always be around to fix everything. I need to do it myself."

I bite my lip. The idea of us being separated next year when we go to college is one I try *not* to think about. What am I going to do without my brother at my side?

"Summer? Did you hear what I said?"

A thick lump forms in the middle of my throat as I jerk my head into a tight nod.

"And," he continues, gaze piercing mine, "if there are things I need to know about, like people messing with you or our car, I want you to be straight with me." He pauses, allowing his words to sink in. "I'm the one who should be protecting you. Not the other way around. Understand?"

"Yeah," I mumble, "I got it."

"Good." His lips quirk before he reaches out and squeezes my hand. "I'm glad we had this little convo."

I roll my eyes. When he knocks his shoulder into mine, I laugh, and the tension between us dissolves. Ten minutes later, the door to the office swings open, and our parents stalk out. Austin and I jump to our feet. Griffin and Eloise don't look happy.

"I'm sorry we had to meet under these circumstances, Mr. and Mrs. Hawthorne. I'll be in touch with more information after I speak with the board tomorrow morning." He turns to the secretary. "Mrs. Baxter, will you please give Summer a pass to third hour? She's missed more than enough instructional time."

I gulp and glance warily at my parents. "What about Austin?"

"For the time being, your brother has been suspended for three days and will come home with us," Mom murmurs in a subdued tone.

"*What!*" I glance at Mr. Pembroke before stepping toward Dad. "But Jasper—"

"The disciplinary action of another student is none of your concern," the headmaster reprimands. "What remains to be seen is if your brother will have any further sanctions brought against him and if he'll remain on the football team for the season."

My mouth drops open. Austin pales but remains silent.

This is total crap!

"Summer," Mrs. Baxter holds out a blue slip of paper. "Here's your pass."

With a somber expression, Dad nods. "Go to class. We'll talk more about this when you get home."

I glance at Austin to get a read on his thoughts. He holds my gaze steadily as a silent communication passes between us.

Go. I'll handle this.

I press my lips together in an effort not to argue before straightening my shoulders.

Fine, I'll go, but this isn't over. Not by a long shot. I have no idea how I'll fix this mess, but there has to be a way. I realize Austin wants to handle his own shit, but this is too important to leave in his hands.

SUMMER

18

The rest of the day passes by with a few sly looks and nothing more. It's a relief when the final bell rings, and I can get the hell out of here. I grab my backpack from the locker and head to the G-wagon. My breath gets trapped in my lungs as I push through the heavy glass door. Weak sunlight struggles to break through the cloud cover. At any moment, the heavens will open up and dump rain on us.

For once, the crummy weather matches my mood perfectly.

There are pockets of people standing around in the parking lot, but none pay me any attention as I hunch my shoulders and weave through the vehicles. As soon as the untouched Mercedes comes into view, relief is expelled from my lungs with a burst. Thankfully, there won't be a side trip to the carwash today.

Twenty minutes later, I pull into the drive before grabbing my backpack from the passenger seat and hauling ass inside. The house seems quieter than normal. Instead of announcing my presence, I take the stairs two at a time and make a beeline straight to Austin's room. I rap my knuckles on the wood before throwing the door wide. I find my brother sprawled out on the queen-sized bed with his hands stacked behind his head as he stares at the ceiling.

Forgoing a greeting, he asks instead, "Any problems?"

I shake my head, relieved I don't have to lie. "Nope, none."

He blows out a steady breath as his muscles visibly loosen. "Good."

I drop my backpack onto the wood plank floor and settle at the foot of the bed. "You're really suspended for three days?"

His lips flatten at the reminder. "Yup. Mom and Dad are pissed."

Join the club. The whole situation infuriates me. "We're not the ones they should be mad at."

"It doesn't matter," he says, fatigue creeping into his voice.

We've been here less than two weeks, and we're exhausted by the constant battle being waged against us.

"Of course, it does," I scoff. Until this morning, Jasper Morgan hadn't even been on my radar. Now, he's public enemy number one and needs to pay for what he did to Austin. It's the only thing I've been able to focus on today. "Here's what I've been thinking. We need to devise a plan—"

"They might expel me, Summer."

"*What?*" Disbelief riddles my voice. This is complete bullshit!

"Yeah. And in the unlikely event that I don't get expelled, they'll kick me off the team. The headmaster is pushing for it and so is the coach. Dad said that I should prepare myself for the outcome."

"No! They can't do that! You didn't start the fight." My brother will never survive this hellhole if they take football away from him.

A wave of grief crashes over him. "Haven't you figured out by now that they can do whatever the hell they want?"

Austin has gotten several looks from major Division I colleges, but the scouting has all been preliminary. No agreements have been made or NCAA paperwork signed. Without a senior season, what will happen to those prospects?

"Can you still get recruited if you don't play?" I force myself to ask.

"Probably not." He stares at the ceiling, refusing to make eye contact. "I'll have to disclose I was kicked off the team. No one will want to take on a player who can't get along with his teammates."

"We can't allow that to happen," I whisper as panic rises in my throat like bile.

Austin flicks his gaze to me. "There might be another way, but I don't want to leave you here alone."

Oh God.

My heart clenches under my breast as I wait for him to elaborate.

"I could move back to Chicago for the year and stay with Max."

Max is Austin's best friend. They've been tight since the third grade. Not only is his father the head football coach at our old high school but he's also the history department chair. If anyone can pull strings and legitimize Austin's residency, it would be Max's father. He was brokenhearted to see Austin leave and had jokingly suggested my brother stay with them for senior year.

When I remain silent, too stunned to say anything, my brother continues. "I've already texted Max."

No!

It feels like I'm being suffocated from the inside out. Any moment I'll start clawing at my neck. Selfish as it might sound, I don't want Austin to leave. The most we've ever been apart is a couple of weeks in the summer when he attends football camp. I know it's unlikely that we'll be accepted to the same college, and I've been preparing myself for the inevitable, but I'm nowhere near ready to be separated from him now. The flipside is that I can't imagine football being taken away from him either. It's Austin's everything. His entire reason for being. What would he do without it?

"There has to be another way," I croak.

Somberness fills his expression. I've never seen him look so beaten down before. "Well, if you find another solution, let me know because this is the only alternative I've been able to come up with."

My teeth sink into my lower lip as I blink away the tears.

There has to be *something* that can be done.

Something *I* can do.

I just have to figure out what it is.

SUMMER

19

I stare at the physics book splayed open on my bed as the sentence swims before my eyes. I've read over the same paragraph at least five times, and I still couldn't tell you what it was about. There's a quiz tomorrow.

A quiz I'm going to fail.

Frustrated with myself and the circumstances, I slam the book shut and hop off the bed. A burst of nervous energy explodes in me, and I pace in front of the window. All I can think about is Austin. He wants me to stand back and let him handle his own problems, but how can I do that when so much is at risk?

I don't want him to move to Chicago and leave me. I'm barely hanging on as it is. Without him...

A shudder slides through me.

Our old school doesn't start until the Tuesday after Labor Day. Max's father jumped at the chance to have Austin come back and play for his old team. My parents spent at least half an hour on the phone with him, hashing out the logistics. It's almost frightening how Austin mentioned the idea a couple of hours ago, and it's already gained so much traction. The only thing stopping my brother from packing his bags and leaving tomorrow is the decision from the board about his future at Hawthorne. If they allow him to continue with the team, then he'll stay here for his senior year. If he's forced to quit, then Austin will probably move to Chicago this weekend, so he has time to register, get settled, and start practicing with his old team. The thought of that happening makes me sick to my stomach.

Tension and fear swirl through me as I swing toward the window and push the heavy drapery aside before peering into the darkness. The stars are out in full force tonight.

I've spent the past five hours trying to come up with a solution to the problem we find ourselves in, but I keep drawing blanks. The only viable option is that Austin should move back to Chicago. Some of my best thinking is done while lying outside and staring up at the stars. If anything can get my neurons firing, it's that.

Otherwise, I'll lose my brother.

I grab the afghan from the chair in the corner and slip out the door onto the small patio off my room. There are definite advantages to having a private entrance to the house, and sneaking out for a breath of fresh air is one of them.

With bare feet, I skirt around the edge of the pool, heading to the far corner of the yard where I've found the perfect spot for stargazing. The little pinpricks of light are so much brighter than the ones in Chicago that it's almost like I'm looking at an entirely different sky. This weekend, I'm going to unpack my telescope and set it up on the balcony.

A whapping noise breaks the silence of the night, and my footsteps falter as I stop and listen, trying to figure out what the sound is and where it's coming from.

Ten seconds later, it repeats.

I tilt my head and prick my ears, realizing after a minute that the noise is rhythmic.

Whatever it is, it's coming from Kingsley's yard. I can't see what's going on because of the thick foliage that separates our properties. It's not a conscious decision to creep closer until I'm all but buried in a clump of bushes and parting the leafy branches so I have an unobstructed view.

My breath hitches when I find a bare-chested Kingsley with a lacrosse stick in hand. He's throwing a small white ball at some kind of standing trampoline. The ball hits the woven canvas and ricochets back to him. He catches it easily with the mesh netting of his stick before flicking the metal pole over his shoulder and releasing it from the pocket.

The repetitive motion is almost hypnotic.

Or maybe it's Kingsley who is mesmerizing.

A soft sigh escapes as his muscles ripple. With moonlight pouring over him, he looks like an ancient Greek god. My core clenches in agreement.

I wince at that damning thought.

No.

No.

No.

He's terrible.

Mean.

Cruel.

He isn't the sweet boy who took me out on his boat. I don't understand what happened to that guy. Maybe he was never real, merely an illusion I wanted to believe in. That thought fills me with so much heartache that it's almost enough to swallow me whole. We only spent one day together, but it was enough for me to start falling for him.

"How long are you going to stand there and watch me?" he calls out, breaking into the whirl of my thoughts.

I straighten and knock my head against a thick branch. "Ow."

Even though his lips tilt at the corners, his attention never deviates from what he's doing. Nor does he break the rhythm of catching and releasing. There's no other choice but to push through the foliage into his yard and show myself.

"Do you spy on me often?" he asks, not sounding interested in the answer.

"No." My fingers bite into the blanket as I clutch it to my chest for protection. How that will keep me safe, I don't know. But it makes me feel marginally better. "I was going to look at the stars." I gulp and force myself to add, "It's a cloudless night, and they're bright."

He catches the ball with the mesh pocket one more time before tossing the stick to the ground and swinging toward me. The heavy weight of his gaze pins me in place. Movement becomes impossible. I don't understand the strange power he has over me. I wish there were a way to shake it off and feel nothing. But I have yet to figure out how to flip that switch.

When he continues to watch me from behind hooded eyes, I clear my throat and blurt, "I like to stargaze at the back of the yard."

"I know."

The fine hair on my arms rise at that acknowledgment.

"I've watched you," he adds without the least bit of shame.

And he accused *me* of spying? How many times has he done that, and I've been unaware? The thought should creep me out, but it doesn't. And that is so many kinds of wrong.

When my tongue darts out to moisten my lips, his gaze drops to the movement before flicking back to mine. Only this time, heat swirls in his eyes.

"I heard about what happened to your brother." There's a pause. "Sucks for him."

Anger bolts through me, and my shoulders jerk as I scowl. "Football is everything to him."

"Then he shouldn't have jeopardized it."

"We both know he didn't start that fight," I grit out, irritated with the comment. "You saw what happened."

He shrugs before closing the gaping distance between us. "Here's what you need to understand, Hawthorne. There are people with power, and then there are those who don't have any." His eyes glitter in the moonlight. "In case you haven't figured it out yet, your family is one of the have-nots."

Why does he have to be such a jerk? "You love that, don't you?"

One side of his mouth crooks. "Actually, I do. It's a nice change of pace. The Hawthornes deserve every bit of their self-induced misery."

As much as I hate to admit it, he's right about us not having any power in this town or at the school.

But you know who *does* have power?

Kingsley Rothchild. He proved it when he stopped Jasper from doling out retribution in the hallway this morning. All it took was one sharp word from him and the other boy was backing down.

Although that doesn't mean Kingsley or his family have pull over the board at Hawthorne Prep. And even if they did, why would he help me when he's delighted by our fall from grace?

"Seems like there's something on your mind," Kingsley drawls, interrupting my thoughts. "Why don't you do us both a favor and spit it out?"

Before I can think better of it, the words are shooting out of my mouth. "I need your help."

"Oh?" One brow slides lazily upward. "Interesting that you would think I'd lift a finger to help you."

Honestly, I don't. But what other choice is there? Kingsley is a last-ditch effort on my part.

"Austin will move back to Chicago if football gets taken away from him." I shake my head and clutch the blanket closer. "I don't want that to happen."

He tilts his head, all the while studying me with an unnerving intensity. "Why should I care about that?"

"Please," I whisper. As much as it pains me to beg, I'll do whatever I have to for my brother.

"I'm flattered that you think I hold so much power." A grin flashes across his face. He is so loving this. "What makes you think I'd offer my assistance even if I could?"

That's an excellent question. One I don't have an answer for.

My shoulders collapse, and I quickly glance away, staring into the swirling darkness of the yard as hopelessness fills me. "I don't."

I sense his movement before I catch it from the corner of my eye. Every step he eats up between us makes my heart pump faster and the adrenaline rush through my veins.

"That's it? You're going to give up just like that?" He makes a clicking sound with his tongue. "Not very persistent, are you?"

"What?" My widened gaze jerks to him as my mouth turns cottony.

He picks up a lock of my hair from my shoulder and twirls it absently around his finger. His movements turn lazy, but nothing about the calculating look in his eyes is idle. Thick tension builds between us as he continues to stare. It's only after the air turns explosive does his gaze flick to mine. "You're going to throw in the towel without even trying to persuade me to change my mind?"

A shudder of unease slides through me. "I don't understand."

Arousal ignites in his eyes as he tugs gently on the heavy strands. "I think you do."

A strange concoction of caution-infused confusion churn inside me. "Are you saying that you'll help me?"

He shrugs, continuing to wrap the inky-colored lock of hair around his finger. "I haven't decided if it's worth my trouble."

What does he want? For me to beg?

If that's all it will take, I'll do it gladly. I gulp and force out the word. *"Please?"*

His eyelids lower. "That's an awfully pretty word falling from your lips."

Nerves skitter along my bare flesh. Attraction tugs deep inside my core. As wrong as it is, I can't stop it from spreading throughout my body like a virus.

"If I make this all go away, what do I get?"

"I don't know," I murmur. It takes everything I have inside to keep the nerves from overtaking my voice. "What do you want?" Whatever price he'll extract will be steep. Of that, I can be certain.

"Everything." He steps closer, his bigger, muscular body dwarfing mine. I crane my neck to hold his steely gaze. "Are you willing to give me that?" There's a pause. "If so, you have yourself a deal."

His hands settle on my shoulders as if grounding me to the earth. His lips hover dangerously over mine. "It's a onetime offer. Once it expires, it's gone for good, and you're on your own."

When he nips my lower lip with sharp teeth, a groan escapes from me, and I drop the blanket from my fingers. An explosion of pleasure-filled pain jolts through my system, shaking me to the core.

His lips curve into a wicked smile. "Sexy little moans aren't good enough. I want to hear you agree to the terms."

What other choice is there?

None that I can think of.

Austin needs to stay in Hawthorne. I can't face these people on my own. Not for the rest of the academic year. "Yes."

"Good girl." His fingers bite into my shoulders as he forces me to the ground. When I resist, a hard glint enters his eyes. "On your knees."

Oh God.

I don't know what I was expecting, but it wasn't this.

When his hands press me lower, my knees buckle, and I drop to the thick grass. As I stare straight ahead, I realize that I'm perfectly aligned with the bulge in his shorts. I swallow thickly before raising my chin and meeting his gaze. The hot look in his eyes has my belly hollowing out.

He lifts one hand from my shoulder and trails his knuckles along my jaw. The other one continues to hold me in place. "How many guys have you blown?"

My tongue darts out to moisten my lips as his gaze fastens onto the movement. My breath stutters as his cock jerks to life inches from my face.

He chuckles darkly at my reaction and repeats the question in a voice that has turned shades deeper. *"How many?"*

"None."

"Hmm." His lips flatten. "I'm not sure how I feel about that."

What does that mean?

Is the deal off?

"I guess I'll just have to teach you." With that, he places his index finger against my lips. "Open."

I don't think about what he's asking. My mouth opens enough for his finger to slip inside. My heart pounds erratically beneath my rib cage as his digit rests against the velvety softness of my tongue. It's such a strange feeling.

One hand lifts from my shoulder before he tunnels his fingers through my thick strands, cupping my scalp before carefully angling my chin upward. His grip tightens as he rocks my head back and forth so that my tongue can slide against the length until we fall into a natural rhythm. As I take over, his eyelids lower, becoming half-mast.

Why does this feel so *erotic*?

That shouldn't be the case when he's forcing me to perform this act. Although, if you want to get technical, Kingsley hasn't *forced* me to do anything. He gave me a way to save my brother, and I took it. Even now, I could change my mind and leave. Confusion whirls inside me, and I avert my gaze. The intimacy of the moment becomes almost too much to bear. I shouldn't feel anything for him except loathing.

"Eyes on me," he grunts.

I force my gaze to his. It only takes a moment before I'm drowning in his dark depths. Even though he keeps his fingers threaded through my hair, I've taken over completely. No longer does he guide my movements. My tongue curls around the blunt digit, sucking it into my mouth before releasing it.

Is this what it would feel like to suck his cock?

It's not an unpleasant thought. Quite the opposite. Heat floods my panties as the image materializes in my mind. Only it would be much thicker. Longer. Without realizing it, my tempo picks up speed, and I suck with renewed energy.

A dark chuckle falls from his lips. "Greedy for the real deal?"

I whimper, my gaze locked on his. All I'm doing is drawing his finger into my mouth, but something about the act is sensual. When he attempts to withdraw, my cheeks hollow, trying to keep him in place. A wicked grin spreads across his face as if he's pleased by my reaction.

The hand threaded through my hair tightens, and I wince. My mouth opens, and his finger slides free. His grip stays firm. My breath comes out in short pants as he carefully traces my parted lips with his wet digit.

"I can't wait to fuck that pretty little mouth of yours." His gaze glitters in the moonlight. "I'm going to destroy you."

I think he might be right.

He *will* destroy me.

But not in the way he intends.

Those thickly muttered words have arousal exploding in my core.

Without warning, he sinks the same finger deep into my mouth before pushing it down my throat. My gaze widens but stays locked on his.

"Relax your muscles and breathe through your nose."

I do as he instructs and focus on drawing air in through my nostrils before forcing it out again.

"Good girl."

Kingsley has given me no reason to trust him, yet for some inexplicable reason, I do. It makes no sense, and part of me wonders if I can trust myself to make smart decisions because of it.

"Swallow."

The muscles in my throat contract around the blunt digit.

"Fuck," he hisses. "Again."

I slow my movement, swallowing with more exaggeration. It's a strange sensation to feel my muscles constrict around him.

He groans and slips his finger free from my mouth before his hand settles on the tented material of his shorts. I watch in fascination as he carefully strokes the covered length. My thighs clench with need as a whimper escapes from my mouth. Anticipation and curiosity rush through my veins. I don't realize I'm straining forward until his grip on my scalp tightens to hold me in place.

"Your eagerness is a real turn-on," he murmurs.

I'm embarrassed to admit that *eagerness* doesn't come close to what's crashing around inside me. With his gaze locked on mine, he drags the waistband of his black shorts down until his thick erection can spring free. The muscles in my throat convulse at the thought of taking his hard length into my mouth. He's so big. A shudder of unease slides through me before pooling in my core. I flick my concerned gaze to him.

The edges of his lips quirk as if he senses my nervousness and is feeding off it. "The only thing you need to remember from now on is that I'm your king."

He wraps his hand around his girth and gives it a few slow pumps before bringing the mushroom-shaped head to my lips. His fingers tighten in my hair as he brings the tip of his cock to my mouth before tracing over it. Hot licks of need engulf me, threatening to singe me alive. How can something so benign be so damn erotic?

Kingsley wasn't mistaken when he accused me of being eager. The need to taste him thrums through me like that of a steady heartbeat. I want to draw him into my mouth and discover his taste and texture for myself.

Once he circles my lips, painting me with slick moisture, he places the tip against them. I'm almost desperate to open wider and flick my tongue over the head. Instead, I remain still, eyes trained on him, waiting for his direction.

"Good girl." His hand tightens in my hair, tipping my head back and exposing the delicate column of my throat. "Are you ready to kiss the crown?"

I pucker my lips and brush them against the head of his cock. The skin is soft, and I'm tempted to nuzzle the tip. A fresh wave of arousal crashes over me, threatening to drag me under. My pussy throbs with painful awareness. All it would take is one stroke of my lower lips, and I would come all over myself.

"Again."

I repeat the caress.

His cock stays poised at my mouth before he flexes his hips. The tip slides across my lips as they stretch around his girth, taking the head inside.

"Now suck."

A flood of warmth rains down on me. If my panties hadn't already been soaked, they would be now. My tongue strokes the flat underside of his head as I greedily suck his cock like I did with his finger only minutes ago.

He groans, and his head lolls back, exposing thickly corded muscles. Who knew a throat could be so sexy? I keep my eyes lifted, wanting to see every nuance of pleasure as it flickers across his face.

"Your mouth feels so damn good," he mutters.

As I fall into a rhythm, my sucking grows forceful as I try pulling more of his length into my mouth. When his grip tightens in my hair, I gasp, and his cock slips free. In one swift movement, he drags the athletic shorts over his erection. Breath coming fast, I stare up at him in question. His fingers loosen, relinquishing their hold on my hair before sifting through the strands.

With a smirk, he steps back. "See you at school tomorrow, Hawthorne."

He turns away from me, sauntering to his lacrosse stick and picking it up from the grass before returning to the house. It's only when the back door slams shut that I snap out of my daze.

A strange mixture of relief and disappointment crashes through me. More disturbing than that, I'm not sure which one takes precedence.

SUMMER

20

My cheeks flush as I add a bit of gloss to my lips. Memories from last night flash through my head as I remember the way Kingsley stroked over them with the tip of his cock. That erotic image has been playing on a constant loop inside my head the entire night. I won't pretend that I didn't want it. His assessment of the situation was correct when he called me out for being eager.

Who was that girl on her knees?

She wasn't anyone I recognized.

The simple act of drawing both his finger and cock into my mouth has unleashed something inside me that feels both wicked and primal. It's a reaction I'm ashamed of.

After I crawled into bed last night, I spent the next couple of hours tossing and turning, trying not to think about the agreement struck under the moonlight. I kept pressing my thighs together, attempting to ease the growing ache between them. Finally, knowing that it would only continue for the rest of the night, I stroked myself to orgasm. Trust me, it didn't take much. A touch or two over my slippery flesh and my body was tightening. Only then was I able to fall into a deep, dreamless sleep.

I woke this morning with the same dull ache between my legs and had to do it all over again. Frustrated with the arousal, I didn't bother to fight it. I simply spread my thighs wide and rubbed my clit until my teeth sank into my lower lip so no one would hear me getting off.

Ugh.

Even after that, my core continued to throb.

I finish applying bronze eye shadow across my lids and pull my hair up into a messy bun. Then I press my hands against my cheeks to cool them. It doesn't work. My face feels like it's on fire. I grab my backpack and step into the hall, glancing at Austin's closed door. With no reason to be up at the butt crack of dawn, I'm sure he's still sacked out.

Nerves dance in the pit of my belly at the thought of not only braving Hawthorne Prep by myself but also seeing Kingsley. He's an enigma, and I don't know what to expect from him.

Friendliness?

Cruelty?

Icy dismissal?

"Hey, sweetie." Mom's lips lift into a forced smile as she sits perched at the island in her robe with a steaming cup of coffee in her hands. "Want me to make pancakes?"

"Nah." My stomach revolts at the idea. I'm way too nervous to eat. "I'm going to grab a cup of coffee."

"Are you feeling all right?" With a frown, her gaze roves carefully over my features. "Your cheeks are flushed."

I turn my attention to the window and the perfectly manicured golf course that lies beyond our property line. "Um, yeah. I'm fine."

The truth of the matter is that I'm far from fine, but she can't do anything to help me.

Mom rises from the chair and walks around the island before laying her palm against my forehead. "Hmm. You don't feel warm." She clucks her tongue. "I really hope you're not coming down with something."

"I'm not sick," I mutter, dancing away to grab a cup before changing it at the last moment to a travel mug and pouring myself some much-needed java to drink on the go. Not that I'm champing at the bit to get to school, but I don't need her bombarding me with questions. I'm already out of sorts without her adding to it.

Once I screw the lid on tight, I head for the front door.

"Have a good day," Mom calls after my retreating figure.

I don't see how that will happen, given the new set of circumstances I have to contend with.

"All right," I say with a wave before walking out of the house with my backpack and sliding behind the wheel of the G-wagon.

The engine purrs to life as I glance at the empty passenger seat, wishing that Austin was here with me. We're a team. Ever since we were little, we've had each other's backs. Without him by my side, I'm lost.

Alone.

Vulnerable.

It's a scary prospect.

I try not to focus on those thoughts as I pull out of the driveway and head to school. Every mile of pavement that gets eaten up by the tires has my anxiety intensifying. By the time I drive through the gated entrance onto the property, I have a death grip on the leather steering wheel.

Since I'm early, it doesn't take long to find a parking spot. Students have already begun to congregate in small groups. Instead of exiting the vehicle, I hang back until there are precisely eight minutes before the warning bell rings, signaling the start of first hour. The plan is to get in, go straight to my locker, and then to class without incident.

I give myself a brief pep talk before gathering my courage and stepping out of the SUV. Even though my hands are shaking, I straighten my shoulders and wipe the fear from my expression. Inside, I might be a tightly wound ball of anxiety, but I'll be damned if any of them see that. As I cut through the parking lot, I avoid all eye contact. My gaze stays focused on the stone building that looms in the distance. It takes a moment to realize that no one is paying any attention to me.

Which is strange. I expected them to fall on me like a pack of jackals.

My heart pounds a painful staccato as I slip inside the impressive three-story structure and slink through the corridor before arriving at my locker. I hold my breath as memories of yesterday morning flash through my head.

Discreetly, I sniff the air, wondering if the same fate awaits me.

But there's nothing out of the ordinary. People aren't gathered in the corridor, and I don't detect anything other than the smell of old books coupled with the scent of lemony polish that permeates the air of Hawthorne.

With trembling fingers, I spin the dial and lift the handle. My muscles tense in anticipation as the door swings open. Maybe it would be best if they suspended me along with Austin. My parents would probably go off the deep end if they had to make another trip less than twenty-four hours later to pick me up. Relief rushes from my lungs when nothing happens. Cautiously, I stare into the locker, inspecting it for anything that looks out of place, but there's nothing. It's exactly as I left it yesterday afternoon. Some of the tension drains from my muscles.

As I grab my lit book from the shelf, a guy sidles up next to me before settling against the neighboring locker. Steeling myself, I glance at him from the corner of my eye. I don't know his name, but I recognize him as one of the football players who had congregated around Austin's locker yesterday morning.

"Hey." A slow grin spreads across his face as his gaze rakes over me.

I don't bother to turn and give him my full attention before snapping, "Can I help you?" It's best to shut this shit down right away before it gets out of control.

"Well, I certainly hope so."

I almost laugh.

Please, as if...

I'm a moment away from telling this guy to fuck off when he's shoved aside.

"Beat it, Wendt," Kingsley growls. There's a sharp edge to his voice. "Until further notice, Hawthorne is off-limits."

The guy's eyes bulge as he waggles a finger between us. "Wait a minute, are you two *together*?"

Kingsley shakes his head. "No, but she's mine just the same. Got it?"

"Whatever you say, man." The beefy football player shrugs before sauntering away.

I watch him retreat down the hallway. "Who was that tool?"

"No one you need to concern yourself with," he says dismissively.

My gaze snaps to him, and I'm slammed with erotic images from last night. They flash through my head like a slow-motion picture show.

On my knees, staring up at him as I sucked his finger.

Him tracing my parted lips with his cock.

The head of his erection pressing into my mouth.

Kiss the crown.

Oh God.

Heat floods into my cheeks as I jerk my gaze away from him. It's not swift enough to avoid glimpsing the knowing grin that flashes across his face.

He leans closer, invading my personal space. The scent of his woodsy cologne assaults my senses. "I'm curious...how many times did you touch yourself last night?"

I slam the locker shut with more force than necessary and lie through my teeth. "None."

The deep scrape of his chuckle slices straight to my core before exploding. Even though I clamp my thighs together to stymie the growing need, it doesn't do a damn bit of good.

His knuckles drag against the strip of exposed skin below the hem of my skirt. "If I slipped my fingers inside your panties, would I find them drenched?"

The huskiness of his voice threatens to send another tidal wave of arousal crashing over me. Kingsley needs to stop toying with me before I burst into flames.

"I have to get to class," I snap, slapping his hand away.

His fingers snake out to shackle my wrist, halting me in place when I try to slip past him. He drags me closer until his face is buried against the side of my head. Electricity crackles through my veins at his slightest touch.

"Don't run off just yet," he whispers near the outer shell of my ear. "I've got something for you."

My heart stutters. I'm almost afraid to ask, but that doesn't stop the word from slipping free. "What?"

He drops something soft on the books I'm clutching in my arms.

What the hell is this?

I glance suspiciously from the pile of fabric to him, but his expression remains inscrutable. Gingerly, I hold up the material and realize it's a white shirt. I blink, staring at the letters boldly stamped across the front in red. It's the same shade that matches the plaid of my skirt.

Property of K. Rothchild

This has to be a joke.

"Forget it." I shake my head and throw it at his chest. He can take that shirt and shove it right up his—

"Excuse me?" He arches a sculpted brow as if he must have heard wrong.

"I'm not wearing *that*," I growl, my voice escalating with each word.

"Hmm." His fingers stroke his chiseled jawline with unhurried movements. "Already reneging on our agreement? You couldn't even make it a full twelve hours? That's disappointing, although I should have expected nothing less from a Hawthorne."

"I can't wear that," I whisper.

"You *will* wear it, or you can forget about my help." He shrugs and leans against the locker as if he couldn't care less about what I do.

And maybe he doesn't. For Kingsley, this is nothing more than a game. For me, it's so much more. I gnaw my bottom lip with indecision.

"Has anyone messed with you this morning?" he asks casually.

My gaze slices to him as my face scrunches with uncertainty. "What?"

He steps closer until I can feel the heat of his body and drops his voice. "I asked if anyone has given you trouble since you stepped foot on campus?"

"No." They've ignored me, which I thought was odd. With a fresh wave of insight, I realize it was all Kingsley's doing.

His fingers slip beneath my chin before tipping it upward until I'm left with no other choice but to meet his gaze. "Has anyone so much as *looked* in your direction?"

I swallow thickly. It takes effort to force out the word. "No."

"Even though saving your ass wasn't part of the deal, that's exactly what I've done." His hand falls away from my face. "Sure seems like I'm holding up my end of the bargain and then some, doesn't it?"

Panic rises inside me.

When I remain silent, he balls up the shirt in his hand. "See you around, Hawthorne."

My teeth sink into my lip, pinning it in place as I watch him saunter away.

One step.

Two steps.

Three—

"*Wait!*" I blurt, unable to hold it in any longer.

A smug smile tips the corners of his lips as he swings back around. "Had a change of heart, did we?"

Not bothering to answer, I hold out my hand. "Give me the shirt."

In the blink of an eye, he eats up the distance between us before pressing the fabric into my outstretched hand. My nails dig into the soft cottony material. With a glare, I drop my book. Humor ignites in his eyes as it hits the marble at my feet with a loud thud. My fingers tremble as I shrug out of the blazer and drop it to the floor before yanking his shirt over my head. People stare as I shove one arm through the short sleeve.

"What are you doing?" he asks.

I pause and scowl. "I'm putting on your stupid shirt."

He presses his lips together before shaking his head. "You need to remove the other one first."

"*What?*" My mouth dries as I stare with wide eyes. Please tell me he isn't being serious.

"You heard me." He nods toward the bathroom down the hall.

"Go change. Or do it right here in front of everyone. I don't give a shit."

"B-but this isn't part of the school uniform." My mind spins, trying to come up with an excuse. "The teachers won't allow me to wear this in class."

"It might be your family's name on the front of the school, but mine is the one who runs it." His eyes darken. "In case you haven't figured it out yet, *I'm* the one in charge." He glances at the digital clock hanging in the hallway. "You've got two minutes before the start of first hour. Get moving. I'm not in the mood to be late."

Tears prick my eyelids. I blink them back, refusing to let them fall before swinging around and taking a step toward the bathroom.

"Oh," he calls after me, "and lose the bra."

My shoulders slump as I stomp away and slam through the lavatory door.

I hate him.

I hate Kingsley Rothchild.

Quickly, I glance around, thankful the bathroom is empty, and I'm alone. Everyone has scurried off to class. I stare at the shirt in my hand before unbuttoning the one I'm wearing and jerking the material away from my chest until I'm standing in front of the mirror in my white lacy bra.

As much as I want to defy him, there's no point. Hastily, I reach around and unhook the clasp until the material springs apart, and I slide it down my shoulders. I keep my gaze lowered as I pull the shirt over my head and stuff my arms through the sleeves. Only then do I chance a peek at my reflection. A dismayed puff of air leaves my lips as I take in the way it hugs my slender curves. This is probably the first time in my life that I've been thankful for B cups. *Property of K. Rothchild* stretches across my breasts. In order for someone to read the words, they need to stare at my chest.

Doubtful that's a coincidence.

My nipples tighten, poking through the thin fabric. It's the dreaded headlight effect. Without a padded bra, there's nothing I can do to diminish my reaction.

A bell rings throughout the building, signaling that first hour is now underway.

Is it too much to ask that Kingsley has already taken off for class?

I'd prefer to make this walk of shame on my own.

Gathering my courage, I push out of the bathroom only to find him waiting in the empty hallway with my blazer thrown over one arm and my book in his hand.

His gaze immediately drops to my breasts. "I like the way my name looks stamped across your titties." He smirks. "Now there won't be any question as to who you belong to."

My hands tighten, the nails digging into my palms as anger bubbles up inside me. "Give me my blazer."

He closes the distance between us before holding it out. I grab the heavy wool and quickly shove my arms through the sleeves before tugging it protectively around my body, trying to cover as much of the shirt as possible. From the corner of my eye, I watch anxiously to see if he'll force me to go without it. I wouldn't put anything past him. When he remains silent, relief rushes through me, weakening my muscles. Then I grab my book before stomping to my locker to toss my shirt and bra inside.

As I'm about to slam the door shut, he reaches into the metal contraption and pulls out the silky material before allowing it to dangle from his index finger.

"What are you doing?"

His lips lift before he stuffs it into his blazer pocket. "Holding on to it so you won't be tempted to put it back on."

"I won't do that," I ground out.

"Please. You're a Hawthorne. Who the hell knows what you're capable of?"

When I open my mouth to argue, he steps closer until his body can press into mine. His hand snakes beneath the wool of the blazer until the palm can settle over my breast before giving it a cruel squeeze. I wince. "You wouldn't want me to do a titty check after each class, now would you?"

"I hate you."

He laughs and withdraws his hand before stepping away. I clutch my book and stalk to class. Kingsley falls in line beside me, easily keeping pace with my stride.

"Now, was that so hard?" he asks.

I gnash my teeth, refusing to answer.

As we arrive at the classroom, he whispers, "Just to clarify, I wasn't talking about the shirt. I meant my cock last night when you were busy sucking it, greedy for every inch I fed you."

I trip over my feet as he strolls past with an evil grin before asking, "You coming or what?"

SUMMER

21

By the time I trudge to my locker after fourth hour, I'm in desperate need of a break. Thankfully, the bell just rang, signaling the beginning of lunch. I can hide out in the farthest corner of the library and lick my wounds in private, all the while pretending for a few minutes that my life hasn't become a total hell.

Mostly, I want to get away from Kingsley.

Every time I passed him in the hall, his gaze would capture mine, and I'd find myself helpless to look away. There's something powerful about him. Something I'm both inexplicably drawn to and repelled by. It makes little sense.

I thought for sure I'd get reprimanded for wearing the shirt under my blazer instead of the standard-issue button-down. It's not a part of the school-sanctioned uniform, yet not one teacher said a word about it. Not even Ms. Pettijohn. They would look at my chest before glancing away. This reaction has only solidified the realization that Kingsley Rothchild holds untold amounts of power at Hawthorne Prep.

Even though I have zero appetite, with no plans to eat my lunch, I grab the paper bag before slamming my locker shut and spinning away.

"Where are you off to, Hawthorne?"

The deep voice that cracks through the hallway has me stumbling to a halt. I gulp and squeeze my eyes tightly shut before whispering, "The library."

Leave me alone.

Just for a minute.

"Sorry, that's not part of the plan. You're coming with me to the cafeteria."

I swing around to face him before lifting my chin. "No." My shoulders stiffen as I get ready to do battle. "I'm eating at the library."

He arches a brow. "Wanna bet?"

Frustrated by the situation and the power he holds over me, I stomp my foot. *"I want to eat in the library!"*

"Unfortunately for you, I don't give a shit. You'll eat lunch with me today and every day after this until *I* say differently. Now, if you want to be done with our little arrangement, all you have to do is say the word."

Grrrr.

My fingers curl, the nails leaving little crescent-shaped marks in my palm while slicing through the brown paper bag in my other hand.

When I remain silent, he snaps, "Make up your mind. I'm starving."

I hate him.

I stomp to his side, glowering the entire time, but he seems unfazed by my behavior.

"You ready?"

"Yes," I grunt between clenched teeth.

"Great."

He saunters to his locker before opening it. I begrudgingly follow, dragging my feet until I reach his side as he shrugs out of his navy blazer before hanging it on a silver hook near the top of his locker. Lunch, I've discovered, is a less formal affair. Most students forgo their jackets, preferring to roll up their sleeves during the thirty minutes of respite we're given. For obvious reasons, I won't be partaking in that particular tradition today. Or any other day I'm forced to wear this stupid shirt.

He unfastens the buttons at his wrists before rolling the white material up his muscular forearms and revealing a smattering of dark hair against his sun-kissed flesh. An unexpected burst of need explodes inside me, and I force my attention away in hopes of dampening it.

"Throw your blazer in here."

My gaze slices to him in surprise. He must be joking. There's no way in hell I'm going to the cafeteria without it.

I shake my head. "No."

"You must have misunderstood me, Hawthorne. It wasn't a request."

I search his face in desperation, already realizing he won't budge from his stance. Kingsley doesn't care if I'm humiliated. On second thought, he probably gets off on it. My heart sinks as I swallow down my rising horror.

Even though I know pleading won't help the situation, I hear the choked whisper escape from my lips before I can stop it. *"Please don't make me take it off."*

In the time it takes to blink, his hands go to the sides of my head as he tips my face toward his. He's so close that I can feel the warmth of his breath drift over my lips. It's strangely intoxicating. But then again, everything about him is.

"The only thing I like more than hearing you beg prettily is when you're on your knees, staring up at me like I'm your fucking king. Don't worry, I plan on making you do it often, but removing your blazer for lunch is nonnegotiable." His hands disappear as he quickly divests me of the uniform jacket before shoving it in his locker and slamming the door shut so there's no chance for me to snatch it back.

"Can I at least wear my bra?"

"Nope."

"I hate you!" Rage bubbles up inside me.

A grin slides across his lips. "Yet that won't stop you from begging for my cock." He takes off down the hall, not bothering to wait, assuming correctly that I'll follow of my own free will.

Turn around and leave.

Austin wouldn't want you to do this.

As if he can sense the inner turmoil swirling through my head, he raises his voice. "Don't make me drag you to the cafeteria, Summer."

Is this humiliation worth it?

Ultimately, yes. If I don't do this, my brother will end up moving to Chicago. Kingsley holds even more power than I suspected. This morning, I got my first real taste of it. If he keeps his end of the agreement, Austin will be allowed to stay on the football team and in Hawthorne for the rest of our senior year.

Is there anything I *wouldn't* do to achieve that outcome?

No.

I fold my arms tightly across my chest and reluctantly trail him. It feels like I'm marching to my death. With every step that brings me closer, my anxiety continues to heighten. By the time we reach the cafeteria, no other students are milling around outside the enormous room. Kingsley stops, smirking when he notices what I'm doing. "Arms down, baby girl."

My tongue darts out to smudge my lips. It feels as if there are cotton balls stuffed in my mouth. How can he be this cruel? *"King—"*

He shakes his head before eating up the distance between us to stand toe to toe with me. His forehead touches mine before he grabs my wrists and physically lowers them to my sides. "Nonnegotiable, remember?"

I want to scream.

Our gazes clash as he reaches out, locking his forefingers and thumbs around the tips of my breasts. He teases my nipples until they stiffen into hard little points that poke insistently against the white fabric.

"Stop," I groan, simultaneously loving and hating how he's torturing me.

He gives each breast a painful tweak before releasing them. "Now everyone will get an eyeful of those pretty little titties."

Asshole!

How can my body be so traitorous?

He steps away, looking completely unaffected. "Are you ready?"

No. With a glare, I remain stoically silent.

Fuck him.

"I'll take that as a yes." Not giving me a chance to escape, he snakes his arm around my waist and steers me into the cafeteria. People turn and stare, but no one utters a sound. My face heats until it feels like I might self-combust.

Actually, that would be more preferable than enduring this hell.

He maneuvers us to the table he's been sitting at since the first day of school. Over the past week and a half, a social hierarchy has emerged in the lunchroom. This table, along with Kingsley and his friends, seems to be the epicenter. Everything fans out from here with the outer rings hugging the perimeter. One seat remains open.

As we approach the table, his friends fall silent. They stare at me before shifting their curious gazes to Kingsley. After a few moments, the swell of conversation picks up again as if I'm not standing here in a shirt that claims me as property. Kingsley looks down at the guy I recognize as the ringleader from yesterday's locker fiasco.

Jasper, the asshole.

"Move over," the dark-haired boy next to me orders.

Jasper turns glaring eyes on me before begrudgingly sliding over another seat. When Kingsley settles on the bench, I do the same before setting down my paper bag.

As soon as my butt hits the smooth wood, he asks the table at large, "Is it cheeseburgers today?"

The guy across from him wraps his hands around a massive burger loaded with the works before raising it to his mouth and taking a bite. "Yup and it's fucking delicious," he says around a mouthful of masticated meat.

"Hmm." Kingsley stares across the cafeteria as he considers his meal options. "All right, that sounds good. I'll also have fries, a side salad with ranch, an orange, and a lemon-lime Gatorade."

I glance around, wondering if there's an invisible waitstaff I'm unaware of. All the chatter and good-natured ribbing dies away as the guys stare at me expectantly.

What?

No way.

My wide gaze shifts to Kingsley. All it takes is one look at the way his lips are twisted into an arrogant smile along with the malicious glint filling his eyes to realize that it's *exactly* what he's expecting.

Bastard!

"You have to be joking," I growl.

"Do you need me to repeat the order?"

I gnash my teeth together before shooting to my feet. There's no point in arguing with him. Kingsley hasn't relented one damn bit this morning, and he certainly isn't going to do it if I challenge him in front of his douchebag friends. For the moment, I'm stuck doing his bidding.

Without a word, I storm toward the lunch line and take my place at the end of it. Even though people haven't been gawking, I fold my arms self-consciously across my chest. Kingsley can kiss my ass.

That being said, I cautiously watch from the corner of my eye to see if he notices that I'm defying his decree. When he rises from his seat, I promptly drop my arms to my sides. Only then does he resettle on the bench.

Grrrr!

I have never hated anyone more in my life than I do Kingsley Rothchild.

You didn't hate him last night.

I shake my head, needing to dislodge the traitorous little voice that keeps popping up at the most inopportune times.

The four older women working behind the counter don't blink as I rattle off the request and tell them to add it to Kingsley's account. I should order something for the entire cafeteria while I'm at it. Doubtful he'd care, or that it would make a dent in his checkbook.

As I walk back with the tray of food, I check the surrounding area for teachers. Or any adult who looks to be in charge, but no one is policing the cafeteria. Apparently, the students of Hawthorne are supposed to prove with this little bit of autonomy that they are mature enough to handle themselves like the young adults they've supposedly grown into.

Ha! What a joke.

"M'lord," I say with an exaggerated flourish before dropping the tray with a loud thud in front of Kingsley. The Gatorade bottle wobbles as the cafeteria china rattles. "Your lunch."

Kingsley's eyes narrow as a few of the guys sitting at the table smirk before hastily glancing away.

I can't lie, this petty show of defiance feels good.

As I'm about to sit down, he says, "Where are the napkins?"

I glare. When he raises his brows, I grit my teeth and straighten to my full height. Sixty seconds later, I slap the napkins on the tray in front of him.

"Careful," he warns.

I press my lips together and fall onto the bench beside him.

"No ketchup? How can I eat a burger without ketchup?"

"You didn't ask for any," I shoot back with exasperation.

I hold his gaze in challenge before dropping my eyes. We both know this isn't a battle I'll win. For the third time, I rise from my seat and maneuver my way through the cafeteria to grab packets of ketchup. As I take a step away from the small counter, I scoop up mustard, mayo, salt, and pepper. Anything he could possibly want.

Kingsley studies me as I return to the table with two fistfuls of condiments before opening my hands and dropping them so the small containers rain down on his meal.

"You want to play games?" An evil smirk curves his lips. "That's fine, we can do that."

The smug smile I'd been wearing fades.

No, I don't want to play games. I just don't want to be treated like a servant and humiliated in front of all your asshole friends.

With his gaze pinned to mine, he says, "Hey, Morgan, you can have your seat back."

Jasper glances at Kingsley and then me. With a sneer, he slides over so I no longer have a place to sit.

I keep my expression neutral. Does he really think I'm going to be upset because I can't sit with him? I want to laugh. Now I can hide out in the library like I originally intended. Honestly, I prefer it. He's delusional for thinking otherwise.

When I shrug and spin on my heels to leave, he snaps, "Where do you think you're going?"

My step falters as I point at the exit. *Freedom, that's where.* "The library," I answer instead.

A wicked gleam enters his eyes as he shakes his head and pats his lap. "No, you'll sit right here."

I stare at his muscular thigh before glancing at him in horror. Without thinking, I shake my head, a denial perched on the tip of my tongue.

"Do you really want to push me, Summer?" He breaks eye contact and looks around. I do the same and realize that everyone's gazes are fastened on me. It's as if they're all waiting for a silent signal to attack. Nausea grows in my belly as I acknowledge how precarious my situation has become.

It takes everything I have inside to shuffle forward until I'm close enough for him to grab me. Instead of forcing me to do his bidding, he taps his thigh again. I grit my teeth and waver.

"Hurry up," he growls, "I'm hungry."

Then eat!

Instead of screaming that, I swallow down my anger before gingerly lowering myself to his lap. My left breast brushes against his hard chest as I twist my body, trying to find a comfortable place to settle. A groan rumbles up from deep in his chest, and an answering response ignites between my legs.

What the hell is wrong with me?

This guy should disgust me, not turn me on!

His hands wrap around my waist as if to anchor me in place. My gaze stays pinned to his, and I get sucked into the strange spell he effortlessly weaves around me.

"Looks like someone's part of the itty-bitty titty committee," one guy at the table jokes.

Kingsley rips his attention away from me long enough to glare at the moron who made the comment. "Shut the fuck up and don't look at her!"

The table falls silent as a thick shudder slides through me.

Please don't tell me it's arousal.

Please don't...

A dull ache throbs to life in my pussy. Unconsciously I shift on his thighs, but there's no relief to be found.

"Stop that," he grumbles in my ear, "before I finger fuck you in front of everyone."

Even though his words are meant for me alone, heat rushes to my cheeks.

"Tell me again how much you hate me," he urges, fingers digging into my waist.

"I hate you," I oblige, but the vehemence is noticeably absent.

"I don't think you do." His gaze stays fastened to mine. "Now feed me lunch."

I grab a fry from his plate and hold it to his lips. When he opens, I press the slim length of potato into his mouth. A reluctant thrill shoots through me when he nibbles at my fingers. It takes effort to bite back the husky moan that threatens to escape as I repeat the process. I don't want to admit how mesmerized I am by what we're doing. As I hold the burger to his mouth, he takes a bite. One of his hands stays wrapped around my waist while the other drops to my thigh.

It doesn't take long before my attention is focused on the feel of his palm pressed against my skin until it's all I'm cognizant of. His fingers glide over my bare flesh with lazy strokes from the edge of my navy sock to the hem of my skirt that rides up my thigh. With every pass, his caress stretches farther up my leg. I break eye contact and glance at the guys filling the table, but no one pays us any attention. They're too busy discussing the upcoming scrimmage next weekend.

"So which is it?" Humor simmers in Kingsley's voice. "Worried I'll make good on my threat or wishing that I would?"

Good question.

I feed him a slice of orange from the tray. "Neither. I'm wondering how long I have to keep this up." It's not a lie. I'm just not sure if I'm counting down the minutes until I can escape his insufferable presence or if I'm enjoying the feel of his fingers.

He studies my face as if he's able to pick through my most intimate thoughts by simply reading my expression. "I think you're lying." There's a pause as his hand slides toward the apex of my thighs. "Should I discover the answer for myself?"

"Please don't." I pop another slice of fruit into his mouth. My fingers tingle as he licks at them.

"Then tell me the truth," he demands. "Are you wet?"

I bite my lip and glance away.

Isn't my silence answer enough?

"Look at me, Summer." The gruffness of his tone strums something deep inside me that I wasn't aware existed. I'm frightened by the discovery and don't know how to make it go away.

My gaze snaps to his. "Yes." I can't take the chance he'll find out firsthand. I wouldn't put it past him to do it either. The normal rules of society don't apply to Kingsley Rothchild. It's intoxicating and disturbing all at the same time.

Fire ignites in his eyes.

When the bell rings, I huff out a relieved breath and hop off his lap without waiting for permission. As I do, my gaze collides with angry blue eyes.

Sloane.

We stare at each other before she whispers something to the brunette who I recognize as her trusty sidekick. Both smirk as their attention returns to me. That girl is going to be trouble. And by that I mean, more of a hassle than she's already been.

As far as Sloane is concerned, Kingsley has painted a big red bull's-eye on my back with his interest. And that's exactly what I don't need.

SUMMER

22

As soon as the last bell rings, I rush to my locker and grab my backpack, along with the white uniform blouse that hangs from the hook inside. I make a beeline to the bathroom and lock myself in a stall before stripping off the stupid shirt Kingsley forced me to wear.

He still hasn't returned my bra. What does he plan to do? Steal them every day? After a week, I'll run out. Not that he would care.

It's a relief when I slip the last button through the hole and tuck the hem of my shirt into my skirt before sliding my arms into the blazer. I've never been so happy in my life to wear a school uniform.

Thank God this horrific day is over, and I can finally get the hell out of here.

No more Kingsley.

With my backpack hoisted over my shoulder, I push out of the bathroom and into the crowded hallway. Students linger in small clusters, chatting and laughing, but no one pays me any attention. A look here and there, but nothing more than that.

The moment I step outside, I inhale a fresh lungful of air and walk to the parking lot before weaving my way to the G-wagon. For the second day in a row, there aren't eggs or shaving cream decorating the hood and windshield. The heavy coils of anxiety wrapping their way around me loosen just a bit.

From the corner of my eye, I catch a group of girls staring. I turn my head more fully only to meet Sloane's narrowed gaze. Four of her friends are standing with her. They're all wearing matching bitchy expressions. I was careful to avoid these kind of girls back home. I had Sloane pegged from the first time I saw her at Rothchild's, and her behavior hasn't disappointed.

When the blonde continues to track me with her gaze, I flip her the bird. One of her clones sputters in disbelief as I stalk past. With a relieved huff, I click the locks on the SUV and slide behind the wheel. The pumping beat of alternative rock fills the cabin. Twenty minutes of this and I just might feel human again by the time I reach our house.

As I'm about to shift the gear into reverse, someone slaps their palm against the driver's side window. Stifling a yelp of surprise, I swing around only to find icy blue eyes glaring at me.

Seriously?

Ugh.

This girl needs to get a life and leave me the hell alone.

When I don't immediately roll down the glass, her scowl deepens, and she smacks her hand against it again.

What the fuck!

I'm surprised she didn't shatter the window.

I stab the button with my finger, and any semblance of safety disappears between us. "What the hell is your problem?"

"*You*," she snarls in response. "*You're* my problem."

"How exactly am *I* your problem?" Before she can answer, I continue. "Did I follow *you* to your car like a stalker before accosting you?" I shake my head. "No, I don't think so."

"You need to stop hanging all over Kingsley." A sneer curls her lip. "It's pathetic."

"Is that what I'm doing?" I pretend to ponder her words. "Hanging all over your boyfriend?"

She presses her lips together as a pink stain seeps into her cheeks.

Hmm. Interesting. I'd wondered if there might be something between them, but obviously, that's not the case, or she would be quick to stake her claim. "I mean, he *is* your boyfriend, right?"

Ignoring my question, she growls, "There's no way he would ever get with a Hawthorne. All he's trying to do is make your life miserable."

Laughter bursts from my lips. I don't even bother trying to control it.

This girl is legit crazy.

"And you're *jealous* of that? I'm not sure what your definition of pathetic is, but that would be mine."

A furious rush of color floods Sloane's face as her minions go silent. When she continues to glower, I decide it's the perfect time to take off.

"Thanks for clarifying matters. I'm glad we had this little chat." With that, I stab the button for the window and watch as her eyes widen at my dismissal. Then I jerk the SUV into reverse and stomp on the gas pedal.

The tires squeal as Sloane screams and jumps away from the vehicle. "You almost ran me over, you stupid bitch!"

"My bad!" I yell. "I'll try not to miss next time!" Then I give her a wave before peeling out of the parking lot.

A smile tickles the corners of my lips as my shoulders shake with silent mirth. Not long after that, a few chuckles slip free. Before I know it, I'm laughing so hard that tears leak from the corners of my eyes. I can barely see the ribbon of road as I drive home. I should probably pull over until the hysteria passes.

I can't remember the last time I had something to laugh about, and it feels amazing. I'm sure Sloane and her minions will make me pay for my insubordination. She's just another name to add to the growing list of haters. In all honesty, she doesn't frighten me nearly as much as Kingsley does.

By the time I pull into the driveway, my laughing jag has subsided. With my backpack hitched over one shoulder, I slam out of the SUV and head inside. I stand in the foyer waiting for Mom to call out her normal greeting, but the house remains silent.

"Hello," I yell.

When there isn't an answering response, I peek in the study only to find it empty. I backtrack to the entryway and peer out the window, realizing the Volvo isn't parked in the drive as usual.

I take the stairs two at a time to the second floor before rapping my knuckles against Austin's closed door. Only now do I realize how much I missed him at school. I was so preoccupied with Kingsley most of the day that I didn't give much thought to my brother. Remorse rushes in to swamp me.

When Austin doesn't answer, I wonder if he went with Mom and Dad to work. I push open the door and peek around the corner. With his back to me, Austin stares out the window while doing bicep curls with a set of fifty-pound dumbbells.

I call his name again, but he must have the music blasting in his ears. Carefully, I step around him, not wanting to get hit with the weights. Once he spots me from the corner of his eye, I wave my hand. He jerks his head in acknowledgment and finishes his reps. With a roll of my eyes, I throw myself on the bed to wait.

God forbid he turn off the music and talk to me. When he wraps up his workout, he sets the adjustable dumbbells on the floor and yanks out the AirPods.

"Hey." His breathing is heavy as he grabs a jug of water from his desk and guzzles half of it. Then he sets it down and wipes the sweat from his brow. "How did school go?" Concern colors his expression.

Under no circumstance will I be telling Austin about the deal I made with Kingsley. If he ever found out, he would lose it.

"It was fine." I give him my most innocent smile and hope he doesn't ask further questions. My lying skills are subpar, especially when it comes to him.

"Really?" His eyes narrow suspiciously. "No vandalism to the G-wagon?"

"Nope." I pop the P and shake my head. "Maybe everything will finally settle down."

My brother snorts out his disbelief. "Bullshit."

"Language!" I snap, doing my best Mom impersonation.

He cracks a smile before taking another drink of water. "You're not lying to me, are you? You didn't have any problems today?"

Ugh.

Let's drop this conversation before I slip up and reveal information he doesn't need to know about. I'm all right telling a slight fib if it helps the greater good, but if he keeps drilling me...I'll end up folding like a cheap house of cards, and then all hell will break loose. I can't take the chance of that happening.

I hop off the bed, fully prepared to retreat. "Everything was fine." Technically, if you remove Kingsley from the equation, that statement is one-hundred-percent accurate. Avoiding eye contact, I flit my gaze around the room. The heat of his stare burns a hole through me, prompting me to add, "Who knows? Maybe Pembroke had a chat with all the guys involved."

His skeptical grunt is answer enough.

I give him a bit of side-eye before moving restlessly around the room. "Did you hear anything about football?" Dread fills me as I spin toward him. "You haven't been kicked off the team, have you?"

"Actually, Mom got a call from Pembroke a couple of hours ago. Since this was my first offense, all I need to do is serve a three-day out-of-school suspension and sit out for the first game of the season." He shakes his head as if he can't believe his good fortune. "That's my punishment."

"Seriously?" The breath escapes from my lungs as a wide grin breaks out across my face. "That's awesome news!"

Once again, I'm floored by the extent of Kingsley's reach. Without him intervening, I have no doubt that Pembroke would have pushed for expulsion. He wasn't interested in hearing our side of the story. Relief floods through me that Austin will not only stay in Hawthorne but also continue to play football.

"We'll see." He shrugs, some of his happiness leaking away. "Who knows how much play time I'll get."

"Why don't we wait and see what happens before you get all pessimistic on me?" I say, heading toward the door. "I have a feeling our situation is about to improve."

"Oh, yeah?" Curiosity fills his voice. "And why's that?"

"No reason." A smile simmers around the edges of my lips. "It's just a feeling."

As he opens his mouth to fire off another question, I slip from the room and close the door before leaning heavily against it.

Thank God.

Even though Kingsley did his best to humiliate me today, it was well worth it. There isn't anything I wouldn't do for my brother.

SUMMER

23

It's the slight creaking of the floorboards that has me jerking awake. My eyelashes flutter as I try to figure out what woke me. It feels like I barely closed my eyes. I had the worst time falling asleep, tossing one way before turning the other with an aggravated huff. Even though I tried not to dwell on the way Kingsley tweaked my nipples outside the cafeteria or caressed my thigh during lunch, the images continued to circle through my mind.

The only bit of good news is that I resisted the urge to touch myself. Instead, I suffered and squeezed my thighs together to stifle the ache until my eyes drooped and my brain finally clicked off.

When the same creaking noise as before breaks the silence of the room, I force my eyes open in time to spot a figure looming over me.

Holy shit!

I inhale a breath, ready to scream the house down. Before the sound can be released, a heavy hand lands on top of my mouth while the other snakes around the back of my skull so I can't slip free of the hold.

You read about this kind of thing happening all the time. Especially in Chicago. That's why we were religious about locking all the doors and windows.

But here?

In bumfuck nowhere?

No way. It's the reason I felt comfortable enough to sleep with the porch door open, allowing more of a breeze to enter the room. Other than Hawthorne, we're pretty far from civilization.

"Quiet," the deep voice rumbles near my ear.

Kingsley?

The breath rushes from my lungs as relief leaves my tense muscles feeling weak. I'm seriously going to kill him! The big jerk took at least ten years off my life!

I growl from behind the hand, struggling against the steely hold he has on me.

"What part of *quiet* don't you understand?" The mattress dips as he settles beside me. "Calm down, or I'll keep my hand over your mouth."

I press my lips together before going limp. As my eyes adjust to the darkness, his features coalesce under the stream of moonlight filtering in through the window.

"Anyone ever tell you that you're not very good at following directions?"

He takes his sweet damn time relinquishing his hold. I'm tempted to snap my teeth at his fingers when he finally pulls them away. Maybe that would teach him a lesson regarding the wisdom of breaking into an unsuspecting girl's room in the middle of the night.

Ignoring the question, I fire off one of my own instead. "Are you crazy?"

"Lower your voice, Hawthorne." Humor simmers in his tone. "We wouldn't want your parents to wake up and find me in your bed, now would we?"

Damnation, he's right. Griffin and Eloise would not be pleased.

I ground my teeth together before forcing out another question. "What do you want?" What I've come to understand is that Kingsley doesn't do anything without an end goal in mind.

He smirks as if I'm finally catching on to the game we've been playing. "Now *that* is a more interesting question."

My belly hollows out as a predatory gleam enters his eyes. "Yet you still haven't answered it."

His gaze drifts down my body as he reaches out to toy with a lock of hair that has fallen over my bare shoulder. Only now am I slammed with the realization that I shed my tank top earlier this evening. The night had turned stuffy, which is why I left the screen door open.

It's not a mistake I'll make again.

Hastily, I tug at the sheet that has pooled at my waist before hauling it up to my collarbone.

"No reason to cover yourself on my account." He continues to stare at my chest as if he has X-ray vision and can see through the tan-colored sheet. "After today, I've become a real fan of your titties."

Heat slams into my cheeks as the asshole's words from lunch echo throughout my head.

Itty-bitty titty committee.

It's not the first time jokes have been cracked at the expense of my breast size, and it won't be the last. Normally, something idiotic like that would roll right off my back, but for some unknown reason, it stuck with me today. Probably because I was forced to wear that stupid shirt, and it made me feel self-conscious.

"There's plenty of reason," I mutter.

"Lower the sheet." When my fingers tighten around the material, he adds, "It's nonnegotiable."

I'm *really* starting to hate when he says that.

"Summer," he warns, hard gaze flicking to mine.

With a huff, I shove the sheet to my waist and glare. Not that he would notice because his gaze is glued to my breasts. My fingers curl, biting into the cotton draped over my lower half.

"Happy?" I growl, embarrassment swamping me. The only thing getting me through this excruciating moment is that the room is cloaked in darkness. It would be so much worse if he were staring at me in broad daylight.

"Extremely."

What I refuse to do is cower before Kingsley. If he thinks I'll give him the satisfaction of making me cry, he's got another thing coming. As that thought circles through my head, I straighten my shoulders and thrust out my breasts.

Fuck him.

He studies me leisurely as if we have all the time in the world. "You don't believe what he said, do you?"

"Who?"

"Axel."

I shake my head, unsure what we're discussing. He reaches out, wrapping his thumb and forefinger around one nipple. Almost instantly, it pebbles beneath his touch as he strokes it. Liquid heat shoots from my breast straight to my core before exploding upon impact.

Every time.

It's like this *every time* he touches me.

My teeth sink into my lower lip to keep the sound buried deep inside. I'm guessing that Axel is the itty-bitty titty committee guy.

"I think your breasts are fucking perfect." His other hand rises, fingers reaching out to play with the other neglected nipple before manipulating them in tandem.

He caresses me until my head rolls back, and I'm unable to stop the whimper from breaking free. How is it possible to enjoy his touch all the while hating him? It's confusing to have so many conflicting emotions warring inside me.

"Does that feel good?" He glances at my face, scrutinizing my expression as if he's genuinely curious. "Do you like when I touch you?" His voice grows thicker, huskier. Until it sounds as if it's been dredged from the bottom of the ocean.

Like isn't nearly a strong enough word, but I'm loathe to tell him that. I don't want Kingsley to realize how much he affects me. It wouldn't surprise me if he turned around and used that information against me.

When his fingers disappear, a mewling protest escapes from my lips. His wide hands wrap around my hips before tugging me down the bed. I yelp and prop myself up on my elbows. The movement causes my back to arch and my breasts to lift. He releases my hips as his hands return to my chest.

"I don't need anything more than this," he murmurs, continuing to palm the soft weight. "You're the perfect handful."

All the other times Kingsley has touched me, it's been laced with anger and a need to dominate as he forces me to submit. This is different. His touch is unexpectedly tender. I'm shocked to realize that as much as I enjoy the way he's caressing me, I also like when he manhandles me. My body responds to the control he exerts as if it's his God-given right. A shudder passes through me as I shove that disturbing thought from my mind, unwilling to inspect it with further thoroughness.

What the hell is wrong with me?

Why am I enjoying something I clearly shouldn't?

When he tweaks my nipples, a strange pleasure-pain shoots through me, and those thoughts disintegrate. A gasp leaves my lips before I cut it off.

"Don't do that," he growls. "I want your moans. All of them." As if to reinforce the point, he pinches the stiffened little buds again. "Understand?"

"Yes," I groan as he soothes my abraded flesh with gentle caresses.

"Good girl." His gaze flicks to mine. "Tell me the truth, do you like the way I touch you?"

There is too much pleasure rushing through me to lie. "Yes, I like it."

So much.

Too much.

No one has ever played with me like this. There were a few guys I went out with in Chicago. There's even been a boob graze or two. At homecoming my junior year, my date worked up the courage to lay his hand over my breast and squeeze it, but I quickly knocked him away, and that was the extent of physical contact for the evening.

What Kingsley is doing is altogether different. He's not asking permission. This is more of a claiming. As if he's making me his. Marking me as his.

Property of K. Rothchild

I should hate the implication and the way he's forcing my body to crave his touch. With every passing hour, my feelings for him become more muddled. The strange relationship we have forged is no longer black and white. Yes, I hate him, but if I'm being perfectly honest, I want him, too. I don't know how to reconcile those feelings.

Warm night air hits my nipple as one hand disappears only to be replaced by the heat of his mouth. The velvetiness of his tongue dances around the areola. Swirling over the flesh without ever coming in contact with the tightened little bud that begs for his attention. His other hand continues toying with my breast. Alternately stroking the tip before kneading the soft weight. With his face lowered to my chest and his upper body caging me in, I groan and shift restlessly beneath him.

When he finally drags the flat of his tongue around my nipple before lapping at the center, I nearly come off the bed. He grunts when my fingers thread through his short hair, dragging him closer. He must understand what I'm desperately trying to convey because he draws the peak into his mouth. I can only liken the pull of his lips to a bomb being detonated, sending shockwaves of arousal straight to my core.

I whimper as he continues to tug mercilessly on the hardened tip.

With a rumble that comes from deep within his chest, he lifts his head before switching to the other side. Fingers vanish as his mouth takes over. Heat gathers in my core, flooding my panties. Sensation whips through my center like an oncoming storm. My pussy throbs to life with a need so sharp that it borders on agonizing.

"Kingsley," I moan, arching my body to get closer.

"Tell me what you need, baby girl," he whispers against my aching flesh.

When he draws me back into the warm cavern of his mouth, I teeter on the edge of the precipice. I don't understand how my body can be so worked up. All he's doing is playing with my breasts. But it feels so damn good.

"More." It's the only thought spinning through my head.

I need *more*.

"You're so fucking greedy," he groans. "I love it."

I've never thought of myself as greedy, but he's right. Where Kingsley is concerned, I can't get enough. I'm not sure if I'll ever get my fill. There is a cavernous well of need buried inside me that he has tapped into. This is a Summer I know nothing about. A sexual being I no longer recognize in the mirror.

He peppers a fiery trail of kisses across my ribs, sliding lower with every flick of his tongue, moving closer to the sheet pooled around my waist. Through heavy-lidded eyes, I watch as he drags the crumpled material away from my body until he has an unobstructed view of my panties.

He groans against my belly before sliding farther down my legs. All I want to do is widen them and give him access to the part of me that throbs with an intoxicating concoction of pleasure-filled pain.

My tummy trembles as his tongue darts out to trace the flesh directly above the elastic band sitting low on my hips. Warm night air kisses my breasts as his hands drift away from them to the cotton barring entrance to my core before he hooks his thumbs under the thin bands at my sides. His gaze flicks to mine, capturing it with a fire that will burn me alive if I let it.

I'm physically incapable of dragging my attention away from him. I felt this strange power the first time I met him on the beach, and the tentative bond was strengthened the day we spent on the boat. And then again, two months later, when I saw him at Hawthorne Prep. I don't understand why there is a connection between us. Every time he lays his hands on me, it intensifies, becoming stronger.

"Are you mine, Summer?" He slides the panties down an inch before nipping at the delicate skin that has been revealed.

"Yes," I whimper. Whether or not I want it, there's no denying that I'm his.

"To do what I want with?"

My teeth sink into my lower lip.

Say no!

I'm my own person. Not a toy he can take out and torment when he's bored.

He pulls the cotton lower so that the top of my mound is exposed before nipping at me. "Answer me," he growls. "Are you mine to do what I want with?"

Not only is the question dangerous but so is the answer. It's the equivalent of handing over my soul to the devil for safekeeping.

When his teeth sink into the plump flesh, I yelp as pain throbs through me before dissolving into pleasure. A heavy wave of arousal crashes over me, flooding my panties with slick moisture. It makes little sense how something so painful can be filled with so much gratification. Something must be wrong with me to enjoy this so much. Some kind of deviant trait he has awakened inside me.

"Yes," I moan, unable to stop the word from escaping.

"Now you belong to me." He tugs the underwear lower, exposing the top of my slit before pressing a kiss against it. A growl rumbles up from his throat before he nips at the flesh. "Do you have any idea how bad I want to eat you up?"

A thick shudder of need works its way through my body as he buries the tip of his nose against me before inhaling. "Goddamn, you smell fucking edible." His eyes glint in the moonlight. "Which is good, because I plan on making a meal out of you."

The words pouring out of his mouth should shock the hell out of me. On some distant level, they do. But not nearly as much as I wish they did. Twenty minutes ago, I wanted to scream the house down because I'd been so frightened. Now I want to scream the house down for an entirely different reason.

"Widen your legs."

Whatever he demands, I'll give without question.

Never breaking physical contact, Kingsley positions himself between my thighs. Even though I'm still wearing panties, I'm spread impossibly wide. His mouth hovers inches from my throbbing center. All that separates us is a thin scrap of material.

"You're soaked." An appreciative tone fills his voice.

I don't think I've ever been this wet or turned on in my life.

He rolls the material down until more of my pussy is exposed. I shift restlessly beneath him as his gaze drops to my center. "Are you a virgin?"

Even though I'm unsure how he'll respond, there's no choice but to tell him the truth. "Yes."

"Good." As if satisfied with the response, he caresses the top of my slit with the fullness of his lips. "Now your cherry belongs to me."

Using his thumbs, he parts the plump flesh, exposing the hidden part of me that throbs with need.

"All this sweetness is mine." Our gazes fasten as he licks at my clit. "You know why?"

Sensation ricochets through me, making it impossible to concentrate on his words, and I cry out.

"Because I'm your king." Another lap of his velvety softness leaves me twisting beneath him. "Do you understand?"

"Yes!" My eyes nearly cross when he strokes over me with the flat of his tongue.

Oh.

My.

God.

The hot rush of pleasure that washes over me is like nothing I've experienced before. It's more explosive. The sensation buzzes under my skin, almost as if it's trying to claw its way out. It makes all the tentative petting I've done under the covers, alone in my bed, seem ridiculously innocent.

A knock on the bedroom door has my eyes popping wide. I stiffen as Kingsley's gaze glitters with wickedness. Instead of hesitating, his tongue swirls with renewed intensity around my clit, and I have to stifle the desperate moan attempting to break free.

"Summer?" There's a pause. "Are you all right?"

Austin.

My gaze stays pinned to the dark head between my spread thighs. He won't stop tormenting my aching flesh. If anything, his attention has become more focused, more persistent with the need to drive me over the edge. It's like he wants to be caught. When I struggle, attempting to dislodge him, his hands tighten around my thighs, dragging them farther apart. His tongue never stops circling, dancing over the delicate flesh.

Oh God!

I can't.

If he keeps this up much longer, I'll end up coming and my brother will burst through the unlocked door. And that, I can't allow to happen. It's that knowledge that keeps me from splintering apart into a million jagged pieces. But that doesn't mean the intensity isn't building inside me, gathering energy like a ferocious storm. Any moment the heavens will open and dump buckets of rain.

"*Summer?*" Austin's voice grows sharp. Less groggy, more insistent.

I clear my throat and squeeze my eyes tightly shut. I can't watch Kingsley lap at my clit while holding a coherent conversation with my brother. "Sorry for waking you. It was just a bad dream."

"Oh." Another pause. "Anything you want to talk about?"

No!

"Nope, just gonna go back to sleep." It's difficult to keep the heavy tension from bleeding into my voice.

"Okay. See you in the morning."

Yes! Morning!

As soon as the footsteps fade down the hall, Kingsley sucks the tiny bundle of nerves between his lips and I nearly come off the bed. A scream builds in my chest as I fall onto my back and grab a pillow, yanking it over my face so that no one will hear me as I'm hit with the most powerful orgasm of my life.

SUMMER

When my alarm goes off the next morning, I stretch against the sheets as a surprising amount of satisfaction reverberates throughout every muscle of my body, and a smile curves my lips. For the first time since moving to Hawthorne, I feel strangely contented.

My eyelids flutter open, and a sigh escapes.

A handsome face materializes in my thoughts.

My eyes pop wide as I jackknife straight up in the bed.

Kingsley!

My lungs empty as memories from last night crash over me like a tsunami.

No!

Someone tell me he didn't sneak into my room last night and play with my body until I screamed out an orgasm so intense that I nearly passed out.

I can't.

It happened.

Oh God, the horror. A tortured moan escapes as I collapse against the pillows. Grabbing one, I drag it over my face before letting loose a long scream. The muffled sound echoes in my head.

Just like it did last night.

I cringe with embarrassment. How am I supposed to face him at school after I let him lick me in the most intimate way possible?

Heat scorches my cheeks, making them feel like they're on fire. I can only imagine that I'll find him loitering near my locker with a smug expression. One dirty word from him and I'll burst into flame.

Everything he said filters through my head.

Now your cherry belongs to me.
All your sweetness is mine.
I'm your king.
Gahhhh!
Know what the worst part is?
I agreed!
Oh God, I agreed with all of it.

Afterward, while I lay sprawled and dazed, he had pressed one last kiss against my soaked flesh before his mouth drifted over my body and claimed my own. His last parting shot had been—*remember to wear your shirt tomorrow. I want everyone to know who owns every inch of you.*

I scream into the pillow again. If only it were possible to smother myself. The humiliation of falling apart under his touch is almost too much to withstand.

You know what?

Screw him.

I'm not going to school today. Not only do I deserve a break after everything I've endured, but I *need* one. For my own mental health or I'll snap, and no one wants that. Least of all me. I need to take a day off and regroup. Maybe find a better way to deal with Kingsley. To keep him at arm's length.

Is that even possible?

A sigh of relief escapes as I come to a decision. Just knowing I won't have to see his smug face today already has me feeling better. I toss back the covers and pull on the tank top I'd discarded last night. Even now, at six o'clock in the morning, the heat of the day is evident. When I grab my robe from the chenille-covered bench tucked beneath my vanity, I find the bra I'd worn yesterday to school neatly folded on top of it. Kingsley must have returned it last night. I wrap the robe around myself before padding down the staircase. My footsteps falter outside the kitchen as I pause and give my cheeks a few hard pinches.

"Hey, honey," Mom says from her perch at the island when she spies me. A steaming cup of coffee sits on the granite countertop in front of her. She blinks in confusion before taking me in. "Why aren't you dressed?"

"I didn't sleep well last night," I mumble, wrapping my arms around my middle.

"Hmm. You look a bit flushed." She rises from her stool, coming around the island before laying a hand against my forehead. "I don't think you have a fever, but still..." Her voice trails off. "If you're not feeling well, maybe you should stay home and rest."

Agreed.

Mental health day, here I come.

But I can't give in that easily.

So, I shake my head and protest. "School just started, and the teachers give so much homework. I can't afford to fall behind."

A stubborn light enters her eyes as she plants her hands on her hips. "Give me a break. You won't fall behind after one day. It's doubtful your teachers would want you to come to school and spread your germs around."

"It doesn't matter. I should go," I murmur before tacking on a long-suffering sigh.

"Absolutely not, young lady!" Mom's voice grows sharp as I continue to argue. "You're going to spend the day in bed resting. For lunch, I'll make your favorite homemade chicken noodle soup. Lucky for you, I have a rotisserie in the fridge. I'm sure by tomorrow, you'll feel better."

Yum...soup! That *does* sound good! Even though I'm not *technically* sick, it's medicine for the soul, right?

Exactly. And right now, it's much needed.

I chew my lower lip and pretend to ponder the decision. "You really think I should stay home?"

She rolls her eyes. Hard. "One hundred percent. Plus, we have that party coming up. I want you well."

"All right." I nod, giving the appearance of capitulation. "I'll stay home."

Now that it's been decided, she shoos me from the sun-drenched kitchen with a flick of her wrist. "Go back to bed. I'll check on you later."

Don't mind if I do.

I practically tap dance my way up the staircase before slipping inside my room and jumping onto the queen-sized bed with an ecstatic bounce.

Screw you, Kingsley Rothchild!

Victory is mine!

A wide smile curves my lips as I imagine the aggravated expression that will flash across his face when he realizes I've managed to outsmart him. It almost makes me wish I could be a fly on the wall in Ms. Pettijohn's classroom to see it for myself.

With an absurd amount of smugness filling me for foiling his dastardly plans, I pull the covers over my body and allow my eyelids to feather closed. In no time at all, I'm drifting off. For the next couple of hours, I float in and out of sleep. Barely do I register Mom laying her hand across my forehead before whispering that Austin will be accompanying them to the office. The soup has been made and is simmering on the stove, ready whenever I want it. I mumble out a response before burying myself beneath the blankets again and getting dragged back under. By the time I resurface, I'm completely rested. I grab my phone from the nightstand and blink at the time.

Is it really nine o'clock?

With a stretch, I throw off the covers and hop out of bed before gravitating to the window that overlooks the yard. The sky is a deep cornflower blue, and there's not a cloud in sight. The sun is shining and it's gorgeous out. Certainly not a day that should be spent in the classroom. Especially Hawthorne Prep.

My gaze is drawn to the sparkling water below.

Yes! Yes! Yes!

The pool company had recently been out to get all the mechanicals up and running. The dark blue tiles have been scrubbed clean, water has been added, and chemicals have been balanced. It's been years since the pool was operational.

Mom and Dad won't be home until later this afternoon. It's the perfect opportunity to enjoy the last dregs of summer before the frigid weather of autumn gets ushered in. It only solidifies what a good idea it was to play hooky. A tiny squeal of excitement escapes as I swing away from the window and dig through the second drawer of my dresser to find a bathing suit. I pull out the first one my fingers come in contact with.

Drumroll, please. And the lucky winner is...

A little black string bikini!

It's not one I wear often because it's a little *too* revealing to wear around family. Dad would probably have an apoplectic fit if he saw me in it. Today, with the fam gone, it's getting worn.

I strip off the tank and panties before stepping into the bikini bottoms and fastening the top. I secure the tiny triangles over my breasts before grabbing a towel from the bathroom and heading downstairs. As if on cue, my belly growls as the aroma of soup permeates the air.

No matter what the weather, there's something infinitely comforting about homemade chicken noodle soup. I chow down an overflowing bowl until my belly is content before dropping the dirty dishes in the sink and exiting through the sliding door to the red stamped patio.

Almost immediately the blistering sun beats down on me, stroking over my flesh. I run inside and grab a can of sunscreen before liberally spraying my front and back. Then I stretch out on a plush lounger and allow it to dry.

I exhale a breath as my skin heats. If I were at school, I would be in third hour, dreading lunch with Kingsley. Yesterday was a nightmare. From the shirt he made me wear without a bra, to the way he treated me like a servant, and then forcing me to sit on his lap and feed him.

Today, the big jerk will have to get his own food.

When a light sweat coats my body, I decide it's the perfect time to take a dip. The pool isn't the standard rectangle. It's custom, more of a kidney shape with an outcropping of rocks where water slides over them creating a mini waterfall. The sound is ridiculously soothing. Near the rock formation is a round stone hot tub.

With my toes at the edge of the blue tile, I dive headfirst into the deep end. Cool, refreshing water envelopes my body as I arrow through the salty liquid before surfacing at the other end.

It's official. I've died and gone to heaven.

I swim a few laps from one end to the other before lazily turning onto my back. With my eyes closed, I enjoy the sun as it strokes over my bare skin. It's only after my fingers turn pruney that I drag myself from the pool and collapse on the lounger with a satisfied sigh. I turn over onto my belly and reach around, untying the knot at my neck and in the middle of my back until the strings slide to the sides.

My eyelids feather closed as the gentle gurgling of the water feature fills my ears. Birds chirp as I drowsily drift under the scorching sun. I don't know how long I doze off for. All I know is that I'm jarred out of my contented state when a sharp slap lands across my ass cheek. I blink away the grogginess and rear up before swinging around. My heartbeat stutters when my gaze collides with a narrowed one.

"Ow!" I cry when he cracks the other side with as much force. "Stop that!"

"Why aren't you at school?"

"I'm sick." When he continues to glare, lips sinking into a frown, I force out a weak-sounding cough.

His gaze meanders over my nearly naked body. "Not that I'm complaining, but this is the second time I've found you with your titties on display. It's almost like you're trying to tempt me into playing with them."

I glance down at the unobstructed view he has of my breasts before dropping my body to the cushion.

"Please, I'm not trying to tempt you into anything," I grumble, wishing he would go away. "I'm enjoying the sunshine. I was in dire need of some vitamin D."

He steps closer, dropping into a squat until he's nearly eye level with my ass. The tiny brief does nothing to cover my cheeks. It's more of a glorified thong, which is exactly why I don't wear it. Clearly, that decision has come back to bite me in the ass.

The moment Kingsley's fingers settle on my warmed flesh, I hiss out a breath. His gaze jerks to mine as his hand strokes over the rounded curve before giving it a squeeze. The tips of his fingers bite into my muscle and I close my eyes as a groan slips free.

Why?

Why does it feel so good when he touches me?

The magnetic attraction is undeniable. Is it because he's the first boy to give me pleasure?

I really hope so. I don't want it to be anything more than that.

Even though I tell myself to be strong, he demolishes that silent promise with the devilish glint that enters his eyes. One stroke of his fingers against my scorched flesh, and he creates a raging inferno within. I have no idea how to flip the switch and turn it off.

Is that even possible?

A more troublesome question—do I want to?

I shove that distressing thought from my head, unwilling to entertain it.

"I missed you," he rasps as if he's as turned on by touching me as I am by what he's doing. "Did you miss me?"

"No." I force the lie from my lips, not wanting him to discover how much he affects me.

"Is that so?" Humor and challenge fill his voice. It's a deadly combination.

Too late, I realize my mistake. Now he'll need to prove me wrong.

A shaky breath escapes as his fingers dance along the cleft between my cheeks.

"I think you're lying to me," he sing-songs, his voice sounding as if it's been roughed up by sandpaper. It scrapes something deep inside me, sparking a thousand tingles that scamper along my over sensitized skin.

A yelp of surprise slips free when he bites the firm round muscle with his teeth. It's sharp enough to send a sizzle of pain scuttling through me, but not hard enough to bruise or break the flesh.

"I don't like when you lie," he growls, warm breath feathering against me.

Another stinging slap lands on my cheek before he palms the muscle in his hand. As he works my flesh, a reluctant groan slides from my lips. My body becomes limp under his tender ministrations.

I'm so relaxed, I don't immediately realize he has pulled the ties at my hips that hold the bikini bottoms in place until it's much too late. Before I can protest, he's back to manhandling my flesh. Only this time, when he pulls at the firm globes, separating them with his hands, there's nothing to bar his view of my backside.

"Kingsley," I squeak, a bolt of panic shooting through me.

"Shh," he grunts, never once letting up on the sweet torture. "I like looking at you."

That acknowledgment sends a second wave of alarm flooding through me.

His hands glide from my lower back to my thighs, not leaving one inch of flesh untouched, as if he's trying to brand every single part of me. It doesn't take long for my anxiety to retreat and I'm once again sinking into the plush cushion. I've never felt so relaxed and turned on at the same time. It's a strange yet addictive combination.

What he's doing is more of a slow burn than last night.

My eyes spring wide when his hands slide around my hips and he drags me up so that my ass is in the air. My knees fold beneath me as the side of my face gets pressed against the lounger.

"*Kingsley,*" I whimper, struggling to rise as I imagine the unobstructed view he has, *"please."*

"You know it drives me crazy when you beg." One heavy hand presses between my shoulder blades to pin me in place as the other strokes over my ass, continuing to knead the flesh. "Especially when you're on your knees."

Gulping down my rising alarm, I watch him from the corner of my eye.

His gaze never wavers as his fingers brush over the lips of my pussy. "So fucking pretty."

Short gasping pants fall from my mouth. I'm torn. What he's

doing feels decadent, but the position is embarrassing. When I finally give in and stop struggling, the firm pressure between my shoulder blades disappears, and he's back to squeezing my ass. The way his fingers sink into the tensed muscle before tugging the cheeks in opposite directions sends a cascade of shivers careening down my spine.

"Every part of you is pretty," he mutters thickly.

I groan when he nips at my flank, feathering seductive little kisses along my hip and thigh before slowly making his way to the inside. My breath hitches, turning into a cry when his tongue dips into my entrance.

"One taste wasn't nearly enough." His warm breath feathers against my intimate flesh, creating a delicious ache. "I need more."

As much as I don't want to be turned on, I am. There is something ridiculously erotic about being out in the open while I'm naked and he's wearing his school uniform. The blazer has been left behind and the first two buttons of his crisp white shirt are unfastened, revealing a slice of his throat. His sleeves have been rolled up to expose bronzed, muscular forearms. The picture we must make is deliciously dirty.

I squeeze my eyes tightly shut to blot out the image of him. There is such a look of intensity on his face as he eats me up with his eyes.

What the hell is wrong with me?

I should be horrified. But not a word of protest slides from my lips. How can it when I'm all but reveling in his touch?

Depraved.

I must be as depraved as he is.

His fingers are splayed wide as his thumbs sweep dangerously close to the most private part of me. I shudder out a breath as his tongue strokes my pussy with unhurried laps. The pad of his thumb grazes over my anus and my eyes fly open in alarm. When I wiggle, attempting to escape the intimate touch, his fingers bite into my flesh, anchoring me to the lounger. His mouth slides up a few inches before his teeth sink into my cheek and his thumb deliberately settles over the puckered muscle where it stubbornly remains.

It's as if he's waiting for me to protest his claim of ownership. There is no fooling myself into believing that he isn't deliberately touching me in such a taboo place. The puffs of air that leave my mouth are harsh and labored. My heart jackhammers a painful staccato under my breast, feeling like it might explode.

Why aren't I screaming bloody murder or trying to roll away?

The truth of the matter is if I wanted to, I could easily escape. I choose to remain still. Folded in submission, with my ass in the air, and the side of my face pressed against the cushion while he explores my body.

Never in my life have I felt so vulnerable.

This feeling of being on display, with the hot sun stroking over my sensitive bits of flesh is one of the most humbling yet strangely empowering sensations I have ever experienced. It makes little sense. Uncertainty swirls through me, creating havoc inside my brain, as my teeth sink into my lower lip.

What is this boy doing to me?

When his finger vanishes, I release a pent-up breath that is tinged at the edges with disappointment. He runs his thumb along the lips of my soaked pussy before sliding it deep inside and pumping it a few times. My inner muscles clench around the intrusion. When he drags the digit from my body, a sense of emptiness takes its place.

He brushes a kiss meant to comfort along my flank before the same thumb that had been buried inside me returns to my backside. I gulp at the slickness now coating his digit as he rubs soft circles against the tight muscle. When I try to wiggle away, his teeth sink into my cheek until my movements cease. He caresses me with unhurried strokes until my body surrenders, accepting this intimate touch. My muscles loosen incrementally, one at a time.

Now that I'm no longer mentally fighting the contact, unexpected pleasure rushes in from all sides, filling every bit of space. Unwilling to inspect the confusion hovering at the outer recesses of my brain, telling me this foreign touch shouldn't feel so enjoyable, I can't help but absorb the wonder of this new experience.

When the blunt tip of his thumb prods the tight ring of muscle seeking entrance, I stiffen beneath his touch. His movement stills, but the digit does not retreat. It stays pressed against me. A reminder that he is not going anywhere. The application of pressure feels both scary and strangely erotic. I'm tempted to give in and relax my body, but I can't mentally let go. I'm clenched against further invasion.

The fingers of his other hand sink deep into my pussy. He repeats the movement until it becomes rhythmic. Delirium floods through me as I'm pushed relentlessly toward climax. As my body tightens, orgasm imminent, he backs off. His fingers slide from my sheath to dance around the drenched entrance.

My core pulses with an awareness that makes everything else seem irrelevant. All I care about is coming. I need his fingers back inside me, stroking me to completion. I squirm beneath him as a whimper of frustration slides from my lips. He knows exactly what I seek but refuses to give it to me. With my hands pressed into the lounger at my chest, I strain toward him.

What I fail to realize is that as I shift in his direction, the blunt tip of his thumb prodding the ring of muscle becomes more insistent. A wave of intensity washes over me as I pause. What becomes clear is that I can not have one touch without the other. His devilish fingers continue to rim me until I want to scream.

I squeeze my eyes tightly closed and make a decision. Actually, there isn't a choice to be made. I need this. I'm much too aroused to retreat now. As I carefully sink into his touch, his thumb breaches the entrance of my anus.

I hiss out a breath when a burning sensation fills me. As if to reward the action, his fingers slide into my pussy, caressing the walls. His teeth scrape against my backside before he bites down, all the while continuing to press farther into the tight space. A strange, but not entirely unpleasant, pressure fills me. The urge to lock my muscles against him pounds through me. When I clench, he nips me again before slipping the tip of his thumb out, but not completely. The sting dissipates as his other hand continues to glide over my heat.

I groan when he pushes the digit back inside my tight hole. This time, the sting is less of a bite than previously. When his fingers caress my outer lips, I push my ass back, trying to get closer. The movement sends his thumb deeper. The way he teases my flesh makes more pleasure bloom inside. I'm so close to coming that it's painful.

When his thumb and fingers move in tandem, filling me at the same moment before retreating and then surging forward again, I lose it and scream out my orgasm. Kingsley doesn't let up on the onslaught until every last ounce of delirium has been wrung from me and I collapse, my body sinking into the lounger as my eyelids droop. I'm almost dizzy as the last waves of ecstasy dissolve.

When Kingsley finally eases his fingers from my body, he gives my ass a sharp slap. My eyes snap open, but I can't work up the energy to glare. All I want to do is sleep.

"Come on, let's go," he says impatiently, rising to his full height. "Fifth hour starts in twenty minutes. I don't want to be late."

"I'm not going anywhere," I grumble, rolling to my side. "I'm taking a mental health day."

"The hell you are." He reaches around, tugging something from his back pocket before tossing it next to me.

With a frown, I pick up the material.

It's another white shirt.

The words—*If found, return to K. Rothchild* are stamped across the chest.

"Oh, and make sure you wear a bra. I don't want anyone else looking at those pretty little titties."

Grrrrr!

SUMMER

25

My feet slow when I find Kingsley lounging against the locker next to mine. For a moment, I allow my gaze to crawl over him while he's unaware. His dark head is bent as he stares down at the phone gripped in his hand. His nose is a bit crooked as if it's been broken and his lips are full. A perfect cupid's bow. A shudder scuttles down my spine as I remember where those lips had been a few short hours ago.

With the navy blazer, white shirt, and perfectly pressed tan pants, he's prep school hot.

I should hate him, not crave him. He's forcing me to do things I don't want to be doing.

Liar! You love the way he touches you.

I'm knocked out of those disturbing thoughts as people push past me. A few give me a bit of side-eye as they continue on their way, but no one utters a peep.

That's Kingsley's doing.

In this realm, his word is law.

It may have taken some time, but I understand that now.

As if realizing that he's being watched from a distance, Kingsley glances up. His gaze fastens onto mine as heat leaps to life in his eyes. In a few short days, I've learned to decipher his expressions. This one tells me he's thinking about what we did earlier and if given half a chance, he'll do it again.

My breath gets trapped in my throat as I recall the way it made me feel.

Like a sexual deviant.

If I close my eyes, I can almost feel the insistent way his thumb caressed the tight ring of muscle before pushing inside. A hot punch of arousal hits me in the core and my panties dampen as if on command.

It's so wrong. Six short hours ago, I could have never imagined someone touching me so intimately yet I allowed it to happen. Barely did I put up a fuss.

What the hell had I been thinking?

A dangerous pattern has emerged. Whenever Kingsley lays his hands on me, all rational thought leaks from my ears and I become nothing more than a walking hormone.

Neither of us move. It's as if we're both frozen in time and place. His expression changes, eyes becoming shuttered. The window allowing me a rare glimpse inside has now been slammed shut. What bothers me most is that I have no idea if this is anything more than a game. Last week, his hatred had been palpable. And now...

I don't know.

If I were smart, I would fortify and protect myself against his onslaught. It's only been a few days and look at me...

I can't stop thinking about him.

Craving him.

All these turbulent thoughts swirl around my head as I push out a breath and force my feet to close the distance between us. His gaze stays pinned to mine as if he's capable of picking through the thoughts in my brain. Instead of allowing him the access, I look away and pretend to busy myself by twisting the combination of my lock.

When he remains silent, a shot of anxiety spikes inside me and I clear my throat. "What are you doing here?"

"I'm going to take you home."

Spending more time alone with Kingsley isn't smart. Already he's messing with my head.

Along with other parts of me.

"Oh." I wrack my brain for an excuse. "Don't you have football?"

He doesn't miss a beat. "I'm skipping today."

It takes effort to remain calm as I shake my head and wave a hand. "You don't have to do that. I was going to call—"

"It's nonnegotiable," a flinty edge enters his voice as he cuts me off, "I'll take you home."

Why does he have to make everything so difficult? He's constantly pushing, forcing me to bend to his will. What I've learned in the limited interactions I've had with Kingsley is that arguing won't do me any good. He always gets his way.

"Fine," I snap, grabbing my books from my locker before shoving them in my backpack with more force than necessary.

His fingers tighten on my arm before he spins me around and forces my back against the lockers. "What's with the attitude?"

My eyes widen as I shake my head. "Are you being serious?"

"As a heart attack." He pushes into my space until his body is flush against mine and I have to crane my neck to hold his steely-eyed stare. "What the hell is your problem?"

His minty breath drifts across my lips. It's nothing short of drugging. All I want to do is inhale a big breath of him.

Focus!

"Nothing," I whisper. "I don't have a problem."

"Could have fooled me," he growls, one hand rising to my throat. His fingers splay wide as they settle over my collarbone. It's almost as if he's pinning me to the locker, but the touch remains gentle. It's always a fine line with him.

"I'm the one who brought you to school today and I'll be the one who takes you home." His lips brush against mine, never quite touching them. Unable to help myself, I strain forward, desperate for the contact. "End of story."

I swallow, wishing he would kiss me so I could forget everything buzzing around in my brain. "Okay."

"Was that so difficult?"

I huff out a slight laugh as the thick tension gathering in the air between us evaporates. "Do you really have to ask?"

His gaze drops to my mouth before he bites his lip and backs away. I suck in a ragged breath before forcing it out again as I slam my locker door shut. When did I start having to remind myself to breathe?

I hitch my backpack onto my shoulder as we walk through the corridor. When we pass by his locker, I ask, "Don't you need your books?"

"Nope." He shoves his hands into the pockets of his pants.

Even though we only have one class together, Kingsley's schedule mirrors my own. There hasn't been an evening that I don't spend at least two hours studying for tests and completing assignments. In the past, I've always performed well in school, but it takes work. From what I've noticed in our literature class, Kingsley is a top student.

So what am I supposed to take away from this?

That he's not only diabolical but also a freaking genius?

Is this the kind of guy I'm dealing with?

How am I supposed to outsmart or stay ahead of someone like that?

It's a daunting reminder that I need to keep my wits about me when dealing with him.

As we push through the glass doors, I stare at him from the corner of my eye. In the past couple of days, I've learned a lot about Kingsley, but I'm no closer to figuring out what makes him tick.

Who is the real Kingsley Rothchild?

He catches me staring as we weave our way through the parking lot. "What's going on in that head of yours?"

I shrug, unwilling to share my innermost thoughts with him. He guards his secrets well. It would be in my best interest to do the same.

Kingsley snakes his arm around my waist and hauls me close before nipping at my neck. "Are you thinking about what it felt like when I made you come?"

I choke on my saliva and sputter. No, I wasn't, but I sure as hell am now.

"'Cause I am." He grins as heat fills his eyes. "I fucking love the sounds you make when you come."

Oh.

My.

God.

As I glance around, praying that no one is eavesdropping on our conversation, my gaze collides with Sloane's narrowed one.

That's all it takes for me to untangle myself from Kingsley before jerking my head toward the blonde. "Your girlfriend seems upset by your lack of attention."

His gaze flickers in her direction. Sloane's expression turns flirtatious as she tilts her head and smiles before flipping her long hair over her shoulder. She finishes the show with a wave as her teeth sink into her lower lip.

Maybe if I'm lucky, he'll change his plans and head that way. Then I can call Austin for a ride. It'll kill two birds with one stone. I'll get away from Kingsley and Sloane will stop channeling all her hatred toward me.

Except, the thought of Kingsley with that blond bitch makes the muscles in my belly spasm painfully. My footsteps stutter at the realization that I'm jealous.

No, that can't be it. This isn't a relationship. He's toying with me the same way a cat plays with a mouse.

Instead of detouring toward Sloane, he jerks his chin in her direction. "Sucks to be her."

All the tension gathering inside me dissolves. I glance at the curvy blonde. If the daggers Sloane is shooting my way are any indication, Kingsley's lack of interest has only stoked her animosity. Yet I'd rather deal with that than watch him give her a moment of his attention.

Once we reach the Mustang, he clicks the locks. Color me surprised when he walks around to the passenger side and opens the door. My gaze flashes to his, but his expression remains inscrutable. Even though uncertainty swirls through me, I tamp down any softness trying to take root and slide onto the black leather seat while he saunters around the hood of the shiny red vehicle. Once settled beside me, he starts the engine. A few minutes later, we're rolling through the gated entrance of Hawthorne Prep and turning onto the main road. My muscles loosen as we leave the school behind.

From beneath the thick fringe of my lashes, I watch as he focuses on the ribbon of black pavement stretched out in front of him. This situation would be far less complicated if we never met at the beach or spent the day together on his boat. If he had never opened up and allowed me to glimpse a different side of him. If I hadn't spent two months pining for him. Fantasizing about him.

Then all I would know is the asshole from Hawthorne Prep. The one who forced me against the lockers on the first day of school in front of a crowd. The one who wrapped his fingers around my throat and squeezed until I thought I would pass out.

That guy would be so much easier to hate. I could close myself off from him with ease. Instead, all of my thoughts and feelings are a tangle.

I stare sightlessly at the passing scenery. When Kingsley parks the car, I blink out of my thoughts, surprised to find that we're not in the subdivision. Instead, we're in the middle of town at a little ice cream stand called the Dairy Barn.

"What are we doing?"

His lips quirk as if it should be obvious. "Getting ice cream."

"Ice cream?" This is unexpected. I would have preferred he drove me straight home. Spending more time together is dangerous. Especially when I'm trying to sort through and separate all the emotions he rouses inside me.

"Sure." He shrugs before winking. A teasing glint enters his eyes. "You gave me a treat earlier. I thought I'd return the favor."

"*Kingsley.*" Even though there's no one to eavesdrop on our conversation, I shift on the leather and glance around. "Jeez."

"What?" His expression turns innocent as a wide grin overtakes his face. "Isn't it the truth?"

"I'm not going to discuss *that* with you right now." Why does he take such perverse pleasure in embarrassing me?

"I enjoyed a creamy dessert earlier, now you get yours." He angles his body toward mine before his fingers drift over my cheek and into my hair. He twists the silky strands of my ponytail around his hand. The more hair he gathers, the higher my chin rises.

It's not painful, just possessive. The simple touch has need bursting to life inside me. The distance between us vanishes until his lips can hover over mine.

"Although," he whispers thickly, "I would much rather feed you something more substantial." With his other hand, he traces the curve of my lips. "Your mouth was made for fucking. And I plan to make good use of it."

The mental image he paints shouldn't arouse me. Memories from the other night tumble through my head. The way he pushed me to my knees and outlined my lips with the tip of his cock. How one firm hand stayed buried in my hair, directing my movements.

Kiss the crown.

A guttural sound escapes from me as our gazes stay locked. His finger falls away as he dips his mouth to caress my top lip with an agonizing deliberateness. The touch is tender, which is at odds with the forceful grip on my hair. He strokes my plump bottom one with the same amount of thoroughness before sucking it into his mouth. When he releases the flesh, I'm moments away from spontaneously combusting.

He tugs the thick strands. When I gasp, his tongue darts out to trace over my lips, licking at them with languid strokes before finally taking my mouth. There is nothing frenzied or out of control about this kiss. It's an exploratory mission of tasting and savoring, as if he is set on devouring me gradually, one heartbeat at a time.

When he finally breaks away, I'm a quivering mess of hormones.

"Ready for your treat?"

God, yes. But not the one he has in mind.

Wickedness glints in his eyes as if he's all too aware of the effect he has on me. His grip disappears from my hair before he exits the vehicle. I press my thighs together to lessen the painful flood of arousal that has gathered in my core.

"You coming?" he asks, voice brimming with humor.

"Yup." I wince and suck in a shaky breath before slowly releasing it, trying to calm the rioting emotions inside me, but it's no use.

Once I'm certain my knees won't buckle, I follow Kingsley to the window of the Dairy Barn and glance at the chalkboard with all the flavors of ice cream. The young girl behind the window beams at him, going all soft in the eyes.

I can hardly blame her for being instantly smitten.

He's gorgeous, muscular, and confident.

It's a potent combination.

Catnip for the female sex.

My mind tumbles back to the first time I saw him on the beach, the sun shining on his dark head, and how completely bowled over I was. The way his eyes sparkled with humor. Those full, sexy lips that begged to be kissed. And then there's the rest of him. Broad shoulders, bulging biceps, hard pecs, and six-pack abs all leading to a tapered waist.

What female in her right mind could resist him?

"Summer?"

The sound of his deep voice pierces the thick web of memories as they slyly wrap their way around me. "Yeah?"

Heat ignites in his eyes until I'm scorched by the intensity burning in them. "I asked what you wanted to order."

"Oh, right." I search the board even though ice cream is the last thing on my mind. "A single scoop chocolate cone, please."

"I'll have the same." Kingsley's attention never deviates from me as he digs through his pocket and produces a twenty.

The cashier takes the bill before returning with his change. Not bothering to count it, he stuffs the money into the tip jar on the counter.

My nerves intensify as I shift from one foot to the other. It's a relief when the girl returns with our cones. Color stains her cheeks as Kingsley's fingers brush against hers.

Instead of returning to the car, he points at a bench at the far corner of the gravel parking lot. "Let's sit over there."

I detour to the park bench shaded by a sprawling oak tree. The leaves are turning red and gold but have yet to fall. He stretches his long legs out in front of him, resting his elbows on the slats of the bench. I settle at the opposite end, needing to create distance between us.

When he takes a leisure lick of his cone, more arousal bursts inside me, and I shift, glancing away.

"What's wrong?" His voice drops, becoming husky. "Remind you of something?"

I watch him from the corner of my eye as he does it again with exaggerated slowness.

All this feels like is a game. One I don't understand the rules for and can't possibly win. At this point, I don't even want to play. This has turned out to be way more than I bargained for.

"Why are you toying with me?" No longer does the cone I'm clenching hold appeal.

His face remains shuttered. "What makes you think I'm toying with you?"

I give him an exasperated look that says *oh, please.*

When my ice cream continues to melt under the sweltering sun, I rise and dump it in the plastic bin near the squat white building. Kingsley's gaze never falters as he continues to eat his cone. I wait, hoping he'll get the hint that I'm ready to leave. When he remains seated, I reluctantly return to the bench. An unsettling silence falls over us as I find a loose thread at the hem of my plaid skirt to pick at.

"I don't understand you," I whisper before pressing my lips together. The thought had been circling through my head, but I didn't mean to voice it out loud.

"What's there to understand?" Even though his legs remain outstretched and his posture relaxed, this conversation feels anything but.

"Do you always answer a question with a question?" When he smirks, I continue. "You're nothing like the guy I met at the beach. It's like you aren't even the same person." This is what haunts me most. It's the only reason I can't close myself off from him completely.

A spark of emotion flashes in his eyes. It's there and gone before I can decipher what it means.

When he remains silent, frustration bubbles up inside me, and I snap, "You know what? I actually *liked* that guy."

Tension vibrates from him before shimmering in the air between us. It's almost suffocating in its intensity.

"Don't you get it? Everything was different at the beach." Irritation explodes from his lips as if I should already know this. "*We* were different."

"That doesn't make sense." I shake my head, trying to wrap my mind around this strange conversation. "Why was it different?"

"I didn't know who you were." A hint of wistfulness enters his voice. "You were a pretty girl I wanted to spend time with. And now..." his eyes clear as he presses his lips together.

"And *now*?" My heartbeat picks up speed.

"And now you're not," he says flatly.

I creep closer on the bench. "That's the thing. I *am* the same girl. Nothing about me has changed. *You're* the one who's different. All I want to know is who the real Kingsley Rothchild is."

His lips twist with bitterness. "Sometimes, I don't even know the answer to that."

My tongue darts out to moisten my lips as my brain continues to spin, trying to figure out a way to chip through the wall he's thrown up between us. Is that even possible? "You're dragging all this history into our relationship that doesn't need to be there."

"What happened with our families will always stand between us. The difference is that I've lived with it my entire life, and you've only become aware of it."

"It doesn't have to be like this between us." Why doesn't he see that?

"But it is." A strange concoction of stubbornness and acceptance settle over his features. "You can't change history."

"You're right, we can't change it. But the present and future don't have to be dictated by it." The need to touch him, to form the same tentative connection we shared at the beach, thrums through me. Before I can think better of it, I reach out, my hand feathering over his. "We can shape it into something different, something better."

His brows slide together as he contemplates my words. It's almost as if I can see the possibilities spinning in his head. I blink and the arrogant mask he usually wears crumbles. For the first time, he looks more like the guy I met in Door County. The one who was so easy to fall for.

I'm tempted to tunnel my fingers through his short hair. Instead, I tighten my hand and resist the urge. These past weeks have taught me to be cautious and watchful around Kingsley. In many ways, he's like an unpredictable animal. Affable one minute and lethal the next.

He tilts his head and narrows his eyes. "How?"

Surprised by his willingness to consider my idea, I shake my head and squeeze his hand. "I don't know, but there has to be a way. We just need time to figure it out."

When his gaze slides away, I release the pent-up breath from my lungs.

"I'm not sure if there's enough time for that," he mutters, darkness overtaking his expression as every bit of light is swallowed up.

"Why wouldn't there be?" I force out a laugh and rise from the bench before extending my hand for him to take.

He considers me for a long moment before wrapping his larger one around mine and straightening to his full height. As gravel crunches beneath my shoe, he tugs me toward him. A puff of air falls from my lips as I stumble into his hard body. My palms go to his chest to regain my balance as his hands cup the sides of my head. When his fingers splay wide around my scalp, I stare up at him and realize how easily he could crush my skull with his strength. Storm clouds churn in his gaze before his lips crash onto mine. Unlike earlier, there is no tenderness, and I find that I don't want it.

Even though we're at the edge of the parking lot and out in the open, it's all too easy to lose myself in the kiss. Only when Kingsley pulls away, resting his forehead against mine, that I become aware of the world surrounding us.

"You make me wish that everything could be different." His harsh breath drifts across my lips. "That you weren't a Hawthorne, and I wasn't a Rothchild."

Something indescribable explodes in my chest. "Isn't it possible for us to be Summer and Kingsley?"

"I don't know." When he steps away, the urge to pull him back pulses through me. "Come on, I'll take you home."

I nod.

The moment is shattered by the sharp screech of tires sliding over pavement. We twist our heads as an SUV skids to a halt in the Dairy Barn parking lot, spitting up gravel in its wake.

Once the dust settles, my stomach drops to the bottom of my toes as Austin slams out of the G-wagon and stalks toward us. Even from this distance, his green eyes flash with rage.

"Oh shit," I whisper as fear pools inside me.

There's no way this will end well.

SUMMER

"What the fuck, Summer!" Austin barks, his hands clench as he stalks closer. My brother has never scared me, but at this moment, his towering fury does.

The two girls loitering at the Dairy Barn window swing around and gape as they watch the scene unfold from a safe distance. Kingsley turns toward the oncoming threat and squares up. The last thing I need is a fight breaking out between them. Austin can't afford any more trouble.

In the blink of an eye, my twin eats up the distance between us with long-legged strides. When he pulls his arm back, I leap between the two, pressing my palms against my brother's chest. It takes all of my strength to knock him back a few steps.

"What the fuck are you doing with him?" Austin growls, not taking his gaze off the other boy.

I gulp as my mind races, trying to come up with a plausible explanation that will defuse the situation. "Kingsley drove me home from school, and we stopped for ice cream."

Austin's gaze flickers to mine. "I thought you were sick."

"I felt better, so I went to school for the afternoon."

"Why didn't you drive yourself?" he shoots back suspiciously.

I don't know how to answer that question.

Before I can blurt out another lie, Kingsley interjects, "I stopped at home to pick something up at lunch and saw that she was leaving, so I offered her a ride."

Austin glowers before shoving me behind his body. "Why would you do that? Aren't you the same asshole who had his fucking hand wrapped around her throat last week?" His voice grows steely as he steps forward. "Maybe she's forgotten about that, but I haven't."

I peek around Austin's arm, trying to gauge Kingsley's reaction, but his gaze becomes shuttered.

The memory invades my brain, and I swallow thickly. It's almost as if I can feel the unrelenting pressure of his fingers pressing against my windpipe, closing off the airflow. Bruises had decorated my skin for days. Makeup had been necessary to camouflage the marks from my parents and while at school.

"It's not that deep, bro." Cruelty flickers in Kingsley's bottomless depths as he smirks. "Don't make more out of it than what it is."

The carelessness of his words cut me with the precision of a scalpel. Whatever fragile bond had been reestablished between us is once again destroyed. It makes me question everything. Maybe I was right the first time, and it was all a giant mindfuck. Not only did I allow him to touch my body, I let him create havoc inside my head.

I'm such an idiot.

How many times do I need to get burned before I learn my lesson? Kingsley is not to be trusted. No matter how much he resembles the boy from the beach, they aren't the same guy. That boy doesn't exist.

The smirking son of a bitch standing before me is the real Kingsley Rothchild. I can't allow myself to ever forget that. Nausea rushes through me. My fingernails bite into my brother's bare arm to pull his attention back to me. I need to escape Kingsley's insufferable presence before I become physically ill.

"Please," I whisper, "take me home."

As if hearing the pain riddled through my words, Austin's concerned gaze flickers to mine. Not wanting to make eye contact with Kingsley, I keep my attention focused on my brother. Stifling waves of tension blanket the atmosphere, making it impossible to breathe. Any moment and I'll start gasping for air.

"Go wait in the car, Summer," he mutters from the corner of his mouth as his gaze shifts to Kingsley.

"Come with me." If I walk away, the situation will only escalate.

Clearly, I can't read Kingsley, but I know my brother. He's spoiling for a fight. And one way or another, he'll find what he's looking for.

"*Go,*" he snaps when I don't budge from behind him. "Rothchild and I need to have a little chat."

My shoulders slump under the heavy weight of the situation. Even though I refuse to glance in Kingsley's direction, the heat of his gaze drills into me.

"Please..." I moisten my lips. "Don't do anything stupid." We both know it's a warning that will go unheeded.

It's only after I've slid onto the passenger seat of the Mercedes that my attention is drawn back to the boys. A shudder slides through me as I cringe, holding my breath. Austin has already advanced on the dark-haired boy and is shoving him in the chest. A low rumble of words is exchanged but I'm too far away to hear them. It's better that way. Anything that comes out of Kingsley's mouth will be specifically designed to inflict pain. I can only hope he doesn't throw our agreement in Austin's face.

It was a mistake to walk away and leave them together. I knew Austin would lose his temper. He's been simmering for weeks. Actually, he's been a powder keg since we found out about the move. The start of school, the hazing, and the subsequent suspension have driven him to the tipping point. It was only a matter of time before he exploded.

But still, I can't allow him to make the situation worse.

As I grip the door handle, Austin yanks back his arm and punches Kingsley in the face. The movement is so swift that the vehicle door is barely open, and already it's over. My hands rise to my mouth as Kingsley staggers back a step before flying forward as the two grapple.

I scream and rush toward them, my shoes sliding over the gravel. By the time I reach the pair, they've already splintered apart and are pacing warily around each other. Neither spares me a look as I grab Austin's arm and haul him toward the G-wagon.

"*Stop it!*" I snap. "*Both of you!*"

Kingsley glares at my brother before lifting his hand to his nose and swiping at the blood beneath it. Bright red splatters dot his white shirt. He jerks his head back, and a chilling menace fills his eyes.

"Stay the fuck away from my sister!" Austin roars in the now silent parking lot.

A slow smirk curves Kingsley's lips, and I mentally prepare myself for the nastiness that will follow. "Can't make any promises, bro. She's a hot piece of ass."

When Austin lunges for the second time, I scramble in front of him, shoving my weight against his body. It's like trying to move a brick wall.

"Let's go!" I wrap both hands around his arm and tug. *"Now!"*

His feet move, and he allows me to drag him away from Kingsley. The more distance I put between them, the more relieved I am. With one final glare, Austin swings around and slides into the SUV. I flinch when he slams the door closed before pounding his fists against the steering wheel.

In silence, I bite my lip and stare out the windshield as Austin guns the engine, squealing out of the Dairy Barn parking lot and onto the main road before fishtailing across the pavement. I grab the oh-shit bar above the door and glance at him with wide eyes. His jaw remains clenched as his gaze stays pinned to the stretch of road in front of him.

"What the fuck were you *really* doing with Rothchild?" he growls. "Because I don't believe that BS story you tried to feed me earlier."

"Language," I murmur, needing to defuse the explosive situation.

He glares and presses his lips together before muttering, "How about you stop being a funny fuck and answer the question."

I wince. There's no way I can divulge the bargain I struck with Kingsley. Austin would turn this SUV around and pummel the shit out of him. The only choice I have is to cover the lie with more lies and hope that the truth never gets dragged into the light.

"It's like he said," I murmur. "He came home for lunch and saw that I was leaving for school. Then he offered me a ride home. We stopped in town for an ice cream cone. End of story."

I'm struck by the realization that it really *is* the end of the story. I can't do this anymore with Kingsley. I can't get wrapped up in his games.

My brother's eyes narrow as he considers everything I've divulged. "Why would he do that?"

"How should I know?" I jerk my shoulders before turning away and leaning my forehead against the glass. Misery floods through me, nearly swallowing me whole, as I stare at the greenery along the side of the road. The town of Hawthorne gets left behind in the rearview mirror.

"Why the hell would you agree to go anywhere with that jackass after he tried hurting you?"

Even though I keep my gaze trained out the window, his stare probes me for details I have no intention of revealing. There has always been a powerful bond between us. Since we moved here, I've been keeping secrets. As much as the guilt gnaws at me, it's better for all of us if Austin never discovers the truth.

"It seemed like a good idea at the time," I mumble, feeling heartsick. "It won't happen again."

That, at least, isn't a lie.

SUMMER

The following Monday, Austin returns to Hawthorne Prep and everything goes back to the way it was before his suspension. Sloane shoots me triumphant looks every chance she gets all the while clinging to Kingsley like a barnacle.

And Kingsley?

He ignores me in class and in the halls. He doesn't make me wear the shirt, force me to eat lunch with him, or sneak into my room at night. I should be thrilled that his interest has become ensnared by someone else.

Instead, a deep sense of sadness fills me.

How's that for fucked up?

No longer are we harassed. It's more like we don't exist, which is fine with me. Even though Austin remains tight-lipped about football practice, he doesn't come home with anymore bruises, blackened eyes, or bloodied noses.

I can't shake the strange energy that hovers over us like a heavy cloud, making it feel like the calm before an impending storm. With every new day that slides by, my anxiety ratchets up a couple of hundred notches. Any moment, I'll come out of my skin.

After fourth hour, while everyone heads to lunch, I slip inside the bathroom and shut myself in a stall. As my finger hovers over the button to flush the toilet, the bathroom door swings open, and a couple of girls stroll in, their heels clicking against the penny round tile floor.

I'm not sure what makes me hesitate.

"God, I hate that bitch."

Sloane.

I would recognize her voice anywhere. There's something about her tone that makes me wonder if I'm the one being talked about. This place has made me paranoid.

"At least Kingsley isn't hanging on her anymore," someone chirps.

"He was never *hanging* on her," Sloane snaps in a haughty tone. "He was *fucking* with her. There's a difference."

My shoulders sink with the realization that I'm not so paranoid after all. They *are* talking about me.

One of them snorts. "I'll just bet he was."

"Shut the hell up, Aubrey! Do you honestly think Kingsley would be interested in that ugly ass Hawthorne girl when he could have *me*?"

Ugly ass?

Ouch.

"Have you ever looked at her nonexistent chest? There are zero boobs to speak of. It's all flat." A smirk fills her voice. "And Kingsley is most *definitely* a breast guy. He can't get enough of mine."

The thought of Kingsley touching Sloane the same way he touched me has nausea churning in the pit of my belly. I lay a hand over my lower abdomen to stymie the discomfort. Why can't these girls leave me the hell alone? I'm not a threat to them. I want nothing to do with Kingsley or them.

"In fact, he stopped by last night," she says with a giggle. "That boy is such a freak in the sheets."

My throat closes until breathing becomes impossible.

Another girl laughs. "Please, slut, you love every minute of his kink."

"Damn right I do," she agrees smugly.

Someone pipes up with, "I heard she gave him a BJ."

Is that idle gossip, or did Kingsley brag about what we did together? A tiny piece of me clinging to the hope that the true Kingsley was the one from the beach and not the asshole from Hawthorne Prep crumbles and dies. Deep down, I knew the truth but refused to admit it. Even to myself.

Especially to myself.

Now I have no other choice but to accept it.

A few girls rattle off sexual acts I supposedly engaged in. Not only with Kingsley but also with several other boys. I've been here a little over two weeks, and from the sound of it, I've really gotten around. It's like they're going out of their way to top the last sexual act mentioned with something more outrageous. All I can say is that these bitches get an F for creativity.

For fuck's sake, if you're going to claim I did something, at least make it interesting.

Fed up with the lies pouring from their mouths, I stab the button on the wall to flush the toilet. If they won't leave, then *I* will. The moment water rushes down the drain, all of the laughter and chatter comes to an abrupt halt.

There's no turning back now.

I suck in a breath, square my shoulders, and paste a pleasant smile on my face before unlatching the lock. All eyes are focused on the stall when the door swings open and I step out.

As soon as Sloane sees me, she scowls. "Well, well, well, speak of the ho."

I force out a laugh. "Oh sweetheart, don't worry, you'll always be the frontrunner in that competition."

Sloane's eyes narrow as she advances on me. "You're jealous that Kingsley is back where he belongs and isn't slumming it with Hawthorne trash."

"Hmm." I scrunch my nose and give her a thoughtful look. "What does that say about you for not being able to hold his interest in the first place?"

She sucks in a sharp breath as her hands tighten. "Why don't you do us all a favor and shut your mouth before I make your life a living hell."

"It's much too late for that. My parents already beat you to the punch by moving us to this backwoods town filled with a bunch of inbred hicks." I clear my throat and give her a pointed look.

"Who are you calling a hick?" she growls.

"I'm sorry, was I not clear?" There's a pause before I force out the rest. "I'm calling *you* a backwoods hick."

With a screech of outrage, she lunges. It's almost a surprise when her body slams into mine. I stagger a few steps and my back hits the bathroom stall. Her fingers tangle through my thick hair, scraping against the scalp before giving it a vicious yank. Tears sting my eyes as I yelp, trying to peel her hands away, but it's no use. She's stronger than she looks.

"*I hate you!*" she shrieks.

We struggle as screams and grunts echo off the walls of the confined space. When she slams me against a tile wall, the air gets knocked from my lungs. All I know is that one moment, she's trying to pull my hair out by the roots, and the next, she's being dragged away. My breath comes out in short sharp pants as my heart thumps painfully against my chest.

Never, in all my eighteen years, have I been in a fight.

I usually leave that to Austin.

Furiously, I blink the wetness out of my eyes until my vision clears. Kingsley has his arms wrapped around Sloane as she struggles against him like a wildcat. Her blue eyes are clouded with fury as she howls out her outrage. With his lips near her ear, he whispers something too soft for me to hear before lifting her off the ground and swinging her away from me.

As soon as I'm out of sight, she goes limp as loud sobs fall from her lips. "*She's horrible, Kingsley! She attacked me for no reason! She's just like her psycho brother!*"

Stunned, I watch as she turns and tangles her arms around his neck, burrowing against the strength of his chest as if she needs to be protected from me.

What a fucking crazy bitch.

I lift my hand to my scalp and wince, gingerly touching the spot where she tried to rip the hair out.

"Come on," he murmurs, leading her from the bathroom without so much as a word to me. Sloane's minions shoot me dirty looks before spinning on their heels and following the pair out the door.

An eerie silence settles around me as I stare in disbelief at my disheveled appearance in the mirror.

Did that seriously happen?

Maybe it was a poor decision on my part to get mouthy, but there's only so much a person can take before they completely lose it. If this episode is any indication, I've reached my limit. Especially where Sloane and her crew are concerned.

With shaking fingers, I turn on the tap and splash cold water on my face before attempting to smooth down my hair. It looks like I've been put through the wringer. All I want to do is go home, but that's not going to happen. I missed half a day last week and can't afford to leave.

The door to the bathroom swings open, and I tense, shifting toward it, ready for round two if Sloane decides to finish what she started. Air leaks from my lungs when I find Kingsley filling the doorway.

He hasn't acknowledged my existence since Austin found us together at the Dairy Barn. Worse than that, I'm not sure which is preferable—his hatred or disregard. It's one more troubling realization where this boy is concerned.

He was screwing with you, Summer.

That's all it ever was.

One giant mindfuck.

Yet pain of his indifference is enough to gut me.

"What the hell was that about?" he growls, closing the distance between us.

My eyes widen at the accusation that fills his sharp voice. Why am I so surprised that he's defending Sloane? It only solidifies my earlier thoughts. *Be relieved that he's done playing games with you.*

"Are you serious?" I press my palm against my pounding chest. "Do you *honestly* think I would start anything with Sloane?" Ever since I stepped foot on the campus of Hawthorne Prep, I've done my best to steer clear of her.

His brow furrows. "She says you attacked her for no reason."

Of course she did.

My mouth drops open, and laughter tumbles out. "She's lying. From my experience, Sloane says a lot of things I hope aren't true." Another prick of pain stabs me before I sweep it away.

His eyes narrow as he takes another step closer. "What the hell is that supposed to mean?"

I press my lips together, refusing to answer. It was all a game. *An agreement.* He helped me and I...

I allowed him to touch me in return.

And now you're going to complain and cry that he's moved on? Pathetic.

I shove all of the pain deep inside, where I can pretend it doesn't exist before straightening my shoulders. I'll be damned if I allow him to see how much damage he's inflicted.

"You know what?" I snap. "It doesn't matter. None of it does."

There's no point in trying to defend myself. Nothing I say or do will change his mind. It's like he said at the Dairy Barn—he's a Rothchild and I'm a Hawthorne. I should have listened to him instead of thinking I knew better.

"The hell it does," he snaps. When I remain silent, his tone grows harsh. "Answer the question, Summer. What the hell did you mean by that?"

I shake my head as a bitter smile twists my lips. I'm done wasting my time. "Nothing."

When I attempt to push past him, he grabs my upper arms and swings me around until my back is pressed against the wall. The air hisses from my lungs when he shackles my wrists and forces them above my head. His body pins mine in place as his mouth hovers inches above my own. Even in anger, I crave his touch. It's disheartening to realize that instead of trying to escape from him, I'm straining to get closer.

"You obviously have something to say, so spit it out."

"There's nothing," I whisper, needing to remind myself that this is not the same boy I met at the beach. They may look identical, but that's where the similarities end.

A deep growl of frustration vibrates in his chest. "I'm not going to let you go until you tell me what's going on."

"You can stop with the games. We both know that there was never anything between us. How could there be when you're a Rothchild and I'm a Hawthorne?" I pause, waiting for him to deny it. When he doesn't, a fresh wave of pain crashes over me. "Because that's all I'll ever be, right? *A Hawthorne.*"

"You don't understand how complicated the situation is," he growls.

I blink back the tears that have filled my eyes. "That's because you refuse to tell me."

Why does this hurt so much?

This boy should mean nothing to me.

There was never anything between us.

It was all lies.

"Summer," he whispers, his lips grazing mine as he forces my wrists up the wall until I'm stretched out beneath him. "Give me time to figure this out."

Instead of cutting me loose, all he wants to do is string me along until there's another punch line. Until he can humiliate and hurt me.

When he nips my lower lip, liquid need pools in my core, and I whimper in frustration. Not only am I angry with him but I'm also angry with myself for being weak and stupid where he's concerned. I know what the right course of action is. I just need to be strong enough to take it.

"The deal we made is over," I force myself to say in a voice devoid of emotion. He's gotten enough from me already. I can't afford to give him anything more. "If you want to make our lives hell, do it."

With that, I shove out of his embrace and fly toward the door.

"*Summer!*"

It takes every ounce of my strength not to look back.

SUMMER

28

I sprint the last quarter mile until the long stretch of our driveway comes into view. Only then do I allow my legs to slow. Running is the only thing that settles my mind, allowing me a rare slice of peace. I push myself until a burn grows in my chest before spreading to the rest of my body like an infection. When thoughts of Kingsley pop into my head, I force my legs to pump faster until all I'm able to focus on is my labored breath. The endorphins kick in, and for a few blissful moments, there's nothing but the road stretched out in front of me.

Once I reach the house, I finish my workout with a few stretches before walking through the front door and stumbling to a halt. Mom is on her hands and knees scrubbing at the marble tile floor. A bucket of water is next to her. I unzip the pocket of my shorts, pull out my phone, and turn off the music before removing the AirPods from my ears.

"Hey." My chest rises and falls with the sharp pants that leave my body. "What are you doing?"

Mom has always kept a clean house, but this is a little obsessive even for her.

"Just making sure everything is immaculate," she murmurs, not bothering to glance up from the spot she's scrubbing.

When she doesn't elaborate any further, I follow up with, "Why?"

She glances up and blinks. "Did you forget that we're having people over tonight?"

"Oh, right." Actually, I did.

My heart sinks at the idea of all those Hawthorne assholes filling my house. I've done my best to push this party to the back of my mind and forget about it. Guess I did too good of a job. I shift my weight and glance away. "Is attendance mandatory?"

If I'm lucky, this is more of an adult affair, and I can skip it.

Her eyes widen as she straightens, sitting back on her heels. "Of course you have to attend! It's important that our family appear as a united front."

I humph out a breath as the edges of my lips draw down. Schmoozing a bunch of townies isn't exactly how I want to spend my Saturday night.

"What's the point of this again?" Exasperation tinges my voice. Before she's able to respond, I tack on, "Do you really think this will change how people perceive us?" I couldn't even change the mind of one person, let alone the whole school. Mom doesn't understand what we're up against. Admittedly, in the beginning, neither did I. I still don't have the complete picture. What I do know is that the history in this town goes way back. And the memories go back even further.

"I hope so," she admits in a tight voice. "We need everything to go smoothly. This has to work."

"What has to work?" I blink as her odd choice of words echoes through my head. "Is there something going on?"

My parents' behavior has grown increasingly strained over the last week. They're both showing signs of cracking. Mom is edgier than usual, and Dad has become even more tight-lipped about the company and the history of this town. Every time I attempt to work a few questions into our conversations, he swiftly shuts them down. If I didn't have so much shit to deal with, I would take the time to dig deeper.

Mom jerks her shoulders and presses her lips together. For a long moment, I wonder if she'll respond.

"Your grandmother," she says haltingly, "was not a beloved figure in Hawthorne."

Ha! From what I've discovered, that's an understatement. She had a difficult relationship with her own son, so it only stands to reason she couldn't get along with other people in her life.

Not exactly a shocking revelation.

"Because of that," Mom continues, "she created even more bad blood with the Rothchild family, which eventually bled over to the town." I'm taken aback by her show of emotion when she buries her face in her hands. "It's all such a mess, Summer."

My eyes widen, and I shift my weight, unsure how to comfort her. This kind of outburst isn't like my mother. She's usually so upbeat and cheerful.

"Mom, I—"

It's on the tip of my tongue to apologize. I shouldn't have questioned her.

She drops her hands from her face before inhaling a deep breath, visibly attempting to wrangle her emotions. "Please, just be there tonight. We need you."

I nod and bite my lower lip. It feels like there's more going on than she's willing to admit. But then again, that's the way everything around here feels. We're all keeping secrets from each other. If given half a chance, this place will destroy the tightly woven fabric of our family. I don't want that to happen.

I clear my throat and push out the question. "What time should I be ready?"

This party will be an ugly wake-up call for them, but nothing can be done about it now. The only thing I can do is stand in solidarity next to them with my head held high.

Her shoulders slump as her face clears. "People will start arriving at seven o'clock."

I glance at my sports watch. That's three hours from now.

"The caterers should be here any moment. The plan is for them to set up a bar in the dining room."

Excellent idea. Mom and Dad need to ply these people with as much liquor as possible.

"Do you need help with anything?" I glance around the foyer and living room. Wood has been polished to a high shine and glass sparkles in the sunlight that filters in through the windows. Mom has obviously spent a lot of time scrubbing the house from top to bottom.

"No, I'm almost done." As she meets my gaze, a strained smile lifts her lips. There are tiny lines of tension bracketing her eyes that never used to be there. "Thanks for asking." Her gaze searches mine before she expels a tense breath. "You're a good girl, Summer. You've tried to make the best of this situation, and we appreciate that."

"Thanks, Mom." Even though there are plenty of negatives about this place, there have also been a few positives. That's what I try to focus on. The house and pool are amazing. I love our G-wagon. And the night sky...

Almost every evening, I stare up at the brightly shining pinpricks of light, trying to find my Zen. Running and the stars. The only two things that make me forget how much I hate it here. Strangely enough, school has become tolerable. From an educational standpoint, it's rigorous and will look good on my transcript.

"I just wish..." Mom's soft voice trails off as she pins her lower lip with her teeth and glances away.

A strange feeling of foreboding fills me.

"What?" My throat tightens as if Kingsley's fingers are wrapped around it, slowly constricting my airway.

"I wish this company had never been founded," she blurts.

The honesty of her words and the threads of resentment woven through them take me by surprise. Sure, that's how I feel, but I wasn't expecting her to voice the same sentiment.

"Then we'd be back in Chicago," she finishes almost wistfully.

"Yeah." I don't understand where all this is coming from. From everything I've seen, Mom has been happy here. So this sudden about-face doesn't make sense. "That would be nice."

For me, it's been a different story. I wish more than anything we could go back to our old life. We've been here less than a month, and it feels like forever. I search my brain, trying to dredge up memories of Chicago. It's disconcerting to realize that some have already blurred around the edges. They aren't as crisp and clear as they should be.

"Go upstairs and get ready, sweetie," Mom says.

As I turn toward the staircase, her voice halts me in my tracks.

"Do me a favor and wear the sleeveless blue halter dress we bought last summer." Her eyes soften as her lips curve. "You look so pretty in it."

I pause on the first tread as my face scrunches. I don't give a damn about impressing these stupid people. They're lucky I'm bothering to show my face at this shindig.

"I'd rather wear the short pink one," I say carelessly.

She shakes her head. "No, that one is too—"

"Too what?" I ask, brows rising in surprise.

Her shoulders straighten. Any tenderness that had been filling her eyes disappears. "It's not appropriate for this gathering. Wear the blue one. You look so sweet and innocent in it."

Sweet and innocent?

What the hell is that about?

Unsure how to respond, I sputter out a disbelieving laugh. "Come on, Mom, you can't be serious."

"Actually," she snaps, "I am. Please, don't argue. Just wear the dress."

My eyes widen in shock. The request is so strange and uncharacteristic that I'm not sure what to make of it.

She's stressed. That's all this is. Tomorrow the party will be over, and we can move on with our lives. Sort of.

"Summer." Her sharp voice cuts into my thoughts. "Did you hear me?"

"Yeah," I grumble, "I'll wear the stupid dress." I stomp up the staircase to the second floor, mumbling under my breath the entire way before slamming into my room. Any good vibes flowing through my veins from the run are long gone.

With hasty movements, I jerk off the athletic top and mesh shorts before stalking to the bathroom and running the tub. To get through this, I'm going to need a long hot bath.

To drown myself in.

I snort at the thought.

The bizarro conversation with Mom continues to play through my head. There's more going on than what my parents are willing to acknowledge. Maybe after this is over, I'll have to snoop around in the study and see what I can uncover.

Once the tub is filled, I strip off my panties and sports bra before sliding into the water. Warmth surrounds me as I rest my head against the smooth porcelain and allow my eyelids to feather closed. Tension seeps from my body as if the water has the ability to leech it away.

My mind wanders, and I end up dozing off. When my eyelashes flutter open again, I'm startled to find Kingsley sitting on the edge of the tub staring at me. I blink, needing to make sure he's not a figment of my imagination. When the vision doesn't shimmer into nothingness, I jerk to a sitting position and draw my knees to my chest before banding my arms around my legs.

"What are you doing here?" As far as I'm concerned, we have nothing further to discuss. I've done my best to push him to the far recesses of my brain and pretend he doesn't exist.

Has it been working?

Not one bit. But what other choice is there?

One side of his mouth hitches into a lazy smile as his gaze drops to my naked body. "You realize that's unnecessary. I've already seen the goods."

True.

"But that doesn't mean you're going to continue to see them," I snap, exasperated to find him invading my space with the same persistence he invades my brain.

The arrogance dissolves from his expression as his eyes soften. "Believe it or not, I didn't come here to fight with you."

Ha!

"Then why are you here?" It takes effort to keep the waver from my voice.

Glancing away, he trails the tips of his fingers through the now lukewarm water. "We need to talk."

I force out a laugh. "In that case, you can leave as quietly as you snuck in because we have nothing further to say to one another."

Ignoring me, he asks, "Did you mean what you said about liking me when we met at the beach?" Uncertainty flickers in his mahogany-colored eyes as he lifts them to mine.

The conversation from the Dairy Barn crashes through my head.

"Yes," I reluctantly admit before continuing, "But that's not the real Kingsley Rothchild, is it?" That knowledge is like a painful vise around my chest, making it impossible to breathe. All this time, I've been holding out hope that the boy from the beach would gradually reveal himself. That has yet to happen, and I've finally come to a place of acceptance that it never will.

He presses his lips together as my heart thuds. "What if I could be? What if it was possible for us to start over again?"

I can't resist flinging his own words back in his face. It's so much easier than allowing them to burrow under my skin, giving me nothing more than false hope. "But that's not possible, is it? There is too much family history standing between us."

"What if I was wrong?" A stripped-down vulnerability I've never glimpsed before lurks in the back of his eyes. "About everything."

Why is he doing this?

Why won't he allow me to walk away?

"I don't understand." Where is this coming from? More than anything, I hate that he has the ability to draw me back in again.

"If I were the guy you first met..." He slides along the edge of the tub. "Could you fall in love with me?"

My mouth tumbles open as his words send my belly into a free fall. How am I supposed to answer that?

"Summer?"

Without considering the consequences, I jerk my head into a nod.

He continues to scoot toward me before dropping to his knees on the other side of the porcelain. Both of his hands slide through my wet hair, holding my head in place before carefully searching my eyes. He tips my face until his warm breath can drift over my lips. My chest expands for the first time in more than a week as I breathe him in.

What is it about him that feels so right?

"Are you sure?" His expression turns serious. As if whatever I say next will somehow seal my fate.

When I open my mouth, he cuts me off. "Don't give me an answer yet. You need to think about it." His tongue darts out to stroke over my lips, and I groan at the contact as my muscles lose their rigidity.

"Do you have any idea how much I've missed touching you?" he growls. "It's been fucking torture."

As much as I've tried to pretend otherwise, I feel the same way. Logically, it doesn't make sense. I've stopped trying to rationalize it in my head. For whatever reason, his touch feels more natural than anything else in my life.

"Give me your tongue," he demands.

It doesn't occur to me to hold back. As soon as my tongue peeks through my lips, he licks it with the velvety softness of his own before drawing it deep into his mouth. Arousal shoots through my core, throbbing to life with a swiftness that almost takes my breath away.

His fingers splay wide as he holds me in place, sucking on me the entire time. Everything he does is so erotic. Even something as simple as this. When he releases me, it's as if I've been drugged. No longer am I able to think; all I want are his hands roaming over my body, branding me in a way he has yet to do.

"Think carefully about what I've said." He presses another kiss against my lips. "I need an answer by the end of the evening."

With a groan, his mouth aligns with mine one last time before he rises to his feet. I don't realize that my body has unfurled from its huddled state until his gaze skims over my naked form, and he plows a hand roughly through his hair. Heat ignites in his eyes as they become dark liquid pools that have the power to singe me alive.

"Tonight," he repeats harshly.

I bite my lip as the sexual haze clouding my brain clears. As he crosses over the threshold into my bedroom, I blurt, "Kingsley?"

He swings around. "Yeah?"

"Tell me this isn't a game." I watch for any telltale signs that he's lying to me. A shuttering of his eyes. A blanking of his expression.

Instead, regret flashes across his face as he stalks into the bathroom, swallowing up the distance between us in four long strides. When he reaches the tub, he falls to his knees, and his hands snake out to cup my cheeks. "This isn't a game. What's happening between us is all too real."

"Do you swear it?" I search his eyes, attempting to sift through every nuance that flickers in them.

"On my life."

My teeth sink into my lower lip before chewing it. "Okay." So badly do I want to believe he's telling me the truth, but the sad reality is that he's never given me one reason to trust him.

His tongue sweeps over my lower lip, and when I release it from being pinned in place, he draws it into his mouth before relinquishing it. "You'll have an answer for me tonight?"

I nod as he rises to his feet. If pressed hard enough, I would give him the answer he's looking for right now. But he doesn't, so I keep my lips tightly pressed together. For whatever reason, it feels as though I should give as much consideration to his question as he has instructed me to.

"Then I'll see you tonight." With that, he disappears from the bathroom. When I hear the screen door slam shut in my bedroom, I know he's gone. My head falls back against the tub as I stare sightlessly at the ceiling.

As confused as I am, there are truths that can not be denied. The way I feel about him is like nothing I've ever experienced. And something tells me that I never will again.

But is it real?

Or another mindfuck?

SUMMER

29

I stare at my reflection in the full-length mirror with a critical eye before twisting one way and then the other. The blue sleeveless halter dress falls to my knees. Even though nothing's wrong with the dress, it irritates me that I don't have a choice about wearing it. I'm eighteen years old; I can decide for myself what's appropriate for an adult party.

A small, stubborn part of me is tempted to change into the short pink tulle dress, but I would never go through with it. The stress of moving to this rinky-dink town, taking over a multimillion-dollar company, and hosting this ill-fated party have pushed my parents over the edge of their sanity.

So, if Mom wants me to wear this dress in a bizarre attempt to impress the small-minded townsfolk, then I guess I'll do it, but that doesn't mean I have to be happy about it.

As soon as I finished my bath, I styled my hair in a sleek ballerina bun at the top of my head.

Mom wants sweet and innocent?

This should do the trick.

Eye shadow and light pink lip gloss are added to complete the look. I glance at the clock on my nightstand and realize it's half past seven. Already the doorbell has chimed at least a dozen times. As much as I'd like to delay the inevitable, I can't put it off any longer. From my closet, I find a pair of matching blue heels and slip them on before leaving the room and knocking on my brother's door.

Since Austin is dreading this party as much as I am, I'm confident he's still hiding out. When he doesn't respond, I crack open the door and poke my head inside, only to find him sitting on the edge of the bed with his hands tightly clasped in his lap.

"Hey."

He glances up and gives me a tight smile before rising to his feet. "You look nice."

"Thanks." I do a little twirl before stacking my hands under my chin and batting my lashes. "Mom requested that I look as pure as the freshly driven snow."

He snorts out a disbelieving laugh before shaking his head. "What the fuck is that about?"

"Language," I sing-song with a wide grin, and his lips twitch.

Austin plows a hand through his short dark hair. "I can't believe we have to do this. It's such a waste of time."

"I know," I huff, dropping my hands. "But it's only for a couple of hours. Maybe we can sneak a few drinks to dull the pain."

He sticks his fingers beneath the collar of his starched white shirt and yanks it away from his neck. "This damn thing is choking me," he mutters before popping the first two buttons. "Fuck it, I'm not wearing a tie."

"I'm sure it'll be fine." My gaze skims over the length of him. Austin has grown into a handsome guy. Maybe the girls at Hawthorne aren't falling all over him like they used to at our old school, but I've seen enough of them eye fuck him in the hallway during passing periods and at lunch to know that they want to. The navy suit only accentuates his tall, muscular build.

"You ready?" I ask, only wanting to get this farce over with.

"Nope."

One side of my mouth hitches. "Well, I guess you're shit out of luck then."

His dimples flash as a slow smile moves across his face. "It might have taken a while, but it's nice to see I've finally corrupted you."

I roll my eyes and nod toward the door. "Let's go."

We're midway down the staircase when the doorbell chimes and more guests arrive. My mother hired a full staff this evening to make sure everything ran smoothly. There is a valet to park the cars on the road, a man in formal wear to greet guests at the door with a silver tray of champagne, and servers to circulate through the party with drinks and appetizers.

As my gaze roams over the crowd, I notice most people already have a beverage in their hands. Mom's plan to get the town trashed looks to be a success. Who knows, maybe she'll pull off the impossible, and by the end of the evening, the Hawthornes will once again be in everyone's good graces.

A couple who look to be around my parents' age step into the foyer. A moment later, a younger couple trails them. Wait a minute...is that Jasper?

Ugh.

What the hell is *he* doing here?

My hand tightens around the wrought-iron railing as I give my brother a bit of side-eye. By the way his jaw clenches, I'm guessing that his rival's presence has not gone unnoticed. I hope he keeps it together. The last thing Mom and Dad need is him getting into a fight when they're trying to prove how wonderful we are.

As my gaze returns to Jasper, I realize Delilah is at his side. Her blond hair falls down her back in a long shiny curtain. Like me, she's wearing a formal dress.

When Austin's footsteps stall, and he lags on the staircase, I turn my attention to him with concern. "Aus?" When he fails to respond, I flick my gaze toward the front door where both couples are being greeted and offered refreshments. "Is this going to be a problem?"

"Nope."

As Delilah glances around, her blue gaze flickers over us until it becomes ensnared by my brother. Another quick look in my twin's direction has me wondering if it was Jasper who snagged his attention in the first place.

Maybe it was the pretty blonde.

Color fills the other girl's cheeks as Jasper slips an arm around his date's waist before steering her into the living room where most of the guests have gathered. A predatory gleam enters Austin's eyes as he watches the younger couple get swallowed up by the crowd.

Uh-oh.

A groan falls from my lips. I don't need twin intuition to tell me where this is headed. Whatever devious plans he's concocting will only lead to more problems.

"I hope you realize that going after her is a bad decision."

His gaze becomes shuttered as a sly smile tugs at the corners of his lips. "You worry too much, sis."

"I don't think so," I snort. Delilah is exactly the kind of girl Austin usually goes for. Now throw in that she's Jasper's girlfriend, and it's a recipe for disaster. I wouldn't put it past Austin to use that poor girl to fuck with the first-string quarterback. Although I hope I'm wrong about that.

As we arrive at the bottom of the staircase, I search the crowd of strangers filling almost every corner of the space. It takes a few moments to spot our parents talking with a tall, dark-haired man. I study the older guy and realize something is vaguely familiar about him even though I know we've never met.

Dismissing him, I shift my gaze to my parents. Neither looks very happy. Upon closer inspection, both have tight lines bracketing their eyes and mouth. Nervous energy wafts from Mom. The muscles in my belly contract as an odd sensation creeps over my skin, leaving a wave of goose flesh in its path. It's the same feeling of foreboding I experienced earlier this afternoon.

I'm about to point out our parents to Austin when he mutters, "I'll be back in a few."

Before I have the chance to respond, he walks away, leaving me alone. Everyone is socializing and appears to be having a wonderful time as they sip their flutes. Like school, even though I'm part of the crowd, I'm still removed from it all. I've been reduced to nothing more than a stranger in my home.

It's a weird, lonely feeling.

From across the room, I watch as Dad lifts a crystal tumbler filled with amber-colored liquor to his mouth before taking a deep swallow. Sheesh. Him tossing back alcohol is a rare occurrence. Once in a while, he'll sit down and crack open a beer at the end of a long day but never hard liquor.

Mom nervously fingers the gold chain adorning her neck as her gaze roves over the sea of people until it lands on me.

Damn.

Unconsciously, I take a step backward as she frantically waves me over. Knowing there's no escape, I suck in a deep, fortifying breath before pushing it out. We've now entered the portion of the evening where I have to pretend to be charming and personable. If for no other reason than to support my parents.

Once I reach the trio, I paste a pleasant smile on my face as Mom slips an arm around my waist to anchor me in place as if she's afraid I'll attempt an escape.

All I can say is that the woman knows me well.

"You look beautiful, honey," she whispers. A slight tremble works its way through her hushed voice, and it strengthens my resolve to do everything I can to help make this party a success.

We're Hawthornes.

And Hawthornes stick together.

"Thanks," I say with forced cheerfulness.

Dad straightens to his full height and runs an agitated hand through his hair before adjusting the lapels of his black jacket. "Perfect timing, Summer. We were just talking about you."

Well, that's not weird at all.

Unsure how to respond, I flick my gaze at the man standing with them before thrusting out my hand for him to shake. No one can say that my parents didn't raise me with manners. "Hello, it's nice to meet you. I'm Griffin and Eloise's daughter, Summer."

There's no answering smile in sight as he reaches out and grasps my hand. His fingers close around mine, swallowing them in a firm grip. "Keaton Rothchild."

Rothchild?

"Kingsley's father?" No wonder he looks so familiar. Now that I realize who he is, I'm able to see the strong family resemblance between them.

Both are tall, with wide shoulders, mahogany-colored hair and eyes. He's handsome for an older man. It's easy to imagine Kingsley maturing to look like this one day. Although, unlike his son, there's a coldness to him that seeps into my fingers before I'm able to pull them away.

"That's right." He gives me a tight smile that doesn't quite reach his eyes as his gaze rakes over me. "I take it you two are acquainted?"

Since I have no desire to share exactly how familiar I am with his son, I say instead, "We have first hour literature class together."

"Yes, I believe he mentioned that." There's no warmth in the murky depths of his eyes as they continue to assess me.

It takes all of my self-control not to squirm beneath his forthright appraisal.

What is he searching for?

"Your parents mentioned that you're a four-point student."

"Yes, that's right." Why would they discuss my grades with this stranger? I give Mom a bit of side-eye, wondering how something like that would come up in conversation. They have never been the kind of parents who boast about their children's achievements.

"And you've been taking college prep and advanced placement classes the past three years of high school?"

Sheesh. They *really* have done a deep dive into my academics. I find it difficult to believe this man is interested in my coursework and grades.

Unsure what to say, I add, "So far, I've taken eight AP classes."

Dad pipes up with, "She also scored a—"

Keaton shoots my father a harsh glare, and Dad immediately falls silent before lifting the crystal tumbler to his lips again and draining the contents.

What the hell was that about?

My stunned gaze snaps back to Kingsley's father when he says, "I heard you're interested in applying to Northwestern, the University of Chicago, and the University of Michigan." I don't get a chance to verify the information before he continues. "What about something closer to home?"

Again, I stare at my parents from the corner of my eye as my brain whirls in confusion. I remain silent, waiting a heartbeat or two for them to jump in and save me from this bizarre conversation. It's only when their desperate gazes stay pinned to mine that I realize they have no intention of intervening.

I'm on my own.

"Umm, I hadn't really thought about any other colleges. Those have always been my top three choices and with my grades and SAT score, I'm confident about my chances of at least getting into one of them."

Keaton tilts his dark head as he contemplates me. Unease pools in the pit of my belly as I shift beneath his unrelenting gaze, only wanting to escape his overbearing presence. The way he continues to grill me makes this feel more like a hard-core interview.

What exactly I've applied for remains elusive.

"It might be something to consider," he murmurs.

Even as he raises his tumbler to his lips, his attention stays pinned to me.

Uncomfortable with the scrutiny, I clear my throat and turn to Mom with a tight smile. "If you'll excuse me, I need to find Austin."

"Ah yes, the heir apparent to Hawthorne Industries." Keaton glances around as if expecting my brother to materialize out of thin air now that his name has been mentioned. "I've heard so many interesting things about the young man."

Shock washes over me, and I glance at my parents to see if they've detected the same snide tone, but their expressions remain impassive as if he has said nothing to give offense.

Dad raises his finger at a passing waiter, signaling for a refill.

Another drink?

What the fuck is going on around here?

Fed up with the forced banter, I slip from Mom's embrace. It takes effort to keep the smile pasted in place as I lie through my teeth. "It was lovely to meet you, Mr. Rothchild."

"Please, call me Keaton." One corner of his mouth lifts sardonically. "We're neighbors. I'm sure now that we've gotten to know one another, we'll be seeing more of each other."

I truly hope not.

"Take care." With a relieved breath, I move through the crowd. The air inside the house has turned stifling with the number of people crammed into the space. Before I realize it, I'm heading toward the back door that leads outside. I'm in dire need of fresh air. After that bizarre conversation, I've earned a few minutes to myself. It's like my parents had given him my pedigree.

Why?

Why would they do that?

Unease slithers down my spine before I banish the peculiar feeling. This party is unpleasant. It's nothing more than that. In a few hours, it'll be over, and these people will get the hell out of my house.

No one bats an eye as I quietly escape through the patio door. As soon as my heels hit the stamped concrete, I pause and inhale a deep breath before slowly releasing it back into the atmosphere.

Then I do it again until the tension leaks from my muscles.

Better.

Much better.

As I move toward the pool, I toss a glance over my shoulder at the lit-up house. A feeling of dread crashes over me. The need to run away pulses through me until it's all I can think about.

As my eyes adjust to the darkness, I spy an oversized towel neatly folded on a lounger I had used earlier this afternoon for a dip in the pool. As soon as the idea enters my head, I don't bother trying to talk myself out of it. I slip the heels from my feet and drop them next to the cushioned chaise before grabbing the towel and padding to the little spot at the back of the property I've claimed as my own.

As I traverse the lawn, the noise of the party fades into the background until it's nothing more than an annoying buzz. I shake out the towel before arranging it on the grass and lowering myself to the ground, mindful not to stain or wrinkle the satin fabric. With a sigh of relief, I stretch out, stacking my hands behind my head as I relax onto the thick cotton material and stare at the black stretch of canvas overhead. My body loses its rigidity as I pick out constellations.

I always begin with the North Star. Then the Little Dipper before moving on to the Big Dipper. With each familiar cluster of lights, my unease dissipates.

There's Cygnus which looks like a giant cross or maybe a bird flying through the sky. It's one of my favorites. I shift my gaze, continuing to search for arrangements. There's Delphinus, which means dolphin. To me, it looks more like a trapezoid or kite with a tail.

Now that everything has calmed, I have even less desire to return to the party. Would my parents really miss me if I stayed out here for the rest of the night? With so many people squashed in there, they probably won't realize I've slipped away.

The atmosphere changes, becoming charged, and I sense his presence long before I see him walking across the lawn. I twist my head until my gaze can rake over him in the darkness. Even with the suit jacket thrown over his shoulder, he's still ridiculously handsome in his starched white button-down and perfectly pressed black pants.

Kingsley Rothchild is much too attractive for his own good.

Mine as well.

Without a word, he drops beside me before lifting his hand and gently tracing his index finger over my lower lip. That's all it takes for a shiver of need to arrow through me before settling in my core.

"Do you have an answer for me?"

SUMMER

30

My breath hitches as his body shifts, stretching over my torso before he places one hand beside my head so I'm caged in. His face looms closer until his lips can dip to mine. Back and forth he brushes them, barely making contact.

It's sweet torture that leaves me whimpering for more. If I want to feel his mouth roving over mine, all I'd have to do is close the distance that separates us. There's no point in being coy and pretending I'm not addicted to the way his lips feel sweeping across mine.

"I need a decision," he repeats, gruffer this time.

The intoxication of his breath is almost too much to bear. Not only do I crave his touch but I also need it.

"Summer," he groans, as if I somehow affect him the same way.

"Yes. The answer is *yes*."

His tongue darts out to swipe over the plump flesh of my lower lip. The caress has my eyelids feathering closed.

"Are you sure?" He presses an open-mouthed kiss along the curve of my jaw, and I tilt my head, baring my neck for his touch. "Once you're mine, I will *never* let you go." He searches my eyes. "Do you understand what that means?"

His words send a sharp thrill shooting through me.

"Yes," I moan.

He bites my lip before his tongue darts out to soothe the pain he's inflicted.

The truth of the matter is that I can't imagine *not* being his. I can't imagine anyone else stirring these kinds of feelings inside me. Maybe Kingsley's words should frighten me. The finality of them. The possessiveness that weaves its way through them. When it comes down to it, we're still in high school and haven't known each other very long.

But still...

Something inside him calls to me. I felt it on the beach that first morning. And then the next day on the boat. A tentative bond as delicate as a thread has been created between us. No matter how many times I've tried to destroy it, it remains intact.

"Then it's done. You belong to me."

His words stir a feeling of pleasure inside me. One of rightness. It's not something I need to question.

He pulls away, putting enough distance between us so that his gaze can rove over the length of my body. The heat of his stare feels very much like a physical caress. From the hair gathered at the top of my head, to the blue skirt fanned out around my thighs, before falling to my bare toes.

"You're gorgeous."

"Do you like the dress? Mom insisted I wear it tonight." The corners of my lips quirk. "She said it made me look innocent."

His gaze flicks to mine as wickedness fills his eyes, making the twin inky pools appear bottomless. "She's right; it does." There's a pause. "I'm the only one who knows what lies beneath all that innocence, aren't I?"

It's not a question that needs to be answered. We both know he's the one who has corrupted me. It only takes the raspy scrape of his voice to have heat settling between my thighs. In a matter of days, I've become conditioned to crave his touch. Restlessly, I shift beneath his gaze.

"You'll give me it all, won't you, Summer?"

Everything.

I'll give him everything.

A bolt of electricity shoots through me as one of his hands settles on the bare skin below the hem of my dress.

"Yes."

"Good girl." As if to reward the response, his fingers trail up and down my flesh. With lazy movements, they migrate toward the apex of my thighs.

When I spread my legs, granting him more access, his lips lift into a knowing smile.

"You need my touch, don't you?"

I moan as his fingertips brush over my panties. It's nothing more than a light, teasing stroke. My hips lift, begging for more. His gentle caresses drive me just as crazy as when he tunnels his fingers through my hair and tugs my head back, rendering me powerless. At first, I was bothered by how much I enjoyed the manhandling. How it would send a rush of liquid heat to my core.

Now, I no longer care.

I want it all.

Whatever he will give me.

"That's not an answer, baby girl," he whispers.

"Yes," I sigh. "I need it."

I widen my thighs as his palm settles over my heat before giving it a possessive squeeze.

"This belongs to me."

How could I possibly want anyone else when he fulfills all my needs? Needs I never realized existed until he carefully stoked them to life.

When he takes possession of my mouth, I open for him until our tongues can meld. His fingers rub soft circles across the cotton that encases my core. Already the material is drenched.

"So fucking wet," he growls against me.

The heated words send more arousal flooding to my pussy.

"For you," I tell him.

"Damn right, it's for me." He presses against the fabric until his fingers sink between my lower lips. "*This* is mine."

"I want you to make me yours," I whimper. *"Please."*

He groans as if pained by the idea. "Is that really what you want, Summer?"

No, it's not what I want. It's what I *need*.

"Yes." My hips gyrate against his searching fingers.

"Fuck," he hisses.

In one swift movement, he shoves the satin of my skirt above my waist. His fingers hook beneath the elastic band of my panties, dragging them down my hips, thighs, and legs before tossing the soaked material to the thick carpet of grass beside the towel. Then his fingers are back, stroking over my bare lips. It doesn't take long for me to grow impatient beneath his touch. The ache pulsing between my legs is already unbearable.

Kingsley slips between my spread thighs before settling on his haunches. He strokes his hands up and down my legs before gently forcing them farther apart. Even under the moonlight, I'm exposed to his gaze.

Completely at his mercy.

That knowledge only heightens the excitement flooding through my system.

His fingers stroke over the delicate skin of my inner thighs until his thumbs can graze the outer lips of my pussy. When he kneads the flesh, I writhe beneath him, silently willing him to caress me. Instead of rushing, he takes his time, toying with me, slowly driving me to the brink.

He rubs a wide circle until his thumbs pause over my lower lips before gently separating them. Cool air rushes over my inner flesh. I'm unable to stifle the moan of impatience growing inside me.

"So fucking pretty." His possessive gaze flicks upward. "And it's mine, right?"

"Yes," I groan. "All for you."

With his fingers still holding me apart, his head dips as he gives my slit a long slow lap with his tongue. I slap a hand to my mouth to stifle the whimper trying to break free.

"Delicious." His warm breath drifts over me as he does it again.

Oh God.

When his teeth scrape against my clit, I nearly come off the towel. His hands tighten around me, holding me firmly in place as he repeats the movement. He nibbles at the tiny bundle of nerves until an orgasm so powerful streaks through me that my muscles tighten, and I scream against the hand clapped over my mouth. Instead of letting up, he teases out every drop of pleasure until my bones turn to jelly, and I stare dazedly up at the brightly lit sky.

I'm still floating on a cloud when I hear the tear of a wrapper, and then Kingsley is moving over my prone body. With his gaze locked on mine, his cock presses against my soaked entrance, nudging my lower lips with his blunt head.

"Tell me you want this, Summer." There's a tautness to his voice as if he won't last much longer.

"I do, I want this." As if to emphasize the words, I tangle my legs around his waist. The motion sends him sliding deeper inside my body. "I want *you*."

He groans as his lips settle over mine. Our tongues mingle as the taste of my arousal explodes in my mouth.

"It's going to hurt," he warns, pushing farther inside.

"I know." A part of me is nervous about the pain he's about to inflict. But I also realize I wouldn't have it any other way. In order for Kingsley to make me his, this needs to happen. He needs to pierce me so that our bodies can be joined.

My breath catches when the head of his cock butts up against the thin membrane of my hymen. With short sharp strokes, he prods it. Our breathing synchronizes as his gaze stays locked on mine.

The way his thickness caresses my inner muscles sends ripples of pleasure throughout my core. I groan and wiggle beneath him, needing more. The feeling continues to build until another orgasm explodes. As I cry out, he withdraws before slamming inside me and forcing his way through the thin barrier. When I scream, his lips seal over mine, swallowing the cry of pain and taking it deep inside his body.

He holds himself impossibly still, allowing me time to adjust to the intrusion. "I need to move," he bites out, his voice whipcord tight. "I have to make you mine."

Yes.

God, yes.

I want that just as much.

Even though pain radiates inside my womb and tears sting my eyes, I need him to take me. With every thrust of his hips, a little more control falls away until his lips lift from mine, and he throws his head back, groaning out his release.

My gaze stays fastened on his face, needing to see the pleasure as it washes over him in heavy waves. It's a heady sensation to realize I'm the one who made him lose control.

Me.

The sharp bite of pain, the sting of his intrusion, was well worth it. I couldn't imagine our joining unfolding any other way. Kingsley marked me in the most primal of ways, and in return, I've done the same.

When he collapses on top of me with a huff, I wrap my arms around his ribs and pull him close. With our bodies locked in intimacy, I've never felt more bonded to another human being.

"Now you belong to me," he whispers harshly against my ear.

"And *you* belong to *me*," I repeat.

And nothing will ever change that.

SUMMER

There is no gradual awakening for me the following morning. One minute, I'm deep in slumber, and the next, I'm being ripped from a dream. My eyelids spring apart, and I stare at the face hovering inches above my own.

"What?" I slur, barely coherent.

"You need to get up," Austin snaps.

I don't think so.

"No," I grumble, eyelids already drooping as I float back into sleep.

All I want to do is roll over and burrow under my blankets until the sun is high in the sky. I'm exhausted. I don't think I've ever felt this tired in my life. I shift my thighs, and a dull ache flares to life between them.

Oh.

A smile curls around the edges of my lips as I remember the way Kingsley made love to me last night. I wanted him to mark me as his, and that's precisely what he did. I have zero regrets about experiencing sex for the first time outside under the brilliance of the stars. It was beautiful and perfect. Exactly the way it was meant to be.

Austin shakes my shoulder, and my gaze flies to him. "Get the fuck up, Summer! It's important!"

Oh, for goodness' sake! Why is he even up? It must be the butt crack of dawn.

"Whatever it is, we can talk about it later," I mumble.

"Hell, no!"

"Why? What's so important?"

I screech when he rips the covers away from my body before

tossing them to the end of the bed. "Mom and Dad were in the study having a meeting with our neighbor. He just left."

I'm about to unload on Austin when his words puncture the grogginess filling my brain.

"*Neighbor?*" I sit up and frown. Last I checked, we weren't on friendly terms with anyone in the subdivision. Not a damn one of them can be bothered to wave when we drive by.

"Kingsley?" My heart skips a beat. Why would he be here, talking to our parents?

My brother's upper lip curls. "No, dumbass. His father."

"Keaton?" My brow furrows as the questions he pelted at me last night flood my consciousness, and the same unease fills me. "Why?"

Something indecipherable flickers in his gaze. "You need to get down there and find out."

And just like that, I'm wide-awake and scrambling from the bed to grab my robe before padding down the stairs to the study. I catch a glimpse of my parents with their heads bent together as they quietly converse. Their gazes jerk to mine as soon as I cross over the threshold. Austin is right behind me, hovering over my shoulder.

"Hi, honey!" Dad greets with a forced exuberance that seems strangely out of place this early in the morning. "Did you sleep well?"

My gaze narrows, darting from one tense expression to the other. Mom has an entire set of luggage under her eyes, and Dad looks like he hasn't slept for a week straight. This is a flashback to how they appeared last night at the party while talking with Keaton.

"Yeah." What little sleep I got. After Kingsley and I had sex, he held me in his arms, and we stared at the dark canvas of the night sky. As cheesy as it sounds, it felt like the stars were shining for us. I pointed out all of my favorite constellations, and a deep contentment like I'd never experienced stole over me as I lay sprawled across his chest.

What we shared last night wasn't just sex.

It was love.

He made *love* to me.

I won't fool myself into believing that I'm madly in love with

Kingsley, but I could definitely get there. The seeds have been sown. All they need to do is flourish and grow.

"We thought you'd sleep later," Mom adds in a strained voice.

The tension filling the study continues to intensify. I don't know what it is, but Austin is right. Something is wrong. What I don't understand is how Keaton fits into the equation.

Yet.

I don't understand it *yet.*

When they remain silent, I ask, "Why was Kingsley's father here?"

A flash of surprise crosses their faces. Neither seems eager to tackle the question. Instead, they glance at each other. A myriad of emotions flickers across their drawn faces. As their silence stretches, I shift restlessly, wrapping my arms around my middle to still the anxiety unfurling inside me like a flower. My nerves stretch taut. I can't take much more of this.

"You need to tell her what's going on," Austin pipes up from behind me.

Dad plows a hand through his thick hair and glances away. "We were actually going to talk with both of you a little later."

"About what?" I ask suspiciously.

"Well..." He pauses, darting his gaze to my mother as if she'll somehow be able to help him muddle through this.

"Say it," Austin snaps. "Tell her what you've done!"

Dad's body jerks at my brother's sharp tone. I've never heard Austin speak to our father in such a disrespectful manner. Sure, he's gotten shitty before, but this is altogether different. There's an undercurrent of disgust and anger weaving its way through his tone.

I wait for Dad to reprimand him. Instead, he ignores Austin, keeping his attention focused on me. "We've come to an agreement with the Rothchilds."

An agreement?

What for?

When he lapses into another silence, I impatiently flick my wrist in a circle, prodding him to continue.

"Remember when we talked about how your great-great-grandfather started the company with Gerald Rothchild?"

I jerk my head into a nod.

Dad clears his throat and shifts in his chair. "I need to fill in some background information so you understand how the arrangement was struck and agreed upon."

Arrangement.

There's something unsettling about the way his lips wrap around that word.

"I wasn't entirely forthcoming with you about what happened with the company. The two men *did* start it together, but after twenty years in business, along with a friendship that had become strained, Herbert decided he wanted sole ownership. Over the years, the company had turned quite a handsome profit, and naturally, Gerald wasn't interested in being bought out. So Herbert, um, went about some nefarious activities to wrestle control away from his partner."

Nefarious activities?

At any other time, such a dramatic description would have me bursting into laughter. Instead, I remain frozen in place as a swarm of butterflies multiplies in my belly.

When he doesn't continue, I prod, "What happened?"

He shrugs. "No one knows for sure, but everyone has their suspicions. The two men attended their long-standing Friday night poker game at a friend's house. Around midnight, Gerald left to return home and was never seen again. Nor was his body ever found. Months after the search, Herbert produced documents showing that Gerald had signed over the company to the Hawthorne family for pennies on the dollar."

When I attempt to gulp down my rising nausea, I realize my mouth has gone bone-dry. Barely am I able to push the question out. "What are you saying, Dad? Do you think your great-grandfather murdered Gerald Rothchild?"

"I don't know." Sadness fills his eyes as he shakes his head. "Do I think there's a high likelihood? Yeah, probably. They were partners for twenty years. Each wanted to take the company in a different direction, and the many disputes led to bad blood. After Gerald disappeared and Herbert produced papers that transferred ownership, the animosity only grew worse. There was a lot of ugly speculation about the Hawthornes."

God.

What the hell kind of people do I have lurking in my family tree? The nefarious kind, that's who.

No wonder Kingsley's family hates us so much. After learning the full story, I can't blame them for it.

"Ever since Gerald disappeared, there has been a rift between the town and the Hawthornes." Dad's voice grows weary as if the burden of our family history weighs heavily on him. "I grew up here, Summer. I know exactly what it was like. And your Grandma Rose didn't help matters." He concedes by adding, "Now, I'm not saying it was entirely her fault. I think the residents treated her poorly while growing up and that skewed her feelings. After she took over the company and moved into a position of power, she wielded her control with an iron fist. It only made them hate her more." He rubs his temples with the tips of his fingers. "It's one reason I left town as soon as I could and never looked back. I didn't want anything to do with the family business."

Holy.

Crap.

I have no words.

A heavy silence blankets the room.

"Why would you think a party could fix this?" I shake my head as it continues to spin. Honestly, I don't know what my parents could do to make the situation better. With the Rothchilds or the residents of Hawthorne who still seem to hate us with the same intensity they did fifty years ago.

His gaze flickers away, almost as if he's unable to hold my eyes. "We never expected the party to fix everything. It was never meant to be anything more than a baby step in the right direction."

I'm not even sure if it was that. I snuck out early. It's always possible that the party ended better than it started. But like he said, it was a baby step. There has to be more to the plan than a cocktail party.

"So what are we going to do? How can we make up for what happened in the past?" I can't imagine my parents spending the rest of their lives in this godforsaken town if nothing changes. Sadder than that, I can't blame these people for how they feel about us. The Hawthorne name is stamped on everything.

The company.

The school.

The town.

It's a constant reminder of what we stole from the Rothchild family and the tyranny that later followed. The whole situation makes me sick to my stomach.

Dad gives me a tight smile. "It's a relief to hear that you're willing to help rectify the past mistakes that have been made."

Is he crazy?

"Of course, I do!" Although I have no idea how we can rebrand the family name. We would have to do something big enough for the entire town to view us in a different light. A better light. Like...give away a certain percentage of our profits every year or set up a foundation that directly benefits the people in town. Maybe create an endowment or a scholarship fund for kids to attend college. Those are definitely ideas to consider, but none seem splashy enough to make an actual difference and turn the tide against our family.

"Since I've taken over the business," Dad says, interrupting my thoughts, "I've spent a lot of time going through old family records, trying to piece together all the historical documents so we have an accurate picture of the past." He waves his hand as he rattles off information. "What the company was worth when Gerald went missing verses what Herbert paid to the family. What were the profit margins each year when it was owned solely by the Hawthornes. Inflation needs to be factored into the equation." He pauses as his gaze shifts from me to my brother and then back again. "The Rothchilds have been cheated out of hundreds of millions of dollars first from the sale of the company and then in yearly profits."

My jaw drops.

"There's no way we can repay that," Austin grunts.

I have to agree with my brother. I'm no chief financial officer, but even I realize that eighty years of lost profits adds up to be an astronomical amount.

Dad nods. "Unfortunately, you're right. The interest alone would bankrupt us."

My head swims with the effort of trying to conceptualize such a number. All this happened because Herbert Hawthorne was a greedy bastard who wanted everything for himself.

"There's one last piece you need to know about," Dad continues.

Good Lord, there's more?

"Apparently, Grandma Rose had a coming to Jesus moment before she died."

My brows furrow in confusion.

A coming to what?

"She decided to make amends for the past. For what her grandfather stole from the Rothchilds."

Finally, a bit of good news.

"A month before my mother died, she set up a meeting with Keaton and shared all the information she had been privy to. Lawyers were involved, and she wrote out a very detailed account of what her grandfather did and then signed an affidavit so it would stand up in a court of law if that became necessary."

A prickle of unease settles deep inside me. Where the hell is he going with this?

"So, she did a good thing, right?" My breath becomes trapped in my lungs as I try to process all of this newly gleaned information.

Dad shakes his head before blowing out a lengthy breath. "I suppose it's good for the Rothchilds. Keaton now has the leverage to legally take the company from us. With all the supporting documents, compliments of Grandma Rose, he can prove that the company was stolen from his family and we'll be left with nothing. Actually, it'll be much worse than that because if he wins, which I assume he will from everything I've looked at, he'll sue us for interest that was lost on company profits for the past eighty years."

What!

How could Grandma Rose do this to us? Why would she deliberately try to ruin our family?

And here I'd thought it was Kingsley trying to mindfuck me. Turns out it was Grandma Rose playing games from beyond the grave. "Is there anything we can do to prevent Keaton from taking us to court?"

"We have one avenue that allows us to avoid losing the company and drowning in debt."

Thank fuck.

When Dad remains silent, Austin mutters, "Tell her."

I glance back at my brother. By the pinched expression he's wearing, I realize he knows what's coming and doesn't like it.

"Tell her what you did!" he shouts.

My father flinches before saying in halting tones, "Keaton will drop the lawsuit if you agree to marry his son."

For a heartbeat, I stare. It's as if all the oxygen has been sucked out of the room, and I can't breathe.

This is a joke, right?

I wait for someone to chuckle. Instead, the tension continues to escalate until high-pitched laughter fills the air. It takes a moment to realize that it's coming from me.

"That's not funny," I croak.

Dad's solemn expression never falters, which only scares me more. "It wasn't meant to be."

"Why would he want that?" It feels as if I'm being strangled from the inside out. "It doesn't make sense. Why would he want his son to marry the great-great-granddaughter of the man who probably murdered his great-grandfather and stole his legacy?"

Dad's shoulders slump. "It's his way of extracting a pound of flesh. The idea is when you and Kingsley have children, it'll be a mix of both our blood, and no one will be able to steal anything from them again."

A wave of shock slides through me.

Marriage?

Children?

With Kingsley?

Are these people insane? I'm an eighteen-year-old girl in her senior year of high school! How can I be expected to get married? I've barely had a boyfriend. In fact, I've only slept with—

Kingsley.

"Sweetie?" Mom clears her throat, and for the first time since this horrific conversation began, my gaze shifts to her. She's been so quiet that I almost forgot she was sitting beside Dad. "I know this is a shock," she bites her lower lip and glances away, "but we need you to do this. Everything we had in Chicago is gone. The house, our jobs, the little bit of savings we had in the bank. It's all gone. What your grandmother left us is tied up in the house and company. With the provisions she added to the will, we can't sell anything for ten years. Even if we wanted to, we couldn't give the company to Keaton. All the proceeds would revert to charity." Her lips twist with bitterness. "It was your grandmother's ultimate parting gift to us. But," she gulps, forcing out the rest in a rush, "as long as you agree to marry Kingsley, the Hawthornes retain ownership of the company and continue to split the profits."

What the fuck?

That's so messed up. How is any of this real? This isn't the eighteen hundreds. They can't marry me off to save themselves.

I shake my head to clear it of the black haze attempting to press in at the edges. I keep expecting them to burst into laughter and scream *—got you! Just kidding*. When they remain sickeningly silent, I realize that isn't going to happen.

"Are you *really* asking me to do this?" I claw at my throat, feeling light-headed.

"I'm sorry," Dad mumbles. "If there was another way..."

"Isn't there?" It takes effort to blink back the tears that prick my eyes. "Isn't there *something* else that can be done?"

"No, the company lawyers have been poring over both the will and the affidavit your grandmother signed with a fine-tooth comb. They're both ironclad. You either marry Kingsley, or Keaton takes the company and bankrupts us. That's the choice."

As the reality of his words sink in, my knees buckle, and I collapse. Austin catches me with a grunt, his arms locking around my chest to hold me up.

This is lunacy. They can't seriously be asking me to marry someone I barely know. When it comes down to it, I'm a kid. My entire life is stretched out ahead of me. I've only begun to work on my applications for...

"What about college?" Am I supposed to give up all my dreams?

"Of course, you'll still go," Dad says hastily.

"But it'll need to be local," Mom adds in a quiet voice.

"You and Kingsley will decide on a school, and that's where you'll attend." Dad twists his hands together in front of him, barely able to make eye contact.

"*Oh my God, you're marrying me off right now?*" A shriek builds in my chest as the walls of the study press in on me.

"No," Dad forces out a brittle laugh, "nothing will happen for a while. You're still in high school."

Well, thank fuck for that.

"*When?*" I push out the question as all of this information whips through my head, making it impossible to think. My reality no longer feels real. Somehow, I've become trapped in a terrifying nightmare.

"Well," he clears his throat, "the terms of the agreement state that it would be a suitable time for you to marry after freshman year of college."

"Oh," I snap, jerking out of my brother's hold, "is that what *you all* decided?" I drive my fingers through the wild tangle of my hair as I pace the width of the study before stopping in front of the window to stare out sightlessly. "I can't believe you've bargained away my future!"

"Honey—"

"No!" A burst of fury explodes inside me as I spin toward my parents. "What you've done is sold me to save yourselves!" Tears sting my eyes. This is so much more than a betrayal. I'll never be able to trust them again.

"Will it really be so bad?" Mom asks. "We met Kingsley last night, and he seems like a lovely boy."

I'm slammed with the realization that he knew about this.

How could he not?

But when? When did he find out?

Has he known the entire time?

God, it really was *all* a mindfuck. I'm so stupid for believing anything that came out of his mouth.

His words crash through my head.

You belong to me.

Once you're mine, I will never let you go.

Bile churns in my gut. At any moment, I'm going to be sick.

He used me.

Just like my parents are using me.

It's all part of the same elaborate scheme.

I stare blindly at my parents.

There are no more words, only emptiness.

Unable to bear the sight of them, I leave the study and head to the staircase.

Like a kaleidoscope, my world has shifted. Only this time, there's no way to make it right again.

Darkness blankets the night as I jog up the narrow staircase to the balcony that juts off the back of the Hawthorne house and leads to Summer's room.

What I need right now is to see her.

To hold her in my arms.

Fuck.

All I could think about today was burying myself deep inside her body. A tidal wave of need crashes over me as I remember how amazing last night felt. In a strange way, it had been like coming home. There was a rightness to the moment that I couldn't have anticipated or explained. As if I'd found something I hadn't realized was missing. Since those thoughts hadn't been entirely comfortable, I'd pushed them away and focused on the physicalness of the act.

The way her body felt wrapped around mine, milking every drop from my cock. Now that I've had a taste of her, I'm insatiable with the need for more. I've slept with my fair share of girls over the years, but nothing compares to being buried deep inside Summer's tight pussy.

Nothing.

It was like having sex for the first time all over again. Even the thought of it is enough to have my dick stiffening. I walked around most of the day with a boner. Now that night has fallen, I can finally see her. We can talk about the arrangement openly and make plans for our future. We can hash shit out between the two of us.

Fuck our parents.

We'll make up our own rules.

Once my feet hit the balcony, I make a beeline for the door, hoping she's left it unlocked. If I need to remove the screen and crawl through the damn window, I'll do it. Nothing and nobody will keep me away from her. It's exactly like I told Summer last night. Now she belongs to me.

It's a relief when the handle turns easily. I pull open the door before stepping inside the darkened room. I like the thought of sneaking in and watching her sleep. She's so fucking beautiful with that mass of ebony-colored hair that tumbles around her shoulders and down her back. I won't lie, I love when she pulls it back into a ponytail. There's no better feeling than wrapping my fingers around the thick length and tugging it so her chin is tipped, and she has no other choice but to stare at me. Instead of fear leaping to life in her eyes, heat fills them.

The first time I pinned her against the wall, I watched both the confusion and lust swirl through her dark depths. It's nothing short of thrilling to stoke that kind of arousal to life in someone. Her desire has been a pleasant surprise. One I can't get enough of.

Luckily, I won't have to.

When my father proposed the idea of marrying Summer, I thought he was out of his mind. You better believe I told him to take that idea and shove it up his ass. All the money in the world isn't worth tying myself to a girl I have zero interest in. I don't give a shit about Hawthorne Industries. Driving her away had been the only thought in my head, but that backfired. The more time I spent with Summer, the more obsessed I became. And now that I've had a real taste of her, I can't imagine not having her. And I sure as shit can't imagine another guy laying his hands on her. I made her mine last night, and there's not a damn thing anyone can do to change that.

Not even Summer.

She had a choice in the matter. Perhaps I should have laid it all out so she would understand exactly what she was agreeing to, but by then, it didn't matter. That girl was always going to be mine. When it comes down to it, Summer chose me of her own free will. Maybe the situation will end up being more than she bargained for, but that no longer matters.

I hope she can reconcile herself to that. Or maybe I'll have to remind her of it. Over and over again. My lips quirk at the idea of fucking her into submission.

The room is swathed in blackness as I creep toward the bed.

Know what the first thing we're going to do will be?

Get her on the pill so I don't have to wear a condom. I don't want anything coming between us. Not even a thin layer of latex. I want to feel her heat against my bare cock.

I'm halfway to her bed, thinking about how amazing it will feel to sink inside her warmth when the overhead light flicks on, illuminating the room. Blinded, I blink as my eyes adjust to the unexpected brightness. My gaze falls to the queen-sized bed only to find it empty.

The bed is neatly made as if—

"She's gone."

I swing toward the deep voice only to find Austin lounging against the doorframe with his arms crossed over his chest. Green sparks of anger fly from his eyes. I brace myself for an attack. That motherfucker has a lot of rage brewing inside him. It's easy to recognize a kindred spirit.

"Where is she?"

His lips curve into a smirk. "Nowhere you'll find her."

My hands tighten into fists as I take a menacing step toward Austin, ready to beat the piss out of the guy if I have to. No one is going to keep me away from Summer.

Including her own flesh and blood.

"Don't fucking play games with me," I growl, advancing toward him.

"Maybe you should talk to your pops. I'm sure he would be more than happy to fill—"

Before Austin finishes the sentence, I'm on him. My fingers close around the collar of his T-shirt as I slam him against the doorframe. *"Where the fuck is she?"*

A ghost of a smile slithers across his lips. I never realized it before, but Austin and I are roughly the same height and build. Unlike most people at Hawthorne Prep, he's not intimidated by me. At that moment, I sense the same kind of deep-seated anger I've always felt swirling around inside me.

"You might be surprised by this, but my sister wasn't nearly as delighted about the prospect of marrying you as everyone thought she would be." He laughs as I press my hands against his throat, slowly cutting off his air supply. "It was the opposite, actually. Summer has plans for the future, and guess what, asshole? They don't include you."

"It no longer matters what she wants," I bite out as hot licks of rage wash over me. "She's mine, and I want her back." I press my weight against him. *"Now!"*

Unfazed by my fury, Austin continues to grin. "Good luck with that, man."

I press my fingers into his windpipe before releasing him with a frustrated growl. As much as I'd like to beat the shit out of Summer's twin, it won't endear me to her. More like the opposite, and I can't afford to piss her off anymore than she already is.

"This isn't over." Dismissing him, I swing around and stalk toward the screen door.

"True that. I have the feeling it's only beginning." He chuckles darkly.

He couldn't be more fucking right.

SUMMER

33

A heavy weight descends, and I wake with a start. Before I'm able to get my bearings and figure out what's happening, my arms are dragged above my head and pinned against the plush ivory fabric covering the headboard.

"Did you really think you could run from me?" a familiar voice growls against my ear, sending a cascade of shivers down my spine.

Actually, I did. Not forever, but at least for a few days.

What I didn't expect was for him to find me hiding out at his house on Lake Michigan. After my parents sprung the news on me, I needed time to think. At first, I had shut myself away in my room, refusing to speak with anyone. Dad finally knocked on the door and said that Keaton had offered their vacation home if I wanted to escape for a while. Even though I had been reluctant to accept the offer, the need to be alone outweighed any of my protests.

So I packed a bag, threw it in the trunk of the G-wagon, and took off midafternoon.

Since there isn't school on Monday or Tuesday because of the holiday weekend, my parents were quick to suggest I extend my stay for the entire week. This is the first time they've ever encouraged me to miss my classes. Both believe strongly in the power of education being the springboard to my future. Guess that tells you what they think my future now holds.

I blink the sleep out of my eyes and stare up at a pissed-off Kingsley.

Well, guess what?

I'm as angry as he is. Maybe more so. He can take a flying leap for all I care.

With a burst of strength, I struggle against the punishing hold he has on my wrists. Even though it's futile, I attempt to buck him off my chest where he sits, pinning me to the mattress with his weight. He doesn't budge an inch. The guy outweighs me by a solid hundred pounds. There's no way I'm going anywhere until he's ready to release me.

"How did you find me?" I growl.

"I tracked your phone," he admits casually as if that kind of stalker behavior is no big deal.

"What?" My movements still as I process his words. "How the hell did you do that?"

Silvery moonlight filters in through the window, illuminating the smirk as it settles across his handsome face. "That's for me to know and you never to find out."

Damn him!

Frustration floods through me, and it renews my energy to dislodge him. *"I hate you,"* I bite out. But the sad truth is that I don't hate Kingsley. Maybe I want to, but I don't. Not yet, at least.

His face dips to mine before he bites my lower lip, sucking the fullness into his mouth before releasing it with a soft pop. "You don't hate me, Summer."

"I do." I gulp in a breath. "You lied to me!" It was all a game.

"Maybe it started out as a lie, but that's not how it ended."

"More lies," I whisper brokenly, twisting my head away from him. "After this, there's no way I'll ever be able to trust you."

Instead of answering, his teeth scrape against the curve of my jaw before he peppers soft kisses along the delicate column of my throat. An unwanted tremor slides through me.

"Stop." How can I be so furious with him yet crave his touch like it's the very breath needed for survival? It's so fucked up.

"Give me one good reason I should stop." Even though his hands continue to shackle my wrists, he moves farther down my body.

"Because..." My voice trails off on a whimper as his lips slide over my bare chest.

When I had arrived earlier, the beach house had been closed up and stuffy, so I'd opened the windows, wanting to feel the fresh breeze and enjoy the sound of the lake crashing against the shoreline. Since the evening had stayed warm and I was alone in the house, I'd decided to forgo pajamas. There's something delicious about the feel of silky sheets against your naked body.

That choice has now come back to haunt me.

A groan leaves his lips as his mouth closes around my nipple before sucking it deep into the warmth of his mouth.

Gahhhhh!

A war erupts inside me. While my brain cries out that this is wrong, my body vehemently disagrees. And it's my body that is winning out as a hot flood of arousal settles in my core. Within a handful of minutes, I'm arching beneath him, restless for more contact.

When he lifts his mouth from me, a reluctant whimper of protest leaves my lips. God, but I hate myself for it. More than that, I hate him for breaking through my defenses so easily. I should be stronger than this. I should be able to resist him.

"How much could you hate me if you ended up in my bed?"

It takes a moment for the sexual haze to clear and his words to sink fully into my brain. Heat stings my cheeks because he's right. I *am* in his bed. And I can't say that it was an accident or coincidence either. Maybe when I walked into the house and looked for a room to stay in, I didn't immediately realize where I'd ended up. But the moment I looked around, I knew it was Kingsley's space. His stamp had been all over the décor.

It wasn't a conscious decision on my part, but being close to him settled something deep inside me. I'd wanted to sleep in the place he had laid his head. And part of me wanted to strip down and enjoy the feel of his sheets sliding across my body.

I never expected him to find out. It was going to be my little secret.

When I remain silent, he nips at my other breast. As soon as I yelp, he laves the flat of his tongue over the throbbing peak, soothing the ache he created.

"Answer the question."

When I press my lips together and try to raise my knee to his groin, he bites me again. Harder this time before drawing the bud so far into his mouth that it feels as if he will never release me. I cry out as the powerful tug of his lips slices straight to my center before bursting into flames.

Damn him!

Damn him!

Damn him!

When he finally lifts his head and releases me, I'm nothing more than a panting, writhing mess beneath him. Worse than that, my pussy is soaked with the need he has all too easily stirred to life.

"You're mine now, and nothing will change that," he growls.

I inhale a shuddering breath and try to settle everything racing madly around inside. I've never felt so conflicted in my life. A part of me desires his possession. *That needs it.* But another piece wants him to let me go and live my life. I have no idea if there's a way to reconcile these opposing views.

Kingsley slides up my body until his lips can hover over mine without ever touching them. All I'd have to do is lift my head a fraction off the pillow, and I could feel the suppleness of them stroking over me. It would be all too easy to give in to the hot licks of arousal that scorch me from the inside out.

Instead, I force myself to say, "I need time."

His mouth continues to ghost over mine until the arousal is so painful that it feels like something is trying to claw its way out of me.

How can I crave him so much?

"Please," I whimper, knowing it's only a matter of time before I cave and spread my legs wide for him.

"All right."

With that, he releases me, his weight lifting as he rolls off the side of the bed. The breath rushes from my lungs as a strange mixture of regret and relief swirls through me.

Wait, is he leaving?

It takes everything I have inside to keep my lips pressed together so the question stays buried where it belongs. Instead of walking out of the bedroom, he strips off his T-shirt and athletic shorts until he's standing before me in nothing more than black boxer briefs. The light that filters in from the windows provides enough illumination for my hungry gaze to lick over him. A shiver slides through me when I realize that he's purposely standing still, allowing me to eat him up with my eyes.

Damn, but he's gorgeous.

And mine.

No!

Dislodging the possessive thought isn't as easy as it should be. With one fluid motion, he shoves the boxers down his hips and thighs until the material puddles around his feet. My gaze drops to his thick erection, and my breath stalls as another wave of need crashes over me, threatening to suck me under.

Kingsley saunters to the bed before sliding beneath the sheets. His hands wrap around my body, dragging me into his arms until my naked flesh is pressed against his. It occurs to me that this is the first time I've seen him naked. Another sharp punch of arousal hits me, making my center throb.

He feathers a kiss against my forehead as his arms band around me. We're so close that the tips of my breasts are pressed against the steely strength of his chest. I'm so tempted to slide my body against him until his hard muscles align with my softer curves. Being naked in bed with Kingsley should feel foreign and strange. I can't explain why it doesn't.

"Stop squirming," his voice rumbles against my ear. "You're making it difficult not to give us what we both want."

As much as I would love to deny his words, I can't. Even though I know it's wrong, I want him buried deep inside me. I want that same feeling of completion I experienced in his arms last night. It was like two parts of the same whole finally coming together. As a twin, I understand that need better than most. What I didn't expect was to feel it with Kingsley.

The warning in his voice should be enough to stop me from

moving against the erection wedged between our bellies. All I'd have to do is arch, and he would slip inside my heat.

With a growl of frustration, Kingsley's fingers bite into my flesh as he flips me around until I'm no longer facing him. He settles against my back, spooning me from behind. His arm snakes around me, cupping my breast. With his thick cock pressed insistently against my backside, a groan slips free as I stretch against him. The tip of his dick paints moisture across my skin as his fingers drift from my breast, over my belly, before sinking between my legs.

As soon as the blunt tips of his fingers separate my already drenched lips, I moan and spread them wide in silent invitation.

"Is this what you want?" He pumps his fingers deep inside me before dragging them out and rimming the entrance. "Answer me."

"*Yes.*"

That one word is all it takes to have him thrusting back inside before circling my clit, which is already pulsing with need. The orgasm streaks through my body before I realize it's happening. I cry out, tightening in his arms. His teeth sink into the back of my neck the entire time, and somehow, that only makes the storm raging inside me more powerful.

A contented sigh is expelled as my body relaxes into the soft mattress. I wait for him to gloat over how weak I am, but all he says is, "Go to bed. We'll talk in the morning."

His hand drifts back to cup my breast as he drops a kiss on my shoulder, pulling me so tightly against him that I have no idea where he ends, and I begin.

Even with the confusion spinning inside me, my eyelids droop, and before I know it, I'm floating off to sleep.

SUMMER

34

I wake to a steady stream of sunlight pouring over me, illuminating the back of my eyelids. Unable to stay submerged any longer, my lashes flutter, and I blink, attempting to find my bearings. For a sliver of time, I don't remember where I am. I'm surrounded by dark blue walls and heavy white furniture. There's nothing familiar about this space. Panic sweeps over me as the memories from yesterday come rushing back. I remember throwing a bag in the SUV and taking off for the Rothchild family beach house in Door County.

This is Kingsley's room, and I'm in his bed. I glance at the other side of the mattress as the sound of crashing waves fills my ears.

Empty.

It couldn't have been a dream, right?

My fingers brush across my nipples, and a dull ache flares to life before settling between my thighs.

Definitely not a dream.

Is he still here? Or did he take off?

I roll from the bed and pause as my gaze lands on the black suitcase parked next to mine. Relief settles in my chest at the knowledge that he didn't leave. Still naked, I walk to my bag and rummage through the contents before grabbing my robe. With the silky material belted securely around my body, I go in search of him, moving steadily through the house, peeking in all the rooms. Even though there's an air of stillness to the place, I sense his presence and know he's near.

It's a peculiar sensation to be so connected to another human being other than Austin. It should disturb me.

On bare feet, I pad through the first-floor hallway. I don't stop to study the pictures that line the walls before arriving in the spacious kitchen. Splashes of gray and blue are everywhere. There is an ocean of white granite counters, dark hardwoods, and stainless-steel appliances. My gaze settles on a red mug sitting next to a fancy machine that looks like something you would find in a high-end coffee shop. I gravitate to the mug before picking it up and staring at the dark brew inside. Steam rises as I lift it to my lips and take a tentative sip. A sigh of pleasure escapes as the first jolt of much-needed caffeine hits my system. As I take another drink, my gaze travels around the adjoining family room, absorbing all the little details I was too upset to notice yesterday. The white shiplap walls, cozy white couches with fluffy indigo pillows that are the identical shade as the curtains.

The sliding glass door that leads outside has been left open, allowing the breeze to waft through the kitchen. With my mug in hand, I gravitate toward the sprawling deck that stretches across the width of the house and faces the water. It's a million-dollar view that's worth every penny.

With nervous fingers, I push open the screen door and step outside. Kingsley is parked at a table, wearing nothing more than black boxer briefs. His muscular legs are stretched out as his heels rest on the chair across from him. In silence, he surveys the deep blue water as the wind whips through his hair, ruffling it. I'm so tempted to reach out and stroke my fingers through the dark strands. To push them away from his face. Every bit of flesh on display is a deep sun-kissed color from months spent outside. There aren't any visible T-shirt lines in sight. Even in repose, his muscles are sharp and defined as if they've been chiseled from marble.

A punch of arousal hits me in the gut before sinking lower.

Kingsley picks up the mug from the table and raises it to his lips before taking a sip and setting it down again. Only then do his eyes flick to mine. "How did you sleep?"

I blink.

I ran away because I'm now promised to him in marriage, and that's all he has to say?

A gurgle of laughter falls from my lips as I shake my head at the absurdity of the situation we now find ourselves in. A crooked smile lifts his lips, and at that moment, he resembles the boy I met on this very beach, and it pains my heart. Does that boy even exist?

"Fine," I say, sweeping away those thoughts. I'm unwilling to admit just how well I slept in his arms.

He nods but doesn't ask any more questions. Soundlessly, I search his gaze, surprised to see the somberness that now fills it.

Arrogance.

Anger.

Hatred.

Lust.

I've experienced a range of emotions from him, but never that one.

What does it mean?

Kingsley rips his gaze from mine before his attention is drawn to the water. "I thought we could take the boat out today." He pauses before tacking on, "And talk."

I busy my fingers by taking another sip of coffee before setting the mug on the table and nodding, surprised by how much the thought of spending time alone with him on the lake pleases me. "All right."

He rises from his chair, straightening to his full height. Not wanting him to notice my interest, I avert my gaze. It isn't long before my focus is pulled back to him. He has a gorgeous body, and I'm fascinated by it. The need to explore him pounds through me.

"We can shower and go." His voice grows deeper. "We'll spend the entire day on the water if that's what you want."

I clear my throat and try to concentrate on the conversation, but it's difficult. "Okay."

My breath catches when he steps closer, invading my personal space. It happens so quickly that I remain rooted in place, unable to move as he lowers his mouth to my ear.

"You asked me last night for time, and I'm trying to give it to you, but when you stand there, eating me up with your eyes, you make it awfully difficult." He pulls back enough for his gaze to fasten on mine. "Now, are you ready to go inside?"

"Yes." My voice comes out sounding more like a squeak.

Kingsley snakes his arm around my waist, tugging me through the sliding door until we're once again in the luxuriously appointed living area. I try to distract myself from the need that has throbbed to life between my thighs by taking in all the finishing touches. The silver candlesticks on the glass end table. The stacked stone fireplace that reaches the ceiling. This might be a beach house, but my guess is that a professional interior designer decorated it. The color schemes, the furniture, the décor. It all flows perfectly. As we walk toward the kitchen, my gaze falls on a family photo framed in silver on the credenza.

My footsteps falter as I inspect the picture.

"What's wrong?"

I glance from the framed photo to Kingsley. "Who's the girl with you?" She looks like a female version of him. Same mahogany-colored hair and eyes. Same high cheekbones and smile.

"That's Harlow, my younger sister."

My head whips toward him as my eyes widen. "You have a sister?" I had assumed Kingsley was an only child. My gaze settles on the other female in the photo. A pretty blonde. Is that his mother? It's not the same woman who answered the door when I tried to say goodbye in June.

"Yup." One corner of his mouth hitches. "Guess you need to ask more questions."

Huh. Maybe I do. My mind cartwheels as I process this new bit of information. Before I know it, we're back in the same place I woke up this morning.

He nods toward the adjoining room. "Why don't you start the shower."

Not questioning the instruction, I step into the bathroom. It's as luxurious as the rest of the house. Clearly, no expense was spared when they remodeled. I walk inside the gray-tiled marble shower that's spacious enough for four people and turn the handle before moving back and waiting for the glass enclosure to steam. With a flick of my fingers, the belt loosens from around my waist, and the silky robe slips off my shoulders before puddling on the floor. I test the water with my fingers before shifting to stand under the hot spray. My eyelids drift shut as water rains down on me from above as well as from the jets that line the interior walls.

Mmm, that feels so good.

As my muscles loosen, Kingsley steps into the shower with me.

"What are you doing?" My eyes fly open, and I'm helpless to stop my gaze from wandering over his naked form. Holy hell, but he's beautiful. Everything about him is thick and muscular.

Everything.

"Showering." A devilish smile curves his lips as he grabs the bottle of liquid soap, squirting a dollop onto his palm before rubbing his hands together. He steps behind me, standing so close that his erection nudges my ass cheeks. My breath catches when his arms slide around my ribs, his soapy hands cupping my breasts, lathering them up. He kneads the soft flesh, pulling at the nipples until they stiffen beneath his fingers.

"You asked me to give you time, and I will," he whispers against my ear. "But that doesn't mean I'll stop touching you. What it means is that you don't get my cock until you're mine."

A groan slides from my parted lips as my head lolls back, resting against the solid wall of his chest. It doesn't take long for his hands to glide lower and for me to keen out an orgasm.

SUMMER

35

I raise my face to the sun as Kingsley navigates the boat out of the harbor. It's a holiday weekend, and the marina is crowded with people who have the same idea. I can't blame them. Everyone is trying to enjoy one of the last three-day weekends that can be spent on the lake before the weather turns chilly.

The wind does its best to whip my hair. It was a smart move on my part to weave the long strands into two thick braids that fall down my back. I settle against the plush cushion on the bench and draw my legs up to my chest before banding my arms around them. My gaze floats over the vast openness of the deep blue water as the speedboat cuts through the waves. The motion is soothing and pretty soon I find myself lost in the tangle of my thoughts.

I have a decision to make.

When my parents sprung this *arrangement* on me yesterday, I was livid. How could they expect me to be on board with such a crazy plan? To blindly accept that I would lose all my freedom, all of my choices so the company could remain in our family? Did they really expect that I would willingly accept my fate as a sacrificial lamb?

They sent me here, hoping that I would come to terms with the new direction my life had swerved in after a couple of days to myself. Yesterday, while sitting on the beach and sifting my fingers through the warm sand, I had contemplated the idea of running away and disappearing. But how is that a viable solution when I don't even have a high school degree? How could I get a job and support myself? Or go to college?

I couldn't.

Now Kingsley is at the beach, dead set on destroying my solitude and convincing me to accept my fate. We have yet to discuss the situation, and already, I'm wavering. His mere presence has me yearning for other things. Things I shouldn't want. A future that isn't in my best interest.

My gaze settles on the dark-haired boy as he masterfully drives the boat over the waves.

Masterful.

That's an excellent way to describe Kingsley. It's shameful to realize how easily he's mastered my body.

And manipulated me?

That's what I need to figure out.

Guess you need to ask more questions.

He's not wrong.

When he anchors the boat about a quarter mile from shore, I remind myself to stay focused. Now isn't the time to get distracted. My mouth dries, and I have to repeat the mantra when he pulls the T-shirt over his head and discards it.

Already I can tell this outing was a terrible idea.

"Summer?"

I jerk out of those thoughts. "What?"

He nods toward the front of the boat. "Want to talk?"

Yes. Talking is good. We need to get everything straightened out between us.

I nod and rise from the bench before stripping off my cover-up. Even from behind the aviators that shield his eyes, the heat of his gaze strokes over me. With my back to him, I bend over, digging around in my bag.

A rough groan leaves his lips.

Good.

Let him see what no longer belongs to him. I clear the smile from my face before straightening and turning around with a plush beach towel in my hands.

"Ready when you are," I say sweetly, brushing past him.

His fingers wrap around my wrist, halting me in my tracks. My eyes widen as he yanks me to him.

"Do you really want to play with fire?" His voice is nothing more than a deep growl that arrows straight to my core before exploding like a firework.

When I say nothing, a wicked grin tugs at the corners of his lips, and my breath slowly leaks from my lungs. Playing games with Kingsley isn't smart. He has the annoying habit of always winning.

When his grip loosens, I scamper to the front of the boat. Nervous energy hums beneath my skin, unleashing a horde of conflicted emotions inside me. Once settled on the towel, I watch him cautiously from the corner of my eye as he drops beside me.

"Turn over, and I'll rub you down."

Hell no!

When I shake my head, he says, "Nonnegotiable."

I press my lips together and flip over onto my front before resting the side of my head against my stacked hands. As he shifts closer, the heat of his body drifts over me, and I squeeze my eyes tight, needing to block out how good his nearness feels.

He picks up one thick braid before doing the same to the other. I expect him to sweep them aside so they're out of the way, but that's not what he does. My eyes snap open as he carefully wraps the length of my hair around his hand until it gently tugs at my scalp, and I have no choice but to lift my head and meet his gaze.

Only when he has my full attention does he say, "You need to understand that I can be gentle, like when I licked your pussy and took your virginity." A whimper leaves my lips as he continues to wind my braids around his palm so I have to arch my neck and upper back. "Or I can be forceful." Almost tenderly, he brushes his lips against mine as I strain toward him. "I know you like it both ways, and I enjoy giving it to you. You might not believe this, but we're the same. A perfect match."

I whimper as his grip tightens, and his mouth grazes the column of my throat. As soon as his hold loosens, my head drops to the towel.

I pant and shake as arousal crashes through me. He sweeps my braids to the side before casually dropping a kiss against my shoulder like he didn't just ignite an inferno in my bikini bottoms.

I draw in an unsteady breath but keep my lips pressed together when he tugs the string at my neck and then the one in the middle of my back before pushing the ties aside, leaving the length of my spine completely exposed. Not that my bikini top offered much in the way of protection, but without it, I feel strangely defenseless.

And with this boy, that's exactly where I always find myself.

At his mercy.

Kingsley starts at the top of my shoulders, kneading them, working his thumbs deep into the tissue before moving lower. Every once in a while, his touch vanishes, and I hear the shake of the bottle before the warmth of his hands returns to my skin. The way he touches me is both calming and seductive at the same time. It doesn't take long before my body is sinking into the towel, relaxing beneath the movement of his fingers.

When he reaches the soft globes of my ass, he pulls and kneads the muscles. Another bolt of excitement slams into me as I recall the way he touched me the day I played hooky. A groan leaves my lips before I can stop it.

"Feel good?" he asks. The scrape of his voice swirls around me, only heightening the desire that rushes through me.

"Yes." Dangerously good.

His teeth sink into my warm flesh, setting off another burst of arousal deep in my core. I hold my breath, wondering if he'll pull the bottoms aside and touch me the same way. As taboo as it was, I loved it. Disappointment courses through me when his hands drift lower, stroking lotion onto the back of my legs until he arrives at my feet.

He gives my ass a light slap. "All done with your backside, flip over."

I am so ridiculously turned on right now that I no longer care if I'm practically naked in front of him. I twist onto my back so that the sun's rays hit my front. His gaze wanders over the length of me before he grabs the lotion and squirts a drop onto his palm before rubbing his hands together. My thighs clench as I watch him from behind my sunglasses.

He starts with one arm before moving to the other, kneading my flesh until I'm once again limp beneath his touch. As his fingers stroke along my collarbone, my heartbeat picks up speed, waiting for him to play with my breasts. They ache for the contact. I bow my back as his fingers dance along my rib cage, but he ignores the silent invitation. Instead, he grabs more lotion and works it deep into the tissue of my belly. Discontentment grows as I writhe beneath him, unable to stand another moment of this torment. It's all I can do not to scream out my frustration.

When a chuckle slides from his curved lips, I realize that all of this sweet torture is intentional. He's deliberately trying to drive me over the edge. His mouth dips to my breast as he presses a chaste kiss against the erect tip. Then he moves to the other side and does the same.

"Kingsley," I whimper, shifting restlessly, *"please."*

"What's wrong, baby girl?"

"I need—"

"I know exactly what you need, but a conversation is in order." There's a pause. "It seemed prudent to remind you of what you're intent on throwing away."

I groan, raising my hands before plucking at my own nipples with my fingers. If he won't touch me, then I'll touch myself.

Screw him.

Kingsley growls, knocking my fingers away as his lips capture one stiff peak before sucking it deep into his mouth as his fingers strum the other tight bud. When I can't stand another moment, he releases my breast before giving the same attention to the other side.

Hot licks of desire rush through every cell of my body as he lifts his head. Then he picks up the bottle of lotion before squirting a drop directly onto my puckered tip. The coolness of the lotion on my hot flesh makes me gasp. He does the same to its twin before allowing the cool cream to sit as I shift beneath his gaze. I become ridiculously aware of the lotion until it's all I can focus on. As I'm about to come out of my skin, Kingsley smooths the thick substance around my nipples before caressing it into my aureoles. After it's been absorbed, he adds more until my breasts are completely covered with sunblock. His fingers pluck at my nipples before giving them a gentle tweak.

"I need to finish your legs."

He massages the muscles of my thighs, stroking over my calves, before moving on to my ankles. By the time he's done, I'm a sexually frustrated noodle.

He presses a kiss against my mouth. "Ready to talk?"

Not really.

I nod. Allowing him to touch me was a bad idea. All I can focus on is the need coursing through me and how damn good it would feel to have him buried deep inside my body.

My gaze roams over him, and the urge to caress all those well-defined muscles pounds through me. "Want me to return the favor?"

He shakes his head as his gaze drops to my naked breasts. "Nope. If you lay your hands on me, I'll have you flat on your back after a couple of strokes. Once you agree to be mine, then you can touch me as much as you want."

His arrogance sends a sharp thrill shooting through me.

I bite my lip before asking, "And what if that never happens?"

A feral smile curves his lips. "We both know that I'm persistent as fuck."

True. As much as that particular characteristic has aggravated me the past couple of weeks, I wouldn't want him any other way. There's something ridiculously sexy about his self-confidence and the way he goes about taking what he wants.

And what he wants right now is me.

Kingsley settles on his side until his face is level with mine before propping his head up on his hand. "If you need more time to work shit out in your head, then I'll wait as long as it takes."

When he tangles his fingers with my own, I realize I don't want to pull them away. I don't want any more distance between us. As much as I want to refuse his touch, it feels right. It was so much easier to be angry with him when he wasn't here in front of me, pushing me to accept my fate and his role in it.

His voice softens. "I know this is a messed-up situation and that you're angry."

That's an understatement. I'm furious this decision has been made without any input from my end.

My brows arch as I throw the question back at him. "And you're not?"

"In the beginning, I was pissed as hell." He smirks. "You might find this hard to believe, but I don't like being told what to do. Maybe if we hadn't met at the beach and spent the day together, you wouldn't have already been an itch under my skin." His eyes grow distant as if he's mentally tumbling back in time. "After the day we spent on the boat, I didn't know what happened to you. I stopped over the next morning to pick you up, and you were gone. I had nothing to go on. No way to find you. No address or phone number." A reluctant chuckle slides from his lips. "I didn't even know your last name."

"That's probably a good thing," I murmur, thinking about our families.

"Yeah, it probably was." He falls silent, pulling off his aviators so that his gaze can pierce mine. "I thought about you a lot after that. I wondered what you were doing in Chicago and if you were spending time with anyone else. Were you letting those guys kiss you the same way I did? It pissed me off."

My heart spasms as I shake my head. "I never kissed anyone the way I kissed you."

"Good." His gaze grows heated. "I don't want anyone else to touch you the way I do. *Not ever.*"

Doesn't he realize how crazy that sounds?

We're too young to be making this kind of commitment. "King—"

"*No!*" he snaps before his eyes narrow. "I want *you*. I don't give a shit about the company or this agreement." He pauses for a beat before rectifying the statement. "Actually, that's not true. I'm fucking thrilled this arrangement gives me *you*. The only reason I'm even going along with it is because I have to have you. We belong together, Summer. I realize that even if you can't see it yet." His voice drops, becoming more of a challenge. "Tell me that you don't feel this between us."

I bite my lip and glance away.

"Summer," he growls, "I'll walk away from the whole damn thing if you can tell me that you don't feel the same way. I'll tell my father to go fuck himself."

If I were smart, that's exactly what I would say.

"I can't." My gaze stays fastened on his. I don't *ever* want to look away from him. "I can't tell you that."

"We belong together," he repeats, stronger this time. "You belong with me, *to me*."

I don't realize how desperate I am to hear those words until they're reverberating in my ears.

When I remain silent, he adds, "I know we're young, and that everything is stacked against us, but we can make it work. I've never felt this way before. I've never wanted—*needed* anyone the way I need you."

Marriage. He's talking about *marriage*. It's no small thing. If I agree to this, I'll be shackling myself to Kingsley forever. A reluctant thrill shoots through me at the notion, but I quickly tamp it down.

I shake my head and whisper, "I don't know…"

"Then I guess it's a good thing I do." With one swift motion, he rolls on top of me. Instead of feeling trapped by the heaviness pinning me to the boat, I'm tempted to wrap my legs around him and pull him closer. There's something soothing about the feel of him covering me. "You just need to trust me."

Does he understand what he's asking?

We will *never* be just Summer and Kingsley. He's a Rothchild, and I'm a Hawthorne. Our families have been enemies for generations. It's doubtful anything will ever change that. There is too much ugly history standing between us.

My feelings for Kingsley have nothing to do with the company. But can he say the same?

Therein lies the problem because that's an answer I'll never know. The insidious little question will always be there, clawing at the back of my mind, creating doubts.

Why is he with me?

Can I live with that? Never knowing for sure?

When I remain silent, he says, "You *are* aware that my family owns a shit ton of stores throughout Wisconsin and Minnesota, right?"

What?

I had assumed there was only one.

His lips quirk into a cocky grin. "Maybe you haven't realized this, but my family has money, Summer. *A lot*. During the early eighties, my grandfather started Rothchild's. The store in Hawthorne was the flagship. Since then, it's continued to grow, and now we have over fifty stores. Every year, a few more get added."

But that doesn't make sense.

"Then why?" I shake my head. "Why is your dad doing this?"

The smile fades from his face as his expression grows somber. "He wants what was stolen from his great-grandfather. He's been obsessed with getting the company back for decades. His thirst for revenge drove my parents apart." He searches my gaze as his voice turns gruff. "There is no way I'd go through with this arrangement unless it's what *I* wanted. I wouldn't martyr myself for Hawthorne Industries." He presses a quick kiss against my lips. "Since the first moment I saw you on the beach, I've wanted you, Summer. And throughout all of this, even when I found out who you were, that never changed. My feelings never wavered. Maybe I wanted them to, but they remained the same, only growing stronger."

"We're talking marriage. Are you willing to put enough stock in your feelings to marry me?" My head spins as I force myself to say, "We're only eighteen years old. Doesn't that scare you?"

No matter how strong my feelings are for Kingsley, that knowledge frightens the hell out of me.

His lips quirk as his expression softens. "How about we take it one day at a time and get through high school first? If our parents can't accept that, they can fuck off. We'll do things our way, when we're ready. Got it?"

I pin my lower lip with my teeth before nodding.

"So, is that a yes?"

I shouldn't...

"Yes." Only now that the word has been released do I realize how much I want this.

How much I want Kingsley.

"Thank fuck." He grins before his lips slam into mine.

And then I do what I've been dying to. I wrap my arms and legs around his body, pulling him tightly to me so there isn't a whisper of space between us.

"No matter what happens, we can make it work," he vows. "I promise you that. You just need to trust me. If you can do that, we'll make it through anything."

Contentment washes over me as I sigh into his mouth. It seems almost unbelievable that I could be this happy. A couple of months ago, I'd had everything worked out in my head. A detailed roadmap of how my future would unfold. That included graduating from high school in Chicago, attending a prestigious college in Illinois or Michigan, and majoring in astronomy. In none of those well-laid plans was there a handsome, domineering boy.

Yet here Kingsley is.

He burst into my life and turned my world, along with all of my plans, upside down and inside out.

And now that I know how he feels...

I won't lie to myself or pretend that I don't feel the same way. Why would I bother when he's everything I didn't know I was looking for?

Maybe we have a lot to figure out, but he's right. There is plenty of time to do that.

As long as we trust each other, nothing will tear us apart.

Thank you for reading King of Hawthorne Prep! I hope you enjoyed this story as much as I loved writing it! Find out how Summer and Kingsley's story ends!

One-click Queen of Hawthorne Prep now!

HE WANTS me on my knees and kissing his crown...

Welcome to the privileged world of Hawthorne Prep. From the outside, the hundred acres of perfectly manicured property seems like an idyllic place to finish out my senior year before spring boarding to the college of my choice.

Unfortunately, like most things in life, looks are deceiving. And I would know that better than most.

Two months ago, my parents moved us to nowheresville, Wisconsin in order for my father to claim his inheritance. Little did we know the town hated us or that there was a decades long feud which would ultimately lead to a forced engagement.

Kingsley Rothchild, the self-appointed king of Hawthorne Prep, has made me his queen. Even though I've bent my knee and kissed the crown, it doesn't take long to realize how easily queens can be cast aside.

If I'd thought all the secrets had been dragged into the light and we would get our happily ever after, I couldn't have been more wrong. I'm about to learn that what they say is true...the higher you rise, the harder your fall from grace is.

One-click Queen of Hawthorne Prep Now!

"I loved everything about this book! I read it in one day. I couldn't put it down. Love Summer and Kingsley's story" -Hanna, Amazon

"Holy hotness! I thought Jennifer's writing couldn't get any better.

Her Hawthorne Prep series are my two new favorite books!" -Jess, Amazon

"I truly loved the back and forth between Kingsley and Summer! This book pulls so much at your heartstrings. But the ending is sure to leave you smiling" -Brittany, Amazon

Turn the page for an excerpt of Queen of Hawthorne Prep...

Queen of Hawthorne Prep

"*Mmm.*" A contented sigh falls from my lips as I stretch against the boy in my bed. His muscular body is in perfect alignment with mine as he feathers seductive little kisses along the curve of my neck. "That feels so good." When he nips the flesh between his teeth, a punch of arousal hits me straight in the core.

Let's just say that if I were wearing panties, they would be drenched.

Is it any wonder I'm addicted to Kingsley Rothchild?

He jogged into my life a couple of months ago, and I haven't been able to evict him from my head since. Not that I want to. He's mine, and I'm his. And that's exactly the way I like it.

Does that mean I'm ready to get hitched tomorrow?

Hell, no.

Thanks to some archaic agreement between our parents to end eighty years of bad blood, my hand has been promised to him. The expectation is that we'll get married sometime during college.

Have I totally come to terms with the new direction my life has swerved in?

Not really.

I'm an eighteen-year-old girl who just started her senior year in high school. I haven't even been accepted to college yet. I don't like the idea of being forced into anything, let alone something as permanent as marriage.

Then I stare at the dark-haired boy with his sexy eyes and a mouth that was meant for all kinds of sin, and I know without a shadow of a doubt that he's the one for me. It's only been a month, but I feel it deep in my bones that Kingsley and I should be together. He completes me in ways I never imagined. And I'm a twin, so I know exactly what that feels like. To experience the same intimate connection with someone other than my brother is mind-blowing.

That being said, there is something unsettling about having my entire life mapped out at such a young age. All the major decisions have been wrestled out of my hands. It all seems preordained.

College.
Marriage.
Where I'll eventually settle down.
And probably where I end up working.

I won't lie, it's that knowledge that continues to claw at me. It's an itch beneath my skin that I can't quite quell. I keep telling myself to let it go and be happy. There are times when Kingsley and I are together, and it sits perched on the tip of my tongue, waiting to explode from my lips. Unsure of his reaction, I haven't mentioned anything to him. He's not aware of how much it bothers me. I've convinced myself it's better that way. If I confide in him, it'll only stir up problems between our families and between us. It's just going to take time to wrap my head around the hand fate has dealt me.

"Know what would feel even better?" he rumbles against my ear, calloused fingers scraping over my rib cage to cup my breast before tweaking the nipple. Shivers dance along my flesh in their wake.

Actually, I do. Desire thrums through me, pounding a steady beat until everything that crowds my mind falls away. As my whimper of need echoes off the walls, there's a soft rap of knuckles against the bedroom door. I freeze, a sharp inhalation lodging in my throat as my eyes pop wide.

"Summer, are you awake?"

Shit.

Mom.

The untimely disruption doesn't stop Kingsley from nipping at my bare shoulder. He doesn't give a damn if one of my parents is standing on the other side of a two-inch plank of wood. What I've learned about Kingsley is that he does what he pleases, when he pleases, and the consequences can be damned.

While I find that sexy as hell, it's not how I live my life.

My mother doesn't know that Kingsley has been sneaking into my room every night to sleep in my bed. Since returning from the beach house a month ago, we haven't spent one night apart, and I love it. I love being wrapped up in his arms. I love when he's on top of me, driving into my body, making me fall apart beneath his fingertips.

There's no better feeling in the world.

A heavy wave of anxiety crashes over me as I claw at his arms, fighting my way out of his embrace. The possibility of Mom finding me in bed with a boy is enough to send me into cardiac arrest.

This is definitely *not* how I imagined starting my Sunday morning.

Instead of relinquishing his hold, Kingsley tugs me closer, locking me in place as his teeth sink into the delicate flesh of my neck. His fingers toy with the erect tip of my breast before grazing the contour of my belly and thrusting deep inside my pussy.

A strangled groan breaks free. *"Stop."*

He teases my heat with sharp, forceful strokes that leave me panting.

"Is that what you really want?" he growls.

Yes.

No.

With the next knock comes another punch of concern.

"Summer?" Mom says, louder this time.

"Please," I whimper, squirming against him. I have no idea if I'm trying to escape or burrow closer. This is exactly what he does to me. Scrambles my brain until coherent thought becomes impossible.

"What are you begging for, baby girl?" He tweaks my tightened bud, a little harder this time. It's enough to send a flash of pain streaking through me before dissolving into pleasure.

Baby girl.

Another shiver of need dances down my spine. I could almost get off on the deep scrape of his voice when he calls me that.

"Hmm?" He continues to toy with me, purposely fanning the flames of my desire.

I'm not sure. And that's part of the problem. He's the only boy I've ever known capable of making me lose my ever-loving mind. How else do you explain my current predicament?

"Should I keep going or..." His fingers drift over my clit before homing in on it like a heat-seeking missile. "Stop?"

In a matter of weeks, he's learned how to touch me to elicit the most amount of pleasure. It's almost as if he takes pride in it. And what he's doing right now is my kryptonite.

My mind spins as my core throbs to life.

When I fail to respond, his hand splays wide over my pussy before giving it a possessive squeeze. "Guess I'll stop. Your loss."

It takes a moment for the sexual haze clouding my brain to clear as air leaks from my lungs.

Mom is waiting.

On the other side of the door.

That's all it takes for my brain to click back on, and then I'm elbowing him in the ribs.

He grunts as a chuckle slips free. "What was that for?"

"You know what!" I hiss before flipping over to face him and shoving my palms against his chest. I'm not sure if I'm angry with him for leaving me hanging or working me up in the first place. Although I won't be admitting that to him because it would only stoke his over-inflated ego. *"Now go!"*

"Why?" He smirks, falling onto his back and lounging on my bed as if he doesn't have a care in the world.

I bite back the sigh that wants to fall from my lips. His dark hair is in sexy disarray. I'm tempted to sift my fingers through the thick silky strands. It takes effort to shake the impulse loose and focus on the moment at hand.

"What do you mean *why*?" I jerk my hand toward the bedroom door as if the answer isn't obvious. "Um, hello? My mother is standing outside the door! She'll flip out if she finds you here." When he doesn't blink, I tack on, *"With me!"* Another beat passes by. *"Naked!"*

My mini tirade only makes the grin on his face stretch wider.

Ugh. So annoying!

I love the guy—wait a minute. No, I don't. Not yet. But my feelings are definitely migrating in that direction. Our relationship has been rocky from the onset. We met at the beach in June and spent one magical day together on his boat before I disappeared, only to resurface a few months later at Hawthorne Prep, where he made my life miserable in an attempt to push me away.

"What the hell does it matter?" Instead of rolling out of bed, he hauls me closer. "We're practically engaged. Who cares if she finds me here?"

Umm, I care. The convo I'd be forced to endure would be seriously horrific. I don't even want to contemplate it.

"Summer?" The knock becomes more insistent. *"Hon?"*

That's it! This boy needs to exit stage left!

"Get!" I grunt, using my hands and feet to eject him from the bed. Kingsley is six foot three and a solid two hundred pounds. He's all steely strength and conditioned muscle. Normally, I love that about him, but not so much at the moment. It takes every ounce of my power to shove him to the edge of the mattress. A moment later, he hits the floor with a loud thump. *"Out!"*

He laughs, staggering a step or two before regaining his balance. "You need to calm down, woman." Kingsley straightens to his full height and scratches his head. "Your reaction is a little excessive, don't you think?"

His sheer masculine beauty is enough to have me losing focus. Even with my mother hovering in the hallway, I can't help but eat him up with hungry eyes. Hands down, he's the most gorgeous guy I've ever seen.

Tall.

Muscular.

Mahogany-colored eyes that match his hair.

And a thick…

Let's just say he makes quite the striking picture in all his erect glory.

I give my head a quick shake to loosen those dangerous thoughts.

"Nope, not one bit." I point at the closet at the far end of the room. "Hurry and hide in there!"

I'm almost afraid he'll brush my concerns aside and jump back into bed. Instead, Kingsley gives me an exaggerated eye roll before taking a step toward the small room when the door handle turns.

The nightmare unfolds in slow motion and there's not a damn thing I can do about it. Before I can screech at the top of my lungs for her to stop, the door is flung open, and in walks Mom with a pink and brown floral basket full of folded laundry. For one sliver of a moment, she's blissfully unaware of the naked boy standing in the middle of the room.

"So, I was thinking—" Her voice abruptly falls off as her gaze crashes with Kingsley who, instead of making a mad dash to the closet, doesn't move a damn muscle.

Shock washes over her features as her feet grind to a halt. Her impression of a deer caught in headlights is spot-on.

Mortification sears my insides, making it impossible to breathe.

I'm not sure who I feel most sorry for.

Her.

Or me.

Want to guess who doesn't seem the least bit bothered by the circumstances?

Kingsley.

He stands buck naked, his erection out there for everyone to see. And trust me when I say that my mother *definitely* sees it. It would be impossible not to. It's long, thick, and…

Yeah.

Twin flags of color stain her cheeks as she hastily averts her eyes. Even so, I'm pretty sure she got an eyeful of what our next-door neighbor is packing. My guess is that if it ever became necessary, she could give an accurate description to a sketch artist.

I'm tempted to throw the comforter over my head and pretend this isn't happening.

"Umm..." Her gaze skitters around the room to avoid settling on Kingsley as she presses her lips together until they turn bloodless. With halting steps, she moves toward the antique armchair in the corner before gingerly setting down the pile of clean laundry. Everything about her movements look awkward and rusty. Like she's the Tinman and her joints are in desperate need of lubrication.

How will I ever look my mother in the eye again?

And you know damn well she'll blab this to my dad. A tortured groan escapes from my lips. And then Austin will find out and I'll never hear the end of it.

Ugh.

With a great deal of deliberateness, she straightens and turns, her attention fastening on to mine like I'm a life preserver in a turbulent ocean. Only then do I remember that I'm also naked. Thankfully, the sheet is still crumpled around the lower half of my body. With shaking fingers, I grab the cotton material and yank it over my breasts, shielding them from view. Although, we can all agree it's a little late for modesty at this point.

I wince at the shock and disappointment that echoes throughout her expression. Heat singes my face as my teeth sink into my lower lip. Kingsley has yet to budge from the center of the room.

Oh my God, why is he still standing there, naked as the day he was born?

The least he could do is grab his boxers and cover up! His hard-on is only making the situation worse. I'm embarrassed to note that his erection has not deflated in the slightest.

"So..." Mom clears her throat before stabbing a finger toward the hallway. "I'm going to, umm, go."

"Yeah." What else am I supposed to say? I want to scrub this moment from our collective memories.

Her feet pad softly across the floor. Hours tick by torturously before she reaches the threshold. Instead of crossing into the hall, she hovers awkwardly in the doorway. "Summer?"

Even though her voice barely rises above a strangled whisper, it breaks the silence of the room like a gunshot, and I cringe. Any hope of coming to an unspoken agreement that the past five minutes never occurred is about to be shattered.

My fingers bite into the sheet as I clutch it to my chest. "Yeah?"

"After you get dressed, I'd like to speak with you downstairs."

"All right," I mumble. "I'll be down in a few minutes."

"Thank you."

As she closes the door behind her, I collapse against the mattress before dragging a pillow over my face and pressing down on it. If only it were possible to smother myself. This episode ranks as a top contender for title of most mortifying moments ever. And just to be clear, the past month has been filled with a shit ton of humiliation.

Light filters through my eyelids when the pillow is removed and chucked to the side of the bed as Kingsley slides beneath the sheets.

"Problem solved." His body shakes with silent laughter. "Now we don't have to hide."

My mouth tumbles open. I'm on the verge of blasting him into next week when he lifts a finger and rims the edges of my lips. "Open your mouth that wide and it's going to get stuffed full."

Oh!

My teeth snap together. "How can you joke around at a time like this?"

"Who says I'm teasing?" He smirks, heat filling his eyes. When he shrugs his broad shoulders, it's almost enough to distract me.

Almost.

A growl rumbles up from deep in my chest.

"Oh, come on, it's not that bad." He laughs. "So your mom got an eyeful of cock. Big deal."

Hearing him say mom and cock in the same sentence has me on the cusp of hyperventilating. "Are you kidding? It's a huge deal!"

He peels back the covers and points at his hard dick. "No, *this* is a huge deal."

Oh my God, I'm seriously going to kill him!

"Do you realize the can of worms you've opened?" When he remains silent, I hiss, "Now I'll have to endure yet another sex talk!"

"Guess you'll have a lot more to contribute to the conversation this time."

Argh! He's impossible!

My lips flatten. "Yeah, I don't think so." I cradle my head in my hands as if it's moments away from rolling off my body. "Given the fact that we'll both have fresh visuals, it'll be significantly worse."

Before I can whine about the situation any further, he pulls me into his arms and presses a kiss against the top of my head. "Want me to come with you?" There's a pause. "'Cause I'll do it. You know I will. It's doubtful Eloise will appreciate my presence, but that's too damn bad."

"No," I grumble, some of my anger melting away as he continues to pepper me with soft caresses. "You'll only make it worse."

"How is that possible when I make everything better?" As he snuggles against me, his boner pokes my thigh. "We probably got a few minutes—"

"Are you serious right now?" What am I asking? Of course he is! "Hell no, we're not having sex!"

"Aw, come on, babe," he wheedles like a petulant child, pouty face and all. "Thanks to her untimely disruption, the cat is already out of the bag." He gyrates his hips, stroking the hard length of his cock against my leg. "Your mom can wait. I won't take long."

Not giving him the chance to convince me otherwise, I shove my way out of his arms before sliding from the side of the bed and stalking to my dresser.

Kingsley sits up and the sheet falls down his sculpted body. "Looking good, baby girl."

He chuckles when I give him a one-fingered salute.

I grab a pair of panties and bra before yanking them on. "You need to go."

"Fine." With an exaggerated huff of breath, he throws off the covers and rises from the bed before sauntering toward me. When he's within striking distance, his hand snakes out, yanking me into his arms. As I land against his chest with a soft grunt, his lips descend. "See you tonight?"

His sharp teeth nip at the plump flesh of my bottom lip.

A sigh escapes from me. "Yeah."

"Same place, same time?"

Those words melt all of my resistance.

Most nights, we lay on the thick carpet of grass at the back of the yard. Tall pines delineate our property from the golf course. With my head pillowed against his chest, we stare at the dark canvas of night sky as it stretches over our heads. I point out constellations, and we talk for hours.

"Yeah," I sigh.

He grins and smacks another kiss against my lips. "Good."

"Now go," I repeat, still aggravated at the situation I'll have to contend with in a few short minutes.

"You gonna let me get dressed first?"

My gaze drops to his cock. It's still impressively hard.

"Don't worry," he whispers roughly, "you'll get that tonight."

Yeah, I better.

One-click Queen of Hawthorne Prep now!

HEARTLESS
SKYE

"Yay! The bitches are back together again and tonight we ride!" Lanie wraps her arms around me and squeezes tight. "It's been too long, girl! *Way too long!*"

A reluctant smile curves my lips. "I know. It's good to be back." The circumstances surrounding my return are less than ideal, but I'm happy to see Lanie again. She's been my best friend since middle school, and I've missed her. Facetime and texting are nice but it's not the same as talking in person. She links her arm through mine as we walk across the open field.

I glance at the cute cowboy boots that adorn her feet. When she told me that we were going to a field in the middle of nowhere, I didn't believe her.

That was my first mistake.

Second mistake?

Not going with sturdier footwear.

Instead, I'm wearing a pair of flimsy sandals. They're cute as hell but that's not going to do me a whole lot of good across this terrain.

Lanie insisted we celebrate my return by dragging me to a bonfire in a farmer's field. Already the place is crawling with drunk-off-their-asses, barely legal adults. Shouting and raucous laughter fills the balmy night air.

Even though I know it won't do me any good, my gaze coasts anxiously over the ever-swelling crowd. Nerves dance across my spine as I silently pray Hunter will be absent from the revelry. Or, if he is here, we'll somehow be able to avoid one another.

If I know Lanie—and I do—she'll be up my ass to cut loose and have fun. How can I do that when Hunter and I now attend the same college? At any given moment I could turn a corner and smack right into him.

The thought of that happening makes me nauseous.

As much as I want to play it cool and act like my ex-boyfriend doesn't matter, the words slip from my mouth before I can stop them. "You don't think he'll be here, do you?" I shoot her a look that's rife with concern.

Lanie doesn't bother to ask who I'm referring to. She doesn't have to. She's all too aware of my past. She had a front-row seat to our relationship. And its demise.

"I don't know," she pauses and pops her shoulders into a careless shrug, "maybe."

"*What?*" My feet grind to a halt as my mouth dries, turning cottony. I'm barely aware of the blades of straw poking my feet through the leather sandals. "But you said—"

Her expression hardens, transforming into one of impatience. "Even if he *is* here, the chances of you running into him are slim." She waves an arm toward the massive group of students who have gathered to mourn the end of summer by drinking themselves into a stupor. "Look around. Half the university is here. There's no way you're going to see him, Skye, so stop worrying about it and live a little."

My teeth sink into my lower lip before I suck the fullness into my mouth. No matter what Lanie says, I'm going to worry.

When I remain silent, my best friend plants her hands on her hips and glares. Here comes Lanie's version of tough love.

"Would you rather sit home by yourself on a Saturday night

because you're too chickenshit to show your face? Afraid that you *might* run into Hunter Price?"

I'm sorry, is that really a question?

From the annoyed expression that flickers across Lanie's face, I decide to keep those thoughts to myself.

"Skye Elizabeth Sinclair!"

I wince as my full name cracks through the air. It brings an unpleasant image of my mother to mind. This is what I get for living with someone who isn't afraid to call me out on my bullshit. Maybe I should have taken Dad up on the offer to live with him.

I decide to go with something close to the truth. "I was hoping to avoid him for a while," I mutter. "That's all."

And when I say awhile, *what I really mean is forever.*

Is that really too much to ask?

Lanie sighs as her expression softens. Marginally. "I know, but you're going to run into him on campus or at a party eventually. It's inevitable. Accept it and move on."

I snort.

Easy for her to say. Lanie doesn't have any ghosts from her past that are ready to jump out and scare her.

I have a carefully constructed plan in place for the year. It involves laying low and flying under the radar, so Hunter doesn't even know I'm here. "Yeah, I guess..."

Unwilling to let me backslide, Lanie loops her arm through mine and pulls me toward the growing group of partiers. "It'll be fine. I promise."

Unfortunately, my bestie isn't in a position to guarantee me anything and we both know it.

The closer we get to the party, the more my anxiety ratchets up. At least night has fallen. The only light that emanates is from the bonfire that flickers in the distance and the stars that twinkle across the dark velvety sky.

For the time being, I'll remain vigilant. There's really nothing more I can do.

I inhale a deep breath before carefully blowing it out.

Maybe Lanie's right and I'm making a big deal out of nothing. It's been three years since we've seen each other, and a lot has happened since then. We've both moved on with our lives. I'm sure he's forgotten all about me. As those thoughts circle through my head, my shoulders loosen from around my ears and my heart stops thumping a painful beat.

The moment we reach the outer ring of people, Lanie is swept off her booted feet and spun around in a tight circle like a rag doll. Her short floral dress flies around her thighs. Laughter rings throughout the air as her arms slip around her boyfriend's neck.

Jaxon Conway has a typical football player's physique. He's a mountain of a man. Tall, broad in the shoulders, and muscular. He looks like he could easily bench press Lanie's VW Bug. I would be intimidated by him but he's quick to laughter and has warm brown eyes. He's like a teddy bear. Big and gruff on the outside but tender and mushy on the inside.

"Missed you, babe," he growls.

"It's only been a couple of hours since we saw each other!"

"Doesn't matter," Jax complains. "I still missed the hell out of you."

"Aww." Lanie's voice softens, becoming dreamy. "I love you so much."

"I love you more," he responds with enough heat to melt the panties off Lanie's body.

Ugh.

Make it stop.

These two are so sickeningly sweet that I get a toothache every time I'm around them. Although, if anyone deserves a good guy, it's Lanie. Like most girls in their early twenties, she's dated her fair share of assholes. Jaxon is almost too good to be true. Kind of like a mythical unicorn sprung to life. He's an athlete who isn't interested in screwing as many girls as he can get his hands on.

Ever since I rolled into town a few days ago, Jaxon and Lanie have been glued together at the hip. I get the feeling he'll be our unofficial third roommate for the year.

Know what's been getting a lot of use?

My noise-cancelling headphones.

Most nights, those two sound like they're auditioning for a porno. Let's hope it calms down soon.

Jaxon and Lanie coo at each other before their mouths fuse together and they start going at it like a pair of cats in heat. I clear my throat and glance everywhere but at them. If we were hanging out at the townhouse, this would be my cue to exit stage left. But we're not at home, we're in the middle of a field a few miles from town. There's nowhere for me to go. No one for me to talk to.

Awkwardness descends as I flick a piece of straw from my shirt.

Maybe I should take this opportunity to grab a beer. There must be a keg around here somewhere. You can't have this many college kids congregating in one spot and not have alcohol. That would be considered sacrilegious, right?

With any luck, by the time I return, Jaxon and Lanie will have stopped mauling each other long enough for us to move on with our evening. It's not like he's being shipped off to war tomorrow and they'll never see each other again.

Sheesh.

My gaze meanders to them in hopes that they've gotten their fill of each other.

Nope. The face sucking has become even more intense. Any moment, clothing is going to spontaneously combust from their bodies.

I don't really want to be around when that happens.

So...a beer it is.

Not that either of them are paying me the least bit of attention, but I point toward the mass of bodies that have multiplied in the fifteen minutes since we've arrived. "I'm going to grab a drink." When my words are met with kissy noises, I say, "Try not to miss me too much while I'm gone."

Lanie waves a hand absently in my direction as they continue to get it on.

"Okay then," I mumble before reluctantly taking off on my own.

The amount of people gathered here is a little overwhelming. Lanie's right, half the university must have shown up. Everyone is talking, laughing, and drinking. In other words, they're having a great time.

Me, not so much.

It takes a good ten minutes to find the keg. Or maybe I should say *kegs*, since there are six of them next to the backend of a midnight black pickup truck that is blasting music from massive speakers. I can barely hear myself think over the thumping beat. Then again, maybe that's for the best. It's a relief to get out of my head, even for a few minutes.

I locate the line for the beer and take my place at the end of it. I'm not much of a drinker, but I need something to smooth out all of the rough edges so I can relax and enjoy myself.

My flesh prickles with awareness and I run my hands over my arms trying to banish the disconcerting sensation. I glance around, scouring the crowd for one face in particular but don't see him anywhere. That alone should alleviate my anxiety, but it doesn't.

My parting with Hunter wasn't what one would call amicable. I don't blame him for being hurt and angry. Whether Hunter understands it or not, I did what needed to be done. As painful as it was, I'd do it all over again. I loved Hunter more than life itself.

Part of me still does.

Probably always will.

If everything I've read online is true, then my sacrifices have been well worth it. Hunter will get snapped up in the NFL draft before graduating this spring. Ever since I can remember, that's been his goal. If there's one person who deserves for all his dreams to come true, it's Hunter Price. Unwilling to dwell on my ex, I shove him from my mind and take in the scene before me.

People are gathered together in groups, greeting one another as if they're long lost friends who haven't seen each other in decades. It's a little surreal to be surrounded by so many people and yet feel so removed from it all. As if I'm more of an observer than a participant. Other than Lanie and Jaxon, I don't know anyone else. I'm sure there are people from high school who attend CU, but after I moved away, I lost touch with most of them.

By the time I make it to the front of the line, I'm antsy and ready to head back to my friends. Even if they're still going at it. Which is really saying something. I'd much rather stand around as a third wheel than be an island onto myself. I dig through my front pocket and hand over a couple of bucks in exchange for a blue plastic cup before it's filled to the rim with golden liquid.

The cute guy manning the keg flashes me an easy grin as his eyes drift over my body. When he's finished with his perusal, his gaze once again settles on my face. Kudos to this guy for not gawking at my boobs like he's never seen a pair of D cups before.

"Here you go, beautiful," he says, handing over the cup with a gallant flourish.

This little bit of silliness lightens my mood. "Thanks."

Our fingers brush as I take the Solo cup from him.

"Next time, cut to the front of the line." He gives me a flirty wink. "I got you covered."

I flash him a grateful smile. Maybe tonight won't be so bad after all.

With my drink in hand, I'm ready to make my way back to Jaxon and Lanie. Only now does it occur to me that they could have moved from the spot where I'd left them.

Who's to say I'll even be able to find my way back?

A knot of unease settles at the bottom of my belly. My fingers go to the purse slung across my chest. It's big enough to hold my phone and that's about it. I could always shoot Lanie a text, but who knows if she'd hear it. And I have no idea how to navigate my way back to our apartment. The unsettled feeling that had taken up residence in my gut turns into full-on nausea.

Only now do I realize that walking away was a bad idea. I should have stuck to Lanie and Jax like glue. But standing around and watching them make-out felt pervy.

And not in a good way.

With those thoughts swirling through my brain, I spin around and slam into a wall of impenetrable muscle. The impact knocks me off-balance and I stumble back a step. Before I can fall, strong hands reach out and grab hold of my shoulders, yanking me forward. My breath catches and my heart pounds at the narrowly avoided tumble.

I shake my head to clear it as beer sloshes over the rim of my plastic cup and spills onto the ground at my feet. I'm lucky it didn't end up down the front of my top or the shirt of the unsuspecting person I plowed into.

How humiliating would that have been?

Ugh...I don't even want to think about it.

"I'm so—"

My voice falls off as I glance up, my gaze colliding with narrowed blue eyes. Hunter quickly sets me free as if his fingers have been burned. Neither of us break eye contact. All of the raucous noise of the bonfire dies away until it's just the two of us standing alone in the middle of a dark field.

This is the moment I've been dreading.

My eyes roam over his face, cataloging the myriad of changes that time has wrought. When I walked away, Hunter had still been a boy, his lean muscles beginning to thicken. Now the transformation has been complete and he's a full-grown man. Hunter has always had size on his side, but somehow, he's managed to grow both taller and broader. He must be somewhere in the vicinity of six three or four. I have to crane my neck to hold his gaze. The graphic T-shirt he's wearing stretches tautly across the wide expanse of his chest and hugs the chiseled strength of his biceps. It's enough to make my mouth dry and my knees soft.

If I have one weakness, it's for thickly corded arms. All that tightly harnessed power waiting to break free...

A shiver of desire scampers down my spine before I stomp it out.

Unaware of the effect he's having on me, Hunter's deep voice cuts through my thoughts.

"What are you doing here, Skye?"

It's the harshness of his tone that has my gaze snapping back to his as heat floods my cheeks. I can't stop myself from staring. The little bit of cyberstalking I've done over the years has in no way prepared me for coming face-to-face with my ex-boyfriend. He's grown into his dark looks, becoming even more of a heartbreaker than he was in high school.

My tongue darts out to smudge my parched lips as nerves dance along my skin. I search Hunter's eyes, looking for any hint of softening but there's none to be found. His gaze is as frigid and detached as I imagined it would be. The tiny kernel of hope that our time apart would be enough to heal our past wounds shrivels and dies inside me.

There is no forgiveness in his heart.

But then again, did I really expect there would be?

Maybe. It would have made coexisting on campus for the next year so much easier.

It's obvious from his terse behavior that Hunter would prefer to pretend I never existed in the first place. As much as I would love to give him that, I can't. Unforeseen circumstances have forced me home.

I straighten my shoulders and attempt to keep my voice level. I don't want him to hear the slight tremble that is working its way through my body. "I transferred to Claremont for my senior year."

His shadowed jaw ticks as he clenches his teeth. *"Why?"*

The way he bites out that one word leaves me wincing.

I take a quick step back and lift my chin, not wanting him to see how much power he still holds over me. Time has done nothing to diminish it. "That's none of your business."

Whether Hunter realizes it or not, he still owns a piece of my heart. It's better for both of us if he never suspects the depth of my feelings.

His hands tighten into fists as he closes the little bit of distance that I've managed to put between us. Instead of scrambling back the way every instinct is clamoring for me to do, I hold my ground until we're standing toe-to-toe. My heart pounds a painful staccato against my breast as his harsh breath feathers across my parted lips.

There was a time when I couldn't get close enough to Hunter.

Now I can't get far enough away.

Sorrow floods through every fiber of my body that it has to be this way between us. Next to Lanie, Hunter was my best friend. He was my first everything.

Date.

Kiss.

Love.

Heartbreak.

Everything we once shared has been blown to pieces and we're nothing more than strangers. Actually, what we are is much worse. His animosity is palpable. It radiates from him in suffocating waves that threaten to choke the life out of me.

"You shouldn't have come back," he growls. "You don't belong here anymore."

That may be true, but there's nothing I can do about it. I'm here. And I'm not going anywhere.

I shift my weight and force myself to say, "Claremont is big enough for the two of us."

"No, it's not. Stay the fuck out of my way, Skye." His eyes flash with barely suppressed hostility. "You won't like the consequences if you don't."

Before I can summon up a retort, he stalks away. Rooted in place, my gaze tracks his movements until he fades into the crowd. Not once does he turn around and acknowledge my presence. I've been dismissed. Relegated to the blackhole that is our past.

Once he disappears from sight, my knees weaken as the pent-up breath rushes from my aching lungs.

I haven't been on campus for a full seventy-two hours and in Hunter's eyes, I'm public enemy number one.

One-click Heartless now!

ALSO BY JENNIFER SUCEVIC

<u>The Campus Series</u> (football)
Campus Player (Demi & Rowan)
Campus Heartthrob (Sydney & Brayden)
Campus Flirt (Sasha & Easton)
Campus Hottie (Elle & Carson)
Campus God (Brooke & Crosby)
Campus Legend (Lola & Asher)

<u>Western Wildcats Hockey</u>
Hate You Always (Juliette & Ryder)
Love You Never (Carina & Ford)
Always My Girl (Viola & Madden)
Dare You to Love Me (Stella & Riggs)
Never Mine to Hold (Fallyn & Wolf)
Never Say Never (Britt & Colby)
Mine to Take (Willow & Maverick)

<u>The Barnett Bulldogs</u> (football)
King of Campus (Ivy & Roan)
Friend Zoned (Violet & Sam)
One Night Stand (Gia & Liam)
If You Were Mine (Claire & JT)

<u>The Claremont Cougars</u> (football)
Heartless Summer (Skye & Hunter)
Heartless (Skye & Hunter)
Shameless (Poppy & Mason)

Hawthorne Prep Series (bully/football)

King of Hawthorne Prep (Summer & Kingsley)

Queen of Hawthorne Prep (Summer & Kingsley)

Prince of Hawthorne Prep (Delilah & Austin)

Princess of Hawthorne Prep (Delilah & Austin)

The Next Door Duet (football)

The Girl Next Door (Mia & Beck)

The Boy Next Door (Alyssa & Colton)

What's Mine Duet (Suspense)

Protecting What's Mine (Grace & Matteo)

Claiming What's Mine (Sofia & Roman)

Stay Duet (hockey)

Stay (Cassidy & Cole)

Don't Leave (Cassidy & Cole)

Stand-alone

Confessions of a Heartbreaker (football)

Hate to Love You (Hockey) (Natalie & Brody)

Just Friends (Hockey) (Emerson & Reed)

Love to Hate You (Football) (Daisy & Carter)

The Breakup Plan (Hockey) (Whitney & Gray)

Collections

Claremont Cougars

The Barnett Bulldogs

The Football Hotties Collection

The Hockey Hotties Collection

The Next Door Duet

ABOUT THE AUTHOR

Jennifer Sucevic is a USA Today bestselling author who has published twenty-four new adult novels. Her work has been translated into German, Dutch, Italian, and French. She has a bachelor's degree in History and a master's in Educational Psychology from the University of Wisconsin-Milwaukee. Jen started out her career as a high school counselor before relocating with her family and focusing on her passion for writing. When she's not tapping away on the keyboard and dreaming up swoonworthy heroes to fall in love with, you can find her bike riding or at the beach. She lives in Michigan with her family.
If you would like to receive regular updates regarding new releases, please subscribe to her Newsletter!

Or contact Jen through email, at her website, or on Facebook.
sucevicjennifer@gmail.com

Want to join her reader group? Do it here -)
J Sucevic's Book Boyfriends | Facebook

Social media links-
https://www.tiktok.com/@jennifersucevicauthor
www.jennifersucevic.com
https://www.instagram.com/jennifersucevicauthor
https://www.facebook.com/jennifer.sucevic
Amazon.com: Jennifer Sucevic: Books, Biography, Blog, Audiobooks, Kindle

Jennifer Sucevic Books - BookBub

www.ingramcontent.com/pod-product-compliance
Lightning Source LLC
LaVergne TN
LVHW040039080526
838202LV00045B/3398